D0495750

PRAISE FOR *SKIN DEEP*

'Skin Deep is a truly compelling, page-turning and evocative novel, with a wonderfully realised 80s setting. The story hooked me, the questions it raised about beauty and art gripped me, and the characters will stay with me for a long, long time. Highly recommended!'

Kate Harrison, best-selling author

'I loved this. Viewed through the eyes of troubled art-student Diana and neglected child Cal, Manchester's Hulme in the 80's is vividly painted and instantly recognisable. Laura Wilkinson's novel asks important questions of us all; about the nature of photography as art, about the ideals of beauty that constrain and limit us, about exploitation, about class. This book will get under your skin.'

Jules Grant, author of
We Go Around in the Night and Are Consumed by Fire

'An engrossing, poignant and wise story that reminds us how we all crave to be seen for who we truly are. I raced through it.'

...lley Road.

CL 1300307 0

WHAT THE READERS ARE SAYING

'This author has a remarkable ability to convey the human emotions, passions and fears so incredibly well. *Skin Deep* is often troubling, sometimes uncomfortable, but completely and utterly compelling...Captivating and beautifully written, *Skin Deep* is a story that will trouble the reader, yet delight at the same time.'

Random Things Through My Letterbox

'*Skin Deep* is such a powerful novel and I still can't get it off my mind. Everything about it was utterly thought-provoking... well written with characters and situations that linger on my mind weeks after finishing the book.'

Book Drunk

'A superb read.'

Northern Soul magazine

'Such a work of art; a beautifully written novel which literally speaks for itself. Heart-breaking yet poignant, heart-warming yet powerful, emotional yet eye-opening; *Skin Deep* needs to be read by everyone, and anyone.'

The Writing Garnet

'This is one of those thought provoking stories that plays on your mind even when you're not reading it. A must-read.'

A Lover of Books

'*Skin Deep*...asks that the reader really considers what is beautiful and what is ugly, whether people can re-invent themselves by changing their looks and does this make them a better person...A thought-provoking and quietly compelling read.'

Portobello Book Blog

'An interesting novel, with a well written thoughtful insight into what makes us, despite our defects, continually search for an elusive perfection.'

Jaffa Reads Too

BOOKS BY LAURA WILKINSON:

Public Battles, Private Wars

Redemption Song

The Family Line

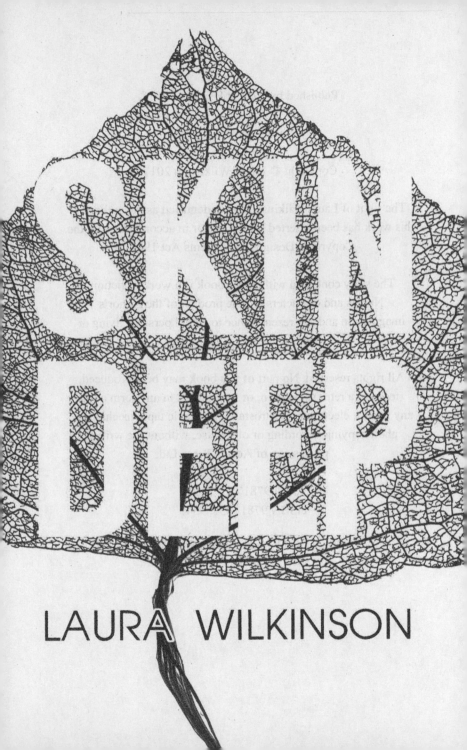

Published by Accent Press Ltd 2017

www.accentpress.co.uk

Copyright © Laura Wilkinson 2017

The right of Laura Wilkinson to be identified as the author of
this work has been asserted by the author in accordance with the
Copyright, Designs and Patents Act 1988.

The story contained within this book is a work of fiction.
Names and characters are the product of the author's
imagination and any resemblance to actual persons, living or
dead, is entirely coincidental.

All rights reserved. No part of this book may be reproduced,
stored in a retrieval system, or transmitted in any form or by
any means, electronic, electrostatic, magnetic tape, mechanical,
photocopying, recording or otherwise, without the written
permission of Accent Press Ltd.

ISBN 9781783758678
eISBN 9781783759545

Printed and bound in Great Britain by
Clays Ltd, St Ives plc

for my three boys, love always

Acknowledgements

I am extremely fortunate to have the support of a great number of smashing people. Thanks to you all. And you, lovely reader, for spending time with Diana and Cal, Alan and Linda. If I thanked everyone personally, these acknowledgements would amount to a novella. Here are those I must mention in relation to this particular novel.

Thanks to Helen Wilkinson who read the first draft and provided encouragement. Also, because you sat up with me late one night as I dissected the plot and characters in forensic (and possibly quite boring) detail. You never once told me to shut up. Thank you, you rock.

To Marian Williams for allowing me to steal a detail from your story and for, well, being my mum. Respect and love.

Everyone at Accent Press who work damn hard for me. Special mentions to Greg Rees – you are my champion and editor supremo, Karen Bultiauw, Kate Ellis and Anne

Porter for wisdom and support, and inspirational head honcho Hazel Cushion. You are quite a team.

Thanks are due to early readers Becky Edmunds, Mark Sheerin, and Sarah Tanburn. Also to members of the Jubilee Writers group and Jenn Ashworth who read sections of the novel. My beta-reading besties: Norma Murray and SR for sage-like advice with this novel (and life). For keeping me going with the writing life more generally I send heartfelt thanks to a host of amazing, talented authors, most especially: JA Corrigan, Shirley Golden, Katy O'Dowd, Sarah Rayner, Kate Harrison, Sue Teddern, Erinna Mettler, Bridget Whelan and Araminta Hall.

To Wendy Jones for her time and advice on procedures and outcomes in Social Services in the late 80s and early 90s. To Sally Atkinson for similar on matters of adoption. I have stretched possibilities to suit the narrative but your advice was invaluable. Thank you both.

And where would authors be without the support and love of the blogging community? Your cheerleading for the industry is awesome; you are reading and reviewing superstars — of a great many books and authors. Huge thank yous. There are a great many of you but again I have to choose a few for special thanks: Anne Cater at Random Things Through my Letterbox and the Facebook group Book Connectors, Anne Williams at Being Anne Reading, Sonya Alford at A Lover of Books, Holly Kilminster at Bookaholic Holly, Jo Barton at Jaffa

Reads Too, Tracy Terry at Pen and Paper, Tracy Fenton and Helen Boyce at THE Book Club, Wendy at Little Bookness Lane, Joanne Baird at Portobello Book Blog, Sandra Woodhead at Book Lover Worm, Sophie Hedley at Reviewed the Book, Rosie Amber and her team, Annette Hannah at Sincerely Book Angels, Vicki Bowles, Kaisha Holloway at The Writing Garnet and Linda Hill at Linda's Book Bag.

Grovelling apologies if I've missed you: my publisher needs to limit the pagination!

And last but by no means least, my Gingers and the BigFella. I love you.

We live only to discover beauty. All else is a form of
waiting.
Kahlil Gibran

I do not attribute to nature either beauty or
deformity, order or confusion. Only in relation to our
imagination can things be called beautiful or ugly,
well-ordered or confused.
Baruch Spinoza

Diana
Winter 2007

He is dying. A scalpel presses against my flesh; a piece of me is being cut away, cut from the deepest, most tender part of me. I took the call moments ago and now I sit silent in the cab, nodding as the driver rattles about the weather, the football results, the dreadful traffic. I do not ask him to be quiet; how could he know? He means well and the babbling is a comfort.

I know how he did it. They didn't tell me; they didn't have to. I see him at the bridge's edge, staring into the middle distance, certain. The city before him. A sea of dense, inviting grey. The shadow of Holy Joe's lingers like incense. He closes his eyes, bends his crooked knees and rolls forward – flying – into the heavy, wet air. Into another world, into freedom.

Cal.

Linda identifies the body, the shell that is not Cal. He dies before I reach the hospital; the traffic is appalling. Never regained consciousness, they said. I am glad of this small mercy.

The corridor is long and beige; it smells of

disinfectant and death. Linda hovers at one end, me at the other. We walk towards each other, like gunslingers at noon, heels tap-tapping, charting our progress. She takes my hand and places the interlaced gold, silver, and bronze ring in my palm and closes my fingers around it, one by one.

Finally, she says, 'He was beautiful.'

He would have loved that. Beautiful, beautiful Cal.

'A note?' I ask, dreading a nod. It is my fault.

She does not answer, embracing me instead, and I fold into our history, mine and Cal's, into youth and beauty and transformation.

PART ONE

Manchester - 1980s

Diana

Autumn 1984

In the soft morning light Hulme looked beautiful –
glorious, technicolour Hulme, also known as Beirut or
bandit country.

Manchester city centre was forever red, and wet
with rain, but Hulme erupted in great random dollops of
colour: yellow, lime and blue municipal doors and
window frames; scrubby grass; retina-aching walkway
graffiti; old punks' hair in cyan and magenta.

We'd arrived at the block with a key for number
fifty-five and a van load of possessions. But the
maisonette was boarded up, the front door covered in
eviction notices, bailiffs' cards crucified on the frame with
rusting nails. Unsure what to do, we leant on the damp
balcony wall and stared across the estate from our
vantage point two storeys up. One of the other crescent-
shaped blocks of flats faced us. Gigantic, it reminded me
of the ruined Coliseum in Rome; black, foul-looking
discharge dribbled from a window, snaking down the
concrete. There were four crescents in total: jerry-built
monstrosities; interlaced blocks inspired by the Georgian
crescents in Bath and optimistically named after great

5

architects and landscapers. Only drug dealers, dropouts and students lived there now. Rents were low, though most of Hulme's inhabitants were squatting.

'What the hell are we going to do?' Linda said. 'We can't go back to Whalley Range. Landlord'll skin us.'

A local boy who'd introduced himself when we'd parked the van, offering to 'mind' it for us, slipped alongside me. He elbowed me in the ribs and said, 'Number fifty's empty. No boards.'

'And how will we get in without a key, soft lad?' Linda said.

The urchin launched himself, shoulder first, at the door. It juddered but did not open. The door to number fifty-one did though.

Out stepped a tall, scrawny bloke, a parrot sitting on his shoulder. A demented scarecrow in a grubby, frilly shirt and torn pyjama bottoms, bloodshot eyes bulging. I jumped.

'Jesus, you nearly gave me a heart attack,' I said.

'Sorry.' He looked wounded and the bird squawked, making us all jump again.

The classy tones of *Your Love is King* poured from his flat. He didn't strike me as a jazz man and Sade's slick styling was at odds with his crazed appearance: a modern day, scummy Heathcliff.

'What's with the parrot?' I said.

'I found it.' He pointed at the ramshackle play area between the crescents and the parrot lifted a scaly leg as if it were about to shit. 'In a tree,' he continued. I wondered where else a lost parrot might hang out and where all the trees were in Hulme. I'd not seen any.

6

'So you took it home?'

'I thought it might starve or something. Freeze. They're tropical creatures; they don't like the cold.'

'Neither do I,' Linda piped up. 'And it's friggin' brass monkeys. Let's get inside.'

'What about the owner?' I said.

'Gone,' Parrot Man said.

'What about you? Can yous get us in?' Linda said.

The boy was attempting to stroke the bird. I shuddered.

'I can try. Let me get my boots,' Parrot Man said.

He disappeared inside, reappearing within minutes, minus the parrot, incongruous in pyjama bottoms and sixteen-hole Dr Martens. He marched over, arms outstretched. 'Move over, lad.' He raised his arms above his head, wrists relaxed, lifted one leg, knee bent, like a praying mantis, then leapt at the lock, foot first. His feet were huge.

The door swung open. We were in.

'Nice one, la. Ta very much,' Linda said. 'What's your name?'

'Alan. Alan Gilbraith.'

'Nice to meet you, Alan,' I said, taking his outstretched hand. 'Diana Brading, Linda Kelly. We're going to be neighbours.'

'Pleasure's all mine, ladies.' And he took a bow, dandy style. 'If you need anything, I'm right here.'

I nodded and smiled. 'You could help us unload the van?'

* * *

7

The boy earned a couple of quid, helping us up drag our stuff up four flights of stairs, and Alan helped out as a neighbourly gesture, or as a way of trying to get into our knickers. He had no chance but we didn't let him know that. After we were done, the boy said his brother could fit a new lock, repair the frame, and then he asked if there was anything else he could get us. He meant to steal whatever we asked for, I was sure, so I replied that we had everything we needed. I would not receive stolen goods and no way would I squat. I was determined to pay rent no matter what Linda said. It would be next to nothing; the council were desperate to let properties here.

'You're different from the other students,' he said.

'How's that?'

'You look like someone famous; he's weird; and she's a scally,' he said, pointing at Linda. 'Got a fag?'

'How old are you? Ten?' said Linda, hands on hips.

'Piss off,' he said.

'She's a model,' Linda said, tipping her head at me.

'Former model,' I said, emphasising former and wishing I'd not told her. I'd done so in a drunken moment at a party when I'd wanted to impress her and gain her friendship. Almost two years older and with a seemingly glamorous history, I'd appeared worldly and sophisticated, and despite the differences between us – background, age, course – we became best friends, inseparable for over a year now.

'I'm not a student,' Alan said.

'Dealer?' the boy asked.

'No.' He sounded offended and I wondered what he

did. On the dole, presumably.

'What are you studying?' the boy said, addressing Linda and me.

I touched my chest, 'Art,' then gesturing at Linda, 'Art History and Literature, books and stuff.'

'Pictures yours?' He pointed at the bundle of canvases resting against the hall wall.

I laughed, throat tightening, stomach tumbling. 'I wish. These are by famous artists. This one's mine.' I turned over a medium-sized canvas. An abstract piece created on my foundation course, the contents of my make-up bag, inspired by Matisse's later works. It wasn't good and I'd produced nothing of worth throughout my first year here either. It was why I was redoing the year, and if I didn't come up with something soon I'd be kicked off for good. I was in the last chance saloon.

'Me brother will be over in a bit.' Shrugging, the boy stepped outside. I followed him and Alan out, and we said our goodbyes. 'See yous around.'

Despite the cold I stood on the balcony and watched the boy shrink as he darted across a walkway and over the adjoining bridge to another block of flats.

Where in this body of concrete bones does he live? Will I see him again?

I gazed over to the play area. In between the broken swings was a pile of burnt-out sofas; a top-loading washing machine lay on its side at the bottom of the slide and torn-open bin bags spotted the grass. Even in the cold air I could smell the dog shit. Man-made ugliness, it was the antithesis of the pretty plastic life I'd led. And living in Hulme was cool. No doubt.

Mum would hate this.

I was fascinated and terrified and excited. I'd found my spiritual home. Here I would recover my mojo. This was where the freaks, the beautiful, and the damned hung out.

Cal

Spring 2007

The nurse says: 'Tell me your earliest memory.'

She's very pretty, in a girl-next-door way. And kind. So I tell her. 'Darkness, total, blacker than black, dark.'

'A womb memory,' she says.

'No, definitely not.' I try to wave an arm. It hurts but I can cope with pain, no problem at all. I've had lots of practise. 'Imagine a box. An enormous black box and you're trapped in it. Alone. Sort of. If you scream and scream someone will come. A washed-out face with colourless eyes which stares at you like you're nothing. You feel like nothing, or you would do if you knew what nothing felt like. That's my earliest memory. Darkness, a face, relief, nothing.'

'The face was your mother?'

'Maybe. Maybe not. Probably not. It feels like a man. Something about the size of the body, and the smell. I've smelt it since and it throws me right back. And it's definitely male. But I might have invented all this. Crazy, huh?'

Her expression is neutral. I can't tell what she's thinking.

11

'Why'd you ask?' I say.

'I'm interested,' she says and smiles, a small, quiet kind of smile.

I feel the morphine taking effect. I close my eyes and other pictures creep in, like photographs developing in a tray, all those chemicals washing over the paper history of my mind. Pictures, pictures, pictures. On billboard adverts, television screens, computers, phones, posters on walls, bus stops, shops, cinemas, magazines, galleries. Flashing, flashing, flashing. I'll go mad for all that colour, for all those faces, all those lovely, lovely faces. Clear blue eyes, sun drenched, peachy skin, shiny, golden hair, long limbs and nails like sea shells.

Diana.

So lovely I dive right in.

Diana

The flat was filthy, junk spattered about like a Pollock. We tiptoed round our new home, poking around, imagining who came before us and why they left so hurriedly. Upstairs, I pushed open the door to the windowless bathroom. The light from the landing was poor but as it trickled into the room I felt movement across the linoleum, dark shapes skittering into the crevices and cracks where the bath, basin and toilet met the floor.

Cockroaches?

I blinked, and looked again. There was nothing but the cheap white enamel of the suite and a *London Calling* poster peeling off the wall. I plodded downstairs.

'Where do we start? It's overwhelming,' I said, draining the last of an instant coffee which Alan had made next door and brought through.

'By getting rid of this crap,' said Linda, pointing at the net curtains, the magazines in the corner of the living room, 'and the fridge and the skanky mattress upstairs. After that we need to get the leccie sorted. I'll bomb to the corner shop and put some cash on this.' She held a key for the meter. Ever practical, she'd sussed out the basics, water, electricity and gas, while I'd mooched around upstairs.

We dragged the rubbish onto the balcony and left it piled up against the door of number fifty-five. I'd harboured fantasies that some of the magazines might be worth keeping, but they were mostly soft porn, *Classic Cars*, and *Jackie*. I'd not seen that mag since I was a kid. A copy with Donny Osmond on the cover was passed round a friend's house shortly before I was transported to boarding school.

We took everything that wasn't ours onto the balcony, except one box. It contained electrical goods and we thought they might be worth testing before we threw them out.

It was almost seven in the evening when there was a knock at the door. I was on my hands and knees scrubbing the skirting boards. The door swung open and in stepped a tall, bleached blond. Rows of silver skulls shone out from his knuckles. He held a toolbox in one hand and a long piece of wood tucked under his arm. His eyes were dark and narrow, his cheekbones high and his lips full. He took my breath away.

He walked in, threw his jacket over the banister and stood over me, legs astride, hands in his pockets. 'Jim. My brother said I'd come round?' I stumbled to my feet, tugging away at my rubber gloves. He jerked his head back at the door, 'To fix the frame, the lock?'

He worked efficiently, refusing all offers of

14

hospitality, speaking only when spoken to. I wished I wasn't so filthy, that my hair fell around my shoulders instead of being scraped into a bird's nest of a bun, that I wore a smattering of make-up. Linda materialised in the kitchen doorway and though she was scruffily dressed she looked amazing: corkscrew curls bouncing out from the confines of a scarlet headscarf, her lean figure encased in a navy boiler suit. She reminded me of the iconic factory girl from the Second World War poster.

We lingered as he worked, making pathetic small talk; we sounded like idiots, especially me. Pampered, spoilt brats slumming it. Except that Linda wasn't a posh girl, and she made this clear, battling for his attention. In the end I walked away and ran a bath. I wasn't going to fall out with a friend over a bloke. He looked like one of those beautiful, cruel men who enmesh women, unravel them, grow bored then, without explanation or apology, move on, leaving the abandoned woman shapeless and without form. If she wanted him, he was hers.

When I came down the stairs wrapped in a towel, I thought he'd gone. I was looking for my hairbrush. He was packing his tools away and I wasn't sure if he'd heard me. I stopped at the bottom of the first flight, on the landing. Before I retreated, I leant over the banister and a drop of water fell from my hair onto the top of his head. He looked up. I should have looked away, but I couldn't. His eyes held me, sucking me in. I could almost feel my pupils dilating, my body humming. Linda came out of the kitchen and broke the

atmosphere with a small, shocked 'oh'. He left. Linda
and I did not speak of his visit.

Space was important to me, important for my creativity.
The right space. Airy, light, clean. So we scraped and
scrubbed and painted. After six days the flat was altered
beyond recognition. Alan had helped out and we'd
thanked him with coffee, tea, biscuits and booze. We
couldn't have done it without him.

'Let's go out,' Alan said, as we stood admiring our
transformed living room, a bottle of cheap fizz on the
coffee table. 'You've been cooped up all week. I'll roll a
joint while you get your glad rags on.'

'I'm knackered,' Linda said, taking another slurp of
wine.

But I agreed with Alan. We needed a change of
scenery. 'Come on. We'll go to the Student Union for a
quiet drink.'

Upstairs, I pulled on my spiky-heeled ankle boots
and biker jacket, tied a bow in my hair with a strip of
black lace. Linda swept some wax through her hair,
clipped on a pair of saucer-sized earrings and changed
from dungarees into a long-sleeved woollen dress: a
sixties movie star, all heavy black eyeliner and pale
lipstick.

It was freezing when we left the Union bar. Home was a
twenty-minute walk away and Alan suggested we call a
cab. At the taxi rank the queue was short, but there were
no taxis about. I dug my hands into my pockets and
stared at my feet and the oily pavement, stomping on the

16

spot in an effort to stem the cold. I lifted my chin at the toot of a horn and saw an imposing figure emerging from the mist. Jim. He stopped.

'Hey man, how's it going?' Alan said.

Jim nodded, looked at me and said, 'Where you goin'?'

'Home. We're shattered,' Alan said.

'This early?' Jim said, still looking at me.

'You got a better offer?' Linda was so brazen. I loved her for it.

'Party, William Kent.'

A taxi pulled up and the group in front hopped in. I could see the orange 'For hire' light of a cab drawing closer. Alan protested that an early night was what we needed.

I'd woken up, and so, it seemed, had Linda. 'Shut your cake hole, grandad.'

The cab slipped alongside us. 'Share ours?' she continued, and without replying Jim opened the door and slid onto the front seat. Alan wedged himself between me and Linda, reluctantly agreeing to come, as if he was doing Jim a favour rather than the other way round.

The party was heaving; the smell of sweat, skunk, and poppers overwhelming. The melancholy tones of New Order floated over the rumble of the crowd. Blinded by air thick with smoke I lost Jim, Alan and Linda to a swarming pride of dancers. I pushed on, acclimatising, moving in to the bowels of the flat.

On the lower level many of the interior walls had been torn down and those left had been stripped to expose the bare plaster boards. The wooden staircase had been replaced with a spiral metal construction, London street signs hung in different rooms.

I spotted Alan's stick insect form as he weaved his way from the main dancing area, his head rising above the horizon of shadows like the funnel of a submarine. I followed him to the kitchen. All that was on offer, other than a glorious visual display on the walls, was a half-empty bottle of vodka and a couple of bottles of Blue Nun. A girl in leggings, a tutu, and an alarming array of piercings bumped into me.

'You know where the beer is?' she said, her pupils so dilated her irises were almost eclipsed.

I shook my head. 'Not in here as far as I can tell.'

A punk with ebony spikes and badly applied lipstick leant over and pointed to the ceiling with his cigarette, and said, 'Beer.' He smelt of stale hops and sweat and the hide of his leather trousers.

I turned to Alan, my head spinning, but he was engaged in conversation with a dumpy girl in a peach cardigan, so I followed Piercings upstairs.

The bath was full of half-melted ice and bottles of Pilsner. I checked myself in the mirror above the basin, wetting my fingertips and brushing them over my brows.

'You look gorgeous,' Piercings said, reaching over, dipping her blue-white arm into the icy water. She pulled out two bottles and handed one to me.

'Thanks.' I turned back to the glass. 'I was admiring the mirror actually,' I said.

'Bloody liar, though it is amazing, isn't it?'

It was. The craftsman had picked a piece of

shattered glass and built the wooden frame around it, or so I was told.

'You know the artist?'

'Sure. Anyone who's anyone knows Pru and Michael. They're like the coolest, you dig? You want some coke?'

I felt reduced. I did not know Pru or Michael. 'Sure.'

She opened a cabinet and took out a razor blade. She spoke as she cut the powder into neat lines. 'They're like Mr and Mrs Hulme, though Michael would hate to be described as an artist. He doesn't buy into all that capitalist shite. You know, labelling and that. He like collects stuff that other people think is rubbish, you know, broken, busted, and makes beautiful things from them.'

'Are they from London?'

She looked blank.

'The street signs...'

'They're like people of the universe, you know. They don't want to be shackled by fascist pretensions like class, national identity, possession.'

I nodded, though I didn't know. I wanted to challenge her on the notion that art was capitalist shite, but she was so stoned I figured I'd be wasting my time and I wanted to keep the offer of the cocaine open. I kept my mouth shut and grunted at the appropriate intervals.

'Michael and Pru, though mostly Michael 'cos he's the real genius, the creative energy behind what they are, likes things stripped to the essentials, you know, pared right back to their very essence, it's the only way to discover true beauty, Michael says.' He was starting to sound like an arsehole.

She rolled a pound note and handed it to me.

'I didn't know there were flats this big in the crescents,' I said, rubbing the crumbs into my gums. She bent down, snorted loudly, took a gulp of beer.

'There aren't. This is two flats, knocked into one. You can't tell from downstairs, it's all an illusion, but there's a doorway through to the next flat up here.' A bloke stumbled in with his flies already open and staggered towards the john. I leapt away. We stepped out on to the landing.

'Where?' I said, intrigued. She pointed at one of the bedrooms before disappearing back down the stairs, shouting, 'No one's allowed in there other than by special invitation. I'm going to dance. I totally dig this track!' I could hear a steady stream of piss hitting the bowl, a flush, then the bloke pushed past me fiddling with his flies. I felt an urge to wash and wondered if Jim washed his hands after using the toilet.

Where is he? Where's Linda?

I was sweating, my heart palpitating. Suspicion stole into me, mingling with the drug. Perhaps they were together. Linda fancied him.

But he likes me. I felt it. Am I wrong?

I finished the beer and raced back downstairs, my heels catching in the metalwork.

They were probably in the main room. Linda loved to dance. Jim would know loads of people; he'd be catching up with friends. I poked my head into the kitchen. Alan was still chatting up Cardie Girl. Unfamiliar faces flashed before me, hemming me in. I backed off, pushed my way through an arch to the open space, and surveyed the crowd. It was hot and dark, the air was heavy. People moved like spectres across the bright spotlights of the disco, which sat on a raised platform in the far corner. I fought my way over and clambered up. The DJ waved me away half-heartedly. The revellers appeared as one amorphous mass. There was no sign of either Linda or Jim. I pictured them kissing, leapt down, pushed my way through and climbed the staircase once more.

Does Jim know about the entrance to the other flat? Perhaps he's there now. With Linda.

People poured from the bathroom; word had travelled about the beer. I forced my way in, the smell of sweaty bodies filling my nostrils, and collected another bottle before crossing the landing. I hovered in front of a bedroom door, uncertain if I could go in, unsure what I might find. Previously, I'd considered Linda's promiscuity a peccadillo, but now it loomed threatening and inimical.

I pushed the door with my index finger. A dozen or so people were slouched on the floor, smoking, prostrate on the carpet. Ennui and addiction hung in the air. I closed the door. There was only one room left to investigate: the forbidden one. I felt the pull and thrill of the illicit. Michael and Pru were strangers, I felt no loyalty to them, but if caught, I would never be allowed into their hallowed circle and I feared Jim's disapproval if I transgressed. He had invited us, they were his friends and an insult to them might be perceived as a personal slight. But I couldn't help myself. The room sucked me in.

Other than the overspill from the hall, there was no light. I felt along the wall for the switch and flicked it down. Nothing. I could just about see a mountain of clothes on a bed, the outline of a small wardrobe and a bookcase. The curtains were drawn. I estimated that I could make it across the room to the window and open the curtains with the available hall light before the door closed behind me, casting me into absolute darkness. I went for it but tripped on a book, or item of clothing, on the way and I yelped in pain as my shin caught the edge of a sharp object. Rubbing my throbbing leg with one hand I tugged at the curtain with the other. The orange hue of the streetlights flooded the room, revealing its character.

It was ordinary, suburban in flavour, quite different from the rest of the flat. An enormous, tired cheese plant drooped in a corner. I looked for a doorway to the next flat. There it was, like an oversized safe door, cut out of the papered wall. Instead of a combination lock, a vertical handle made from Perspex jutted out. There was no keyhole, no lock.

I grasped the handle and tugged. It made a clicking sound, like cheap wardrobe doors, and swung open. I hesitated, my body like a tinder stick, ready to ignite, every synapse and nerve ending crackling. The thrill was unbearable, and I almost turned back when I heard a noise. Like a bark, or a howling. I peered forward and waited for another sound.

Nothing.

It must have been one of the many stray dogs that

sloped around the estate, foraging. With the heat from my pounding heart bursting through my ribs, I ducked my head, stepped over the lip, and crossed into Pru and Michael's private space.

~

The tangerine of the street lamps lit the room just as they had its opposite number. The room resembled an elderly man's shed-come-junk shop. Shelves stacked up, one on top of another, bowing with the weight of the flimflam of an artistic life. I tiptoed in, fear threatening to devour me until I dispersed it with a reedy 'Ahhh' as a figure in a wide brimmed hat materialised before me.

It was a dressmaker's dummy, wrapped in a stinking fur coat: an indoor scarecrow, or security guard. Relieved and petulant, I flicked the hat off before bending to retrieve it. The decapitated form unnerved me and I plonked the hat back on the stump of the neck.

I moved onto the landing. A bare bulb threw out an unforgiving light. I could hear nothing but the drone of the party downstairs. There was no one here, of that I was sure, and I was both relieved and a little disappointed. Why I felt relief was easy to identify – I hadn't stumbled upon an entwined Linda and Jim – disappointment less so. Pru and Michael intrigued me. Perhaps I wanted to discover something revealing and intimate about the couple, something I could purloin, a key, a way into their bohemian world. Something I could use to distinguish myself from their numerous acolytes, to prove that I was a true artiste, a life rebel, like them. I wanted something they had, and I didn't mean the space.

I poked my head around the door of the adjoining

room – a futon sat in the middle of the floor, a clothing rail hovered beside it. The heady scent of Rive Gauche permeated the air. I moved out, there was nothing of interest after all. Their bedroom, if it was Pru and Michael's, was quotidian, functional, just like most other student bedrooms. If they were students. Disappointment descended and I went to return to the party without even looking in the bathroom and third bedroom.

As I moved towards the adjoining wall, my narrow heels clacking on the floorboards, I heard a cry. I stopped and turned to the dummy. 'You trying to freak me out?'

I was sure it came from behind me, that it had not come from downstairs, or outside as I had thought earlier. The sound was too close, as if I might reach out and touch it. I listened again, but heard nothing. I went to step forward, then froze. There, it came again. It was impossible to say what could create such a sound. Not a human, not a dog or a cat, or other domestic animal. Perhaps it was a bird. I shuddered, but I did not move. I reached out and pulled the dividing door open but instead of clambering through it, I remained where I stood and shut it once more, attempting to trick whoever, or whatever, lay beyond into believing I had left. I heard a skittering, a scuttling, a grunting. The noises were coming from the far room, the room I had not entered. I was not alone.

Even as I stole towards the howling, the mewling, I was aware that I mimicked a scene from a schlock horror film. The heroine, a young woman – blonde – stupidly moving towards the terror awaiting her, the audience yelling, 'Don't go there!' Perhaps it was the cocaine that pumped me with courage, or recklessness. Who knows?

My breathing was shallow and fast, and I was acutely aware of how noisy it was. As I pushed my face against the bedroom door, listening hard, I held my breath. The wood pulsed beneath my cheek, my palms. I heard nothing but as I waited a smell slipped out. The hairs on the inside of my nose tingled, tears pricked my eyes, the outer layer of my brain dissolved with the power of the acrid stench of piss pouring from the gap between the door and the floorboards. It wasn't only urine; there was another smell. More difficult to identify; ripe, sour sweet, almost fruity. A child. The smell reminded me of my half-brother.

Whatever lurked in that room was waiting for me just as I waited for it. The smell was strong but it was more than that. A presence reached out, leached through the hollow wood. Neither of us moved, or spoke, or even breathed.

I pushed the door, gently. I did not wish to harm whatever lay behind it but the door did not ease as I had expected it to. It was locked. I checked the landing for a key. I ran my fingers along the architraves and found nothing but dust. I wiped it off on my jeans.

Sadness descended. The room was sepulchre-like and whatever was in it was trapped, buried alive. No wonder this quarter of the flat was out of bounds. What dark secret lurked there? My mind raced, I had forgotten all about Linda and Jim. I heard the slurred, muffled echo of voices. There were people nearby. The gateway door clicked open and I rushed into another bedroom, tucking myself behind the door.

25

'You left the lights on, babe. You silly cow.'

'I never did, you must have.'

'Where's Jim stashed the gear? I can't find it.' The couple scrabbled around in the junk room. I guessed it was the eponymous Michael and Pru. What was their poison?

'In the Impressionists. I moved it, what with the party and all. In case we get done over,' Pru said. I was surprised that a couple so bohemian and free-spirited and disparaging of capitalist values like possession would protect against theft. I heard a book being dragged off a shelf; a pot or jam jar crashed to the floor.

'Bollocks.'

'Do you think that'll have woken him? We don't want him kicking off now,' she said.

'I'll go check. It'd be good to unlock the door, in case of fire, or something. He'll be asleep now.'

'Forget it. I've got a key in my pocket, he'll be fine.'

Him.

'I'll go check.'

They fumbled around for some time. I heard the striking of a match, the smell of phosphorous and skunk and one of them staggering closer. My legs turned to jelly. I tried not to breathe, struggling to remain upright.

Footsteps louder and louder.

She was so close I could smell her. Rive Gauche.

The rattle of a key, the click of a door being unlocked. A whispered, 'You all right?', the door closing and footsteps drawing nearer still.

Nausea rose. I clamped my hand over my mouth and pressed down, tensing every muscle in my body. I could not vomit. I would not.

Footsteps faded, clomp–clomp–clomp, a door slammed and I breathed once more.

Above the rasp of my breaths came the sound of shuffling from behind the wall. Instantly alert, I crept out onto the landing. Crouched low, I pressed my face against the door, rapped with my fingernails. The shuffling grew louder still. I tapped three times and waited. I did not want to frighten him by entering uninvited.

Nothing.

I tapped again, twice. And then it came: two taps, clear and distinct, from the other side. I tapped three times. Three followed. Then two, then one.

'Can I come in?' I whispered. 'Do you understand?'

A slap against the door.

A yes.

I thought of my half-brother, Tom, his fragile, milky skin and sticky sweet smell. The sensation of cheek on cheek, huge great hugs, love swirling in the air around us, the high sweep of his shiny forehead.

Sitting up, resting on my haunches, I took hold of the handle, pressed down and pushed the door ajar. Light pooled from the crack. I whispered at the gap, 'Hello, I'm Diana, a friend.'

An arm emerged, chubby flesh creased around the wrist. Long smooth fingers, black dirt forming stripes underneath jagged nails. It was such a beautiful hand. I reached out and touched. Despite the cold it was warm, the way only children's flesh can be. I pushed again at the door.

27

He stood before me.

There was a snuffling, followed by screaming, mine at first, as I fell backwards onto my bottom, trying to push myself away with my arms and legs, like a crab. As I beheld the child before me I burst into tears of horror and pity.

~

Unsteady on my feet, I clambered down the staircase. I hoped the party might have thinned but, if anything, it seemed busier than ever. Shocked and in need of my bed, I was in no state to stay. My stomach churned, my vision was hazy. Disconnected, I scanned the room searching for Alan, Jim, and Linda. It was like watching a film, one the projectionist hadn't bothered to focus.

Violent crime was shockingly high in the city, and nowhere more so than Hulme. It would have been foolhardy to walk home alone, but I couldn't bear to stay. Leaning against a wall, I shut my eyes, remembering. Tears pricked.

My cries had merged with his, and he'd disappeared, closing the door behind him, retreating to his tomb, and I'd slumped back against a wall, his face imprinted on my mind. The sloping forehead, bulging, wide set eyes, like a fish, mouth stuffed with crooked teeth and a flat, almost concave face. In the murky light, he looked like a primitive doll, like those used to ward off evil spirits by African tribes.

'Diana! Hey, man, where've you been? I've been looking for you everywhere.'

Alan: all swollen, stoned eyes, looking concerned and kind. I could have kissed him.

28

'Around. Upstairs.' I only just found my voice.

'Weird. I looked for you there,' he said.

'I tell no lie when I say I was up there.' I'd stayed there for ages after the child had skittered back into his room, and I'd neither seen nor heard anyone.

'You don't look so good,' Alan said. 'You want to go home?'

'What about the girl, the one in the cardie?'

'She made her excuses a while back.'

'Tough luck. You two seemed to be hitting it off.' I touched his shoulder, genuinely sorry, wondering if he ever got lucky. He felt stronger, more solid, than I'd expected him to.

'She wasn't my type really.' He became very serious. 'It's hard not to measure women against you and Linda. You're both so lovely. Different, but lovely. A bit...' An enormous bloke shoved past and crashed into Alan, propelling him towards me.

'You're pissed. I need to go,' I said.

'Then let's.'

'What about Linda? Have you seen her? Or Jim?'

'Not for ages. He'll make sure she's OK.'

Alan didn't want to trust Jim, but deep down he knew Jim was alright. Certainly, he couldn't prove Jim wasn't, and I admired him for acknowledging this.

The journey back was short. Descending only one staircase, we didn't touch ground level, sticking to the walkways. Alan held out a rolled up *NME* he'd withdrawn from his jacket pocket as we turned the blind corner on the stairs. As defence against muggers and thieves, he said, though how a bit of paper might offer protection against a knife or crowbar was a mystery to me. But I was too shook up to protest.

Mine and Linda's flat door shone like a beacon, an oversized number fifty painted in purple gleamed against the lurid pink of the background.

'Want a cuppa before you hit the sack?' Alan said.

I'd not seen the inside of Alan's place and neither did I want to. I dithered.

A cup of tea would be nice. But that bird...

'I'll come in and make it for you,' he said, as if reading my thoughts. 'Joey's fine for a bit.'

'Joey? Original, huh. He caged?'

Alan nodded.

'You spend so much time at ours, we should think about bashing the walls through, like Pru and Michael.' I was kidding but Alan leapt on it.

'Oh, man, that would be ace. Gets lonely.'

'I'm knackered.'

'You get ready for bed. I'll bring your tea up. Let myself out.'

'That'd be great, thanks,' I said, waving him in.

He pointed at a coat hanging over the banister. 'Linda's back.'

'I'll go check if she's awake. She might want a drink too.'

But her bedroom door was shut and the light was out, so I prepared for bed. I wiped away the remains of my make-up – most of it had dribbled off with sweat and fear and tears – and cleaned my teeth. I was still flossing when Alan knocked.

'I've put it on the *Vogue* next to your bed. Night-night,' he whispered through the door. He pattered down the stairs and I heard the click of the front door closing. His scent hovered in my room, not as unpleasant as I'd have expected.

Eyes closed, trying for oblivion, I lay awake for hours. I couldn't stop thinking about the child. Our meeting – if you could describe it like that – whirled round and round my head. And though I tried to stop them, other memories rushed in.

Of a dark cupboard, me, crouching, howling, chest heaving, an unbearable pain. Bunny yelling behind the locked door, 'You want stay in the shadows, baby? You stay right there. I'm not letting you out. Not until you beg.' Later, hours or minutes? Sunlight blinding me, Bunny's arms around me, the scent of her perfume like ambrosia, melting into me. Then we're wrenched apart, her fingers pressing under my chin, insistent, so hard it hurts, lifting my head. 'You need to be displayed, honey, paraded. Enjoyed, celebrated. Bunny knows best. Remember that.'

'I love you, Mummy. I love you.'

I opened my eyes, disorientated, the memory of Bunny impossible to shake off. Her image drifted before me, like cigarette smoke: too much make-up, too blue, too pink, too coral. All too much. Her image mingled with that of the boy.

When I woke my room was bathed in the silvery sheen of a December sun. It was difficult to see the time on the travel clock sitting on the other side of the room. I clambered out of bed, knocking over the half-empty mug of tea. It seeped between my toes. I staggered to the clock. Almost ten.

'Crap.' I had a lecture in half an hour with the most fearsome tutor on the course, and I'd skipped the previous week to sort out the flat. I'd be in deepest shit if I missed another. I was so close to being kicked off. If I rushed I would only miss the beginning and this would, I hoped, be considered acceptable. After drying my feet on my dirty underwear, I grabbed some clean knickers from the pile on the floor, making a mental note to go and buy a dressing table at the weekend, and poured myself into last night's outfit. I left my hair unbrushed but couldn't bear the idea of not cleaning my teeth.

As I dashed across the landing the bathroom door swung open and a tall figure emerged, stark naked. The nude coughed a throaty rumble that sounded like, 'Sorry,' and disappeared into Linda's room. Winded with shock, I leant against the bathroom wall before grabbing my toothbrush, unable to vanquish the image of Jim's semi-erect penis from my mind.

Cal

The whirring of a fan is the first thing I hear. I'm not sure if I'm imagining it or if it's real; it sounds like it's coming from inside a machine. A computer, or my brain knocking against my skull, shaking off the drugs, like a dog shakes off water.

It's a monitor. I remember where I am. A hospital in South London, or is it Surrey? Not that the location matters. Not to me.

The nurse is here. She leans over me, checking if I'm conscious. Her perfume smells lemony, though the scent of alcohol pervades. I sniff greedily, like an addict. I open my eyes, and it takes a while to focus. Everything is blurred. I fix on a button on her uniform. It feels as if her chest is in my face. What is she looking at? Something above my head? She has big round breasts and I want to bury my face in them. I imagine releasing them from the buttoned-up, thick cotton of her drab uniform, seeing them encased in a pretty lace bra with fiddly hooks I'll struggle to undo. Heavy-lidded, I close my eyes again and drift.

~

Outside the bike sheds, leaning against the concrete, smoking a joint, Radiohead on my Walkman, I watch Stanley's mouth moving up and down, up and down. He's going on about a girl he went out with last night. It's all he's talked about. Non-stop, and I mean non-stop. Dave Lownie chucked him out of class because he couldn't shut up. Now that's weird. Lownie's about the most laid-back teacher in school. So laid-back most of the time it seems like he don't actually give a shit. I've heard about this girl like a gazillion times already and I can't listen no more. China's nodding like one of those plastic dogs people put on the back shelf of their cars. She's totally wasted.

She lifts my headphones.

'You want?' She waves the spliff in my face, before placing it between my lips. I draw deeply, breathing in the weedy, herby smell. It's good stuff.

Judging by the shape his hands are making, Stanley's talking about her tits again. Not China's, his date's. I forget her name. Thom Yorke's howling about fake plastic trees, and I wish Stanley would shut the fuck up. God knows how China can stand to listen to him talking like that about another woman. She says she's a feminist. Girl. They're girls, not yet women.

I catch China looking at me a funny way. I crease my eyebrows. She lifts the headphones again. 'You want a feel?'

'You what?'

'You can feel my tits if you like?'

'You're shitting me?'

'Go on.' She sticks her chest out – China's what Alan would call well-developed – and I look at Stanley. He's trying, and failing, to look totally not bothered. I reach out, hesitate, and China moves forward so that her tits bounce off my outstretched hands. She pushes forward and I move in, touching her. I don't look at her face; I can't. Despite her thick jumper – one of those flecked, shapeless ones like fishermen are supposed to wear – I can feel the fleshy expanse of softness. It is nothing like my own body, which is hard and unyielding. It's a fantastic feeling.

'Can I have a go?' Stanley interrupts. I'd forgotten he was there. I pull away.

'Get lost,' China says.

'Why not?' He looks wounded.

'You can feel whatshername's,' she says, a tremulous edge to her voice, and I realise that China likes Stanley more than she lets on, that maybe she is trying to make him jealous. And being kind to me. Maybe.

He shrugs, checks his watch and then pulls a face. 'Fuck. Late for Spanish.' And even though he's really, really stoned, he moves pretty quickly. Impressive.

After he's gone I say, 'Thanks.' Feeling like an idiot.

'It's nothing,' she says, bending to gather her bag and coat, slumped on the floor at her feet.

And I think: Nothing to you. Everything to me.

～

The nurse is smiling, revealing crooked teeth. It'd be so easy to fix them I wonder why she hasn't bothered. English teeth, I love them. I love that this pretty nurse has not whitened or fixed them. She's natural.

'Don't you ever go home?' I say.

'You've only been out of theatre a couple of hours,' she says. She's wearing a name badge: Sister Eve

35

Markham. 'Would you like something to eat?'

'Not hungry thanks, Sister. Or can I call you Eve?'

She laughs. 'You can.'

What's funny, I wonder.

'You should eat, it will help you recover.'

I shake my head. 'Pureed baby grub? No thanks.'

'Have something to drink?'

'If it'll make you happy.' I like her smile.

She nods and turns to leave. I sink into my pillow. Before the op I expected to feel something – a faint throbbing, dull ache, if not out and out pain. But the drugs are good. I can't feel a thing. The steady tick-tock of a bedside clock fills the air around me. Outside I hear birdsong, the distant roar of traffic, horns honking. Normal, everyday beats.

Eve returns with a mug of tea. White, no sugar, strong, with the teabag left in. And a straw. I can't drink properly. I say thanks and wonder who else she cares for in here. What she does for them. She has fed me, watered me, checked my catheter, turned on the radio, that sort of thing. She helps me with the tea; it is an effort to drink.

When I'm finished she takes the mug and places it on the tray sitting on the table. Bedside tables usually have books on them, get well cards, a picture of loved ones. Mine's empty apart from that cheap, noisy little clock.

'Do you feel your talents are wasted here?'

'How do you mean?' she says, leaning over and smoothing the sheet that covers my body.

'You trained for three years, yeah? To do tea and

sympathy…'

She nods. 'I enjoy it. Caring for people, helping them get better.'

'So you're sure I will get better,' I say.

'You will.'

I say nothing.

'It might not feel like that now, but things will improve,' she says.

'You sound so sure,' I say and I close my eyes; I'm exhausted. I hear her clogs tapping against the tiled floor as she makes her way to the door.

'See you later, Cal.'

I try to reply but she's gone before I can formulate words.

Diana

Drenched from a downpour as I made my way up Cavendish Street, I decided against sitting in a crowded lecture theatre and headed to the studios instead. While walking to college I'd been unable to shake the image of Jim's dick and at one point I'd laughed out loud. If nothing else it had dispelled the boy's face, if only for a brief spell.

The studios were quiet, with only a handful of finalists working in there. No doubt everyone else was at Elspeth Dartnell's lecture. Work by current and former students hung on the corridor walls. Brave, brilliant pieces. I paused in front of one, humbled. Would I ever be that good? I wanted to be.

I set up in the smallest studio at the far end of the building. From my folder I dragged out some work with batik dyes I'd done weeks ago, along with magazine cuttings of tribeswomen. The photographs were extraordinary, but I didn't know how to use them. I flicked through rough sketches, my ideas. Rubbish. Derivative, buy-it-at-Athena rubbish. A droplet of rain fell from my hair onto the page, soaking into the weave, spreading like a stain. Furious at my artistic incompetence, my mother's derisive words ringing in my ears, I tore the sheets apart, marched to the door, and punched the paper over and over down into a large bin. When I came up for air I was face to face with Elspeth.

'You decided against the lecture?' she said, mouth a tight thin line, green eyes cold.

'I thought ...'

She wafted a jewel-bedecked hand in the air, fingers like claws. Arthritis had claimed her ability to paint. 'Scott's talking abstract expressionism instead. There's a finalist I wanted to see.' She peered over half-moon glasses. 'And you. I need to see you, Diana.'

My gaze dropped to the shredded paper and my guts clenched. She'd seen it.

From the bin she plucked several pieces and hobbled to the nearest board, where she laid them out, piecing them together like a jigsaw puzzle. She stood back and observed. The fragmented pieces looked better than my work had ever done whole.

'So ... you have produced *something*, at least. Why trash?' The insertion of the occasional Americanism was another oddity of Elspeth's, though I'd heard she spent some time there as a young woman.

'It's terrible.'

'At least we can agree on something.' She swept up the pieces and screwed them into a loose ball, and returned them to the bin. Elspeth was good on humiliation. 'Christmas is almost upon us and still you have nothing of value. Nothing at all, if we're being frank.' She stared at me.

This was it, I faced the firing squad, and I could think of nothing, nothing, for my last words. 'Elspeth …' My voice shook.

'Diana.'

I looked into her eyes, the sting in my own blinding. 'I …'

She gripped my wrist with a force that took me by surprise. 'What disturbs you? What do you dream of at night, during the day? What are you uncomfortable with? Shock me.'

The boy's face flickered before me. 'Trolls.'

Her brow furrowed.

'The grotesque, the macabre, the freakish.'

She smiled. 'Now we have something, a grain. I feel your passion.'

Passion. She was right. There was passion there. I hadn't known it, but it was there, lurking behind the doorway of my conscious mind.

'In the library, the history section, you'll find books on Victorian circuses, freak shows. Fairy tales, go read Grimm and Andersen,' she said, her grip tightening, 'and create. Create.' With that she turned and shuffled to the door. I rubbed my throbbing wrist. For a woman with a crippling condition, she could hurt.

Before leaving, she turned, one hand resting on her back. She jabbed a crooked finger at me. 'But this is it, Diana. You have until the New Year or you're off my course. And now I must go get some goddamn painkillers.'

Shaking, I staggered to a chair. I had prepared for the worst and like an escapologist I had slipped the knot.

40

But there would be no next time.

I did not need to visit the library. Elspeth had unlocked something. With an energy borne of inspiration, and perhaps desperation, though that had done me no favours before, I gathered materials and began to draw.

I swept charcoal across paper, pressing down heavier and heavier, until the page was covered and almost black. Rubbing at the charcoal with my fingers till they stung, a picture emerged: a clover-leafed head with fish eyes the size of saucers, a plump arm, hunchback and unbalanced shoulders. Oils, wax and crayons came next. I experimented with them all. Everything around me faded as I immersed myself utterly and it was only when I felt a sharp tap on my shoulder that I surfaced from the world I was creating: the boy's world, as I imagined it. I'd scribbled and scratched and painted like an individual possessed. It had felt good.

'Time to clear up. You've made a right mess.' It was another student, one of the finalists, a bossy girl, sneering down at the bench. I stepped back and saw what she saw: a car crash of paper and materials, a caricature goblin. My spirits crashed; I was deluded. Useless and talentless.

I looked again. A glimmer of hope: yes, this was awful, but I *was* onto something, I really was. But studying books and pictures was no good; I wanted to study the boy, my very own fairy tale creature. I had to see him again.

It was dark outside; I'd not even noticed the lights coming on in the studio. The clock read quarter past six.

I'd been absorbed for over seven hours. It was a start.

Thank you, beautiful freak, thank you.

'Hellooo?' I shouted up the stairs. I heard the lock on the bathroom door slide open, the patter of feet and Linda's familiar tones.

'Be right down. Give us a minute!'

I went into the kitchen and put the kettle on, and watched the steam curling from the lip. I was pouring water into mugs when Linda breezed in.

'Tea?'

'Ta, I *so* need this.' She looked tired but happy. Her eyes glinted; there was a glow in her cheeks and an angry scab on her chin.

On the journey back, I'd been fretting about how it might be between us. Would she sense my envy? Was I envious? Would she ask where I'd been half the night? Had she searched for me as I had her? But with her, in front of me, all filled up with love, or lust, and desperate to share, I couldn't be angry or resentful.

But I didn't want to know the gory details either.

'How was your day?' she said.

For something to do, I sipped at the tea though it was way too hot. I felt a blister forming on my gum. I pressed against it with my tongue. 'Fine.'

'Were you late? Sounded like you were in a right hurry.'

'It was OK. You been here all day?'

'Pretty much.' She paused. 'I felt like shit. There were so many drugs there! Did you get any?'

'Huh, huh.' I took a gulp and felt another blister

forming on my inner lip.

She was about to burst. 'He said he saw you ... well, you saw him ...' Our eyes met. She burst out laughing, deep and dirty.

'Oh yeah, I saw him,' I said, and we both laughed. She put down her tea and looked at me.

'Diana, he's amazing.'

And she talked and talked. But not like she did the last time she slept with a bloke, when she told me all about the poor sod's quirks. No. She shared nothing of their sexual antics. She talked about how intelligent and thoughtful Jim was, how different he was to the rest of his family (how she knew this I couldn't be sure, he seemed as slippery as his brother and we'd not met the others), how they had so much in common – music, books, plays (I kid you not, I could hardly believe that someone like Jim even went to the theatre), films – how their zodiac signs were compatible. The girl was infatuated. Finally, she stopped and stared at me.

'You didn't fancy him that much, did you?'

'Who says I fancied him?'

'That day, when he came to sort the lock...'

'He's not my type,' I lied.

She laughed, complicit in the deceit. 'I came looking for you last night, and when I couldn't find you I figured you must be in one of the bedrooms ...' She had no idea how right and yet how wrong she was. 'There were so many gorgeous blokes there!'

'Were there?' My mind was on the boy.

'Are you kidding me? I didn't know who to choose.

But when Jim came onto me ... Jesus, even Alan tapped off!'

'He didn't actually.' I stared into my mug. 'I'm happy for you.' And I was. 'Are you going see him again?'

'I friggin' hope so!' she squealed.

'How could he resist you?' I murmured. Bare-faced and tired, she gave the illusion of a beautiful child.

'Have you seen Alan?'

'Nah. You OK? How's college?'

'Better. I feel like I'm meant to be here, finally. That there's a reason, other than to totally piss my mother off!'

Linda collected our mugs. 'More tea?'

We stood in the kitchen and I watched her make the drinks. 'When you were looking for me, at the party, you looked upstairs?' I said, watching her warm the teapot.

'Said I did.'

'You know there are still two flats upstairs?'

She reached for the sugar bowl and emptied two heaped spoonfuls into her mug. 'Jim said, though one's private.' Stirring slowly, she turned, her eyes wide, and said, 'You did not? You're friggin' kidding me?'

'What do you take me for?' Lunging forward, I took my tea from the worktop and blew across the scalding surface. I wanted to tell her, but I couldn't. 'I mean, it would be so disrespectful ...'

Her eyes narrowed; I wasn't entirely sure if she believed me, and I was about to ask for more milk as distraction when there was a loud knocking on the door.

'Are you expecting anyone?' I said.

'No.' Her eyes glistened; she hoped it was Jim. She bolted to the hall just as a familiar voice floated through the letterbox.

'Anyone home? Diana? Linda?'

Alan. He saved me from an interrogation. I followed Linda into the hall and opened the door. I wanted to kiss him, the hopeless, useless bugger.

~

The next morning, I was first out of bed. Alan had been upset. He'd returned home after a long walk to find Joey on his back, curled claws in the air, stone-cold dead. 'It must have been the weather. He was a tropical bird.' Alan had looked as if he might cry.

'You've no idea how old he was. Could have been ancient,' I said, touching his shoulder. I felt the outline of his collar bone. He placed his hand over mine and the cool softness of his fingers surprised me. I'd expected his hands to be rough.

To cheer him up, we'd bought a take-away and a bottle of cheap cider, and watched TV most of the evening. Alan had crashed on our sofa.

As I crept into the kitchen to prepare coffee I could hear Alan's gentle snores.

On the counter was the Leica that he'd carried in last night, when he'd interrupted me and Linda, when I'd almost told her about the child. I stroked the camera, its metal dulled and scratched. It looked well-used. I picked it up. It was satisfyingly heavy and I peered through the viewfinder. Blackness – the lens cap was on.

Alan appeared in the doorway, startling me, and other than his hair being a little more dishevelled than usual he looked much the same as he always did. Perhaps he often slept fully dressed.

'Where'd you say you found this?'

'Bailey uses one.'

'I'm not so sure.'

'Capa definitely used a Leica.'

I flipped off the lens cap, lifted the viewfinder and aimed at the window.

Alan's face filled the view. 'Nice, isn't it?' he said.

'What you going to do with it?'

'Take pictures?' He shrugged.

'What of?' I had no idea what made Alan tick, what he did all day, what excited him.

He acted embarrassed.

'Go on,' I said, 'otherwise you can't have any coffee.' Alan had developed a taste for our percolated coffee; he was forever popping in for a cup.

'The estate and the people who live here.'

I didn't respond, waiting for him to explain.

'As a record, of what it's like. So that when they knock it down and say it'll never happen again, and anyway it wasn't so bad, was it, there'll be a record. Proof.'

'You're bearing witness? Like a photojournalist?'

'Yeah, right. Like a photojournalist!' He was like a kid with a new toy, and his enthusiasm was infectious.

'I could start today. I bought film and everything, and I got it checked over. Come with me,' he said, and with nothing planned other than a visit to some junk shops I said yes. Dressing tables and dining tables could wait.

* * *

We walked about the Hulme estate and Alan took photo after photo.

'Funny that estate also means a stately home, isn't it? You couldn't get much further from ornamental gardens, gilded mirrors and roaming stags. Though this place has its own kind of beauty,' I said.

'You think so?' He shook his head. 'Think I'm more traditional than you on that front.'

He took pictures of the syringes and Kit Kat foils on the stairwells – the detritus of the addict's life – the boarded up shops, the dogs tied to bollards with string outside The Spinners pub, the old PSV club, the girls in the line for the cash point with their turned-out toes and gently curved arms, dancers-in-waiting from The Northern Ballet School, trying to be regal and graceful in the middle of all this gorgeous, vital ugliness. We stretched towards the edges of the community, noting the distinct change in character once normal society was within reach. The blocks of flats were lower, the disaffection and alienation less marked; this was a better class of slum, and the inhabitants considered themselves lucky to be outside the crescents.

The sun was setting as we crossed the bridge spanning the motorway and made our way back into the bowels of the estate. In the distance, the warehouses lining the river Medlock were backlit by the dying sun.

Alan stopped and lifted the camera, then dropped it down again. 'The whole area was built on swampland, below the water level. They never bothered to drain it when the first lot of slums went up. In Victorian Manchester, Irish immigrants would regularly wake up to a dwelling ankle-deep in polluted river water. And when they tore those slums down they still didn't bother to drain. Built right on top again. It's as if the rich and powerful hope that the earth itself will swallow up the human waste dumped here.'

'Rotten foundations?'

'The foundations for anything need to be right, don't they?'

I nodded. I'd not heard Alan so serious. He was angry and sad, and he moved me.

The child; human waste.

'I found something at that party.'

He turned away from the view to look at me.

I continued. 'I was somewhere I wasn't meant to be.'

I told him everything I knew, or guessed, or imagined.

He shrugged. 'It's no secret they have a boy.'

How does Alan know this? Off-kilter Alan, who doesn't have any friends other than me and Linda, and doesn't seem to work, or sign on, or be connected to anyone worth knowing, let alone Mr and Mrs Super-Cool of Hulme.

As it transpired Alan was not the loser I'd assumed he was. People talked to Alan; he gained their trust. When Cardie Girl had deserted him, he'd got into a conversation with the scarlet-lipped punk who'd spilt all sorts about Pru and Michael. They were junkies, rich kids from Chelsea who'd stayed on after they dropped out of university in the late seventies, later 'working' as artists and rebelling against the Thatcherite regime. Purportedly, they ran a small printing press and published a Marxist magazine that was distributed on

48

campus – I'd never seen it – organised parties and marches and generally made a nuisance of themselves. I wondered how a couple of junkies managed to squeeze all this in between fixes.

'So everyone knows they've got a kid. Do they know they lock him up?'

'Not everyone. And they might not always lock him up. It might have been a one-off, you know, 'cos of the party.'

I saw the boy's hand in my mind's eye, dredged up the hazy image of his body. He'd been rounded, fleshy, not starved. They fed him. 'Anyone seen him?'

'Not many people have.'

'No bloody wonder if they keep him locked up. It's not right.'

'He's a spastic. People make fun. They keep him out of the way for protection.'

'That does not make it right.' I was shouting. 'It's wrong to trap a kid. Force them to do things they don't want to.' My voice cracked and I heard how strange and overblown I sounded.

'Force them to do things they don't want to? We don't know that Pru and Michael do that. Diana? You OK?'

I was crying.

Alan couldn't have understood where my tears came from, but he pulled me to his chest, and I didn't object to the stink of his armpits or smelly old jacket. At least not at the time; I complained bitterly later.

Bunny made me do things I didn't want to. She'd locked me in a wardrobe and told me she'd let me out only when I was ready to be beautiful. Having inherited my mother's stubborn gene I'd stayed there for hours, belly griping with hunger, bladder aching. In the end I'd pissed on her shoes and I got a beating for that too.

Alan pulled a tissue from his pocket and I noticed the ring on the little finger of his left hand. It was made of white gold, I was sure, and had an expensive, handcrafted look about it. I shook my head, refusing the tissue, wondering where and how Alan had acquired such a lovely piece of jewellery. I dug a tissue from my own pocket and sniffled into it. 'Don't tell Linda. They're Jim's friends.'

'I won't. Look, if they lock him up, then it is definitely not right, but it might have been a one-off and even if it wasn't I'm not sure what we can do about it,' he said. 'They're the parents, we don't even know them. It's none of our business. You've got to try and forget about it.'

'I'm not sure I can.' I wiped my eyes and smiled weakly at him, and he pointed the camera at me.

'You look lovely when you're upset. Different, vulnerable. Let me take your picture.'

'I HATE my picture being taken!' I grimaced and turned my back on him.

'But you were a model, a beauty queen…'

I started walking towards the crescents, his footsteps echoing on the paving slabs as he lurched after me.

'That's why I hate it,' I said. 'I spent my childhood smiling so hard my cheeks ached, my eyes watering from

50

the glare of the flashbulbs. I'm surprised I didn't develop epilepsy or something.'

'I'd have thought most girls would have loved it, the attention. Linda made it sound like it was amazing.'

'The attention wears thin after a while, and it couldn't make up for the hours spent getting my hair and nails done when all I wanted to do was hang out with my friends, play with my Barbie dolls and other normal stuff.' I couldn't look at him.

'You didn't tell your mum you weren't happy?'

It was so rude to keep my back to him, he deserved better. I turned. 'I tried to, but she never listened. And the winning competitions and getting jobs was nice, when I did, which wasn't always...'

He raised his eyebrows and opened his eyes so wide I could see white all around his irises. He said, 'You didn't always win? No way!' It took me a while to realise he was teasing. I smiled at my arrogance and wondered if I was losing my appeal. First Jim, now Alan.

'Hey, we need to keep moving if we want to keep hold of your camera. It's getting dark,' I said, linking my arm in his, 'muggers'll be out soon.'

'Today's been great. Thanks for coming with me.'

'My pleasure. Sorry about the outburst.'

We strode along, our long legs and broad steps carrying us home faster than most. Alan talked about using his bathroom as a dark room, and asked if I'd like to watch him develop the shots he'd taken. As we marched along the curve of the crescent I saw a figure outside number fifty: Jim. Linda would be pleased. And a lightbulb came on in my head.

Jim! He's the way into Pru and Michael's world, the way to the boy. Today has indeed been good.

Blisters sprouted before my eyes.

'Herpes,' Linda said, bluntly.

I squealed in horror.

'Not THAT type. Commonly known as cold sores. Our kid gets them. Nasty.'

'How do I get rid of them?' I was close to tears.

'Only thing you can do is dry them up. Try perfume.'

My mouth was still stinging when Alan dropped by. 'My man's away,' he sighed, as he sank into a chair. He picked at foam poking out of the threadbare cover.

'Jim'll get you some,' Linda said.

Alan cheered instantly.

'I'm seeing him tomorrow.'

'Not sure I can wait that long, scouse. You know where he is tonight?'

'Pru's.'

'I didn't know they dealt,' I said, heart rate increasing.

'Only to support their habit.'

'Only? Christ!' I said. There was nothing 'only' about drug dealing; it was disgusting. End of. No way did I want to be associated with dealers. But the boy was Pru and Michael's. 'I fancy getting out,' I continued, sweeping up our empty dinner plates. 'They won't mind, will they?'

'They don't like people pouring in and out of the place. Too obvious,' Linda said.

Alan and I yelled in unison. 'You can't go alone. Too dangerous.'

So we all went, and once again I was more thankful to Alan than he could have guessed.

Unsurprisingly, the flat looked different empty of party-goers. The grubbiness was visible even in the poor light. A collection of bean bags and cushions formed a kind of sofa in front of which sat an extremely low coffee table laden with the accoutrements of addiction and a bottle of cheap vodka. Michael and Pru were recumbent, almost moribund. They did not sit up or greet us as we crept across the floor, shy and reverential. There was no sign of the boy, or any evidence that a child lived there. Not a teddy, piece of Lego, or tiny shoe. Nor was there any sign of Jim.

Ashamed of my ugly, blistered lips, I kept my chin low to my chest, though I need not have bothered on Pru and Michael's account. Their pasty faces were dotted with the lesions and sores common to addicts. A trace of beauty lurked behind Pru's atrophied features, though the image of her future shone clearer. Michael was rugged rather than classically handsome; he reminded me of a gypsy, though he too was a shell. Pointing at the vodka, he waved at the floor. The three of us sat down but no one took a drink. Then began the usual, pointless, small talk before the deal was struck. Both of them talked obsessively about themselves, utterly self-centred.

Through her mumbling the cut crystal ring of Pru's accent was clear. She sounded like a hoarse Celia Johnson. They were full of crap and I had nothing but contempt for them. My face hurt like hell, and my thoughts scrambled for a way to see the boy.

'May I use your bathroom, please?' I said.

Michael gestured to the downstairs loo.

Damn it.

'Does it have a mirror?' I said, hoping it didn't, 'I need to check these.' I pointed at my sores.

'Upstairs.' Pru wrenched herself up and handed me the vodka. 'Use this on them.' I snatched the bottle from her skeletal fingers and bolted upstairs.

For courage I took a swig as I climbed the stairs. The alcohol hit my throat with a bang. I didn't go into the bathroom, of course. I made my way to the secret entrance, stopping before I went through.

Ready?

When I'd first discovered him, I was shocked, horrified, grossed out. I'd reacted exactly as many others would. Pru and Michael didn't mean to be cruel, I rationalised; they were protecting him, but even if they had the will, and I had no evidence to prove that they didn't, they didn't have the resources – emotional or physical – to give a child anything other than the bare essentials.

Children need love.

I resolved to hug him, if he'd let me, instead of screaming and recoiling from the sight of him.

After a deep breath I pushed open the gateway door. The dressmaker's dummy stared at me. It wouldn't be long before I was missed downstairs. How could I avoid scaring the poor kid half to death? On the shelf I caught sight of a few children's books and a couple of jigsaws.

He had toys. As I stole through, I heard a child playing: happy noises, like tinkling music on a glockenspiel or xylophone. I was so close.

I caught a flicker of movement in the corner of my eye, like a shadow crossing over a mirror. I glanced towards another bedroom. The door was ajar and there was Jim crouched over an open suitcase. In amongst the clothes were packets of what looked like cannabis.

Jim looked up. Gargoyle-faced. Within seconds he had hold of my arm, dragging me into the room, his nails digging into my flesh. Words flew like bullets from between his tight lips. 'What the hell are you doing?' He pushed me against the wall.

'I could ask the same of you,' I said, indignant. So Jim was Pru and Michael's supplier. Or was he stealing from them?

'Don't get clever with me.'

I considered inventing some dismal excuse about getting lost, but that would never fool Jim, and I was scared.

'I know about the boy,' I said, mouth dry, sores throbbing.

'And?'

'I've seen him.'

Jim let go of my arm. 'That explains a lot. We thought he was making it up.'

'I only wanted to see him. To say sorry, if I frightened him.'

Sensing my fear, Jim relaxed; he was back in control, and in repose he was beautiful once more.

'You, frightening him?'

'They'll be wondering where I am,' I said, the change in atmosphere offering an escape.

'You say nothing of this. Nothing.' He gestured towards the suitcase of hash. 'And I'll keep quiet about you creeping around. You get me?' he said, pointing, his index finger spiking my chest.

I nodded and rushed back downstairs, bitterly disappointed I'd not seen the boy again.

But I had something on Jim now, even if I wasn't quite sure what it was. And he was my route to the boy.

Cal

I drink a cup of tea and I'm knackered it's such an effort. It leaves a peculiar taste in my mouth – a metallic film coats my gums and tongue. Something in the milk or the painkillers perhaps. The milk could be UHT. It tastes like the milk from little white cartons you find at railway station cafés, those that are impossible to open. I loved those cartons as a kid; they signified journeys, adventure, something new.

It hurts to move my head, twist even a centimetre or flinch a muscle. I can flex my fingers and toes without pain and that's about it. The drugs are wearing off. Physical pain's nothing. I can put up with it. Anyone can if they have to.

There's a match on the television: Spurs versus the Gunners. The commentator is very excited. Arsenal have just scored. I can't lift my head and I can't be arsed to call the nurse who isn't Eve to ask her to prop me up. I listen instead, pretend it's radio. I'm not all that keen on football. Not really. Not anymore.

I fall into something that could be sleep, or a daydream, or memory. I can't be sure which.

~

Big blocks of Lego litter the floor. The remains of a sandwich curl on a paper plate. I take a bite as I pass. The xylophone is calling me. I tap the wooden stick against the red and pink keys. I like the noise it makes. I hit it harder and harder, and then in between the tings I hear another noise, from behind the door. Moving about, pushing at the door, tapping on it, pulling the metal handle. I run towards it. It swings open, almost knocking me over.

There he is: the golden man with the silky voice. He picks me up, under the arms, and swings me round and round and round. I am dizzy and sick and happy. He stops, puts me down; I stick to his legs, feeling the warm of him against me. The bone of his knee presses against my chest and it's time to let go. I'm a good boy. I want him to hold me, cuddle me like grown-ups with kids on the telly. 'Hug. Hug,' I say. But he just stands. He is nice. He brings me sweets, talks to me and sometimes he brings me toys. An Action Man, a ball and some skittles. Today he has an orange woollen blanket. What a silly present. The ends are stitched with white wool. It has some holes in it and he tells me that it is a very old and very special blanket. It is cold today. We sit on the bed on the floor, next to each other, watching telly, me cuddled in the blanket, looking at the orange falling from my shoulders, wrapped around my legs. He loves me very, very much.

~

I snap awake. I hear the clock. What time is it? The remnants of the dream hang around me. Was it real? Did this really happen, or have I re-imagined it, as an adult, the way we do. Filling the gaps and tears in the truth with all sorts of nonsense. Nonsense to make us feel better, because the truth hurts too much.

Diana

As the end of the academic term drew closer the noose of expulsion grew tighter round my neck. The morning I received the letter from my mother, much of my optimism about my future had already faded. I'd attended every lecture, shown up at the studios regularly and still I struggled. What little I did produce ended in the bin. Whenever our paths crossed, which was thankfully infrequent, Elspeth tipped her chin, but did not smile. My dreams, when I slept, were full of the boy. On waking, his image dissolved immediately and it was becoming increasingly difficult to recall his face at all.

Running late, I swept the envelope up off the mat and rammed it into the back pocket of my jeans, before running out of the flat. I almost forgot about it and later wished I'd acted on my first impulse to chuck it. My mother wanted something. Bunny never wrote. It'd been over two years since I'd left home, since she left husband number two after catching him once too often in a compromising situation with a colleague, secretary, nurse. He couldn't keep his hands to himself and, in fairness, Bunny was a total nightmare so not altogether blameless in the disaster zone that was their marriage.

I trudged across the sopping wet park grass to the library, intent on finding books on fairy tales, when I saw a homeless man, palm outstretched. I reached into my front pocket to retrieve some loose change and felt the rustle of the envelope in my back pocket.

In the library, I sat down and read the letter. After waffling on and on about how awful Dad – husband number one – was, she came to the purpose of her communication. She was short of cash, though only until the details of her divorce were finalised. 'But heaven knows how long that will be! You know what the courts are like!' She understood that students had no money, but she had a contact in a new agency; she'd shown her my old book, and this agent would be delighted to send me to castings. Only classy work – 'No catalogue rubbish' – would be considered, so I wouldn't have to do much and she'd pay me back, with interest, as soon as she was solvent. She was desperate.

Jesus.

Bunny had received a more than healthy settlement from my father, but her lifestyle had always outstripped her means and she'd clearly not learned from past mistakes, though perhaps this was yet another attempt to lure me back into fashion. Furious, and upset, I banged my head on the desk until someone asked me to be quiet.

I read the letter again.

It did sound bad. Poor Bunny. She could lose her home; she'd already sent her car back, and she loved her car. And she was frightened for Jasper. Jasper was her dog, our dog. She'd had to cancel the insurance and recent vet fees had been colossal. But I couldn't model again. I felt sick at the thought of parading myself; I was more than that, wasn't I? Next month, Dad would send another cheque to top up the grant cheque I'd receive. Bunny could have some of that. I'd manage.

To get a grant, you have to be on a course, you fool.

I found the books I needed and rushed over to the studios.

All manner of demonic sprites, elves, pixies, ogres and goblins lay before me. The troll that lay in wait for the goats in *The Three Billy Goats Gruff* reminded me of the boy with his curved spine, large, distorted nose, and wide set eyes. In truth, the troll was less alarming than the boy. I opened a book on the fairies of the flowers and woodlands. How exquisite, delicate, and pretty they were. An idea formed: I would transform the trolls and fairies. The beautiful would become ugly, the hideous lovely, or something in between, something that was neither. I took hold of a pencil and began to sketch.

'Illustration really isn't your thing, is it?'

Elspeth. She moved as inconspicuously as a ghost despite her crippling condition. I stared at the page, not daring to look at her.

She wafted her hand across the open books, a ring large enough to contain poison on her index finger. Her joints so swollen it would stay there forever. 'Tell me where you're going with this. The concept. If you can.'

Stammering my way through an explanation, I did as she demanded.

'But surely you're not going to draw these creatures?'

'No,' I blurted. 'Photographs. I'm going to use photographs.'

She huffed. 'Now there would be a thing: photos of fairies. It's been tried before. All fake.'

'This will be real. Real monsters, freaks, fairies.' I had no notion what possessed me. Desperation, of course. I would take photos of the boy, gather photos of myself as a girl, angel-faced and spangly in tiaras and satin gowns, all dressed up with nowhere to go, gather images of American pageant queens I'd seen in Sunday supplement magazines, early modelling shots of my own.

Elspeth laughed loud and throaty. '*This*, I look forward to seeing. Well, Diana, you might just save yourself.' And she walked away as silently as she'd arrived.

I scribbled away for as long as I could bear it, nausea building with every stroke, every crappy, hopeless sketch. After a while, I shoved them into my portfolio case and staggered outside. There was little point staying.

On the pavement, I lit a cigarette, panicking. The sky darkened and it began to drizzle. I dithered whether or not to hail a cab. By the time I'd finished my cigarette, it was lashing it down. No way was I walking over the bridge, not with my portfolio to haul. I crossed the road to the bank. As I turned away from the cash machine, I saw Jim beneath the glow of a street lamp.

'What are you doing creeping about round here?' I'd not seen Jim since the night I caught him rifling through the suitcase packed with drugs at Pru and Michael's, and my aggression was an attempt to cover my nervousness. Why did this bloke always catch me when I looked a complete sight? It'd been a stressful day, what with Bunny's news and then Elspeth pitching up and me making all kinds of insane promises. My face was probably covered in charcoal smudges, my hair was scraped back into a severe ponytail, while he looked magnificent, his blond hair glowing like a halo.

'On my way home. Dropped in for a pint.' He jerked his head towards the Union building. 'You going back?'

'Don't you need a student card?' I began to walk down the road. Without waiting for an invitation, Jim ambled alongside me.

'Easy. Nicked one.'

'I should have guessed.'

I'd overstepped the mark. He said, 'Is that what you think of me? Robbin' git?'

'No—'

'It was a joke. I walk right in. Nobody stops me, it's all about believing you have the right to be there—'

'Sorry. I've no idea why I said that—' I couldn't look at him.

'Because you're ashamed, and embarrassed.' Linda was right. He might have left school without qualifications but he was smart.

'Look, I can't believe I did that ... snooping round someone else's home.' Icy drops of rain whipped my forehead and cheeks; there was no hood on my second-hand mac. I turned up the collar.

'You shouldn't have gone nosin—'

We crossed the road, jumping over puddles, and dived for shelter underneath the halls of residence entrance, and looked out at the rain.

'How is he? The boy?'

'His name's Cal.'

Cal. Lovely name.

'Why do they keep him hidden away?'

'Why do you think?' He emphasised the 'you', enunciating correctly.

Despite the finality of his tone, I added, 'It's not right.'

'You wanna share a taxi?'

'Sure. Are you going to our place?'

Jim breezed into the halls of residence and asked the porter to call a cab. As he leant across the counter his leather jacket rode up and I could make out the curve of his backside in his tight jeans. He pulled a comb from his back pocket and ran it through his hair, twice, easing it into an upright position again. I wanted to talk more about Cal, find out what was wrong with him, but Jim was having none of it. 'Stay out of it. None of your business.'

A taxi pulled up and Jim stepped into the rain and held open the door. We flopped into deep leather seats a safe distance apart. 'Charles Barry Crescent, mate,' Jim said, and the driver swung the cab round in the road. We lurched into each other; his thighs felt damp and firm. As I prized myself from him, I muttered an apology. Jim shrugged and shifted in his seat without actually moving. Our thighs no longer touched but I could feel his shoulder against mine. I wiped the steam from the window and stared out.

My restraint didn't last long. 'You talk to Linda about Cal?' I said.

'Why would I? Nothing to do with me.'

'I'd like to make it up to him.'

'No you wouldn't. You wanna say sorry so that you can feel better about yourself.' Contempt washed over his features, and I hated him. What he said was true: I did need to feel better, but it was more than that. I had to see Cal again. And if I wasn't to be kicked off the course and have to go back to Bunny, and modelling, with my tail between my legs, I had to find inspiration and produce some work. Elspeth expected photographs.

The cab pulled up outside the crescent and we both climbed out. I had no idea where Jim lived. He insisted on paying. We stood on the pavement, neither prepared to make the first move to leave.

'I'm sorry 'bout before,' he said, kicking the ground.

I was confused.

'I was out of order, what I said about you wanting to make yourself feel better and all that about Cal.'

'You want to come in for a coffee?' I didn't fancy being alone. Linda was out with her mother, who'd come over from Liverpool to do some Christmas shopping. They'd be sitting in a café, sharing news, being mother and daughter, and I couldn't imagine how that might feel. I wanted to know what it felt like for someone, a mother, to really care.

'I got things to do,' he replied.

'Sure—'

'Maybe a quick one.'

It was one of those rare days when the lift worked. It stank of an unholy mix of urine and bleach. We didn't speak as the lift groaned its way up two storeys. It juddered to a standstill and the doors creaked apart before jamming. Through a gap of about six inches I saw a teenager, a child really, loitering, knife in hand, and what looked like plastic pants on his head – the sort you put over a nappy to protect the baby from the safety pins. I started to laugh and said, 'You have got to be kidding me!'

Apparently incensed by my laughter, the boy leapt forward and waved the knife through the gap shouting, 'Give us your money or else!'

Jim stepped into the boy's line of vision. 'Or else what?' Jim said in a voice as hard and mean as metal, 'You'll what, Dave Pritchard?'

The boy froze, fear sweeping over his features like a rash.

'I'm waiting,' Jim said.

'Sorry, Jim, sorry.' And he ran.

Jim prized the doors apart and I almost fell out behind him, legs wobbly. The boy had been afraid of Jim, the sort of fear that comes from knowledge. What was it about Jim that inspired such terror? He was a small-time drug dealer; I'd not seen evidence of anything more sinister. But still I shuddered. Jim took my arm as we made our way down the walkway. That old saying about the fire and the frying pan kept flashing in my mind.

In the flat I put the kettle on and told Jim to make

66

himself at home. Upstairs I fussed with brushes and changed my clothes, a tight feeling in my chest. When, finally, I emerged, two mugs of steaming coffee in my hands, Jim was sitting at the dining table flicking through my sketches. A mixture of annoyance and embarrassment made me almost drop the drinks. I dumped them on the edge of the table and began to sweep up the sheets that Jim didn't have hold of. His assumption that he was privy to whatsoever he pleased angered me, but the words I needed to express this escaped me. I found myself stuttering, 'These aren't for public viewing, they're rough sketches, terrible really, rubbish. No one's meant to see them.' I took hold of the sheet he held.

'Aren't artists supposed to show their work?' His voice as sharp as a paper cut. He did not relax his grip.

I tugged. He pulled the paper towards him and said, 'They're not rubbish.'

'Well, they're not for public consumption.'

'I'm hardly "public". You know me, I thought we were friends.' He held my gaze with those dark eyes, the faintest flicker of a smile across his lips, or was it a sneer?

'You're my flat mate's boyfriend.'

'Does that mean we can't be friends?'

Heat rushed through me. 'Of course it doesn't …' I spoke too quickly, too defensively. I stopped and told myself to get a grip. 'But I didn't mean for anyone to see them.'

'I've already seen.'

I let go of the sheet at the same time as he did and the drawing dropped to the table. 'So you have,' I said, defeated. I sat down and took a sip of coffee.

'They're good.'

'Art expert are we, as well as mugger vanquisher?' Ignoring me, he lifted another sketch, one of goblins with long, downy hair, like gossamer, on cheeks and hands.

'This looks like Cal?' He stared at me.

'Does it?' Linda wasn't the only one who could be brazen.

'It wasn't deliberate?'

'Not exactly.'

He sat back in the chair, his shoulders spilling over the sides, his chin tipped up, face cocked on one side, demanding an explanation. I detected something resembling tenderness in his tone when he mentioned Cal. This was my opportunity to get closer to the boy; I was not going to squander it with lies and ego.

'The concept, changelings, was inspired by Cal, I think. You can never be sure of these things,' I said.

'The artistic impulse moves in mysterious ways,' he said, mocking again.

I guffawed, choking on my coffee, and said, 'Sound like a jerk, don't I?'

'Yeah.'

I flinched; his honesty was brutal. He picked up another drawing, a charcoal, gazed at it, his skin melting before me, transforming him into a man I no longer recognised but liked. He continued. 'It's great. Weird, extraordinary, beautiful.' It was as if he was talking to himself.

'He is,' I said.

Jim looked up at me, as if to check that it wasn't me

68

who was mocking this time.

'Extraordinary,' I whispered.

'Yeah, right. A weirdo, freak, spaz.' The spell was broken. He took a gulp of his drink and slammed the empty mug down. The sound echoed round the flat.

'I'd like him to see them,' I said, hurriedly, worried the moment had passed. 'Perhaps Pru and Michael might like to see them too?'

'Thought you said they weren't ready? Rubbish?'

'You've changed my mind.'

He stood and brushed imaginary dust from the front of his jeans and said, 'They wouldn't be interested.'

'But Cal would?'

He shrugged, but the gesture betrayed him. 'Not sure he'd get it.'

'He doesn't have to "get it". He can enjoy them. I'll make up stories to go with them—' I was persistent. I felt a connection with Cal. As a child I'd been isolated, unloved and unhappy.

'What is it with you? Why can't you just leave him alone?' he snapped and turned to go.

I wasn't about to spill my guts to Jim. But possessed by a morbid curiosity, fascination, and desperation to make good my promise to Elspeth, I cried out. 'Because it seems that everyone leaves him alone!' I grabbed Jim's arm and he swung around, eyes blazing. I'd gone too far, touching him like that, but it was too late.

He shook himself free so violently that my arm rattled in its socket, hurting.

'Why does it matter to you?' I was yelling.

He looked startled, like I'd slapped his face or

something, then he regained his composure and said, 'It doesn't.'

'You're lying.'

'You don't think much of me, do you? Liar, thief ... You think I'm scum.'

I rubbed my shoulder and said, 'I don't.' We looked into each other's eyes.

'You OK?' He went to touch me. I flinched and stepped back, frightened that if he touched me, gentle, kind, I'd want to touch him and then there'd be no stopping it.

'I'm fine.'

'I'll talk to Pru and Michael. You'll have to be discreet.'

'When?'

'Tonight. Seven-ish. Bring your pictures, all right?' And he left, slamming the door behind him.

~

Pru and Michael's flat lost even more of its appeal on my third visit. I felt ever so clean and shiny in their living area. The gleaming leather of my portfolio looked out of place in this room of recycled, overused junk. Jim mentioned something about preparing space for the goods and disappeared. The way he moved around the space, like it was his own, almost ordering Pru and Michael about surprised me. And then I understood: the suitcase full of drugs in the bedroom, he *was* the source. Their pad was his shop front, loaned in exchange for a regular supply of heroin.

Michael gestured for me to sit. The floor was littered with tobacco, torn-off roaches, used matches, and the odd bit of unidentifiable old food. It looked like they'd had noodles though they could have been maggots. My stomach turned as I forced myself to sit. I needed to keep them sweet.

Michael and Pru were sober though judging by the open bottle of whisky on the table that state wouldn't last. The whisky was a cheap blend, the sort Dad would be sniffy about, and they drank without ice or a mixer. The atmosphere was fraught, though neither of them were hostile nor unfriendly, more confused. In many ways, they seemed so normal: two down-on-their-luck toffs, boring, and bored of each other. Michael made an attempt at small talk. He spoke at length, and with some passion, about a desire to travel.

'Piss off then,' she snapped. They were about to have a row and I couldn't bear the idea of a petty domestic squabble. I'd had enough of that as a child. A painful silence followed. I stood and admired the glazed wall.

Pru talked about the décor of the flat, the inspiration behind it. She described it as conceptual, like an installation, and compared it to the Haçienda, the coolest club in town. I almost laughed; she was such a phoney – pretentious and humourless. Where was Jim? Had he mentioned that I wanted to meet Cal?

Michael interrupted Pru. 'Jim says you're an artist, that you want to show Cal your paintings. He'll like that.' He shook, all edgy, pulling at his fingers.

I nodded. So Jim had been true to his word.

'How do you know what he'll like,' said Pru, 'you never take any notice of him.'

'Nor do you,' he replied.

71

I tuned out while they bickered about Cal, the flat, everything. Finally, Pru staggered out. Michael took a gulp of whisky and lay down. He stared at me and I hoped he wasn't about to make a pass.

Then he spoke, slowly, dreamily. 'Not long before she was due, she became very odd. More so than usual,' he said. 'She started saying that she didn't want him to come out, that she wanted to keep him inside her forever, just for her. Understand what I mean?'

'Like she didn't want to share him?'

'Exactly. And when he came out she couldn't bear to keep him. To have him anywhere near her.' He knocked back more whisky.

'But she did,' I said.

He continued as if I hadn't spoken. 'It was months before she held him. Post-natal depression, the docs said. But I knew it was more than that. He was so special to her when he was inside, a part of her, that when he came, like that, it was like he'd been conning her all that time, laughing at her. She said it was punishment for something bad she'd done, but she couldn't think of anything that bad, something bad enough to warrant him looking like he did.' His voice strained, with something like love, and fear and disappointment. I wondered if Cal's birth, and condition, was what had turned them onto heroin, or whether the drugs came first, were responsible.

'She doesn't love him, she can't. She doesn't know how.'

'What about you, Michael? Do you love him?'

He reached forward, averting his eyes, but before he

did I detected a tremble in his cheeks, a crumpling around the mouth. Whether it was love or shame I wasn't sure. 'I look after him. Feed him, clean him, take him to the doctors.'

'One person's love can be enough,' I said.

He didn't reply, instead he stood up and announced that he needed a fix. He staggered out.

I felt small and cold, alone in the vast room. Unsure what to do, I was about to wander upstairs when Jim returned.

'You can come up. Don't be nosin' in any other room.'

I picked up my portfolio and said, 'I won't stay long, it's late.'

'Stay as long as you like. He's like an owl, mostly nocturnal.'

Upstairs, the lights were dim. Everything was fuzzy round the edges, as if I was viewing it through a jar of honey. Jim knocked on the bedroom door.

'All right, Cal? She's here.'

A muffled voice said, 'Come in, Jim. Come in, Jim,' with an underlying delight that hinted at an awareness of rhythm. I hesitated. There, in front of the door, invited in at last, I wasn't sure that I was ready. The boy was monstrous. Would I be able to control my disgust? Perhaps I was the monster. Jim held the door open and I forced myself to step inside.

He was crouched in the middle of the room surrounded by scraps of paper and brightly coloured pencils and Lego. He had his back to us, matted hair falling to his shoulders, downy hair dusted his back, his figure cast a strange shadow on the wall. As we stepped forward he shuffled round and pushed himself upright. He wore nothing but a pair of swimming trunks and other than his barely discernible twisted stance and being a little small for his age – Cal was four, less than a year younger than my half-brother Tom – from the front his body looked perfect. His legs were long and chubby. His skin was never-seen-the-sun white and his stomach retained the swell of infancy. I longed to squeeze it, or kiss it, as I did Tom's. He wore a plastic mask, the sort you'd buy at a tacky toy shop. It was supposed to be a monkey but it was so cheap I couldn't be sure. Would he take it off? I needed him to.

He stood still and offered a well-rehearsed, 'Hello, Diana,' like children do on stage at school assemblies when presented with a prize. His voice sounded as if he didn't know where to put his tongue, or as if his tongue was too big for his mouth. I pictured it dangling, fat and crimson, out of his distorted lips and tried to recall his mouth in detail. I couldn't.

'Hi, Cal. Good to meet you.'

Ignoring my outstretched hand, he nodded and sat back down again, and I noticed again how large his head was. How flat. He picked up some Lego bricks and began to build.

'I like your mask,' I said.

He continued building without replying. I crouched and asked if I could join in. He ignored me, and adjusted the mask, before returning to his work. Disappointment unravelled from my knotted centre. He wore a mask and now this. I'd hoped he might be pleased or excited to meet someone new. Someone who was interested in him.

But what had I expected? For him to fall grateful into my benevolent arms? Even normal children, children that went to nursery, had friends, family and ordinary social interaction, were mostly uninterested in adults, shy of meeting strangers. Like Tom, and me when I was only a little older than Cal.

A few months short of my sixth birthday I was taken to my first casting, pushed into the limelight to be admired and flattered, and criticised by strangers. That first time, I was shy. When the photographer asked me questions my mind emptied. Despite hours and hours of priming, Mum forcing me to pout and strut and twirl I could not remember what to do or say. My mouth was dry; I couldn't get any words out. All I could see was Bunny's furious face. According to Bunny, it was because of my silence I wasn't offered that first job, despite being '*so* much prettier than the other girl. Why, she was overweight. I don't mean to be cruel, but the girl was fat!'

That was the first time Bunny beat me.

By seven, I was an old hand at the modelling business. Used to being primped and fussed and cooed over. Used to the occasional slap if I didn't get a job. I lost my shyness, as well as my childhood.

I picked up a drawing. It was typical of a child of Cal's age in form and composition. Two figures, filled out stick men, battled with lightsabers, one red, one blue. I recognised it instantly. 'Darth Vader and Luke Skywalker.'

Cal made swooshing, chinking noises, and began to breathe heavily, like Vader did. His impersonation was

75

spot on. My eyes scanned the room and I saw the television and VCR.

'I'd love one of those,' I said, 'I'd watch films all day.'

'Science fiction and fantasy are his favourites,' Jim said. He made me jump. I'd forgotten he was there.

'E.T. is one of my favourites. Have you seen it?' I said. I heard the hollowness in my voice, the desperation to please. It was almost true. Tom loved it and I'd watched it with him.

'Phone home,' Cal said in a shaky voice, pointing a figure at the ceiling. I smiled, and wondered if he identified with E.T. Jim had said he was perfectly normal in other ways, tapping his head. I took that to mean that the boy wasn't retarded.

I pulled out my drawings and pushed them along the uncarpeted floor towards Cal. He showed no interest, so, hiding my disappointment, I put them to one side and began to play with Lego. After a while Cal skiffled over to the pictures and leafed through them.

How uncomfortable that mask must be.

He pointed at a figure and said, 'This me?' He was left-handed. His fingers were beautiful, flawless, despite dirty nails, and as he pointed I noticed a mole on the web-like skin between his middle and ring finger.

'Kind of. I thought of you when I drew it. Do you like it?'

He shrugged.

This was good. He was honest, like all kids. I was surprised he recognised himself. I looked round the room, properly this time, and there in the corner behind me, a full-length mirror, attached to the wall. It seemed

76

cruel, somehow, to remind him. Surely he would compare himself to characters on TV.

'You,' Cal said.

He handed me a figure made from bricks. The head was a ready-made one with yellow hair and a straight red mouth. It looked very serious, if not actually miserable. It made me laugh. I looked over at Cal, the fixed expression of the monkey mask unnerving me. I longed to read his emotion. I couldn't make out his eyes in the cylindrical holes in the plastic.

'Do I really look that cross?'

He didn't reply, but shuffled closer. I could have touched him with outstretched arms. I wanted to.

'I like your hair,' he said.

'Thank you.' And I smiled. 'May I draw you?'

He shrugged, and Jim said maybe another time.

'That OK with you, Cal?' I said. I needed the boy's consent and to my delight I registered a small, definite, tip of the mask. I felt as happy as I'd been in a long while.

Jim said it was time I left.

Jim abandoned me at the bottom of the stairs, disappearing into the black night, leaving me to walk home alone. But I didn't care; I had no fear of what might await me out there.

Another time. That's good. I must have been a hit.

~

A note on the doormat greeted me as I pushed open the flat door.

Baby doll. I looked for you at the school of art and when you weren't there I got directions from the concierge. I risked

77

my life to come to this Godforsaken hole to find you. Where are
you? Call me. Midland Hotel, Room 518. 061 299 5050.
Bunny.

Concierge! I ask you. No date. No kisses. No I love
you, I'm worried about you.

'Welcome to Manchester, Bunny.' I slung my bag
across the hall and pondered whether or not to take my
coat off.

'Hellooo.' I peered up the stairs.

'All right there?' Linda's face appeared over the
banister. Seconds later she tottered down the stairs. She
wore a mini-dress with half a dozen coloured beads
draped around her neck and a pair of extremely high-
heeled ankle boots.

'You look nice. Where you off to?'

'Haçienda. Fancy it?'

'Not sure. Bunny's in town. I really should go and
see her.' I held up the note.

'I never heard any knocking.' Linda played music
loud enough to shatter eardrums.

'No worries. She probably didn't try too hard. You
had a lucky escape.'

I didn't feel up to seeing Bunny, fighting off her
demands and pleas for financial help, though if I didn't go
I'd only be delaying the inevitable. I knew my mother; no
way would she slip away quietly.

'I'd like to meet your mum.' Her brow furrowed.
'Why'd you call her Bunny?'

'It's her name.'

'Why not Mum?'

'Cos I don't see her as all that maternal. More like

78

an agent.'

'Funny name, Bunny.'

'Funny Bunny, ha ha. Except she's had a sense of humour bypass and she's nothing like a bunny rabbit.'

'What is she like then?'

'A Rottweiler.'

She laughed. 'Go and see her. You can't not go. She's come all this way.'

'I'm not sure I can face it. I've no idea what she wants,' I lied.

'To see you? Maybe she just wants to see you.'

How I wished that were true. 'Bunny always wants something.'

The bus came quickly, too quickly, and the journey was too short. There appeared to be no traffic that night. Images of Bunny flashed before me: her enormous orange face and huge blonde hair; her spiky lashes and frosted eyeshadow; teeth gnashing, threatening to gobble me up. She was talking, always talking. Instructing. 'Smile, baby, smile. Big, big smile. Chest out, tail in. Work it, baby, work it.' Mascara dribbling down her cheeks like tar as photographers snapped away, as she turned the pages of glossy magazines looking for her darling girl, her doll. The warmth I felt basking in her pride. Then, a crack reverberating in my skull, a throbbing in my cheeks, a distorted face, all chin and nose, screaming at casting agents: 'What's wrong with you? Are you blind? My baby's the most beautiful, the best...' In rage, her accent slipping, unmasking her Dagenham origins.

And then her face merged with Cal's. What would

she make of someone like him?

The Midland was glitzy and expensive, seriously expensive. She was supposed to be broke. On the pavement opposite, I checked my watch: quarter past ten. I couldn't use the hour as an excuse not to drop in, but at least the visit would be brief by necessity. Bunny had always retired before midnight.

I'd been elated after spending time with Cal, but the journey and thoughts of Bunny allowed disappointment to surface, to merge with my excitement and temper it. After all, he'd not removed his mask and I needed to see his face. On top of that I needed to persuade him to let me take photographs. But, I reminded myself, it was a start; I was hopeful I'd see him again. And Elspeth was off my back for a while.

My mood was shifting. I aimed to be as bright as the hotel lights. From a distance, the doorman sneered at my shabby clothes, but his expression altered as I drew closer and he positively melted when I threw him one of my megawatt smiles.

What a pushover.

The receptionist dialled Bunny's room, but there was no reply. 'I'm sorry miss, you could check—' she said, in a thick Mancunian accent.

'The bar. I'll check the bar, thanks.'

Sure enough there was Bunny, on a high stool, legs crossed, thighs exposed, cellulite visible below the hem of her stone-washed denim skirt, a thin cigarette gripped between pink-tipped fingers. The stink of artificial mint hung in the air. She looked incongruous here in northern England in mid-winter, with her heavy tan, white teeth and exposed limbs. She'd freeze to death if she ventured out. Despite an aura of tawdriness she looked good for woman a couple of years shy of forty. The moment she saw me, she leapt down from the stool and opened her mouth. Full throttle.

'Sweetheart! Why didn't you call to let me know you were coming?' She made a great show of kissing me on both cheeks, holding me at arm's length and checking me over. 'You look so pretty, baby. Even in these rags.' She flicked the collar of my mac.

'Good to see you too, Mum. Nice place for someone who's broke. Can you afford to buy me a drink?'

'Why of course. Martin, are you going to offer to buy my beautiful daughter a drink, sweetie pie?'

It was only then I noticed a man, maybe late forties, standing at the bar, a short distance away from the stool Bunny had vacated moments ago. He was notable only for his size. Tall and broad, and though not fat he was in possession of an inappropriate amount of bulk. Like a weightlifter or boxer gone to seed. Bunny had wasted no time finding company.

We sipped cocktails bought by 'Martin' (I wasn't convinced this was his real name; I'd clocked the band of gold) who had the grace to leave before he'd finished his. He said goodbye after pushing a business card across the bar. 'If ever you need a new kitchen, Bunny, you know where to find me.'

We watched him walk across the bar towards reception.

'So… what brings you to Manchester?'

'Why, sweetie, to see you!'

I nodded and smiled, wanting to believe her but waiting for her to mention money. After asking about her journey and friends from London, I talked about my course, about the work I was creating, the positive feedback I'd received from Elspeth (a half-truth admittedly), about Linda and Alan, and how she would barely understand a word Linda said. Bunny nodded in roughly the right places, and made all sorts of 'Uh-huh' noises, but I could tell she either wasn't listening or wasn't interested. Not really. A fierce pain skewered my chest, a fire burned in my throat.

I drained my glass, pulled out the cherry, swallowed it and said, 'So enough about me. What's new with you? How's the money situation? You look great.'

'Thank you, sweetie. Such a lovely daughter.' She pinched my cheek.

Why are you here, Bunny? What do you want?

She babbled for a while about her latest venture, an idea. She would become a scout, maybe even set up her own agency. She talked about the fifteen-year-old daughter of a friend she introduced to an agent. The girl was already earning a small fortune treading the runways of Paris and Milan. She mentioned, casually, how the agency had said their UK office was on the look-out for older girls for catalogue work.

'It's not glamorous, sweetheart, but my God it pays well! And there's lots of it. Especially now. The market is exploding.'

Finally we were getting to it. My throat tightened again. My eyes stung. I fought a desire to cry.

'I'd pay you back,' she said, touching my knee.

82

'We both know it's not about the money.' My eyes swept the room.

'You'd be helping me, your Mummy.'

'I'm too fat.'

'The fashion is for bigger girls now.'

'I'm too old.'

'You're only just out of your teens.'

'What about my course?'

'Take time off. All work and no play... It's my big chance, to do something with my life, something for me. I can prove myself to these people.'

I continued to make excuses, vacillating between desperately wanting to please, to help her, and wanting to fulfil my own ambitions.

'This is a sure thing, Diana. Not like this silly hobby.'

I snapped. 'This is not a hobby. It's my life.' I took a cigarette from her packet and struggled to ignite the lighter. The bartender leant over and offered me his and I was glad for the expensive, classy hotel and its emphasis on service. I shook as I inhaled.

'What kind of a life, baby? You'll never earn a decent living. Think of all those French painters, that poor, stunted little man.'

'Toulouse-Lautrec. A genius.'

'Penniless. He died penniless,' she screeched. She went on and on.

'Some artists earn. Why not me?' I choked, the words catching in my throat.

'You need to get a grip. Take a reality check,' she said, shouting. The argument grew more heated, and people turned to the source of the disturbance, flicking back to their original poses as sharply when I stared right back.

'You're not talented.' She checked herself. 'Not talented enough. "Artists" like you are ten a penny. You can't even draw properly.' Softening, she added, 'Sweetheart, your looks won't last for ever, so you're better off making the most of them while you can.'

What a philistine. She'd never understand. I didn't bother explaining that you don't have to draw brilliantly to be an artist, but I did explain that when I was famous and making millions of pounds there was no way she was getting her sticky, fat fingers on any of it, as she had with my modelling earnings. Calling her fingers fat hurt; I knew it would.

'I'd have killed for the opportunities you've had, Diana. You have no idea. I was a child myself when you came along. I gave up everything. And what do you do? You throw it back in my face. You selfish, stupid little bitch. You break my heart, baby. You break my heart. I should have had you aborted, like everyone told me to…'

I heard the bartender gasp, though she couldn't have. She continued screeching, but I didn't hear the details – I'd heard them all before – because I was marching towards the exit, her voice reduced to a buzzing in my ear: you're rubbish, worthless, pathetic.

On the steps I played with the cigarette I'd swiped as I left, hands trembling, trying to block out the words. A white Rolls-Royce pulled up, and I expected a rock star to tumble out. The window slid down and an arm beckoned me forward. Without thinking, I leaned in.

'You got a light?' There was something familiar about the voice.

He wasn't old, not bad-looking. Clean shaven, nice teeth, smelt expensive. He didn't want a light; we both knew that. It would have been easy to climb in, and I wondered what it'd be like if I did. Would he treat me nicely? Buy me a drink beforehand, be gentle? It was tempting to find out. It'd be crazy and risky and wild. Like the times Mark, my first boyfriend, and I had sex in my room while Bunny and Roland watched TV downstairs. Roland. The geezer in the Rolls reminded me of Roland, an ex-boyfriend of Bunny's, one of many wedged between Dad and husband number two.

Roland was different from most of the sleazeballs who hung around the shoots. He had power. Bunny encouraged me. 'He wants to meet you, baby. In his office, to talk publicity. You're good for the business, he says!'

He sat me on his lap, ran his hand up my leg, stopping mid-thigh, and held out a glass bowl of sweets wrapped in brightly coloured paper. I was thirteen years old. Too old to be tempted by chocolate. I refused. 'It makes me fat,' I said, rolling my eyes, like he was stupid not to think of that.

Uncle Roland, as he insisted I call him, became very friendly with Bunny. They started dating. Roland would catch me in the bathroom, my bedroom, and touch me in places he shouldn't: top of my head, my waist, my knees. I could tell he wanted more, but was too chicken-shit scared to push it. Thank God. I didn't want to spoil things for Mum. Not for the sake of letting some old bloke squeeze my little tits. She was happy for the first time since Dad left. Mentioning what he did hardly seemed worth the pain it would cause her.

Bunny and Roland split when I was just turned fourteen, and though I was glad to be shot of Roland's clumsy fumblings, Bunny was sad and she took her sadness out on me.

'I'm not what you think I am,' I said to Mr Rolls-Royce at last. No way was I climbing into a car with a man who reminded me of Roland, but I craved a kind of loving.

He smiled. 'Buy you a drink, anyway, beautiful.'

'Thanks, but no.' I pushed myself upright and watched the window close. I threw the cigarette on the ground, turned and walked down Oxford Road, the self-loathing tempered a fraction as I neared Hulme, a reminder that I would see Cal again.

Fuck her. I will find inspiration. I will make my mark. People will love my work.

~

Determined not be dragged down by Bunny and to use the time before the Christmas break productively, whether I saw Cal again or not, the next day I bought a load of dolls from a charity shop: Tiny Tears, Barbie, Pippa Dolls, a Sindy. I dressed them in sequined bikinis, ridiculously high-heeled shoes, stuck on long glossy locks, even on the 'hey-I-just-pissed-my-pants' doll, and made sashes to drape across their bodies: 'Miss Shit Face 1984', 'Miss Mini Whore-Bags', 'Miss Sold to the Highest Bidder'. I found a blow-torch in the studio and blasted Sindy's face. The point at which her sweet, innocent-forever smile began to collapse was so good. The others I lined up in front of an old two-bar electric fire and watched as their noses, eyes and mouths fell away from their faces. I stood the finished articles in a row and called it *Parade*. I had Bunny to thank for the inspiration behind that piece.

'Whoa! That's spooky!' Alan stared at *Parade* – I'd left the dolls on the table, along with more sketches of fairies and gnomes. 'I'd love a coffee.'

'You could buy your own. Just a thought. Radical, I know.'

'Cheers. Three sugars today please. Got a stinking hangover. Did buy biscuits but got the munchies and ate them all last night.'

'What kind?' I asked, swilling out a couple of mugs.

'*Viscounts.*'

'You bastard.' I heaped sugar into his mug. 'You'll lose your teeth.' I paused, waiting for him to comment further on my work. He didn't. I pointed, heart thrashing. 'What do you think?'

'Freaky.'

'Bad?'

'No, no. In a good way.'

I breathed out. 'I'm so glad you like it. I'm pleased with it, I think.'

'It's great, man, great.' It was Alan's turn to sound nervous. 'You want to see my photos?'

'You bet!'

After we'd finished our coffees we went next door. It

was the first time I'd been into his flat and it was as spartan as I'd predicted, though unexpectedly clean for a man who looked like an A grade scumbag.

He showed me a contact sheet of photographs he'd taken of children on the estate – kids like Jim's brother.

'Al, these shots are incredible,' I said, as we stood over the developing tray in the reddish, warm glow of the bathroom-come-darkroom.

'You really think so?' he said, all wide, primary school-eyed.

'No, they're awful,' I said, watching him pull another print out of the tray, allowing the liquid to dribble off before taking a clothes peg and clipping the image to the string stretched across the bath. 'I mean it! You've a gift.'

'Oh man, that means so much to me,' he said, his sincerity embarrassing me. He bent down to a box tucked under the basin and placed it on the closed toilet seat. He pulled out a 10x8 black and white image and handed it to me. 'Remember that day, when we walked round the estate—'

'I do.'

'Most of the landscape shots were pathetic, out of focus, the composition all wrong; light dreadful... but this one...'

The photograph was of me, standing on the bridge, after my outburst, the silhouette of the city behind me. I didn't recognise myself immediately; my face was shadowed, my left hand draped across my forehead as if shading my eyes from a blazing light. The sun was behind me, falling below the skyline, the shape of the buildings black and dramatic, with over-exposed rays of light, like white gold, shooting out from the towers and church spires. I'd always seen myself as essentially modern looking, a twentieth-century girl. But in the photograph, with my bleached hair scraped off my face, little if any make-up left after the tears, my coat indistinct in the fading light, there was a timeless quality to this woman, this stranger. Almost androgynous. She could have come from anywhere, any time.

'Doesn't look like me,' I said at last.

'Does to me. Different to the usual you, but still you. Daguerre called the photograph the mirror with a memory. We see ourselves as others see us.'

'Get you!' I smiled at him. So he'd been studying the history of photography as well as the craft. 'Actually, I prefer John Berger's summary that it's a "trace of appearance seized from the normal flow of the eye".'

'Then this is a trace of you that we don't often see. The camera never lies.'

'It lies all the time. It captures and freezes images that don't register in the normal, everyday flow of seen life. That's what makes it so amazing.'

His eyes widened, the whites yellow-red and vampire-like in the light. He looked extra-specially weird.

'Can I have it?' I asked. 'I might use it somehow.'

'I'll do another print. I'd like to keep it, if you don't mind.' He turned away from me to admire the 10x8s drying on the line.

'Can I have copies of these?' I asked, pointing at the shots of the estate children.

'Sure. What do you want them for?'

'I'm going to transform them into mythical creatures. Ugly, misshapen, hairy, warty, grotesque and lovely.'

'Classic,' Alan replied, and once we'd retreated to my flat for fresh coffee and warmth, I found myself showing him some of my 'Cal' sketches. I needed to make sure they were good enough to share with Elspeth, and I valued Alan's opinion. Much, much more than Jim's.

Cal

'Do you remember your mother?' Eve says, busying herself with the drip.

I am sitting up in bed, playing patience with the cards laid out on a tray on my lap. I love card games, especially poker. But you can't play alone and it's so much better with a single malt, a cigarette or two, but beggars and all that.

I'm good at it. Poker, that is. We used to play a lot, Diana, Alan and me. They introduced me to it and then I taught China and Stanley to play in Sixth Form. We used to pretend that we were Butch Cassidy, the Sundance Kid and Etta Place. It was China's favourite movie. Me? I wasn't all that keen on westerns. Preferred horror: *Village of the Damned, Candyman, Interview with the Vampire.*

Anyway, I like the way card games focus the mind, allowing you to think of nothing but the hand before you. It's liberating, absorbing. Better than meditation and other hippy shit, though it depends how much you smoke and drink while you're at it.

I wonder if this question about my mother is

gamesmanship on Eve's behalf. She's lied to me and though I should be angry with her, I can't. I stare at the cards deciding what to do. My head is beginning to hurt. If I answer and engage with her then she will tell the doc that I'm on the up, getting better and all that. I might be released early for good behaviour. But I'm not sure I'm ready to leave; I like this prison.

'You know about my past. You said you didn't.'

'I lied,' she says, 'Sorry. I thought it might make you feel better, to be anonymous.'

'What changed?'

'I'm not sure. It felt wrong.'

I pull at a bandage and Eve raises a hand to stop me. 'No,' I say.

She is puzzled, so I add, 'I don't remember her. My mother.'

'Does that bother you?'

'No. She appears sometimes…'

'Like in a dream?'

I shake my head. 'More like a movement in the corner of my eye, but when I turn there's nothing there.'

'Did Diana talk to you about her?'

I flinch at the mention of Diana, pain skewers me. I can see her, hear her, smell her. Eve looks bothered and I don't want her to feel guilty, to feel that she's upset me.

'She didn't know much. I wasn't overly interested. I think she made her – my mother – out to be better than she was, trying to be kind. Said she was creative, clever—'

'That could be true. Look at you. Gifted, they said.'

I try to smile, but it hurts. 'Some of it might be true.

But what does it matter? She's dead. I feel nothing about her.'

'Nothing?' She comes closer and I can smell her lovely fresh scent, a smell all her own, something human above the stench of hospital-ness.

'It pissed me off sometimes. That Diana didn't tell me the truth.'

'And what is the truth? Your truth.'

I raise my voice. It's bluster, to cover my fear. 'I was so repulsive that my own mother couldn't love me. Spare the monster's feelings, his life's crap enough as it is.'

I've said too much. What a stupid, stupid idiot I am.

'Sorry for swearing.'

She returns to the drip and finishes what she's doing; she'll be cleaning her hands next.

'Your life isn't crap,' she says, lifting her brows as she says 'crap' and sure enough she's over at the sink, pumping on the anti-bacterial soap. It's either almost empty or she's pissed off with me. She's hitting it hard. I'm surprised at her swearing; it doesn't suit her. There's something so pure about Eve. Diana washed her hands a lot.

Diana. Her name's like a time machine, throwing me into the past.

~

It is night-time and the moon is fat. I am staring out of my window when the man called Jim comes in. He's brought me sweets: Black Jacks and Dolly Mixtures. Brightly coloured sugar lumps that I gobble greedily. They taste like the best place in the world, like a galaxy far, far away. My head goes all fizzy.

'There's a lady who'd like to meet you,' he says.

'Why?'

'She likes you.'

'Why'

'Dunno. You'd like a new friend, yeah?'

I nod. Jim does not come to see me every day and he stays for very small minutes. He is a busy man.

'What's her name?'

'Diana.'

'Like a princess?'

'If you like.'

'What she like?'

'She likes to draw.'

I'm not much keen on drawing. When the telly goes all fuzzy, all black and white, and sparkly and hissy, I play my xylophone and hit my drums. I don't much like quiet.

'You must look your best. I've brought you something special to wear,' he says, moving over to the mirror.

I nod and scramble across. Presents are the best. I stand in front of the glass, all tall, and Jim holds up two masks: a monkey and a leopard.

'Which one?'

I pick up the monkey mask and look in the mirror. I look funny: half boy, half beast, and I laugh and jump about making monkey noises.

'You like this one best, yeah?' Jim says.

I nod and swing my arms like the monkeys I've seen on telly.

'You wear it all the time when she comes, Cal. You understand me?'

'Understand.'

'Good lad.'

'When she come?'

'Soon, Cal, soon.'

The lady is gold and white. I look from behind my mask, my chin low. I do not lift it and I do not talk to her. My voice is broken, I am so shaky and funny feeling. She smiles lots, but only when she knows I am looking. I do not know what to do, so I sit, mouth shut, and play. I don't like quiet.

She shows me pictures. Of me, she says, but I don't look much like me. I make a Lego man of her.

After Jim gives me a sweet and says that I am a good boy. 'If you're really good the nice lady will come again, Cal. You'd like that, yeah?'

'Yeah.'

Jim looks happy, but the lady Diana is sad when she thinks I'm not looking.

I will make her smile. Watch me.

Diana

In the January murk of the stairwell I dragged my suitcase into the lift. Lonely in Highgate, I came back to Manchester well before the start of term. I'd seen no one from college on the journey from Piccadilly station to Hulme. I felt as grey as the sky.

It had been Dad's turn to have me for Christmas. But, a total workaholic, he'd spent the bulk of the holiday at the hospital. New wife Louise went out a lot. I'd played with Tom when he didn't have friends round, which was nearly always, and I resented the time they took him away from me. With other children around I transformed into another boring grown-up, and I couldn't help comparing Tom's hectic social scene with Cal's lonely existence.

I'd not seen Bunny at all. Not because of a lack of desire on my part: she was away, skiing with a new beau. He paid, I had to assume.

As the lift doors slid apart I gasped. Jim. In a woollen overcoat, he looked stylish and devastatingly handsome. Linda was one lucky girl.

'Taking a risk, aren't you?' he said, as an opener,

stepping aside as I dragged my case out.

'Figured muggers might take a holiday once in a while,' I shrugged.

'Hope you've nothing valuable in that.'

I laughed. 'Hardly. What you doing here?'

'Taking care of some business.' He smiled and took the case from me. Our fingers brushed against each other. 'Let me help you.' He lifted my case. 'Fuck me, this is heavy. What you got in there?'

'Presents. For Cal, mostly.'

'Presents?' He seemed surprised.

'Christmas?' I said. 'I'd hoped to see him before, and then when I didn't... I picked up something else at home.'

'You like to see the spastic now?'

'That's a hateful word.'

'Sorry.' He seemed genuinely contrite so I took the opportunity to ask what had caused Cal's deformities. If he knew.

'Born that way. It happens,' he said.

'That's totally shit. Can anything be done? Surgery?'

'He's had some. When he was tiny. Would have died otherwise, or been retarded or something.'

'Will he need more?'

'Possibly. Once he's grown. No point doing nothing till then.'

'Plastic surgeons can do amazing things.'

'There ain't no surgery that can sort him. He'll never look right.'

I hadn't dared hope I might see Cal so soon but

97

meeting Jim felt like a sign. A new term beckoned; time was running out. I had stupidly promised Elspeth work involving photographs and I had no idea if Cal would be agreeable.

'I'd love to see him now,' I said. 'I could dump my stuff and we could nip round?' I intended to collect my camera while I was at it.

He shrugged, implying agreement. My spirits soared.

Jim climbed Pru and Michael's stairs. I went to follow him, unsure of the protocol in this dysfunctional, drug-den. Michael appeared in the living room doorway, startling me.

'He's in here.' He gestured over his shoulder.

'The lounge?'

I was surprised; I hadn't realised they allowed him in there. I was also disappointed; I wanted Cal all to myself. But then I realised that he might not have his mask on if he was with his mum and dad, and I smiled.

'What's funny?'

'Nothing.'

I followed Michael in.

The curtains were drawn and it took a while for my eyes to adjust to the gloaming. Pru lay in her customary position, recumbent on the sofa, watching a black and white portable television, which perched on the coffee table. Michael plonked himself down next to her and offered me a drink. I shook my head.

Cal was sitting in the far corner with his back to me, tapping on an upturned plastic bin. It wasn't sound for sound's sake; there was a distinct rhythm and beat. It sounded familiar but I couldn't place it. My mind searched for childhood nursery rhymes and songs but still it wouldn't come. It was too sophisticated for baa-baa black sheep and all that.

'Hey, Cal. It's me, Diana.'

'Where's your mask?' Pru sat upright and screeched across the space before falling back to her usual position. I was surprised that she'd even clocked me or Cal.

He stopped banging, dropped his chin and lifted his hands to his face.

'No mask,' he said, his voice quivering.

I crouched behind him. 'You don't need your mask. Not for me.'

'But Mummy say…'

'I'd like to see you. You mustn't hide away.'

'Mummy say people don't like my face,' he whispered.

'I like it.' I slung my bag over one shoulder, reached out with my free hand and took hold of his wrist. 'Shall we go upstairs?' I turned to check this was OK, and Michael gestured that it was. Pru remained staring at the ceiling.

'I have presents for you.'

He gasped and said, 'I like presents!'

'You keep your mask off. Yes? You'd like that wouldn't you?'

I tugged at his wrist, gently, and he pushed himself up, and we walked, slowly, across the room to the door, his head hung low, his long dark hair like curtains over his face. I didn't look at him. As we left the room I

99

turned. 'See you in a bit,' I said to Pru and Michael, though neither bothered to reply.

Nothing prepared me for seeing Cal's face again. Nothing could have done. He led me up the spiral staircase, the dark metal contrasting with the pale flesh of his bare feet. My bag bounced against my hip. Dressed in a tatty T-shirt and long shorts, his face obscured, he could have been any child, save for the curve high on his back and his lop-sided, ape-like gait. I wondered why he moved like this; his legs, straight and smooth-skinned, looked perfect. At the bedroom door, he pointed, head still low, indicating that I should enter first.

The room was lit, albeit dimly, and before I turned to face him I tried to recall our first meeting, at the party, to conjure his features. I could not. I caught a glimpse of him in the mirror. He must have seen his own reflection and seen me looking, because he covered his face with his hands. I followed suit.

'Peep-o!' I said, as I pulled my hands apart and back together.

Peeking through the gaps in my fingers I waited for him to do the same. He did not. I could just see the odd shape of his skull. I tried 'Peep-o' again. And again. I was about to admit defeat when he snapped his hands away.

'I see you,' he said.

Up went his hands. I turned and crept towards him, taking my time, ensuring he knew I was coming. I crouched before him and poked his belly. 'I see you too!'

And he pulled his hands down from his face, slowly, revealing eyes, nose, mouth, chin. It felt like an age, though it was only seconds. I looked properly, fully, for the first time.

I observed his skull, shaped almost like a clover leaf, the wide set fish eyes, one dropping down his face, as if it had melted like the dolls left in front of the fire, the flat, almost non-existent nose, fat lips, the strange growth on his jaw line. He looked as if he'd been flattened against a wall, like a two-dimensional drawing. I tried to disguise my repulsion, my fascination. I tried to be normal. I reached for the presents.

'For you.' I handed him the largest.

He didn't snatch, as most children would have, or tear at the paper in a frenzy. He held it carefully, with both hands, and lowered himself to the floor. He placed it front of him and stroked the surface of the shiny paper, which glimmered in the light.

'I like this paper,' he said, head tilted to one side, to better see the gift with his more normal eye, I guessed. Carefully, he picked at the tape, peeling it away before folding the paper back to reveal a tape deck.

'It's a music player.' I'd seen it in a market in London and, knowing it was perfect, gave the book I'd originally bought for Cal to Tom instead.

'I know!' he said, and I felt foolish.

Don't patronise him.

'Do you like it?' I asked.

'Yes! Yes!' He said, standing up and jumping on the spot, squealing with delight, smiling, revealing a mass of crooked, rotten teeth.

They're milk teeth. No permanent harm done.

'You don't like my face,' he said.

101

'I do. It's yours, and I like you.' I handed him the second parcel, a cassette.

'It's a band called Orange Juice. Like the drink,' I explained as I showed him how to load the machine. 'Press this button, here.'

For a second-hand deck, it didn't sound bad.

'Happy music!' He was dancing, jigging about the room, unself-conscious, the way only kids can be, and I thought of midnight gnomes and elves.

He jumped towards me. I crouched. He touched my nose, clumsy. He stroked my hair and said, 'I like your hair best.' And he leaned in and cuddled me, his head resting on my shoulder, the sticky sweet smell of milk and sugar filling my nostrils, the warmth of his body spreading through me. I stiffened at first, unsure. I kept my arms by my side, held my breath. He clung on and slowly, I wrapped my arms round him. His disfigurement wasn't contagious. It felt good to hold and be held, so good. I filled up.

'Cal, I'd like to take a photograph of you. I'll ask Mummy and Daddy.'

'Like the doctors?'

'Kind of. It's for my pictures. Like the ones you saw before. Is that OK with you?'

'You like me?' he said.

'I told you I did.'

I took the camera from my bag and pointed it at Cal. 'Pose for me?' I joked.

He smiled, tipped his head, and put his hands on his hips, a hint of joy mingled with puzzlement behind his hooded eyes. The camera shutter clicked.

102

*   *   *

There was no sign of Jim when I left. I'd put Cal to bed, read him a story and sang with him. My singing voice was horrible but Cal didn't seem to mind; he laughed whenever I hit a bum note. He had a great musical ear and I decided to look out for a child-sized keyboard for him. I virtually ran all the way back to Charles Barry Crescent, clutching the camera against my chest as if it were the crown jewels. To me, it was. It contained Cal.

My inspiration, my muse, my future.

Diana

Spliced photos of Alan's feral estate children, me, Linda, Cal as goblin, elf or changeling and other outsiders lay scattered across the dining table. Like a butcher I'd carved each person into their constituent parts. I was shuffling the images about, rearranging the composition, when I heard a familiar rap at the door. Linda was out with Jim; a friend in Fallowfield was holding a barbecue. I'd waited for her to invite me, but she never did. As I opened the door a tepid breeze brushed my bare shoulders.

'Hey, how are you doing?' I was pleased to see Alan. I'd not seen him for days, which was unusual.

'Cool,' he replied, though he didn't look it. His pale skin was dewy, his cheeks blotchy. He looked like someone who'd come back from a long run. 'Went out for a walk,' he offered.

'Lucky you.' It was a beautiful evening and I'd been in all day.

I'd thought I was a fast walker till I met Alan. Walking quickly was a habit I acquired in puberty when I started to develop curves, changing from an über-skinny waif to something resembling normal for a fourteen-year-old. It was an attempt to burn calories, encouraged by Bunny. I was underweight for my height and frame, but she weighed me weekly, had done since I turned ten or eleven, and if I so much as gained a pound she'd ban chocolate and have me on her rowing machine for an hour or more each evening. I hated that machine so whenever I sneaked a bar of chocolate on the way home from school or ate chips for lunch I'd walk like an Olympic pentathlete for days. Habits are hard to shake off.

I offered Alan coffee, but he refused, choosing instead a glass of water. Back at the table, he sat opposite and played with the scissors. When he didn't say anything, I continued to work and began to tear more pictures. I preferred the effect to the neat lines of the scissor cuts. Usually, we were comfortable with silence but that evening there was an awkwardness about Alan, or more so than usual. He was never completely at ease, a part of him was always twitching: a foot, a finger, something. No wonder he was so thin.

'You OK?' I stared at the top of his bent head. I could see his scalp between the dreadlocks and wondered if he'd go bald as he aged. He picked at the corner of the table. It was split, exposing a raw, yellow pulp.

'I saw you the other day.' He lifted his head but not his eyes.

'Good for you,' I said.

He didn't smile. 'You didn't see me.'

'That stops you saying hi?' I didn't understand.

'With Jim,' he said, and he looked at me. His eyes

weren't bloodshot, as they so often were, and the startled expression that commonly adorned his features wasn't there, replaced with a sadness and confusion that made my stomach curl. I shook my head, still not understanding.

'I tried to catch up. Thought you'd be on your way home. I figured Jim was going to see Linda and you'd bumped into each other...'

The implication hit me like a punch. I was offended, and angry. I remained silent, unable to find the words. He was going to have to say it, to accuse me directly.

He hesitated, blundering, and I realised that Alan had been avoiding me all weekend. His absence had been deliberate.

'Did you follow us?'

'I was on my way home.' His voice cracked. 'You turned off, towards The Spinners.' My anger retreated as rapidly as it had risen.

'You think there's something going down between me and Jim?' My voice was as brittle as charcoal sticks, smudged with defensiveness. There was something going on, but not what Alan thought, and I was hurt.

But what else was he to think? He didn't want to believe it, that much was obvious.

'I don't know what to think. But you two were...'

'What?'

'Comfortable together... I had a really strong feeling it wasn't the first time... sounds mental. Tell me I'm wrong,' he said, his voice heavy.

'You're not wrong,' I said, in a way relieved to tell someone my secret, 'but it's not what you think.'

Alan slumped on the table, his head resting in his hands, like he was about to cry. He kept his head down as I explained about my friendship with Cal, why I'd kept quiet, how I understood that it could appear weird, how inspiring Cal was, how I loved him, and that Jim helped set up the meetings, talked to Pru and Michael on my behalf. Once I'd finished he lifted his head. Relief blanketed his features. I felt lighter and said that if my behaviour had been strained of late it was the result of keeping a secret from those closest to me. I apologised profusely and lit a cigarette, the first of the day.

He picked up an image of Cal's mouth. 'So these are Pru's boy? I thought you'd got them from a medical journal or something. Wow.'

I couldn't tell if he approved and was too scared to ask. 'Jim and I are not having an affair.'

'You're a good person ... I never honestly thought you capable of *that*.'

'Yes, you did. You're a hopeless liar. Good people are capable of doing bad things,' I said, and it dawned on me that Alan's fear Jim and I were having an affair might have had less to do with Linda's feelings than his own.

And I was flattered. Being considered attractive mattered to me. It was the only thing I could be sure of.

'And bad people are capable of good,' he said.

'Meaning?'

He hesitated.

'You think Jim's a bad person?' I'd never heard Alan speak ill of anyone. He was wary of Jim, but he'd not bad-mouthed him at any point, loyalty to Linda perhaps.

'Not bad, exactly, but...' He struggled to find the

107

word. 'Untrustworthy.'

'The drug dealing? That's kind of hypocritical. You buy your gear from him.' I offered him a cigarette and watched the way he held it between his second and third fingers, like a dandy.

'I get the impression he never tells the truth.'

'We all lie.'

'What are his motives?'

I knew what Alan was driving at but I wasn't ready to admit it to him or myself.

'Dunno. You're just jealous, 'cos he's so good-looking and charismatic and all that.' My tone was bright, dismissive, and Alan responded appropriately.

'Probably. You want to go out?' he said, flicking his cigarette stub out of the window.

From the bridge the city was bathed in a golden mist of sunlight and centuries worth of pollution. 'I've got to tell Linda.' I held Alan's Leica, preparing to take some shots.

'If you don't and she finds out she'll be really hurt, maybe even angry,' he said.

'Oh, I do not want to make her angry!' I meant it light-heartedly, but Alan's face dropped.

'You don't. This is hard to say, but something like this could turn Linda against you.'

Baffled, I shook my head as I replaced the lens cap.

'She thinks the world of you, but she's threatened by you; jealous. You have everything she doesn't: money, privilege, well-connected parents.'

'Well-connected parents! Those two are no use whatsoever. Not in the art world at any rate! And

Bunny's allegedly still broke.'

'Look, I'm not saying it's true, I'm saying it's how Linda perceives it, right or wrong. And she knows Jim fancies you. I've watched her watching him watching you.' His eyes bored into mine.

'He doesn't fancy me.' I pulled my sunglasses down from where they rested on the top of my head, over my eyes.

'Half of Manchester fancies you.'

I blew air from my mouth, 'Pfff.'

'Point is, Linda could get it all wrong, and her love for you could turn to hate.'

Alan was spot on, and I realised that, in part, I'd kept it from her because, deep down, I knew she would be threatened. Not by my friendship with Cal, but that Jim facilitated it.

'I'll tell her as soon as I see her,' I said. Guilt had weighed me down for months and though I was concerned about telling Linda, life appeared much lighter. My mood was as bright as the evening sun.

As we walked, I talked and talked about Cal. Neither Pru nor Michael were ever interested in what I did with Cal but Alan was. He wanted to meet Cal, and I told him Cal would like him.

'I've never had you down as a kid person,' he said.

'I'm not really, I'm a Cal person. He loves me, and I love that. It's a great feeling.'

The gothic buildings peered down at us as we crossed Albert Square and headed towards St Anne's Square and the Royal Exchange. We carried cider, swigging from the bottle as we walked. The square was empty apart from a gaggle of ragged pigeons and we rested on a bench at its centre. They pecked and waddled closer. Dirty, stupid, ugly birds; it wasn't as if we had seed or bread. I took a photograph of Alan's enormous hand clutching the bottle, a close up, and one of his ear. I noticed dirt in the curls and folds of the cartilage, and I noticed that it didn't disgust me as such slovenliness normally would.

'Cal feeds me, my work. I can't explain. Since I met him my work has improved ten-fold. Elspeth has noticed. I've a way to go, but I'm getting there, and it feels good.'

'It's not all inspired by him?'

'No, but he's like... I don't know... my muse. And every great artist has a muse!'

I kicked at a pigeon that'd strayed too close. It flapped its ugly grey wings and I lashed out again.

'You're going be a great artist then?'

'You bet. Just watch me.'

Drunk on cheap cider, I charged at the birds, frightening them away.

~

'I'm taking Cal out.'

'You what?' said Jim.

'Taking him out. Into the world – this place you, me and others enjoy.' I swept my tanned arm across the clammy air. We were walking over the bridge, cars zooming below, sweating in the scorching heat. Across the city, layer after layer of clothing had been discarded. The skinny goths and lanky art students ill at ease with their exposed, alabaster skin, their jeans and T-shirts exposed by the unforgiving sun as a faded moss green. Kohl pencil dribbled into crow's feet formed from squinting in the unfamiliar Manchester sun. Flattops, spikes and backcombed hair wilted. I wasn't bothered; the heat suited me with my golden skin and bleached blonde hair.

'They'll never agree to it,' he said.

'They already have.'

'He's been out before you know. Operations, doctors, hospitals.'

'Hardly ever.'

'There's a good reason for that.'

I tutted and Jim said, 'To protect him, not others.'

'He's ready. He's five years old. Let him be normal. He's curious, and it's wrong to keep him inside that rank apartment all the time. Doctors'll want to see him again soon. This will prepare him,' I said.

'Bollocks.'

'We're taking him to the cinema.'

'Doctors can't do nothing for him.'

'It's decided.'

The prospect of going to see a film on the big screen quashed any nascent anxiety Cal might have had about going out. I was nervous and excited. My stomach churned like an actress's on opening night. What would Cal make of this world? A world outside a few trips to hospitals and the doctor's surgery. A world with smell and touch and taste; a world different from that he'd seen on his videos and in the books we shared. A world of grey, not black or white, goodies and baddies. And I

111

wanted to see how others would view him, react to him. An idea was forming.

Michael was tightening a makeshift tourniquet round his upper arm when we came through to say goodbye. One end of the rag gripped between his stained teeth, blue vein bulging, expectant. The syringe perched on the table. I don't know why we bothered really; maybe habit, or misguided good manners. He glanced up, eyes wild like a rabid dog, then plunged the needle into his bruised skin, his eyes glazing over before us. The needle was filthy.

He was alone. Pru was ill in bed with some kind of 'flu; she'd been ill a lot, but I figured pumping poison into your veins with relentless regularity was bound to take its toll sooner or later.

It was seven o'clock and the sun still shone when we emerged from the stairway. At first, Cal shielded his eyes from the glare, then he tipped his head to the sky and asked why all the fairies were out. He pointed at the sparkling, sunlit, dusky air. The rainy city had been dry for weeks. The landscape was bleached, faded sepia, like an old photograph left to rot in a crumbling album.

'It smells funny,' he said.

'Dirty, and smoggy, and smelly, and champion!' said Linda.

'It smells big. And it sounds HUGE!' he said.

People stared as our gang of four stepped off the bus in the city centre, Cal flanked by Alan and me, Linda huddled behind. Some did it openly; others walked past and then turned back when they thought we wouldn't notice. Linda stuck out her tongue. It struck me that we could be viewed as an expression of the divine and the grotesque, as if we were constituent parts of one strange, magnificent creature. I lifted Cal's hand to my mouth and kissed the back of it, relishing the sensation of his small hand in mine, sticky and soft, so trusting, so reassuring.

At the end of the film we left through a side door. The stairway to ground level was uncarpeted, bare concrete steps and grey walls smelling of disinfectant. The illusion and magic of the silver screen well and truly shattered. We were spewed out into a dingy, rubbish-strewn alley. Linda dropped the empty bottle of cider we'd shared during the film and we picked our way to the main road where a bike lay on its side, seemingly abandoned.

'A Chopper!' Alan said.

I looked around. The city was throbbing in the heat; crowds milled on the streets. I felt trapped by the mass.

'Let's take the bike,' I said, grabbing the handlebars and picking it up off the floor.

'Oh man, we don't know whose it is,' said Alan.

Linda roared with laughter. 'Classic!'

'We're borrowing it. I'll bring it back,' I said to Alan, 'hop on, Cal.'

He tilted his head to one side and scrutinised me, perplexed.

'Like in *E.T.* – you sit on the front, I'll ride. Trust me,' I said.

'But the owner might need it tonight. You can't take it,' protested Alan.

'Get away with you. Hop on, our kid,' said Linda,

giggling. 'I'm dying to see you ride this thing, Diana.'

'Your skirt's very short, and you've been drinking,' Alan said. Linda and I turned and stared at him, before we collapsed into fits of laughter. He stepped forward. 'Let me. I did my cycling proficiency at school.'

'Get 'im!' Linda said, and we laughed again.

Alan was awful. Linda insisted he prove to us, especially Cal, that he was a competent rider. He wobbled and weaved up and down the alley and almost caused an accident between two black cabs as he careered onto the main road. He looked ridiculous, like someone in a Heath Robinson drawing, his spiky arms jutting out at right angles to the bike, shirtsleeves billowing in the breeze like a listing galleon, his knobbly knees grazing the handlebars as he pedalled. I wished I'd brought the camera.

After he dismounted I said, 'Let's get a taxi.'

'I am totally skint, like, totally,' Linda said.

Cal had remained silent, and serious, throughout this episode. When he spoke, in a voice like a penny whistle, he said, 'I don't want to go home.'

'Then we shan't,' Linda announced.

None of us wanted the evening to end. The adults had assumed that Cal would want to go home but he was a night bird, with wide-awake eyes gleaming, ready for more adventure.

And so we wandered.

Alan hoisted Cal onto his shoulders and off we went, towards the north east and the Arndale centre, with more and more people staring, gasping, holding a hand to their mouth, sounds of shock and revulsion cutting through the hubbub of the throngs. Cal was too high to hear, I hoped. I studied the faces as we walked.

The crowds thinned as we neared the shopping centre. I loved shopping centres after hours, and car parks, places with their guts ripped out. We pressed our faces against the windows of McDonald's, the round tables bolted to the floor like the ballerina trapped in a musical box. I promised Cal that I'd buy him a milkshake one day and described how thick and icy and sickly sweet they were.

We walked on through deserted Shudehill and Smithfield, the streets narrow, sometimes cobbled, with cabbage leaves and squashed tomatoes in the gutters, the discarded remains of a day's market trading. Old-fashioned rag shops with dated clothes on orange-brown dummies rubbed shoulders with trendy flea market, Affleck's Palace. The façade of the Victorian fish market washed-out and exhausted in the hazy light. Cal looked and looked. We played peek-a-boo in the creases and tucks of the market place. The moon lit the area like a drenched watercolour and in the warmth of the summer evening everything appeared to run.

And Alan, Linda and I tried to explain the world around us to a boy whose primary experience of it was formed through TV, film and books. We stopped for a rest, mostly for Alan's benefit, and sat on the kerb, with only the smell of the drains for company.

'It used to be like a circus here, Cal, a long, long time ago,' said Alan.

'Like in fairy tales?' Cal said.

'Kind of. They called them night markets. They

115

were magic, like a dream, full of entertainers, dancers, singers, people throwing balls and riding bicycles with one wheel, people standing on boxes and talking on and on and on.'

Cal giggled, though he can't have understood half of what Alan was saying. Maybe he caught Alan's sense of wonder that this forsaken place was once vibrant and alive, host to burlesques and cabaret, dancing bears and bearded ladies. I watched him as he listened. Even in the bizarre surroundings of the market place at night, he appeared strange and alien. I wasn't exactly used to the way Cal looked, though he no longer appeared freaky. But it was as if I was seeing him for the first time and I don't know if it was Alan's tales of Victorian entertainers, orators and quacks but I felt the shadow of the city's heyday; the cruel and insensitive way that those who were different or disabled were paraded like animals or playthings for the amusement of the ignorant. I shuddered; it wasn't so different today.

People are fascinated with difference, abnormality. Our disgust mingles with pity and an overwhelming sense of relief: Thank God it's him and not me. Cal unsettles people because his appearance is subversive, threatening. It undermines our sense of human-ness.

'My head hurts,' Cal said.

Linda crouched to his level. 'It's good to see you out and about, our kid, but it's time to go home.'

'Hurts here,' he repeated, pointing between his brows. He dipped his head; shy, coquettish almost.

'When I've a headache, I like someone to rub it. Can I touch you?'

116

He nodded and she ran her slender fingers through his thick mop. 'You've got gorgeous hair. There are people who would pay a lot of money to have hair like yours,' she said, natural and easy. He reached out and stroked her wiry curls. 'It feels dead different to yours, doesn't it? That's 'cos my dad's from a place called Jamaica, a long way from here.' I felt a prick of jealousy; Cal had always loved my hair.

'Like space?' said Cal.

'Warmer.'

'Is everyone there pretty, like you?' Cal said.

Alan stepped forward and offered his hand to Cal. 'C'mon. Take a ride home.'

'We're ugly,' Cal said.

'Hey man, beauty's in the eye of the beholder.'

'He doesn't understand what you mean, Al,' I said.

Alan crouched and folded his huge form, arms locked round his knees. 'What I mean is that everyone thinks different things are beautiful. I love this dirty old market place though some people think it's horrid. To me, it's gorgeous.'

'And I love Hulme – your home – and car parks. The concrete, the boxiness, the grey,' I said, 'but other people say they're ugly.'

Linda joined in. 'And I love Liverpool! A dirty city past its sell-by date whose people are among the best in the bloody world!' She was shouting, arms outstretched, spinning round and round. She was drunk.

I took hold of Cal's hands. 'What we mean is that ugly to one person is beautiful to another. To me, you are beautiful.'

'And me.'

'And me.'

'I love Darth Vader,' Cal said, smiling at last.

'There, you've got it,' I said.

'But you're pretty to everybody,' he said, and pointing at Linda, 'You too.'

His insight silenced us.

'Princesses never ugly, or Princes.'

And I thought of all the books we'd read together, with their flaxen-haired heroines and tall, squared-jawed heroes and squat, warty goblins.

'You know *Beauty and the Beast*, yeah?' Alan said.

Cal nodded, and I wanted to kiss Alan. Like I said, we were all a bit drunk. 'Beast isn't ugly inside, is he? And Beauty loves him for him, not what he looks like.'

Linda skipped over and kissed Cal on the cheek and said, 'You're our little Prince, our kid!' I had never kissed Cal on the face. I wondered if it was the alcohol, because she was so drunk, or whether it said something about me. Was his deformity a barrier?

As I leant over and stroked his cheek, I heard the slurred, aggressive singing of drunks rising from a nearby street.

Despite her intoxication, Linda's survival mechanism was finely tuned; she leapt up and Alan hoisted Cal onto his back, piggyback fashion.

'Time to go,' I said, and we headed off back towards Tib Street. We'd not gone far when Cal squealed that he'd forgotten his lightsaber. We'd made it together days earlier, from kitchen roll and tin foil and he'd carried it the entire evening. We stopped. I could hear the drunken singing and shouting. I didn't want to go back and judging by the silence neither did Alan nor Linda.

'We'll get you another one,' Linda said, 'we need to get going. It's late.'

'I want that one, that one.' He was insistent.

'I'll go back. They may have gone a different way, turned off—' I said.

'No,' Alan said, firm. 'We all go, or none of us go.'

Cal continued to murmur and cry, 'Lightsaber, lightsaber, lightsaber—'

My mind was made up. 'Don't worry, Cal, we'll get your lightsaber.'

My stomach flipped right over as we turned into Carpenter Street: there were at least half a dozen of them, arms draped over shoulders, swaying, cans of beer dangling from limp wrists, loafer clad feet kicking at the rubbish on the pavement. They appeared as one foreboding mass and I experienced fear in a way that I had not before.

Our pace slowed, but we did not stop and I whispered to the others, 'Keep walking, don't make eye contact, move aside as they get closer.'

'They might be harmless,' said Alan.

'And I'm Mahatma Gandhi,' I hissed.

They stopped before we did. They were precisely where Cal had dropped the lightsaber. I could almost hear the blood draining from our bodies and try as I might to keep my fear in check, for Cal's sake, I trembled.

Alan swung Cal off his back and without allowing Cal's feet to touch the ground handed him to me. Cal wrapped his legs around my waist.

'I'll get it,' Alan said. His lips were chalky white.

Cal's fingers dug into my shoulder.

'It'd be better if I went, Al. Less threatening, being a girl and all that,' said Linda, stepping forward.

Alan grabbed her arm. 'No.'

'I've met twats like this a million times. I know how to handle them,' she said, shrugging him off, but her voice quivered. 'You stay here and look after Cal, and Diana.' She no longer sounded drunk.

We moved forward a couple of paces, and then Linda marched ahead. The pack was leering and jostling for a fight, buoyed up with beer and bravado. They spread out, opening like a fan.

'All right, love?' one said.

'I dropped something,' replied Linda, pointing to the spot where the lightsaber lay. They did not turn or step aside.

'Nice skirt.'

'Thanks. It's there.' She pointed again, waiting for them to part. My heart roared in my chest, deafening. Cal clutched harder. I could hear Alan's breathing.

'Nice legs,' said another.

'What was it you dropped?' An insolent voice. 'Your knickers?' A few laughs, pathetic-sounding. Linda didn't respond. They closed round her, and we shuffled closer, imperceptibly, instinctively. I wanted to rush forward, to help her, but knew I could not. I had to protect Cal. For a brief moment I hated Alan, for not going instead, for not rushing to Linda's defence, but I knew that would be foolhardy. They were playing with her; they wouldn't hurt her, surely?

'I just want to get our kid's lightsaber and I'll be off.' Her voice was too loud; the volume compensating for her diminishing nerve.

It was as if they'd not really noticed Alan, Cal and me hovering in the near distance. At the mention of the lightsaber they raised their weak chins and peered.

'Fuck me, it's Darth Vader,' said the insolent one, breaking away from the gang, one hand on his narrow hips. 'Da da da, da da da da da da,' he sang. I held Cal even harder, pressing his face into my shoulder, and shifted half a pace back.

These thugs must not see his face.

'Is this what you're looking for?' Another boy in a checked shirt, yellow gold chain at his throat, held up the lightsaber. It looked fragile, and cruddy, the tin foil creased and split, a cheap homemade toy in the harsh, unforgiving light of the youths' bullying. Snake Hips snatched it from him and offered it to Linda. She reached for it. He pulled it away, teasing.

'How about a kiss for me trouble?'

'My boyfriend wouldn't like it.'

'Him?' He jerked his chin at Alan, scornful, pugnacious. 'Go on, just a little one. You know you want to.'

Linda stood her ground, palm outstretched, not responding.

'Scrubber,' said another voice.

'Nigger.'

I almost heard Linda's patience snap. It's difficult to be precise because I was twenty, maybe thirty yards away and everything was a bit of blur, but I knew that

121

things had gone from bad to disastrous and it was all about to turn very, very ugly. Linda lunged forward and snatched the saber. She called Snake Hips a skanky twat, then yelled, 'Run!' at Alan and me.

In an instant we knew what to do: I ran one way, he ran another and, I learned later, Linda ran in another direction entirely. As I scurried along, hindered by my stiletto heels and Cal bouncing up and down on my hip, I could hear Linda calling those yobs all the names under the sun. And from the other direction Alan hollering, 'Come on, you bastards. Fight a man, why don't you? Or are the girls all you can handle?' I remember thinking that this was an extremely good ploy to entice the thugs to chase him, confusing them, their muddled thoughts possibly slowing them down, given that Alan had stood by while Linda confronted them. And Linda was clearly doing the same.

It worked. For despite being the easiest target I had stumbled only a few streets when I realised I was not being followed. Cal whimpered, but did not complain and only when I reached Piccadilly Gardens and slowed down did my legs begin to throb and my sharp, shallow breaths rasp at my throat like acid. I had wet myself, and the dampness at my waistline told me that Cal had too. I hailed a cab, despite my lack of money, asking the driver to stop at a cash point en route.

He could see my distress, and Cal's, and he was kind. 'Are you all right, love? What happened?'

I couldn't tell him, not fully, but I blurted enough for him to understand. 'Shall we go look for your mates?'

'If we could ride round the block—'

'Consider it done, love.'

We drove for fifteen minutes, that lovely cabbie and me, but we didn't find Alan and Linda. I was sick with worry and imagined them in all kinds of states: beaten, raped, you name it. Funnily enough I fretted more about Alan than Linda. He felt so much more vulnerable.

As we pulled up outside the crescent the cabbie offered to walk us up to the second floor. 'I know what this estate's like. My dad lived here before they built these monstrosities. Bloody tip then an' all. Nothing changes.'

'What about your cab?'

'I'm insured. Let me carry the little fella, you look done in.'

'He's nervous of strangers.'

At the door of number fifty he took my key from my purse and opened up. I promised to forward the fare to him, if he'd give me his licence number. He refused.

'I'll pay you back,' I said, 'somehow. You never know, I might jump in your cab again one day.'

'Stranger things have happened, love. Stranger things.'

I shut the door behind me. Cal was a dead weight, and the dampness in my knickers and on my T-shirt was uncomfortable. I couldn't wait to take them off. I pushed open the living room door with my bottom. Jim rose from the sofa – I couldn't tell if he'd been sleeping – and hissed, 'Where the hell have you bin?'

He'd let himself in with Linda's spare key. What was I thinking of, he asked, and where the hell was Linda, and that pillock, Alan? He didn't raise his voice – I'd never heard Jim raise his voice – but his anger, fear and frustration were palpable.

I laid Cal on the sofa. He whimpered as I peeled off his wet shorts and covered him with a crocheted blanket. Linda's mum had made it when she was pregnant and used it as a cot blanket, and Linda had kept it ever since. Cal murmured and I stroked his head, hoping he would fall into sleep.

Only once he was quiet, drifting away, did I tell Jim what had happened. He paced the room as I spoke, smoking. I wanted to say that it wasn't good to smoke round children, but knew it wouldn't go down well.

'You looked for her, right?'

I repeated that I had.

'What did the bastards look like? If they've laid a finger on her, I'll kill 'em.' And I knew that he meant it.

The force of his emotion was shocking. He cared about Linda, really cared. I'd understood that he liked her, enjoyed her company, fancied her like mad, but until now, I'd not thought that his feelings ran much deeper than that. He was such a cold man. Had he been wealthier, better bred, he would probably have been described as aloof, or suave. As it was most people thought him rude and arrogant.

Does anyone worry about me, care for me, the way that Jim worries about Linda?

He didn't ask about Cal, though it was clear Cal was all right, and Alan didn't get a look-in. I worried for Alan instead.

Minutes crept round the brass clock on the wall. We

stared at it as if by watching we could guarantee them safe passage home. Thirty minutes went by and Jim was ready to go out looking, or report them missing to the police. He was buttoning his jacket, lighting yet another cigarette, when the door burst open.

Linda staggered in, barefoot, her shoes in one hand, followed by a bedraggled Alan, limping slightly. Jim wrapped his arms round her, comforted her, and whispered in her ear. Alan and I looked on, embarrassed at being privy to this intimate moment, before I reached across and we hugged. 'Thank God, you're all right. Thank God,' I said through strangled tears.

Linda held her arm aloft. She was clutching a single shoe and not a pair as I'd thought.

'Your favourites,' I said.

'Bastards. They were fifties, vintage, totally irreplaceable, like.' Her voice quivered.

'What happened, babe?' said Jim.

'The heel snapped, the shoe slipped off my foot. My favourite shoes, my friggin' favourite shoes. They were my gran's.'

'To you, you silly cow. Not the bleedin' shoes.'

She began to cry.

Linda had evaded her pursuers absolutely. She'd kept on running till she came to a taxi rank, then realising that she hadn't enough money and no plastic, she hobbled to the all-night bus stop. Alan had been less fortunate. Four of them came after him and though his great long strides outran them for a while, he lost his sense of direction and ended up cornered in a dead end. He kicked out a lot, he said, but fell to the floor and was taking blows to his lower back and legs when a police siren scared them off.

'It was miles off, but, hey, I'm not complaining. It saved my bacon.'

'You should get checked out. They might have damaged your kidneys, or your liver,' I said, worried.

'My liver's taken worse hits on nights out than the feeble slaps those kids gave me.' I knew he was putting it on; his face was etched in pain and he'd aged about ten years but I didn't want to show him up in front of Jim. Instead I whispered, 'Be careful,' as Jim and Linda turned away in another embrace.

'Little man's OK then,' Alan said, watching Cal sleep.

'He's fine. Shaken, but fine. Next time we'll take him out during the day.'

'Pru and Michael'll never agree to it. Not after this,' Jim said.

'It's so unfair to keep him hidden away,' I said.

'Says who?' Jim said.

'Let's talk about this another time. We should call the police,' Alan said. He looked done in.

'No way. No pigs,' Jim said. His eyes were like flint, his tone granite.

A chill washed over me.

Upstairs I tore off my sodden clothes and ran a bath. Warm and fragrant, the water caressed my battered flesh. I lay back and stared at the cracked bathroom ceiling. No matter what had happened I didn't regret it, not one bit. Cal had a great time. I wanted him to be

126

normal, see the world like a normal kid, experience things, and for the world to experience him. So what if he freaked people out? They needed to be shaken from their stupor, their notions of how people, children, should look. Shocked into a new way of seeing. This was only the beginning. I didn't have to only photograph Cal or draw him. He could *be* the canvas on which I worked. Their reaction could be a project. I could film it, photograph it, interview people about their reaction to him.

The clock showed shortly after three when I climbed into bed. Dawn was breaking before sleep claimed me.

Diana

The unlit cigarette was a great help – it gave me something to do with my fingers. I twirled it, rolled and tapped it from hand to hand. I glanced across at the trestle tables, covered in starched tablecloths, fold lines still visible beneath the legions of glasses, two-thirds full with white, red and pink wine. A wine rainbow. Half of me longed to grab a glass and take a gulp, though I felt so queasy I wasn't sure I could stomach it. The white wine wasn't chilled; this was a degree show private view, after all, not the Tate, Pompidou, or Guggenheim. I closed my eyes and pictured myself at such revered places, champagne flute in hand, a posse of sycophants scurrying behind me, as I waltzed, diva-like, round a retrospective of my work.

At night and in my waking dreams, I'd composed my Turner Prize acceptance speech. I imagined a glamorous life in a trendy area of London, Sunday Supplement articles praising my work. I had been admired, viewed as a winner in my modelling days but I feared my luck had expired. And this was something inside of me, not fluke genetic good fortune. I longed to succeed so much it hurt.

'Big night. Happy?' It was Elspeth, small and bright, cigarette holder in one hand, glass in the other.

'I'm proud of it. I hope others like it,' I said.

'It will provoke a reaction, and that's what counts. I hope to introduce you to some people, important people, who could help you on your way.'

'What, dealers, buyers?'

'Maybe. Angels, supporters of the arts. That's what you need. They have been invited, but whether they come is another matter entirely.' She turned her hands with their gnarled fingers and swollen joints outwards, palms facing the ceiling, skilfully avoiding spilling a single drop of wine.

For the first time, I almost regretted my decision to come to Manchester. I had not applied to such hallowed institutes as Goldsmith's or St Martin's. Studying in London would have meant living at home with Dad, after Bunny kicked me out, and I was desperate to escape. And it suited Dad to have me out of the way so that he could play happy families with his new wife, and Tom. I was a reminder of an unpleasant episode in his hitherto unruffled existence.

'I've invited people too,' I said.

'Good for you; very entrepreneurial.' She said entrepreneurial as if it were some kind of affliction, or disease.

'People won't come to you, you've got to get out there and drag them in,' I said.

Elspeth laughed. 'You're a new breed. What this changing world needs.'

129

'I've offered to pay train fares. Or petrol. I figured none of them would take the coach.'

She laughed again. 'Then let's hope they don't all show up. You'll be bankrupt.'

A couple will be enough.

'I like your confidence. And business acumen. It'll stand you in good stead.' Elspeth drew on her cigarette, and through a fug of smoke, looked directly at me, with her piercing green eyes. 'Why didn't you go to the Slade, Goldsmith's? I've never asked.'

'I didn't apply,' I said, admitting that it was nothing to do with Dad. Not really. My confidence was a façade. 'I wasn't good enough. My foundation course tutor said so. I was afraid they'd say no.' My voice shook a little.

'You little fool. But I'm glad you came here. Good luck.' She waved at someone across the room, a block of ash dropped to the floor, and she hobbled away, oblivious, her velvet frock coat dragging behind her like a wedding train, a trail of ash smudging the floor.

More people pushed their way in to the gallery. I spotted Louise before Dad – though he looked just as incongruous – the brass buttons on her Chanel jacket almost as dazzling as her enormous hair. She looked extremely pink, and blonde. In fifteen years she'd not be dissimilar to Bunny, and I wondered if Dad realised this. He sauntered a few paces behind, looking hot in his suit and tie. They were both tanned and although he appeared uncomfortable I had to admit he cut a fine figure; he was a handsome man. I searched for Tom's small form.

Something resembling a smile cracked across

130

Louise's features and she threw an instruction over her shoulder. My mouth was dry. I leant in to kiss him, hug him, desperate to hold on to someone, but we didn't quite make contact. I kissed the air in front of his cheek and he patted my back, like you'd pat the flank of a racehorse or show dog.

'Where's Tom?' I said.

She answered. 'We didn't think it a good idea to take him out of school, did we, darling?' She looked to my father for support. He nodded apologetically, eyes fixed on the parquet. 'To drag him all the way up here. It's an important time for him.'

It was an important time for me. 'He's eight, not sixteen,' I said. 'But hey, there'll be other opportunities. When I'm rich and famous.' I was intent on an unsullied evening. At least Dad had come, which was more than could be said for Bunny.

After our last, disastrous, meeting I'd wondered if it was worth inviting Bunny, but I had to – I couldn't stop myself. And if I'm honest, I wanted her there, if only to show her that I'd done it: graduated, and with a first class degree. I wanted to rub her face in it, stick two fingers up at her. See, I am more than a pretty face. Look at me. Look at all this.

'What have you done to your hair, Diana?' Louise said, flicking her mane over her shoulder. Dad coughed.

I didn't deign to answer. I'd cut it months ago, on impulse, with the clippers Linda had borrowed from a friend to do Jim's hair. It had grown considerably since, but I'd swept the longer section on top back over my crown and waxed it down with some Black and White. I

131

loved the smell: almond sweet, it trailed the wearer like a loyal dog. The sides of my head I shaved regularly. I wore scarlet lipstick, heavy eyeliner and false eyelashes, a man's suit, complete with braces, and no shirt.

Neither Dad nor Louise had moved forward to take a look at my work. We stood there, like lemons, as Linda would say, struggling for something to say. Thinking they might be waiting for an invitation I lifted my arm towards the table and said, 'Help yourselves to a glass and take a look round.'

You'd have sworn I'd offered Louise a glass of my own piss judging by her expression, though in all fairness my piss might have tasted better than the wine. She scrunched her pointy nose, tittered and said, in her faux-posh accent, 'I'll think we'll pass on that, won't we, darling? It's a tad early.'

And then, under his breath, so quiet I thought I might have imagined it, Dad said, 'Never stopped you before, Louise.'

She blanched, laughed, a bit too loudly, and I wondered if my father was on the first step to divorce number two. I thought about Tom, and my heart stopped. If they separated, no way would he have Tom, and where would that leave me? How would I get to see him?

Dad coughed. 'Righto, give us the guided tour.'

'I'm not a bloody estate agent,' I said, waving them on, 'take a look, I'll hover behind, you can ask me anything you like.'

I can practise on them, though I doubt either of them will have anything intelligent to say.

My father was a clever man but had never before

proved he had any artistic sensibility. His idea of culture was reading the *Sunday Times*. Louise was a philistine. I just wanted them, him, to see what I could do, and to like it, even.

'There's not much actual painting, is there?' she said, her head jerking about as if a fly buzzed round her face. She was looking to see who was watching. Christ, she was vain. 'I thought art was paintings, drawings and stuff.'

'This is the "and stuff",' I said, smiling.

I caught sight of Dad, his narrow eyes following those people who paused in front of my work, as if he was monitoring their reaction. To guide his own perhaps. My ears were as finely tuned as a bat's and I captured hushed comments. Most were complimentary, some pretentious, others uncomprehending, and shocked. Dad was shot through with a burning, like a glowing ember, something that, for a brief moment, I thought resembled pride. I allowed myself to believe that he might say to a passer-by: 'My daughter created this. Isn't she clever? Talented?' Not waiting for an answer because he already knew.

He didn't, of course. He was his usual reserved self, but he touched my shoulder, gave it a gentle squeeze. And that was enough. He approved, and in that second it would not have mattered to me if the rest of the world said it was utter bollocks.

Louise studied a photograph of me dressed as a fairy, reduced and superimposed over an image of Cal's hairy back, as if I was riding him. You wouldn't know it was Cal, but it was clear that it was a child's back, if not

133

entirely clear if it was real or photographic trickery. The next hanging was one of my hairy fairies: a self-portrait with my cheeks covered in gossamer and down. I looked leonine, with my enormous, mystical mane. Louise was uncharacteristically quiet.

'What does it make you think of?' I asked.

'An animal. It's grotesque,' she said.

'That's a big word,' I said. She scowled, but before she could retort I added, 'Good. Exactly the reaction I hoped for.' And I smiled. One of my best "I'm a little princess" smiles, the sort I'd perfected years ago.

'They're almost beautiful. Arresting. Quite, quite alarming,' Dad said, out of the blue.

It was as close to praise as I was ever likely to receive from him, and I was so shocked I couldn't even thank him.

I'll make you proud, one day, Dad. I will.

I wished that Cal had been present to hear my father say he thought the work was beautiful. When I'd shown Cal the picture that's exactly what he'd said, and I'd replied that it took both of us to make the picture lovely.

'Will you join us for supper later? At our hotel?' my father said, as he turned from my final piece. 'You'll need to wear a shirt.' He'd so studiously avoided looking below my neck that I'd thought he'd not noticed I was shirt-less. It wasn't indecent. After all, the braces covered my nipples and I'd fastened the buttons of the single breasted jacket despite the heat.

'Sure. I have to stay till the end. I'll be through sometime round nine. I've got friends coming, and you never know... Take a look around, there's some interesting stuff.' I stared at Louise as I said 'stuff,' but instead of feeling triumphant about showing her up, my father taking my side for a change, guilt gripped me. Maybe it was the insecurity behind her eyes, the desperation. Maybe she knew she was losing her hold on him, that he'd desert her as he had me, and Bunny, and that, after all, she loved him more than he did her.

I watched them cross the hall and leave.

Dinner would be painful. Dad would sit there avoiding talk of anything that mattered. He'd drone about some paper or other he'd read about the latest techniques in eye surgery, going into ludicrous, arse-achingly boring detail, then he'd talk about some enlightening documentary he'd seen on the box, the poor service in the provinces. He wouldn't ask about my life, what made me miserable or happy, who my friends were, my hopes and desires. He'd make pronouncements about the best way forward now that I'd completed my degree. A career in teaching, further education if I'd knuckle down to an MA. Administration was 'not to be sniffed at'. He might ask if there was a 'young man' on the scene. I imagined telling him the truth: I've been sleeping with a guy doing Philosophy, but it's not what you'd call going anywhere. He's the sort of bloke that left a chunk of himself in adolescence. No, that's being too kind. Let's say he's got the emotional age of an eleven-year-old. You'd get on well. But no, there's no one you'd call special, Dad.

She'd blather on about her soap opera of a life and look startled when I asked after Tom, like I'd reminded her of a favourite piece of jewellery she'd not worn for a while. The evening might even end in a row. That was always a distinct possibility; usually dependent on how energetic I felt or how much expensive wine I guzzled to alleviate the boredom.

It was past seven.

Where were my friends? I'd expected them to appear almost as soon as the doors opened. Then I thought of Linda fussing over what to wear before affecting a 'this old thing?' attitude when complimented by an admiring Alan, watched over by a studiously uninterested Jim.

People took in my work: fellow students, their family and friends, professors, tutors. There were even a couple of visitors I didn't recognise. They might have been important. I chatted when spoken to, polite, self-assured, opinionated without seeming arrogant, my eyes returning to the clock periodically. It was a long hour.

~

Ten minutes before close. Small clusters of people huddled round the drinks table, loud laughter, plumes of smoke. No longer feigning interest in the art they treated it like a pub. Disappointment at my friends' no-show seized me. Anger swiftly followed disbelief, then pain. I watched a couple stagger to the exit, arms across backs, supporting and destabilising each other simultaneously. I pulled my lone cigarette from the tin, eyes locked on the departing couple. Were they heading home for leisurely, drunken sex? Was it love or lust? Were they just good friends, or a brother and sister, affectionate, secure, needed?

As I turned to light my cigarette I noticed a small

figure standing before my hairy fairy pieces. In a grey business suit and stacked heels, he carried a briefcase and looked more like a surveyor than an art fan, but this innocuous man was important. I felt it. I put my cigarette away.

'Do you believe in fairies?' I said, slipping alongside him.

'What I believe in doesn't matter, Miss...?'

'Brading, Diana Brading.' I offered my hand. He didn't take it, and I left it there, hovering in mid-air before curling my fingers and stroking my fingernails in a pathetic attempt to cover my unease.

'Some of your work is interesting, Miss Brading. Underdeveloped, but interesting nevertheless. Promising.'

'Thank you, I think.' I wanted to ask what he meant by underdeveloped, but he continued.

'The piece with the boy. Fascinating. Most unusual.' He held out a card, which I almost snatched, fingers shaking, afraid he might withdraw it before I had purchase.

'Yes, he is,' I said, glancing down. A London address, Chelsea, wealthy part of town. Scadanelli Art. No Christian name, no title.

'Stay in touch. Contact me when you have more work like this.' Stunned, wondering if I'd heard correctly, I managed a nod. 'I might even try this piece in the gallery. I'll sleep on it.' He flicked a limp wrist at the photograph of me riding Cal, the flick morphing into a wave, and walked away without saying another word. Unsure what to make of his final comment,

I remained silent, head spinning, heart punching against my chest. Finally, I squeaked, 'Till tomorrow, then? The name's Brading, Diana Brading.' He turned, unsmiling. 'I know,' he said, before disappearing into the crowd.

I stared at the card, turned it between my fingers. The other side was blank. He was *that* classy. I slipped the card into my breast coat pocket, enjoying the sensation of the stiff paper against my heart. The exchange reeled over and over in my mind, like a stuck record. It was an offer. 'Stay in touch,' he said. 'Contact me.' Blood rushed to my head: This was it, a break. A break that might lead to a big break. And it was down to Cal. I would make the film project I'd conceived some time ago, Cal would enjoy it and recording people's reactions would be fascinating. My imagination spooled. Filled with excitement, gratefulness and love, I longed to rush home and tell him, swing him in my arms round and round, the way he liked it.

Brimming, I went to light my cigarette. As I battled with cheap matches the doors burst open and in stepped Alan and Linda. They appeared ruffled as they scanned the hall. From a position nestled behind a display flat I watched, unobserved, still shaking, unsure if I could speak.

They're here! They came!

They turned to study the exhibition map. Linda radiated an almost preternatural beauty. She had never looked more lovely; she was an exotic pre-Raphaelite nymph, oozing excess, temptation, sex. She was predicted to do well in her finals, but she had no concrete career plans after graduation. Unsure what she wanted to do with the rest of her life, other than she didn't want to return to Liverpool or teach – the natural and most straightforward choice for a young woman with a humanities degree and no contacts in the much sought-after and glamorous worlds of publishing or advertising – she'd settled on the idea of hanging out in Manchester waitressing at a fancy restaurant in King Street, raising money to travel in India and the East.

Alan loped over. He carried an aura of excitement and purpose, despite his chaotic appearance. He'd found his vocation.

He's imagining himself in three years' time. Where he'll be, what he'll be doing. Just as I am.

For the second time that evening I found myself searching the room for a third party in the group: Jim. He'd promised he would come, that he would bring Cal, but there was no sign of him. I so wanted Cal to see my show, his part in it.

Perhaps they'll follow on. Better get a move on though. Time's running out.

I watched Linda charge over to the wine table, knock back an entire glass in one go, and collect a second. Someone either said something or pulled a face, because Linda stuck out her tongue. Reaching over for yet another glass, she passed it, ever so slowly, to Alan, who shrugged apologetically then took a sip and turned in my direction. He fiddled with the roll-up tucked behind his right ear. The dreadlocks had gone. His hair curled in shiny locks before resting above his square shoulders. He'd had a shave and his chin gleamed white, his puckered flesh reminding me of a plucked chicken. He caught my eye and waved enthusiastically. He brought a wide grin to my face.

Linda kissed me on the cheek as she hugged me, squeezing me so tight I could barely breathe. A delicious tang of tobacco, alcohol and perfume swarmed round me. I went to say something but she held her hand across my mouth, the other gripping my shoulder.

'Don't say anything. I want to look round like a stranger, seeing it for the first time,' she said. She removed her hand then rubbed the corners of my mouth. 'Smudged lippie. Give us a sec.' She licked her finger and wiped again. 'Done. Perfect!'

I might have resembled Robert Smith, or a clown. I didn't care.

'Oh man, Diana, that's have a look. Sorry we're so late,' Alan said, staring at my chest, as if willing a button to pop off and reveal my breasts.

'Cheers. Thought you'd approve.' I waved him on. 'Go on. Enjoy. Before it's too late.'

I held onto my news like a delicious secret. I wanted to relish the telling, to hear their views of my work, before I shared Scadanelli's. Or what I imagined his view was given that he'd not exactly spelt it out. I didn't mention Jim and Cal's absence.

'Friggin' hell, Diana, it's amazing. Amazing.' Linda turned from each piece and looked at me, mouth wide, eyes popping. 'Like, on the walls, here, it looks, just, like, so much better.' She checked herself. 'I mean, it was brill before ... but, like this ... Wow!'

Alan said nothing. He caught my eye and smiled, tipped his chin. It meant more than any overblown exclamation.

'Right. We all deserve a drink. Especially you.' She pointed at me and winked.

'It should be champagne,' I said, almost a whisper, lifting the card up.

'Damn right it should,' Linda insisted. She wasn't looking and hadn't seen the card. Alan had. He leapt over. I held it up, over my mouth, almost kissing the back of it, as he studied the words.

He stared into my eyes, his own glistening, brimming with delight. He knew. 'Oh, Diana.'

It was as if a dam had burst. I screamed out my news, fists clenched, jumping up and down on the spot, as Cal did whenever he was excited. Linda and Alan hooked their arms over each of my shoulders, forming a tight circle and joined in. We screamed and jumped until we were breathless.

'Gonna be huge, Diana, HUGE! Think of the dosh!' Linda said.

'You bet,' I said. 'Now how about some lighter fluid?'

Linda fetched the wine glasses and we raised them.

'To us. To being young and ambitious. To life.'

Linda turned to Alan, 'I can't wait to be toasting your final success.' She kissed him, and he glowed, he really did. He looked almost handsome.

'Nor me,' I said. 'You're going to be great, Al. Just great.'

After months of nagging, Alan had applied to and been accepted on the photography degree. He was to begin in September, and he was going to be brilliant. Of

141

this I was certain.

The wine hit my empty system like speed. A rush to the head, a shiver in my throat, a spin in the stomach. I longed for the cigarette, the one I'd failed to light earlier, to feel the rush, another brief high, once more.

'Where's Jim?' I asked as casually as I could, glancing at three people milling round my space. 'He said he'd bring Cal.'

'I have no friggin' idea. That's why we were late,' Linda spat. 'We waited for ages and ages, then I thought sod the stupid git, we're not missing Diana's party for nothing.'

My guts twisted.

Should I be worried? Or is it just Jim being Jim? An unreliable, controlling bastard.

'On the plus side, you missed my dad and Louise,' I said, toxicity snaking through my veins.

'I'd love to have met them. No Tom?' Linda dashed to the drinks table and took the last three glasses of wine.

I shook my head. I'd hoped Cal and Tom could meet. Tom was a kind boy; Cal would like him.

'Shame,' she said, 'I can't believe I've known you two all this time and I've never met either of your folks.' She looked at me and Alan.

'I have to meet them for dinner. Come.'

'Won't they mind?' said Linda.

'Possibly, but Dad'll be far too polite to say anything, and she doesn't count,' I said. 'C'mon. It'll be a laugh, and there'll be plenty to drink.' The wine was having an effect. It was nine o'clock and the private view was officially over.

I said my goodbyes to Elspeth and a few other tutors, grabbed a T-shirt from my bag – I hadn't planned on walking home bare-chested – and ushered my friends outside. Alan stopped on the bottom step.

'I'm not coming,' he said, 'your dad's expecting you, not us.'

'He won't mind,' I insisted. 'He'll be glad. He never knows what to say to me. He can lecture you,' I said to Alan, 'on the improbability of making a decent living in the arts and,' turning to Linda, 'letch at you.' I linked arms with Linda and pulled her towards All Saints. 'And that has the added benefit of pissing off Louise,' I ended with a self-satisfied flourish.

'How can you be so horrible?' Alan said.

Linda and I looked at each other and raised our eyebrows. 'What's with him?' I mouthed.

'Bin in a funny mood all day,' she mouthed back.

Alan wasn't looking at us. He stared at the pavement, and kicked the concrete.

'Without him you wouldn't be here,' he said, a peculiar edge to his voice. I assumed it was the drink, or dope.

'Durgh,' I said.

'Here. Manchester. Finishing a degree. Support, a home to go to.' His voice rose higher and higher.

For support I read money. Big mistake.

'Huh! He's got pots, doesn't mean anything. He pays to keep me away.' Linda let go of my embrace and took out another cigarette, changed her mind and stood there in the road looking lost. I couldn't work out what Alan's problem was. After all, money was even less of an issue for him. He didn't work, he didn't collect dole, he said, or a grant cheque. Clearly his parents stumped up too, and he didn't have to beg the way I did from time to time. It was always there.

'You never give him a chance. Or Bunny.'

The mention of Bunny pushed what could have been a minor disagreement into something more serious. Had Alan known this? Was it a deliberate tactic on his behalf? Everything we'd known for the past three years was changing, and he needed to start afresh. Sometimes, we unconsciously engineer rows when the need to dispose of emotional baggage becomes great.

'And what the hell would you know?' I screeched. The evening's tension, the wine, the excitement, the fear that Scadanelli would reconsider, decide that I was not a winner after all, the even greater fear that I couldn't live up to expectation, the buried hurt that Bunny hadn't come, that Jim hadn't brought Cal, the fossilised feeling that I was worthless, a sweet-looking shell with a hollow centre, always close to the surface, rose once more.

'You never give them a chance,' he said.

'Why should I?'

And then it was Alan who was yelling, 'Because you can! Because they're here and they might not always be!'

We'd never seen Alan angry, and his raw fury was alarming. Linda and I stood there, frozen despite the heat. Passers-by skittered to the other side of the road, circumnavigating us. He kicked the concrete again, and stormed off towards Loxford Halls of Residence. I went to make chase.

Linda held out her arm, to stop me. 'Let him go.'

'I can't.'

We found Alan leaning against the sidewall of Cavendish, facing Hulme. He must have wanted to be found and been convinced that we would follow him; it was only round the corner.

Not confident that I'd say the right thing, I let Linda approach him. I hung behind like a naughty, contrite child.

'What happened to your folks?' she said.

'Car accident. Drunk driver. They died instantly, the police said.'

Alan's parents had been killed four years ago that night. The drunk driver walked away from the scene unhurt, and after the inquest Alan walked away from the life he'd known. He left leafy, prosperous Alderley Edge and began a new life in Manchester, burying himself in dope and drink. He was twenty-one and all alone in the world with a small fortune in the bank. His father had been a conservative, prudent man, with a good life insurance policy.

'Everything's changing,' he said. He was calmer, shame-faced, though he had no need to be. I couldn't believe he'd kept this to himself. That three anniversaries of his parents' deaths had been and gone, and Linda and I hadn't noticed. Alan's Spartan lifestyle, his secrecy, his overblown sadness at the parrot's demise, the way he walked the city over and over, all made sense: walking was his way of dealing with pain. I wondered if he walked away from his pain or into it.

'You won't be left alone, Al,' Linda said, 'I'll be here.'

'Me too. Only once I've a body of new work will I stand a chance of making it down in London.'

'Not for long. Not for three years,' he said.

'Quit the self-pity. It's really unattractive,' I said.

'And there's Cal,' he said.

The atmosphere thickened at the mention of Cal; I thought we might never be able to move on from that moment, like we'd been varnished or trapped in amber. Cal, alone in his room. He was only seven years old. How could I ever leave Manchester? But one day I'd have to. I felt my heart stop.

Linda hooked her arm through Alan's. 'He'll be taken care of when we all go and that's not going to be for ages.'

But all I could think was that no one could care for him like I did. I touched my jacket pocket, checking that the business card was still there. I wanted to split myself in two.

In the distance I heard a clock strike; I had to go. Dad would be waiting, hungry. Worried about me, maybe. I hugged them both goodbye. Alan held me like he'd never let me go. I prised myself away and hailed a cab, waving like an idiot from the open window, like I was leaving them for good rather than a couple of hours.

~

It was gone midnight when I arrived home. I'd not expected Linda to be in; I figured she'd have found Jim, so it was a surprise to discover her sitting in the dark, drinking from a chipped mug. Despite the open windows the place stank of fags; the ashtray in the middle of the rug struggled to contain the butts. She was perched on the edge of the sofa, elbows resting on her knees, chin cupped in her palms, legs bouncing up and down, jiggling on the balls of her bare feet. She didn't move as I crossed the room. She looked as if she were in a trance. Her eyes were glazed, her pupils dilated. She stared at me, without really looking. Something was very, very wrong.

I crouched down and placed my hands on her knees; her skin was sticky. 'Linda?'

'Pru's dead. Jim's with the police.'

I fell onto my knees, the cheap carpet prickling through the worn fabric of my trousers. I shook her knees. 'Cal? What about Cal?'

'Social Services.'

I let out a deep sigh, my head resting on her knees, my knuckles boring into my forehead. 'Thank God he's safe. What happened?'

'Overdose. Michael's in hospital, he's going to be OK.'

Why was she here and not with Jim? Of course. She'd been waiting for my return, to tell me, because of Cal. Uneasiness swept over me and I couldn't identify why, and then it punched me, hard, in the pit of my stomach. 'Where are the cops?'

Her face scrunched up; she looked at me as if I was stupid. 'At the flat.'

'Oh Christ, Cal, Cal...' I stood up and paced the room, talking to myself. My mind raced. If the police were at the flat, they'd know, about the drugs, the dealing. Cal would never be allowed to stay with Michael

– and I was nothing to Cal, not in the eyes of the law. Until now, he'd slipped through the net; how could the authorities have known? He wasn't ill-treated – far from it since Alan and I had become close to him – but a home visit would have revealed his environment as a drugs den, as risky. Why had I never seen it as such?

Cal would be taken into care; Social Services already had him. He'd be institutionalised, fostered – if anyone would have him – I'd never see him again. I needed him. He could never be loved by anyone as much as me. The thought was unbearable. My lungs struggled for air. I crossed to the window, hyperventilating, gripped the windowsill and hung my head outside. The humid air felt fresh after the fug in the room. Stars appeared before my eyes and I retreated, afraid that I was about to pass out.

My panic had the opposite effect on Linda. She snapped out of her stupor; she stood, grabbed my shoulders and shook me. I was still babbling and she raised a hand to slap me. That shut me up. She spoke to me like I was an imbecile.

'I'm going down to the cop shop. I'm going to take Alan, see if we can help Jim,' she said, slipping on her stilettos, before changing her mind and dragging a pair of pumps from under the settee. She pulled them on as she headed, hopping, towards the door.

'They know he's involved?' I said, following her through the hall.

'God knows. But he's not.'

I admired her faith in Jim and considered her blind simultaneously. Jim worked with Pru and Michael: he was the supplier, higher up the chain than they could ever be. But I fretted for Linda. She'd be devastated if anything happened to Jim, and she could be implicated. She was his girl. She spent loads of time with him; they might think she was involved. They might think I was. And Alan. We spent time at the William Kent flat. I'd known they dealt for years, Christ, we bought gear from them ourselves, but I'd kidded myself that it had nothing to do with me. How deluded I was.

And I thought of Cal: all alone, in a strange place with no one who knew him, let alone loved him. He would be terrified. I had to see him.

~

Ten minutes on the train from Piccadilly was Stretford, a quiet suburb that fancied itself more Cheshire than Greater Manchester. The house was red-brick, with a steeply pitched roof and a black and white tiled path through the front garden to the door.

So this is where all the unwanted kids are sent.

A white doorbell stared at me, daring me to press it. I glanced at my watch: five-thirty. What a terrible time. The kids would be having tea. I was dying to see him, and dreading it all at the same time. I closed my eyes and pressed.

'You must be Diana. Do come in.' An imposing woman stood in the doorway. Her smile was as friendly as the yellow and brown batik print of her head wrap.

'Sorry I'm early,' I stumbled.

'No problem. Come on in.' She waved her arm, stepped aside, and ushered me through. Her colossal breasts barred my progress and I had to squeeze myself past her. I wondered if Cal had been buried in an embrace in all that flesh, and if he'd enjoyed it. Jealousy piqued.

The querulous prattle of children wafted through the hall as the woman bounded up a wide flight of stairs.

'Should be eating his tea. I'm hoping he's almost finished it. Not eaten a scrap of dinner or breakfast.'

'He's having his supper in his room?'

Surely the dining room isn't upstairs?

'We thought it better. For the other children,' she said.

I wanted to holler didn't he suffer enough, without being isolated from the other kids, but I realised that perhaps it was better after all. Cal wasn't used to other children; he knew little of their casual cruelty, the pecking orders, the game playing. Despite the searing heat I shuddered and hoped that he'd not come out of his room at all. He'd been here less than forty-eight hours.

The woman stopped outside a door on the landing, lifted a fist, preparing to knock, and then turned to me and whispered, 'He's expecting you, but maybe I should check first?'

I nodded; it might frighten him half to death if the door opened suddenly. She tapped, opened the door and popped her head through the gap. I stared at a poster on the landing wall: a horrible illustration of a woman's face, well made-up, black spiky hair, supposed to be a pop star or something.

I heard Cal's voice; my spirits lifted and the poster didn't seem so ugly any more. 'Diana, Diana!' He was screaming. Excited, upset, angry. So many emotions contained in my name.

'Now you watch your supper, little man. You'll tip it

all over the carpet, you will.'

I followed her into the room and overtook her as Cal tumbled towards me, arms outstretched. I dropped to my knees, and encased him as he fell onto my chest. He didn't smell like Cal anymore. His hair stank of coconut milk and honey, the scent of the detergent used to clean the strange clothes he was wearing tickled my nostrils. His strength astonished me, he held me so tight, and then he started thumping my back, harder and harder.

'Why you did you leave me? Why? Why? Why?' he screamed. I sensed the woman approaching, pulling him off me.

'It's fine. Fine. Leave him. Leave us,' I said, turning my head a little and looking up at her. I felt Cal's anger recede and his body convulsed with great thundering sobs.

'I cannot leave you with him. It is not allowed,' she said, sitting herself on a chair in the corner.

Still holding tight onto Cal, rocking him gently, I glanced round. My back still thrummed from the force of Cal's beating. The room was spacious, the walls Moroccan sky orange and though there was nothing specific it felt like a girl's room. The curtains were purple, and a line of soft toys sat at the end of a single bed. Perhaps it was the only room available.

What does Cal make of this?

It was colourful and bright and light, everything the flat in William Kent Crescent wasn't.

Stroking his hair, I whispered in his ear how much I missed him, how much I cared for him, loved him. We stayed there, in our own little world, for ages. Rocking back and forth. I felt his breathing return to normal, the shaking at his core subside. I held him at arm's length. 'It's good to see you, kid.'

He did not smile. 'I want to go home. Go home,' he said.

Instead of answering I pulled a book, some plastic figures and a couple of bars of chocolate from my bag. I expected him to go for the chocolate, but he seized on the figures, before scuttling over to the bed, pulling out a shoebox from underneath it and carefully placing the figures in, before sliding it back.

'You want some chocolate?' I said, holding it out.

He shook his head, but took it all the same.

'I want to go home. With you.'

'Oh Cal, I'd love that. I'd really love that. But right now, it's not possible.' I reached towards him, but he slid back, his face distorted with rage. I didn't know how to reach him. I wanted to scream. The woman watched, nodding her head knowingly, a faint smile in her eyes. Was this a scene she'd witnessed a thousand times? I couldn't remember her name.

'Shall I read to you? *Stig of the Dump*. It sounds great.'

He didn't reply so I opened the book and began to read, glancing up occasionally to check if he was listening. Before I'd reached the bottom of page two he said, suddenly, 'There are cars here.'

'Sorry?'

'Cars. I hear cars. I watch too. Out the window.' He pointed. 'And birds. Tweet, tweet,' he mimicked.

'What else do you hear?'

152

'Shouting. Crying.'

'Laughing?' How I longed for him to hear something nice.

'Sometimes.'

I smiled and he shuffled next to me, tucking himself under the crook of my arm. I continued to read, my heart rate slowing with the warmth of him next to me.

We sat there – not playing, not talking, not doing any of the stuff I'd imagined we'd do – reading, listening, just being. And it felt like forever and no time at all. Peaceful, at one with the world.

'It's time to go, Miss Brading. I am sorry.'

Jolted out of our private world Cal grabbed hold of me and began to scream. 'Don't go, don't go, don't go!'

She prised him off me, restraining him in a massive bear hug, her arms crossed over his little chest. His face red, sweaty, wet. I took hold of his shoulders and looked into his eyes. Big and brown and beautiful.

'I'm going to get you out of here.'

'Promise?'

I glanced up at the woman.

'Anything's possible,' she said, smiling.

I looked back at Cal. 'Promise. I promise.'

~

The police were interviewing Michael in his hospital bed when I pitched up with a bag of grapes he'd never eat. I'd have brought him fags if I'd thought he could get away with smoking. Anything to soften him up. After much deliberation, I'd opted for fruit and a very short, cheerful-looking dress. It was bright orange with pink and white spots, a slash neck and no sleeves, and as of days earlier, it was my lucky dress.

Scadanelli had been as good as his word. He'd not visited the exhibition again, but he had left a message with Elspeth's office: 'Tell Ms Brading that I will be interested in seeing more of her work when she is ready. Do not sell, give away or destroy *Fairy Rides Boy*. I want to see it as part of a larger body of work.'

As it transpired, dressing up for Michael was a waste of time; he didn't take any persuading. He burbled on and on about 'poor Pru', about the shock of watching her die.

'Her lips went blue. Blue, Diana. Blue. I thought that was all bollocks, made up.'

'There was nothing you could have done,' I said in an attempt to console him.

'Jim slapped her, real hard. But she didn't even open her eyes. Her head lolled from side to side.'

'It was too late. Stop torturing yourself.'

He spoke about moving away from the flat, from Hulme, going straight. I wondered if the medics were giving him a substitute opiate, to prevent him going cold turkey. Time and time again he returned to Pru's death. The moment was very much alive for him. He relived it over and over, refusing to talk about little else other than his plans to kick heroin, refusing to face the truth: the only place he was going was Strangeways, or some other jail.

He never once mentioned Cal.

I let him talk, knowing that it was all shit and he'd be back on smack within months, if not days, of release. Assuming he couldn't get hold of gear inside. And that was some assumption given what I'd heard about prison.

Fed up of waiting for him to ask me what I wanted, why I'd come, I launched into my request. My offer of help.

'I could care for Cal.'

Michael looked blank, as if he'd forgotten who Cal was.

'I'd like to.'

'He'd like that,' he said, and immediately returned to his plans for when he was discharged from hospital.

'I went to see Michael.' I leant against the wall of the degree show hall, next to a sketch of William Kent Crescent in charcoal. My hands were folded across my chest; I could feel the heat building beneath my breasts, the thick cotton of my vintage dress sticking to my ribs.

Jim continued to stare at another picture. A trickle of sweat ran down his forehead, his temple and onto the stubble of his sideburns. I'd never seen Jim so unkempt and the contrast of his dark beard with the bleached yellow of his flat top made him look sexier than ever. The strength and expanse of his facial hair surprised me. Although it was obvious he wasn't a natural blond I hadn't expected such a growth. Something finer, patchier, less strong. The dense stubble confirmed his virility, visual evidence of his masculine power.

'You should take your jacket off, it's hot,' I said, glancing down at my legs, one bare foot in front of the other, my electric blue toenails bright against the wooden floor.

'You wanna watch no one steps on your toes. It

155

could hurt,' he said, turning to face me.

I looked at his boot-clad feet, then his face and said, 'I'm careful.'

'I bet you are.'

I sighed. The heat had built steadily throughout the week, and everyone was tired. I was exhausted with the stress of seeing Cal, talking with social workers, the not knowing what the hell was going to happen to him, and through all this attempting to juggle my commitment to college and the degree show.

People dragged heavy legs round the gallery, fanning themselves with the exhibition catalogue. I was glad of my cropped hair and exposed neck.

The cops had questioned Jim but there was nothing concrete to link him to the drugs and so he'd been released after a few hours, with the caveat that he might be called for further questioning once the coroner or pathologist had established the exact cause of Pru's death. It appeared to be a clear-cut case of yet another junkie getting greedy, and as far as the police were concerned they had their man in the pathetic form of Michael. He would be convicted as a dealer, his cottage industry closed down. A rare success story in a catalogue of police failures to deal with escalating drug crime in the city.

I stared at Jim who stared at my work.

How did you secure Michael's silence? Maybe you didn't need to exert any pressure? Perhaps Michael believes it's all his fault, that you are blameless, despite your involvement in the trade?

'And then I spoke to Social Services and told them

what Michael said, and you know what?' I said.

'What?'

'Michael has no say. No rights at all.'

'He's a crim.'

'And his name's not on the birth certificate. Came as a bit of a shock to Michael by all accounts.'

Jim remained silent, expression blank. He continued to look at my work.

'So what do you think?' I said.

'Weird. Best in the show. Looked at the other students' stuff. All shite. Bollocks.'

'Say what you think, Jim.' I basked in his praise, though I tried to disguise it, annoyed that I cared so much. I had my offer from Scadanelli. It didn't matter one iota what Jim thought.

'So is Michael even Cal's father?' I continued, studying him hard.

He took a white handkerchief from his pocket and wiped his brow.

'Any ideas?' I continued.

'Nope. Who says it isn't Michael, just 'cos his name's not on the certificate?'

I stood in front of him – there wasn't a bead of sweat on him now – and said, 'Well, he won't have any say in what happens to Cal.'

'And neither will you.' He started to leave. 'You shouldn't have used him,' he said gesturing at *Fairy Rides Boy*. 'He's not a circus animal. Or in a zoo.'

'Zoo animals are cared for. Only way to protect some of them,' I said.

'People staring at them all day.'

157

'They enjoy it.'

'But do they, eh?'

'Cal enjoys it.'

Fuck Jim. Fuck him.

'You sure about that?' he snarled, walking away.

I peered out of the window and watched him head for the pub; we'd agreed to meet once I'd wrapped up. Nausea waved through me.

Cal.

Stuck in a strange place. Away from me and Jim and Linda and Alan and everything he knew. Scadanelli was interested in the Cal work; work that needed further exploration. I still had to prove myself. The real work was about to begin.

I met Jim outside the pub. He was taking me to the William Kent flat. I'd promised Cal that I would collect more of his belongings and bring them with me on my next visit.

'I'm going to apply to look after Cal,' I said.

'You what?'

'My chances are fair.'

'Says who?'

'Social Services. We have a relationship, he knows me. That's what they try to do these days. Keep children with friends, family. I'll get a social worker.'

He kicked an empty can as we trudged on towards the crescents, a tinny rattle echoed across the wasteland.

'There's no family. Pru's parents don't want to know. Disowned and disinherited her years ago. So a friend it is, according to Cal's social worker. I met one yesterday, said she might be mine. Her name's Jennifer.'

'And the friend's you?' He snorted.

'Why not? I love him, he loves me.'

'You're a student, single, in a council flat in Hulme.' He burst out laughing.

'Ex-student. With prospects.'

'No prospects without Cal. Think I don't know the kind of deal it is?'

So Linda had told him. I couldn't blame her; I hadn't asked her not to. Why wouldn't she share with her boyfriend? I should have been more circumspect.

'I'm moving out of the flat, and there's Alan,' I said.

'You're fucking kidding me!'

We were outside the flat. Plastic tape hung from the doorframe, torn pieces scattered the walkway.

Inside it was a tip. The police had searched the place, or most of it, and it seemed as if either the cops or other scavengers had picked clean the bones of Mr and Mrs Hulme's life. It smelt like any other home that had been uninhabited for days. I found this disconcerting. Something wonderful happened here, and something terrible, and it was an affront to decency that it smelt so normal.

All the electrical goods had gone, stolen no doubt. Jim wondered if his brother had anything to do with it. 'Little git, I'll kill 'im.'

I collected the remainder of Cal's toys and books scattered about his room and was about to leave when I caught sight of a Darth Vader mask hanging on the wall. I was surprised I'd not noticed it earlier and gave thanks that it hadn't been stolen or crushed and destroyed in the ransacking. I unhooked it from the nail knocked into the plasterboard.

When I came down the staircase Jim was standing in the middle of the enormous living room with his back to me, smoking. I coughed to alert him to my presence.

'You goin' to tell Cal the good news right away?' Jim said, sarcasm rolled round every word like pastry.

'Are you crazy? It'll take time to sort out. Need to get a new place, get some cash from Dad—'

'Talk to Alan?' He smirked.

'He'll do anything for me.'

'If he has to pretend to be your partner, he might insist upon his rights.' He moved closer. I could smell the beer on his breath.

'Alan's a gent,' I said, nodding at the cigarette packet poking out of Jim's top pocket. 'May I?'

He handed me the pack. 'Nothing's certain. You might not get him. *I* wouldn't give you custody or whatever it's called.'

'You're not the judge.' I wanted to slap him.

I dropped the bag of Cal's things on the floor, the mask on top, and lit a cigarette, vacillating between petulance and determination. I wandered to the far wall and leant against it. I would work, take care of Cal, Alan would help. Maybe Linda too.

Jim walked forwards, stopping in front of me. He looked like an Olympian god. His mouth drooped a touch, put on for effect. 'You've got it all planned out, haven't you?' he said.

I blew air out of my nostrils but said nothing. He

160

was glad I'd be staying, even though he would never say it. 'I didn't say that,' I replied.

He took another step forwards. I pushed myself against the wall. A puddle of sweat gathered at the base of my spine. Sunlight shot between us like a veil. The wall felt as slippery and yielding as my flesh.

'Why did you cut your hair?' he said, stroking the top of my head. 'I liked it long.'

'You never said.'

He sniggered, perhaps realising how old-fashioned he sounded. Our physical proximity was unsettling, but compulsive, and neither of us wanted to break apart. I ran my hand along my neck; it was sticky and tense.

'Why are you staying in Manchester?' he said. I caught sight of his tongue as he spoke, the tips of his front teeth. They looked sharp.

'For Cal.'

'What if he's sent somewhere else? Some nice little family in Chorlton-cum-Hardy? You'll piss off then?'

'I'll stay. Visit him. Work here.'

'Cheaper than London, isn't it? Till you sell your work.' He moved closer; our feet touched.

'You're glad I'm staying.'

I felt his hand sliding up my thigh, his fingertips rough against the soft, pliant flesh, my short dress, confusion and desire presenting no barrier to his progress.

'You're nice to look at.'

'Even with short hair?' I slapped my hand over his and pressed hard, holding his hand steady. He leant in, as if to kiss me, stopped, our lips almost touching.

161

'Why Linda?' I said, 'Why did you choose Linda?'
My arm was shaking from the strain of halting his
progress up my thigh.

'She's uncomplicated,' he said, pushing his hand
higher. Stronger than me, his fingers reached my
knickers, where the softest flesh blended into damp folds.
I left my hand on his, but without pressure, compliant
and complicit.

'You're a bastard.'

He bit my earlobe, sucked on my neck, pulled down
my knickers. I grabbed his cheeks as we kissed, pressing
my thumbs onto his cheekbones, hard like metal. I could
taste the beer on his tongue. He fumbled with his belt,
the flies of his trousers. He released himself quickly and
lifted my legs around his waist. My head hit the wall
over and over as he rammed into me in that abandoned,
desolate flat.

It was over in minutes. He came with a small, silent
shudder and pulled away so fast I fell. I scrabbled on the
floor for my knickers, drenched in shame. I wanted to
vomit.

Jim fastened his trousers, tucked in his shirt
carefully. I turned away and checked my dress for tears. I
had no voice, a cacophony of words lodged in my throat,
choking me, and if I'd found my voice I would not have
known what to say. It had happened as if in slow motion.
I had been fully conscious of what was going on, willed
it, even though I knew it to be disgusting. Some would
say we behaved like animals but that would be doing
animals a disservice.

How could you betray a friend like this? Are you so afraid of being ignored you need to seduce a man you don't like, let alone trust?

In a matter of days I'd fallen from intoxicated joy and optimism about the future into a pit of darkness and misery that felt impossible to escape. What if Jim was right and Cal was taken away? I'd never see him again. No one loved him like I did. My work would suffer, which meant the offer from Scadanelli would come to nothing. And I'd betrayed a friend. Friends. Alan would be devastated.

They'll turn their backs on you. You need their support. They must never know.

I dragged myself to the bathroom and threw up in the soiled pan. I wiped away Jim's stinking residue with my bare hands, washed, and in the cracked mirror hanging above the sink smoothed my hair and wiped away any traces of make-up.

Jim materialised behind me in the reflection. I had not locked the door; modesty seemed inappropriate. 'You look fine,' he grunted.

'This will never happen again,' I said.

'It's been coming a long time. You were gagging for it.'

I resisted the urge to turn round and thump him. He would have hit me right back.

He didn't ask me not to tell Linda; he didn't have to. I pushed past, collected Cal's bag and made my way to the door. The metal of the lock was cool against my burning flesh. I wanted to walk to my flat alone but he would not let me. We were silent. Words whirled round my head: *You stupid, disgusting bitch. You shallow, worthless*

163

cow. You deserve nothing. You are nothing.
Words I'd heard so many times before.

164

Cal

'Are you religious?' Eve asks, shaking a thermometer. She caught me looking at her breasts so I asked about the gold crucifix round her neck. It looks real pretty. I'd like to run to my fingers over the silky skin of her neck all the way down to the stiff collar of her uniform. I'd like to run my finger along the neckline, feel the hard contours of her collarbone.

'I had faith once,' I say.

'That's not quite the same thing,' says Eve. 'It's not what I meant.'

'I know.'

'Is there anything that takes you out of yourself, fills you up?'

'Music. Music does that for me.'

'That's art, not faith.'

'Same thing.'

'There's a radio here.'

'Cheers, but I can't stand the crap they play.'

'Better than nothing.'

'Is it?'

~

Light is everywhere in my new house. And sound. Music pours from every corner. It is so different to my old house, where everything was crushed and dark and tumbled down all around me. The dreams where the walls move in, shrinking the room, have stopped and I am surrounded by air. Standing on a chair I press my face against the glass and gaze out. The sky goes on and on and on, and if I stare too long my eyes start to hurt.

'There's magic out there,' Diana says.

'I don't want to go anywhere without you.'

'I won't leave you.'

'Never?'

'Never ever.'

'Then I would like to go to space,' I say.

'There's enough to explore here on earth,' she waves her arm about, 'and within ourselves without bothering with all that space crap.'

'I like space crap.'

'Don't swear. It's rude,' she says.

'You did.'

'I'm a grown-up.'

Alan joins us looking out of the window.

'Take no notice, mate. The universe is infinite, goes on forever and forever, and we will never know even a fraction of it, but that's not to stop us trying.' He spins and turns up the volume on the cassette player. 'Man, I LOVE this track.'

Diana groans. I know this song. Alan plays it a lot: *A Kind of Magic*. The name of the band is funny – Queen. I know all the words and me and Alan sing along, clapping our hands and spinning about. It's fun. Diana walks out of the room. I hope that she's not angry with me. I want her to visit again. I love their visits. Being with Alan and Diana is boss. I hate it here. Hate it.

~

'Cal? Cal?' Eve is touching my shoulder.

I open my eyes.

'Thought you'd nodded off. I can get a CD player,' she says.

'That'd be nice. Thanks.' There are good people about. Like Eve and Mr McKenzie.

She smiles, but her hazel eyes are troubled, her curls have lost their bounce. She knows I sense her sadness, that her mask has slipped, but she's not going to share. Not yet.

Marking my chart, she says I'm making progress.

'Not too long before these bandages can come off,' she says, briskly, back to her professional, nursey self. 'You should get outside while you can. No reason to stay in bed all the time.' Then she is gone. A smart clicking of shoes, like a soldier, and she has vanished.

I am alone again.

The sound of footsteps echoes outside my room and I am thrown back to another white room, in my past, the walls adorned with images. Of me. All me.

~

There are so many pictures. I don't know where to look first. I feel a smile cracking across my face, the sound of footsteps. Heels on a wooden floor. I spin round. It is Diana, smiling, turning her head, taking in the pictures.

'What do you think, Cal?'

'I dunno.'

167

'Do you like them?'

I shrug. I'm really not sure.

'Just imagine... lots and lots of people will be here later. Looking at you! Talking about you!'

'Wow!' It's hard to imagine, and it makes me feel funny inside. Good funny, I think.

'You can come and meet the people if you like? I'll buy you a present.' Diana is crouched, holding onto both my hands.

Again, I shrug. What would I say to grown-ups? They always ask questions and I never know what to say. But it's good to have everyone treating me nice, looking at me – but not in a bad way – talking to me. Like on birthdays, or Christmas when I'm opening all my presents.

'Only if you want to, Cal. No pressure.'

'OK.'

Diana kisses my hands and we hug each other.

'I love you,' she says.

'I love you too.'

'Three.'

'Four.'

'Five.'

~

I enjoyed the attention as a child. I did. It made me happy and it made Diana happy. When did all that change?

Diana

Harry's skin was an extraordinary shade of orange and in the dull light of an overcast Manchester morning he looked more out of place than ever. He stood before us: gatekeeper to the former warehouse. I looked down the canal, films of grease mercurial on the water in the dank spring air, a low, dirty sun. It reminded me of a Vallette painting. Alan flung open the van doors and we began to unload the cargo. I touched Scadanelli's card in my back pocket, now dog-eared and yellowed, but no less precious.

When I'd called the number on the card to invite him to the show I'd recognised the wheezy tones of the little man from my degree show immediately.

'Mr Scadanelli?' I said, unsure of the correct form of address.

'Scadanelli's private secretary speaking.'

'Oh.'

So you've not been dealing with the organ grinder.

I composed myself, determined not to allow my error to derail me from my purpose. I invited Scadanelli to my show.

The little man was polite, if not what I'd call friendly, and thanked me for the invitation. When I pressed for confirmation he'd replied tersely that Scadanelli never attended shows personally, unless it was a private view (and by this he meant a showing with Scadanelli and Scadanelli alone, without the usual coterie of friends, family and hangers-on) and that he, the little man, would have to consult his master's diary before making a firm arrangement. He was puzzled by the address. 'I've never heard of this gallery, Ms Brading,' he'd said, 'is it new?'

'In a manner of speaking,' I'd replied.

Harry touched me on the shoulder. 'Wakey wakey, darling. No rest for the wicked. We need to get this work unloaded.'

Van empty, I watched Alan jump into the cabin and turn on the engine, ready to return it to the hire company. Invitations had been sent out to the great and the good of the Northern art world – courtesy of Alan's inheritance – but I had no idea whether any of them would turn up. In truth, my hopes all hinged on one dealer. I kissed Scadanelli's card and whispered a private prayer. How I hoped the mysterious dealer's minion would attend. If he did, this was going to be one of the most important days of my life.

'Cheer up, darling. What's the worst that can happen?' Harry said, pulling me into the warehouse.

'I wish Linda was here,' I whispered, almost to myself.

'What, to admire your pieces? Or lug this stuff?' he

said, picking up one of the smaller boxes. 'The others'll be here soon. Fear not.'

It had been a tough year. Linda had gone travelling as she'd planned and, concerned about my welfare, a female living in a Hulme flat alone, Alan had moved in. Though I'd protested, I'd not done so convincingly. I welcomed the company, the protection he offered, and having a live-in 'partner' was good for my ongoing appeals to foster Cal.

I missed Cal so much it hurt. Visits to his current foster home were allowed, and arranged, but didn't happen nearly often enough. Not for either of us.

'Heard you were hoping to bring the boy later?' Harry said, as we entered the main space.

'His carers have agreed. He's so excited.'

'Really?' Harry pulled a face. 'Does he like everyone staring?'

You don't know Cal like I do. You don't know him at all.

'People will be sensitive,' I snapped.

'Steady.' He raised his hands in surrender. 'I'm sure they'll try. Now, let's get to work.'

As Jim had predicted, another barrier to fostering Cal was my address. Though we were legitimate – paying the rent monthly (surely the only tenants in Hulme to do so) – Alan and I needed to move out. But money was tight, for me. I'd slogged part-time in a bar to contribute to the household budget as well as beavering away on creating enough work for an exhibition. Alan paid the utilities bills, bought food, fags, and materials, but I could not, and would not, tap Alan for any more money.

171

Harry surveyed the space, as he had a dozen times before, and so did I. This was it; it was finally happening.

The gallery was not a gallery in the conventional sense. It was one of a long line of cathedral-like buildings off Whitworth Street; former warehouses, built during the city's manufacturing hey-day, now derelict and defunct. The future belonged to those bold enough to shape it. Collectives in Hulme trail-blazed, organising huge, illegal, pyrotechnic displays, community arts events or 'happenings', but I did not want to confine my first show to an outpost of the city, and I would never attract the big guns to Hulme. Walking home from the city centre late one evening, I'd noticed dim lights in one of the warehouses. I crept round the back, to the canal side. There were shadowy couples, snogging, embracing, pressed up against the walls. A middle-aged woman approached and asked if I needed company. She had an open, generous face. I asked if she knew why light was spilling from the warehouse and if she knew a way in. She took me by the hand to an unlocked door, and led me into the building, to the foot of some stairs, where she abandoned me once more. I picked my way through the debris of addicts' materials, used condoms, and pigeon droppings, climbing up and up, spellbound by the grandeur and scale of the place.

On the top floor the rooms were vast, with high ceilings and exposed pipes. Underneath the tall windows, each divided into small squares of glass as if light itself needed to be broken down and controlled, sat squat radiators, like those at my old school – wide enough to sit on and burn your bum in minutes. There was more pigeon waste, dust and rubbish, but I saw the potential. Painted white, or grey, it would make an incredible space to show my work. Subversive and sublime.

Alan had been enthusiastic immediately and it hadn't been difficult to gather a committed group of like-minded artists. The building manager was grateful to see it used, if only for a brief period. We even managed to garner funds from a government initiative to stimulate the local economy. It covered the cost of the reduced rent with money spare to clean up and paint the space. Pandering to his colossal ego, and promising him a hefty commission on any sales, I'd persuaded Harry, who ran the Cornerhouse centre, to curate the event. I wanted him for his talent – not inconsiderable – and his impressive contacts. In the end it was space for his boyfriend to exhibit that clinched the deal, and it was a relief to discover that the bloke's work was good. He and Alan were to display work in the smaller room next to the one where mine would be displayed.

It had taken months and months to negotiate the space, tart it up and finally promote the event. But here we were, and it felt good and terrifying.

Our small army of unpaid helpers carried most of the work up, Harry barking instructions. He reminded me of a Chihuahua: spoilt, bad-tempered, and faintly ridiculous, but I had a soft spot for him, as I did those silly dogs.

Back from dropping the van off, Alan charged in with bacon sandwiches for the workers and I put the kettle on. We needed refuelling before the real work began.

'Did you call Jennifer?' I asked. 'Everything still on for Cal coming this evening?'

He nodded. 'Far as I know. She said his foster family...'

'The Georges.'

'Would bring him later, after his tea. Said they'd get here around seven.'

'You went home too?'

He nodded, unable to speak with a mouth crammed with sandwich.

'Any post?' I didn't have to spell it out.

He shook his head and squeezed my hand.

I'd hoped for a card, wishing me luck, from Dad, maybe even Bunny. They'd both been invited, though I'd not heard a peep. I was very easy to forget, it seemed. Even Linda hadn't been in touch. It hurt. Not a single postcard letting us know where she was or what she was up to. When I'd mentioned it to Alan he'd said that I shouldn't take it personally, Linda was a 'no turning back' kind of girl and if we were meant to meet again in the future, then we would. I'd never have had him down as a fatalist, but there was a lot about Alan that surprised me.

Jim had threatened to drop by, though he'd not been sent an invitation. I'd half wondered if he might come onto me after Linda had gone but he didn't. This had left me with a hollow, worthless feeling; I'd wanted the opportunity to turn him down. He and Linda hadn't officially split up but given she'd not said when, or *if*, she would return, it was clear that it was all over. I'd heard he was shagging a second year History student; a former friend of Linda's.

With so much to do before opening, the hours whizzed by.

'Diana, darling. Finishing touches. What do you think?' Harry said, pointing at *Two-Faced*. *Two-Faced* was a series of images of me and Cal wearing plastic masks on the backs of our heads. It was one of the first pieces I'd created after leaving college, after Linda left and Cal was taken into care. My mask was a grotesque, Cal's was preternaturally beautiful – at least that was the effect I was aiming for. I'd moulded the masks from latex to give the impression of real skin, then Alan shot a series of photographs in black and white, and colour, and the finished results were better than I had expected. 'A little higher? Lower?' Harry asked.

I motioned upwards and he nodded approvingly. 'Are you sure there's enough wine? Looks pretty pathetic to me,' I said, gazing over at the table.

'Darling, those that count don't guzzle the booze. Control your friends and we'll be just fine.'

But I didn't have many friends. College friends had gone and there was no time to make new ones in between creating art, working at the bar and visiting Cal.

'Now go and put some lippie on and make yourself look pretty. You look like a boy, albeit a devilishly handsome one.' He winked before planting a reassuring kiss on his boyfriend's cheek. Harry's boyfriend had drifted over after setting up his own work in the room next door. He spoke with a gruff Rochdale accent that gave the illusion he was permanently pissed off. He had

175

talent. I liked him immensely and he and Harry were well suited.

'Off you go,' Harry said flicking his wrists, and, obediently, I grabbed my bag and headed for the door. Alan had already left on a last-minute mission.

~

Alan stepped into the space, clutching the exhibition catalogue, watery blue eyes glazed with excitement. 'Oh man, this is champion, absolutely champion.'

He leant in to kiss me on the cheek, which was kind of formal given that we lived together, but it suited the occasion. We moved awkwardly, as we often did − not knowing which cheek to kiss first, if we were going for a kiss on both cheeks, or a kiss on one followed by a great, big hug. We chopped and changed from one to the other so that neither of us could ever anticipate the correct approach and invariably got it wrong. I needed the reassurance of a bear hug so I leant forward but Alan had clearly decided on a continental kiss.

I realised my mistake too late. I moved towards his other side, but without the necessary conviction and consequently Alan landed a kiss on my astonished lips. I gasped, then laughed as Alan brought a hand to his mouth.

'Sorry,' he said. 'I've smudged your lipstick.'

'Do I look like a clown?'

'Hardly. But, hey, we have to agree on the kiss thing.'

I laughed, but the kiss hadn't felt bad, not bad at all.

You need a boyfriend. Jesus, how desperate are you?

He became very serious and, lifting the catalogue,

said, 'I am so touched that you give me this credit. My resume I knew about —'

'You wrote it.'

'But the dedication... oh, Diana.' He leant in and hugged me and we stood there, holding each other tight, until I heard a forced cough. It was Harry's boyfriend. 'Harry says you shouldn't stand at the entrance. Looks desperate or something.' He looked uncomfortable, and I didn't want to embarrass him.

'Tell him to cool his boots, I'm moving,' I said as I pulled Alan further into the space.

'Shame Cal can't be here to see it like this,' Alan said.

'Like what?'

'Empty. No people, just the work.'

'I'm just glad he'll be here. This is all down to him.'

Hands on his hips, Alan spun on his heels, admiring. 'It's down to you. I'd better check next door.'

'You mean you came in here first?' I said, surprised. I'd have raced in to give my own show a final once over before anyone else's and yet Alan had to come to me first.

'Saw it before I popped back. But I do need to...' he pointed.

'Course you do. Looks great, Al, really great. Hard to believe you've not even completed your first year.'

I wasn't exaggerating. Alan's photographs were incredible and I wondered what he could be learning on his degree course, if anything.

People drifted in. Some I recognised as inhabitants of the canal side, here to check out this new colonisation of their stomping ground, to see the transformation for themselves.

I'd prepared for no visitors, absolute failure, but instead they kept on coming.

Alan and I watched, trying to work out who everyone was, and their relative importance. Harry hovered like a humming-bird, enthusiastic and knowledgeable. He waved me over when he deemed it worthwhile to introduce 'the Artist'. I kept one eye on the existing visitors, the other constantly on the lookout for Scadanelli's private secretary, assuming the little man made the trip up north himself.

When a gap in the proceedings allowed, I drifted over to a window and cast my eyes towards the sky. I wasn't sure what I was looking for; it was still a little early to expect Cal. When I turned around I found myself gazing down at a bald patch. The skin was pink and raw, as if a cheese grater had been run over it, flakes of dry skin curled from tiny sores, like ant bites. I was fascinated and repulsed, and I recognised it immediately: Scadanelli's secretary. Nerves, excitement, joy washed over me, and my face must have said as much.

'Your evening is going well, Ms Brading.'

'Thank you.' I composed myself. 'I'm delighted you made it. Can I show you round?'

Harry waltzed over, all flushed cheeks and dilated pupils. He'd either got a whiff of a sale or had been stuffing charlie up his nose. 'Diana, darling, there's someone you simply must meet—'

He obviously didn't recognise Scadanelli's man from my description. I gave him my best 'this'd better be good' scowl and said, 'Harry, let me introduce you to

Scadanelli's private secretary, Mr...' I realised I did not know the little man's name.

'Jones.'

Harry did one of his fabulously grovelling greetings, Dickensian in style, bending so low one could be mistaken for thinking he'd dropped something. 'I'm an enormous fan of Scadanelli.' He tittered. 'Everyone is. Such a progressive.'

'Will you excuse me a moment?' Jones said, and disappeared towards the unisex bathroom. I prayed he wouldn't find it in bad taste. We'd slapped white paint on the bare brickwork and decorated the cubicles with a montage of glamour models and stills from porno movies – the 73FF bosoms of Chesty Morgan the centrepiece of every other cubicle door. The alternate doors were focused on the not inconsiderable charms of male porn star King Dong.

'Diana, my love, this is beyond exciting! Scadanelli's man. Indeed!'

'He's been interested in me for some time.'

'Good God, darling, wish I'd known, I'd have had more commission off you,' he said, taking a gulp of champagne.

'You did know. I told you.'

He draped an arm across my shoulders. 'Let me deal with this, darling. I know how to work these things.'

But Harry would be a barrier; I'd noticed the little man's distaste at Harry's vulgar, ostentatious personal style. I wondered if the trip to the bathroom was an excuse. Was Jones slipping out of a side door as we spoke? Panic set in, my heart palpitated. I would not let anything, or anyone, ruin this opportunity.

Amongst the crowd, I spotted Alan and flagged him over, still pretending to listen to Harry's excited ramblings. Harry was planning what he would do with the commission from, at this moment, an entirely speculative sale.

Diverted by an extremely handsome punter, Harry turned away. I whispered in Alan's ear. 'Can you get rid of Harry? I need to be alone when Jones returns. If he returns.'

'That was *him?*' Alan exclaimed. 'Who'd have thought? They say don't judge a book ...'

'Please, Al. Now.'

'Champion. I'm on it.' And sure enough, smooth as, Alan linked arms with Harry and steered him away. I wanted to kiss him.

Within seconds Jones reappeared. He wasted no time on niceties. 'I have seen enough. I have clear instructions.'

Blood cursed through my veins, growing hotter and hotter, as if it were coming to the boil. I fried. I needed this man to like my work, to take it on, at Scadanelli's gallery, sell it to their buyers. I needed to show that I could earn, seriously earn, if I was to stand any chance of caring for Cal, to continue working as an artist. I craved the validation.

Smile. Be positive.

'Which pieces are you interested in?' I said, as nonchalantly as I could muster.

From the corner of my eye I saw Alan waving his arms; he looked desperate. I had no idea how long he'd been flaying about. His eyes flitted from left to right like a cornered animal. I followed his gaze. From opposite directions of the room Harry and Bunny were converging on me and Jones. I realised, with dismay, that it was me who was trapped, not Alan.

I had not seen Bunny in well over a year. We hadn't spoken in months after our disastrous meeting at the Midland Hotel, but I finally relented, guilt getting the better of me, and called her. Our subsequent conversations had been strained at best. The last time we spoke I had been unable to resist crowing about the sale of a minor work – the charcoal of the crescents shown at my degree show. I'd virtually given it away, I was so thrilled that someone wanted to part with money, real money, for anything I'd created. That'll show her, I'd thought, but Bunny had sniggered and said that fools and their cash were soon parted and that it was more than likely a one-off. I'd sent an invitation to the show, with a note explaining that I didn't expect her to make it, but if she fancied mixing with a different set of fools to her usual then this was the place. Never in a million years had I expected her to turn up.

Harry and Bunny almost collided as they rushed towards me arms outstretched. They stopped abruptly when they realised they were both heading for the same object – me – like bargain hunters at a jumble sale both clutching the same garment.

'Mr Jones, let me formally introduce Harry McNulty, our curator. Harry, Mr Jones, my mother – Bunny... Which surname are you using now? Husband number one or two?'

Bunny slapped my back in that 'what a joker' kind of way, but really, really hard. She'd wanted to hurt me and her heavy rings ensured that she had. 'Sweetheart, you are *so* cute!' She leant in for a kiss and though I arched backwards there was nowhere to go; she had me.

After a kiss that felt more like a sting, she turned on Harry. 'De-lighted to make your acquaintance, Mr McNulty, and you too, Mr Jones.' Judging by the dismissive way she wafted her jewelled fingers at Jones she evidently considered him of no importance. Like a vulture considering her prey she sized up Harry, and I realised with some amusement that she found him attractive. He was obviously gay but Bunny always had been a lousy judge of character. If you ignored Harry's sexual orientation they almost suited each other; they were both brash and self-centred with skin an outlandish shade of orange.

Harry puckered his lips and plonked a kiss on the back of Bunny's hand. 'The pleasure's all mine, and I'm sure people say this all the time, Bunny, but you two could be sisters.'

Bunny guffawed. 'I don't believe you for one instance, you old charmer, but say it again anyway.'

Harry laughed obligingly. 'Now, Bunny, darling, I hate to be rude but if you could excuse us for one teeny, tiny moment I need to talk business with your beautiful daughter and Mr Jones.'

Jones had been throwing withering looks at them both, but they were too wrapped up in their little charade to notice.

'Harry, Bunny doesn't appear to have a drink, and I

just know that she'll love Stephen's work. You might even be able to persuade her to buy,' I said, winking at Harry. Bunny's idea of art was the back view of a naked man walking towards an oversized pair of swan wings. She would hate Steve's work (it was only Harry who called him Stephen), but she would never acknowledge her unrefined taste in public or that her purse would never open for something as frivolous as art. With that, I virtually shoved them towards the refreshments and the next room.

I turned to Jones, who was visibly relieved, and flashed a killer smile.

Returning my smile, Jones said, 'Scadanelli does not wish to purchase any work.'

I was crushed. Despair choked me. I tried to force my heart back down into my chest and fought the liquid feeling in my gut.

Who did you think you could fool? You can't do this. Bunny's been right all along. You're nothing but a pretty face.

'At least, not directly,' Jones continued. 'Scadanelli wishes to offer you the use of a studio, and materials, an assistant, living expenses. Whatever you require to carry out your work. As your benefactor.'

I was puzzled. What would Scadanelli receive from such an arrangement?

Jones continued. 'In return, he will have the right to exhibit whatever you produce during your time as the recipient of his generosity exclusively in his gallery, to his buyers. In the first instance we are suggesting a twenty-four month contract.'

I could not breathe; it sounded too good to be true,

like a dream. My very own angel. Jones's gaze was fixed on me, those impenetrable eyes, his expression registering only mild amusement and impatience, like rich men's butlers in old films. 'Does this meet with your approval?' he said at last.

'Oh yes. Yes. Yes. Yes. I'm speechless,' I gasped.

'Hardly, Ms Brading. If I have your agreement a contract will be drawn up and forwarded to you in due course. I will make all the necessary arrangements.' He held out his hand and I realised that he expected me to shake on it and it was only as he strutted towards the exit in his Cuban-heeled boots that a maelstrom of questions surged. I ran after him, weaving through the crowd.

'Mr Jones! How will you contact me?' He held one of my cards aloft and I hoped he'd not noticed the mimicry of Scadanelli's in the design. But of course he had. 'Where is the studio? When do I start? Do I have to produce a minimum number of pieces?' He shook his head, like a parent with an exasperating child. 'Scadanelli's primary residences are in New York and London. I imagine he will want you in our capital. The finer details can be thrashed out. Now is not the time. Good day, Ms Brading.' And with a jaunty wave of his hand he was gone.

I surveyed the exhibition. It didn't matter anymore. If I sold work, if I did not. If the critics came, if they did not. I wanted to laugh out loud.

I floated about the space, buzzing.

Harry was disappointed. He couldn't take commission on such an arrangement, but he cheered up when I pointed out he could use the deal to his benefit – building his reputation as a talent-spotter and man with his finger on the artistic pulse.

'And we might sell yet,' I said.

I saw Bunny and waved her over, dying to tell her my news. Alan should have been the first to know, that's what I'd have preferred, but he was busy with his own guests. She would have to do and I looked forward to telling her.

She tried, and failed, to hide her astonishment. It transpired that Harry had filled her in on Scadanelli's importance as well as filling her wine glass several times.

'I'm so proud of you.' She patted Harry's shoulder. 'I always knew she had it in her.' I raised my eyebrows. Compliments came easy when other people applauded. She'd revelled in my successes – reflected glory – but she'd punished me for the failures, and when things were really tough she was nowhere to be seen. But I'd made her happy again momentarily and it felt good.

'You'll never make serious money of course, Diana. You should use your true talent while you can. Won't last forever, baby.' Addressing Harry again, she said, 'You know, models can earn a thousand pounds a day.'

'What's an agent's cut?' he said, razor-sharp as ever.

'Never enough,' said Bunny, winking at him.

'It's not something that will concern you,' I said through gritted teeth. 'Would you like an orange juice?'

'Sweetheart, I can't stand the stuff, you know that.' She polished off her wine and looked as if she were about to throw the glass over her shoulder. Harry retrieved it from her clutches. She draped an arm over his shoulders

– possibly as a gesture of bonhomie, or to steady herself – and whispered, loudly, in his ear. 'She needs me. Can't admit it, but she's nothing without me.'

I laughed. Perhaps I'd had a glass too many too.

'Gave her the best years of my life. To make something of her, give her opportunities I never had,' she slurred.

'Opportunities I never asked for or wanted,' I said.

'And this is how she repays me! What a waste. Ungrateful little bitch.'

Harry stood between us, rooted to the spot, his head ping-ponging from side to side like a spectator at a tennis match. He didn't know how to extricate himself.

'I hated the modelling, the beauty competitions. You loved it, not me.'

'I was Miss Butlin's 1962! I could have been a model, an actress. I never got the chance. Pregnant with you, at eighteen. You took the best years of my life…' Some people were staring; others tried to focus on the art.

'You had nothing else. That was not my fault. You punished me. If you'd been a half-decent mother you'd—'

The crack echoed round like the room like lightning. I felt the windows rattling, though that could have been my brain bouncing off my skull. My cheek burned, and I was backstage at a beauty competition again, ten years old, and locked in the bathroom with my raging mother. I remembered the scent of artificial apricots lingering over the stench of a recent bowel movement, the thick air of the unventilated room, the smoky brown mirror over the basin. I'd refused to twirl and smile and pose on stage; I'd been sullen, rude, and made no effort. I'd been

186

defiant, and I'd not made the final round. Bunny was livid, but I remained rebellious. I have no idea why; no idea what triggered such insubordination. I was usually such a compliant child. She dragged me into the bathroom, and slapped me repeatedly. Left cheek, right cheek, left cheek, right cheek, until I promised never, ever, to do that again. To be a good girl.

The gasps of onlookers ricocheted off the walls, tears stung my raw cheek. I stared at Bunny, her eyes glassy from the alcohol. I wanted to slap her back, but could not. 'You promised never again. Get out. Now,' I hissed.

The onlookers' shock must have penetrated the walls because Alan pushed his way through. Harry steered Bunny towards the exit as Alan wrapped his arms around me. I cried on his shoulder and when I looked up he dabbed at my eyes and cheeks with a tissue. He was gentle and protective.

'You were right. What a complete cow.'

Senses still ringing I was overcome with another, altogether different, sensation. Alan patted away at my tears. The world around me froze, like a video with the pause button on. There was nothing other than him, his watery blue eyes fixed on my face, concentrating on his task. Had I not noticed how strong the line of his nose was before, his delicate ear lobes, the small mole at the hairline on the left of his brow? I took hold of his wrist and he stopped, confusion and uncertainty obvious in the ridges forming across his forehead. I tugged on his wrist and the furrows on his brow faded. There was nothing and no one in that room apart from Alan and me.

Nothing else mattered. I pulled again, bringing him towards me. Our lips met, eyes wide open, only closing as we opened up for each other.

We kissed.

For how long I have no idea. It might have been seconds, or minutes; it could have been hours. Time disappeared.

Cal

When Eve comes in I'm sitting on a chair staring out of the window. From here I can see a flat-roofed, many-windowed building in the distance. There's a large expanse of grass in front. Must be a school. It's good to see her. She's been away and I've missed her smile, her conversation. My mind is jumping about all over the place.

Eve checks the charts and drip. It's sunny and warm outside, I think. I'd like to feel the sun on my face. I've forgotten how that feels.

'Good to see you out of bed,' she says.

'Yeah.'

She checks my dressings, busies herself with the sheets. She's loitering.

'Did you like the CDs?'

I shrug and try to smile. The CDs are stacked up on the bedside table: Dido, Norah Jones, Sarah McLachlan. God help me.

'Not your cup of tea?' she says.

I don't want to hurt her feelings. 'Not really. But thanks all the same.'

'I could ask my brother. He's about the same age as you.'

'You can't be much older. Making yourself sound ancient.'

'I'm three years older than him.'

'So not much older than me then.'

'No.' She moves the conversation back to music. 'What are you in to?'

'All sorts. Bands mostly, dance music. Trancy stuff. Aphex Twin. Nirvana.'

'Oh he'll definitely have some of that miserable, angry stuff!' She smiles, and I try to smile back. It hurts. 'Let me take you out.' She checks the watch hanging on her chest. 'I've got time.'

Outside the breeze is cool on my bare arms. I should have worn a long-sleeved top. I can hear the faint sound of children screaming. The school. Eve places a chair on the terrace and gestures for me to sit. 'I'll wander round for a bit.'

'Good idea.'

I'm drawn to the echo of the children.

~

I'm ten years old and it's my first day at proper, normal school. My tummy aches but it's a good ache. I think. The gates are grey and thick with a giant padlock. Diana presses a button and a crackly voice splits the air. One of the gates clicks open and we go in. As we cross the playground a boy and his mum – I suppose it's his mum – pass us. The boy turns back and stares. I hear him say: 'Look at THAT.' He jolts, like a puppet or rag doll, as his mum yanks him towards her. She glances over her

190

shoulder but blushes and turns back when I catch her eye. I'd like to stick my tongue out but know that I mustn't. That isn't nice and I should always be nice.

I think about Mrs Reed, the lady who has taught me at home, and how terrified I am of her. The whites of her eyes shine like billiard balls and when she expects an answer they grow wider and wider, till it looks like they might pop out of their sockets and hit me in the face. Sometimes I think I might give her the wrong answer just to see if they do pop out, but I always bottle out. And here, right now, at these big grey gates I am not afraid of her at all. I wish I was sitting in our front room, at the table, with Mrs Reed tapping the ruler against the wood making me chant my times tables. I want things to go back to the way they were. I want nothing to change. I am terrified.

The building is scruffy, with writing on the walls, nice writing, graffiti art Diana says, and the window frames are painted yellow and pink. It isn't a real normal school; it's private and the kids are all sons and daughters of successful musicians, actors, artists and hippies, according to Diana. I step through the swing doors, Diana at my side, the flooring honeyed and slick. A dozen or so kids stomp from a classroom. None of them look like those on the telly. They smell sweet and sticky; a fug of body odour, farts, surrounds them. They stop and stare. I'm aware that I am different, but it doesn't bother me, really it doesn't. I step forward and the children part.

An adult steps out into the corridor: a teacher. She is tall and she wears a long skirt and rings on every finger. She smiles widely and says that I must be Cal and tells the children to say hello. Some of them do as she asks. A fat

boy steps forward with an outstretched hand and I can't
bring myself to shake it. My palms are all sweaty. I feel the
little crowd recoiling.

At lunchtime I eat alone, away from the other
children. I'm at a table for two, side on to the rest of the
canteen. When I peel back the plastic lid of my lunchbox I
find a neatly cut brown bread sandwich filled with cheese
and salad and mayonnaise, a banana, a packet of cheese
and onion crisps (my favourite) and a carton of apple juice.
Alan whistled along to the radio as he made it this
morning.

I am about to bite into my banana, the bitter smell of
the peel hovering before my nose, when in my peripheral
vision I see a group of girls nudging each other. Peripheral
is a new word; I learnt it this week. I take a bite, enjoying
the soft squishiness in my mouth when a girl with long
blonde hair walks over and asks what happened to my face.
I wave my hand in front of my mouth, to indicate (another
new word) that I'm not quite done yet. She turns back to
her friends and giggles. Before I can finish chewing she is
dragged away by a short, heavy-legged girl with a deep
voice.

'Leave him alone, you bitch.'

'Aw, shhhrup, China. You ugly cow.' I want to tell the
blonde girl that I don't know what happened to my face.
And the girl with the lovely voice that she's not ugly. Not at
all. But I still have a mouthful of banana. I leave my crisps
and sandwich.

For the next two days I eat alone; other children will
not sit with me, though I make sure my manners are
perfect. Eating is so everyday, so normal, I do not

understand, and this hurts. I wonder if the act of eating, a basic human need like sleeping and breathing, is too human for a freak. It reminds them that I am human and not so very far removed from them after all. When I tell Diana this she says that I'm too clever for my own good, that I'm special, they're jealous, and the girl China sounds nice and why don't I find her at lunchtimes?

At school I begin to understand the true power of my difference.

People are fascinated and repelled.

~

I'm all grown up now, at a secondary school, and I travel alone on public transport. People stare, some more openly than others. I stare back, forcing them to turn away before I do. I always win.

My schoolmates have grown accustomed to my face and no longer stare. I am used to being studied; I am the subject of Diana's work, her model. She sketches me and paints me and photographs me. I inspire her. Why would others not wish to look at me?

Diana

Alan and I weren't embarrassed when, finally, we stopped kissing. No one appeared to have noticed anyway. Too busy admiring the art. Alan and I made perfect sense. He wasn't the kind of man I'd imagined myself with. He was crazily romantic, with horrific taste in clothes and music. He was seriously quirky-looking. Men like Jim blinded me with their beauty and style; I'd wanted Jim when all the time I'd needed Alan.

Where do we go from here? Are we now boyfriend and girlfriend?

As far as the authorities, Social Services and the like, were concerned, we were already an item. We lived together; we often visited Cal together. Two 'parents' were considered better than one, though I'd have argued it depended on the parents. Michael and Pru, anyone?

Cal. Where's Cal?

I grabbed Alan's wrist to check the time. The Georges were late.

'There's still time. Don't panic.' Alan stroked my palm and I managed a smile. There was over an hour before the end of the evening.

The urge to run away and hide after the scene with Bunny was strong but I resisted. Instead, I disguised the red slap mark on my cheek with pan-stick and, bolstered by Alan's support, the deal with Scadanelli and the excitement at showing Cal our work, I determined to spend the time before he arrived usefully: promoting Alan's pictures.

It wasn't hard; they were amazing. Raw, visceral and unsettling they cut to the heart of city life with deceptive simplicity. There were photographs of Jim's brother and his mates standing on the roofs of burnt out cars, arms folded, chins high and proud, like hunters resting their feet on the haunches of a stag. Images of overflowing rubbish bins on the crescents, their strange beauty mesmerising, angry mobs challenging rows of policemen with riot shields, faces distorted with rage and hatred.

While I'd been fending off Bunny and dealing with Mr Jones, the editor of a local newspaper had taken a brief look around the exhibition and offered Alan a job on the spot. His photographer had resigned recently, and he'd been using freelancers.

'It'd be good to have a steady job. Social Services look very favourably on that kind of thing,' Alan said, when I pulled a face.

'None of the mega-famous photographers went to college,' I said, 'but don't sell yourself short. A local paper?'

'I've got my eyes on a bigger prize, long-term. The experience will be good.'

I shook my head. I'd not told him about Scadanelli's offer. I opened my mouth to speak but Harry interrupted.

'Well, well. Who'd have put you two together? Not me, darlings. But you fit, weirdly enough. A talent-match at least.'

Harry's right. We're a good fit.

Alan liked the way I looked, but he liked me for who I was too, and that felt brilliant. I took hold of his hand. 'I have something to tell you,' I began, excitement surging as I tried to form the words, only to be stopped once again by Harry.

'Alan, my love, a gentleman – that one over there – would like to buy three of your pictures,' Harry said, pointing. He offered more champagne.

'Which ones?' Alan gasped, breathless.

'Strike series. He was born in Wapping, father was a printer. He lives in London, wants something to remind him of his heritage, he says. A broker, darling, loadsa money!'

I whispered in Alan's ear, 'There's more money in the south, you'd sell there.'

'Oh man, London gives me the heebies. It's so big. You can get lost there,' Alan said.

'Not always a bad thing.'

For the third time I tried to tell him about Scadanelli, but this time, I stopped myself.

Cal.

My balloon burst. My guts twisted. If we moved to London, what would happen to Cal? Could we keep trying for adoption? Would we even stand a chance against families like the Georges, with their steady income, big house and children of a similar age? But if I stayed, would the Scadanelli deal be off? How could I choose between art and Cal? They were one and the same thing, arteries feeding one heart, one body.

'You all right? You've gone ever so pale,' Alan said. He touched my forehead with the back of his hand.

'Something amazing and wonderful and awful has happened,' I said, stopping at the sight of Jim in my peripheral vision. I didn't feel pleased, or flattered that he had graced me with his presence, only irritated that he was here, sullying my event. He'd not been sent an invitation; he'd been crossed off my guest list long ago. His roots were showing; his hair seemed orange-yellow in the bright gallery lights, his skin was sallow and the lines from his nose to his mouth were marked, giving him the appearance of a fairground puppet, those menacing clowns in glass cases that revealed your fortune if you paid ten pence. He looked sleazy and rough.

How did you ever find him attractive?

He was studying the sculptures of a crouching figure, Cal, exchanging words with the couple to his left. The woman glanced up and pointed at the photographs of Cal. Jim said something and her face lit up. An uneasy sensation built. I couldn't hear what was being said, and I couldn't lip read, but something didn't feel right. I made my excuses and wandered over, aiming for casual in my tone and gait.

By the time I'd reached the sculptures Jim had moved on. The couple remained, studying the catalogue. Once I'd stood next to them I had no idea what to say. But the catalogue was open on the page with the artists' resumes. My photograph gave me the opening I needed.

197

I introduced myself. We chatted a while but nothing relevant was divulged and I could find no way of asking what Jim had been saying without appearing like a paranoid weirdo.

Jim stood with a group huddled round the drinks. I sidled up to him. A wiry man in grey slacks, loafers and white socks said, 'Do you know where the boy's from? Bloody extraordinary, isn't he?' Clearly he didn't recognise me. 'Like something out of *The Elephant Man*, eh? You seen the film?'

The crowd rumbled: where did the artist find the boy, was there nothing that could be done to help him, what did the way he look and the way we respond to deformities say about the modern world and its obsession with perfection? Were my self-portraits post-modern or post-feminist? It seemed everything was post-something or other, the usual pseudo-intellectual, pretentious crap. It meant nothing to me.

I steered Jim downstairs on the pretext of needing a smoke. 'Alan thinks I've given up,' I said. I didn't want to be alone with Jim but I needed to find out what he was up to.

'I'm so glad you could make it,' I said as we walked down the staircase.

'Strange that. I never got an invite.'

'Bizarre. It must have got lost in the post.'

'Yeah. Must of.'

Outside he offered me a Marlboro and flicked the top off his Zippo. The petrol fumes masked the smell of the canal for a brief spell. I inhaled deeply and relished the rush; my head spun. We stood in silence staring at the black water.

'So how's it going?' he said.

'Good, good,' I mumbled. 'People seem to like it.'

'Not your work. With Cal. Heard you want to adopt.'

Who's he heard this from?

He continued, 'It'll get harder with him. Easy when they're little.'

'How would you know?'

'Got a brother, haven't I? Little bastard.'

I'd not seen Jim's brother round the estate in months and wondered what he was up to. 'I'm not sure what you mean,' I said after a pause.

'Cal'll be a teenager before you know it. Wanting to go out, try all sorts of stuff, girls...' He lit another cigarette with the butt of the one he'd been smoking.

'I'll protect him. And no one's said yes yet.'

We stood in silence again.

'Where would you be without him?' he said at last, lips pinched.

'Who?' My mind had drifted inadvertently to Alan; how strange and tender and wonderful his kiss had been.

'Cal, you stupid cow. Who else?' He meant to be light-hearted but his words sounded harsh and cruel.

'I'm not following you,' I said, my mind flitting from the kiss with Alan to where Cal could have got to. I was worried; it was getting late.

'You'd be nothing without him. You'd have no work. All this stuff,' he waved a dismissive arm above his head, towards the gallery space.

'There are pieces that aren't him.'

199

'All inspired by him. He should get the credit, not you.'

'It doesn't work like that.'

We talked on, in this manner, until his cigarette burnt down. I was getting nowhere and beginning to feel cold, despite the numbing effects of alcohol. Losing patience, I asked him directly what he'd said to the couple.

'Those posh gits?' He pulled a face. 'I knew you and the boy. That I introduced you two,' he said.

'You want the best for Cal, don't you? You care?'

'Why d'you ask?'

I told him about Jones's offer, that I was moving to London, that I'd do anything to ensure Cal's happiness, that I'd already applied to adopt him, that the social workers said my chances were fair, and they'd just got better. I'd have money, financial stability. My mind raced and it all spilt out, there, on the canal bank, like factory effluent.

Jim remained quiet as I spoke, his dark eyes narrowing a fraction. When at last I fell silent, he lit another cigarette. He did not offer me one. 'You make a lot of money tonight?' he said, blowing smoke in my face. I resisted the urge to cough.

'It's none of your business.'

'You need Cal more than he needs you.' His shoulders squared in the dim light.

'What do you mean?' Panic rose; I could not bear to think of life, and work, without Cal.

Jim threw the unfinished cigarette on the ground, and shoved his hands in his pockets, thumbs resting on the outside, illuminated in the murky light. 'You don't get it, do you?' He stepped forward, a sly smile stealing across his face. Nauseous, I did get it; I'd worked it out long ago but I'd blocked it out.

Pru had been lovely before heroin ravaged her. Jim was a sucker for a pretty face. There was a frisson between them. They'd had an affair; she fell pregnant. Too stoned to have an abortion, she'd kept the child and passed him off as Michael's. Cal looked like no other; no one would suspect.

We were alone on the canal bank. I'd told no one where I was going. The orange glow of the still smouldering fag was my only witness. It was dark. The canal was deep and dirty. He might be carrying a knife, a gun, for all I knew. He was involved in the gangs running the drugs rings in the city. I knew nothing of what this man was capable of. In the distance I heard a faint scream, or was it drunken giggling? I focused on the sound of my own shallow breathing and the rapid thumping of my heart. I stepped back. The cigarette had fizzled out.

He took his hands from his pockets. Looking down on me, mouth curled, chin jutting forward, he said, 'I'm Cal's father.'

'So?' I said, barely a whisper.

'I could make things difficult for you.' He took a step closer. On the 'you' he poked his index finger at my chest, hitting me in the fleshy area below the clavicle. It hurt, though I disguised my pain.

'How? It wouldn't be easy.'

'I'll get a solicitor. The best.'

'Why now? You've never loved him enough to own him, or admit he's yours. You've never fought for him before. You stood by and let them treat him like a dog,' I said, 'What is it you want? Money?'

We stared at each other.

'The law will favour me, whatever you might think,' he said.

'I'm not sure it does. We've already put in an application. We stand a good chance. We do.'

'Trying to convince yourself?'

'It just got better, remember? And I don't imagine the law will look too kindly on a "father" who's denied his son's existence for eight years, who makes a living selling drugs and God knows what else. How would you stack up against me, Jim? I've a wealthy father—'

'Who pretends you don't exist—'

'A career, a benefactor, a history of caring for Cal.'

Jim lifted his arm and I braced myself for my second slap of the evening, perhaps even a punch. He took another cigarette from his breast pocket.

Just as I began to relax, he shoved me, hard, with both hands. I cracked against the wall, like a whip, and bounced back off. Winded, heart sprinting, anaesthetising the pain, I watched him walk away. He stopped and turned.

'You wanna take the risk?' he said.

I felt myself shrivelling before his gaze. 'You know I'd do anything for Cal.' I stressed the 'anything'.

He laughed. 'I've already had you.'

'What do you want? Money?'

He raised one eyebrow. 'I'll let you know how

much...' Then he followed the line of the canal until the descending mist swallowed him up.

I slumped against the wall and slid onto my haunches. I was trembling and aching, but I had a victory, of sorts. But the feeling that this wasn't the last I'd seen of Jim, no matter how much money I gave him, hung in the air like a November fog: penetrating, chilling. Moisture seeped through the brickwork into the fine silk of my evening jacket and onto the tingling skin of my back, spreading slowly, like a stain.

Shivering, I pushed myself off the wall and clambered to my feet. Where was Cal? Upstairs, I filched some change off Harry and went back outside to make a phone call. There was a telephone box across the road. It was littered with prostitutes' calling cards and stank of piss and who knew what else. I prayed the damn thing worked and that vandals hadn't rammed a foreign coin into the slot, blocking it. Shaking with cold, worry and fear and I dialled the Georges' number. It rang and rang and rang.

Back in the gallery, I made polite conversation with the local press and an unknown visitor for roughly the time it might take to travel from leafy, suburban Didsbury where the George family lived to Whitworth Street West. There were only minutes left before the exhibition closed.

Where are they?

Ignoring Harry's protests, I hoofed it over the road again, dismayed to find a man in the phone box embroiled in what was clearly an argument with a stack

203

of coins sitting on the metal shelf next to the telephone directory.

I waited. And waited.

I banged on the door, mouthing a request that he wrapped up as soon as possible.

I dialled the number and it rang and rang and rang. I don't know how long I let it ring before I hung up. It didn't matter. They weren't at home and they weren't here.

Where are you, Cal? What's happened?

I threw up in the gutter and staggered back to the exhibition.

Cal

I'm welded to this bed. It's like a slightly unwelcome appendage, something I've grown used to despite myself, something I can't shake off, unsure if I even want to, because no bed would mean it's time to leave and I sure as hell am not ready for that. It's not that the bed's uncomfortable. Quite the contrary. It's wide and long, spacious, encased in Egyptian cotton sheets. Not that I knew their type till Eve told me, when I commented on how soft they were compared to the starchy harshness of those in other hospitals.

'Are you complaining?' she said.

'No,' I replied. 'Not about these or the NHS's.'

The room is all right, posh, as you'd expect. I have it all to myself, no sharing here, with fresh flowers in a vase in the window, which has a view of the gardens. Classy. The cut flowers are a pathetic extravagance, what with the view and all. The garden's full of flowers and bushes and trees. Never see any people in that bit though. The main lawn is out front and visitors are roped off from wandering round here. There's probably a sign: Keep Off the Grass. It's all show.

My legs tingle, itching, aching to move. I feel so heavy, as if I've sunk into the mattress, an invisible weight bearing down on me. I have to get up, move about properly and not just from bed to en-suite bathroom. I will go for a walk, up and down the corridor. I'd like to go outside but I don't know if I'll be stopped and I've only my gown, no clothes, nothing. If my bandaged face doesn't scare people – which it really shouldn't in here – the sight of my hairy arse hanging out of the gown will. No difference to state hospital attire there.

From the safety of my room, I peer up and down the corridor. It's empty. I move my head too sharply and I see stars and clutch the doorframe hoping to Christ I don't pass out. My head is heavy, with dressings, stitches, bruising, I suppose, and it feels huge, like heads in children's drawings, like I might topple over with the sheer weight of it.

With an outstretched arm touching the wall, I creep down the corridor. Noise is muffled by the bandages covering my ears and face, as is smell. Because some senses are impaired, others are heightened. The tiles are cool against the soles of my feet; I am aware of the air brushing my calves, leg hairs standing on end, though it's not cold. Air circulates around my buttocks, genitals, reminding me I am naked beneath this gown and vulnerable. More vulnerable.

A child emerges from a room further down the corridor and skips towards me. I am too far from my room to get back before he reaches me. I think it is a boy; it's hard to tell, he has his head down, studying the floor, arms swinging like mad. Will I frighten him?

He stops before me. It is a boy. He is about nine, I'd say, with shoulder-length dark hair, like mine used to be.

'What happened to you?' he says. He looks at me directly, confident, not at all alarmed.

I don't know how to answer.

'Mama's had her face done. She looks an absolute fright, but she will be prettier afterwards, like she was when she was a girl, she says. Is that the same for you?' he continues, staring at me intently.

What can I say that he will understand? He does not give me the opportunity.

'I bet you're horribly ugly under all that.' He skips past, unconcerned and I remember how cruel children can be.

~

Mrs 'call me Sally' George tells Aaron and Naomi to be nice. She pushes me into the place they call the playroom. As on my first day, the floor is covered in toys. There are cars and dolls and jigsaws and Lego bursting from every corner. And figures – Star Wars figures! I can see Luke Skywalker and Vader and R2-D2. They weren't here yesterday! Naomi has dolls in a circle and a teapot and cups. There are sweets on plates in front of the dolls. Stupid. Dolls can't eat. Aaron has a wooden hammer which he is banging down on some cars over and over and over. Stupid. The cars will break and then he'll be sorry.

'Now, I'll make something to eat and then we'll get ready,' Mrs George says. 'Don't scoff those sweets, otherwise you won't eat your tea.' She points at me, which is funny 'cos they're not my sweets. 'Isn't it exciting? We've never been to an art exhibition before, have we? Aaron, Naomi?'

The children grunt and Mrs George closes the door behind her. I don't know what to do now they're in here as well. These are not my toys. Aaron carries on bashing and Naomi picks up a sweet and puts it in her mouth. 'Yummy,' she says, looking at me, before turning away. She doesn't like to look at me; she's told me this already, lots of times.

I turn around and crouch down.

'It's rude to turn your back on people,' she says and Aaron sniggers.

I shuffle round but keep my head down. They carry on playing for a bit and I pick up some bricks and stick them together. Aaron snatches the block from me and throws it across the room. 'Not yours,' he says.

'Sorry,' I say and I crawl to the seat by the window and stare outside. It's a nice road, like those on the telly, with lots of shiny cars parked in driveways.

Naomi is eating another sweet. She chews loudly. That's rude. From the corner of my eye I see Aaron taking one. My tummy rumbles, really loudly.

'Ugh. Sounds like a drain. A stinky, smelly, ugly old drain,' says Naomi.

My tummy hurts even more and I lift my eyes to the ceiling to stop myself crying. Diana showed me how to do this and she said that she did it all the time when she was little so people didn't see she was upset when she didn't want them to know. Thinking of Diana makes me want to cry even more.

'I don't want to go to any stupid f-art show,' Aaron says. He makes a fart noise with his mouth and his spit lights up in the air.

'Nor do I,' says Naomi. 'It's boring. Boring, boring, boring.' She eats another sweet, and another and another.

Mrs George's head pops round the door and she says that tea is ready. 'I've got a smashing outfit for you to wear, Cal. For your special night,' she says as she takes my hand and leads me down the stairs. Mrs George is kind.

On the third step Mrs George stops and shouts for Naomi and Aaron to hurry up. There is a terrible cry, a scream and Aaron rushes out of the room. 'Naomi swallowed a Lego brick,' he yells. Mrs George lets go of my hand and rushes back to the room. 'How big was it?' she shouts. I hear Naomi screaming that her belly hurts, her throat hurts. Mrs George is thumping Naomi's back.

'It's OK, darling. You're not choking, no blocked airways,' she says, but Naomi is screaming and screaming and screaming. She won't stop.

'We have to go to hospital, Cal. I'm so sorry, but Naomi is hurting and we don't know if the Lego will come out.' Mrs George is crying.

'It's OK,' I nod, wiping snot from my nose, trying to catch my breath through my tears. 'Poor Naomi.' Even though it's not OK, it's not OK at all.

'If only Tony was back from work. I'll leave a note and he can come and collect you from A&E. Take you to the show.'

In the car, Naomi stops screaming. She's moaning instead and Mrs George says, 'There, there, everything will be all right, darling.'

I turn from my front seat to look at Naomi because even though I know she doesn't like it I think it will be OK this time. Aaron has his arm around her, her head rests on his shoulder, the other clutches her tummy. They look at me and Aaron smiles and so does Naomi.

Worm smiles.

They're lying. This is a game. There is nothing wrong with her. Nothing. I will miss Diana's show because of them. And Diana might forget all about me and then I'll be stuck here for ever and ever.

I think I will explode. I can put up with the pinching and punching and nasty words but this... This is too horrid.

I begin to snivel and Mrs George tells me to stop but I can't. She snaps at me to be a brave boy, tells me that I'll see the show sometime. I want to punch Naomi, in the belly, the face, everywhere. And Aaron.

I hate it here. I hate them. I hate her. I want Diana.

We sit in the hospital for ages, waiting. Mr George turns up but it is too late to go to the show.

Too late.

I'm telling. I'm telling about the names they call me, the punches, the slaps, the pinches, the way they steal my sweets, spit in my food when Mr and Mrs George aren't looking. I will tell on them.

I will.

PART TWO

London – 1990s – 2000s

Diana
Winter 1995

Cal's eyes flickered and he smiled, something like admiration bursting through his mangled features. Puberty often wreaks havoc with appearance as childish features shift into their adult form, but for Cal it had been especially cruel. Alan wanted to investigate cosmetic surgery; I did not.

The gallery had closed early and it was just me and Cal. He'd made it clear this was the only way he would attend my latest exhibition – free from the prying eyes of a public greedy for spectacle.

'It's interesting,' he said, pausing before the first in a series of sculptures. Shop dummies with contorted limbs, melted breasts and extremities, dressed in provocative underwear, ugly words and phrases scribbled, like tattoos, on the orange-hued plastic flesh. A pen on the floor invited guests to make their own mark on the dummy's form.

I moved beside Cal, folded my arms, and stared at the mannequin, trying to see it as a stranger might. It was impossible. All I could see was me; my desire to shock, incite a reaction, appreciation. 'Shame no one else

215

feels the same way. Everyone wants you – you!'

Footfall had been poor, the critics had all but ignored the show and buyers were rare, if non-existent. Scadanelli hesitated to call it a disaster, though that's how I was experiencing it, and his interest in my latest work was lukewarm at best. It was disappointing, especially after the dismal ratings of the TV show profiling me and a couple of other risqué artists. I'd hoped it would propel me into the premier league.

Cal's face darkened, the smile rubbed off as easily as pencil. 'I hated the stuff about me.'

'You used to love it!'

'Not anymore.' He walked to the next dummy, gave it a cursory glance and moved on. I trotted after him. 'I could murder a drink,' he said.

'There's tea or coffee. Might even find some Coke.'

'Cheers. Not tea.'

I scurried to the kitchen, relieved to escape. Cal could look around without me watching his every move, every reaction. He couldn't stand being watched now. He was close to the unnamed series of photographs of different parts of my body, from my bare breasts to a shot of my head with my scalp peeled back to expose my 'brain', a price tag attached to each body part (my brain being the most expensive). It was an intimate piece and I figured he'd prefer to see it alone – if at all.

An empty Coke bottle poked from the top of the bin. Coffee would have to do. In the cupboard were new mugs, large and off-white, the colour of putty. The colour reminded me of an old piece, *Ugly Mugs*, and the delight Cal had taken in the project. *Ugly Mugs* had been a focal point of my *Beauty and the Beast* exhibition, along with *Two-faced*. It was a series of giant misshapen ceramic mugs onto which I'd superimposed photographs of Cal, me, and random strangers pulling faces. We'd laughed and laughed pulling those expressions. My heart swelled at the memory.

Two-faced was a series of images of me and Cal wearing plastic masks on the back of our heads. Mine was a grotesque, Cal's preternaturally beautiful. Cal had been fascinated by the latex, stroking and sniffing it repeatedly, and had initially placed the mask over his face. I recalled the disappointment in his eyes when I explained that I wanted to see his face too, in profile, straight on, as well as from the back. Whenever we weren't shooting, he'd spin the mask around and admire his reflection in the mirror. I winced at the memory and focused instead on stirring the coffee.

Beauty and the Beast had been a success. Hailed as an up and coming artist with a promising future, I'd been ecstatic. Cal enjoyed the attention. He had. Alan had been wrong when he'd said that I shouldn't parade Cal, that I shouldn't exhibit him like a rare bird, for 'all in sundry to stare at'. When Cal didn't want to be part of my work, I didn't use him.

My chest tightened.

Work without Cal at its heart wasn't as interesting, as vital, dynamic. No one paid any attention.

'Have I lost my mojo? ' I said, offering the steaming mug. Cal was leaning against the arch of the entrance to the main space.

'Why'd you do this? Mess things up?' He said,

217

cradling the mug.

'Mess things up?'

'You sell other stuff. Nice pretty stuff. Your portraits, prints of the city, the river.'

'That's the money work. This is the art. You know that.'

'You enjoy doing the money work?' he said, stepping forward, reading the plaque beneath the photograph on the wall.

I nodded. It was satisfying to sell, to imagine prints on stranger's walls, in homes, and offices. I made a decent living, which was just as well given the monthly 'commission' I paid Jim for his silence. 'But it will never get me a reputation as a serious artist. My Cal work gets me that. Got me that.' I meant to laugh, meaning it light-heartedly, but it came out as a displeased 'pfft'.

'This is a lovely picture,' he said, pointing at my portrait, a black and white shot taken in Clissold Park. 'Alan take it?'

I nodded.

'It's so you.'

It was a candid shot. I leant against a tree, rough bark in contrast to my smooth, healthy skin, the wind whipping strands of hair across my face. I looked serious, but relaxed, happy even. 'You like it?'

'Who wouldn't? It's you.' He took a noisy slurp of coffee.

I was confused. 'It's not what I am.'

It's how I appear.

'Isn't it?' he said.

'Absolutely not. This,' I waved my arm over the

space, 'is who I am.' A puerile impulse to stamp my feet and shriek, 'I am more than a pretty face. I am. I am,' Threatened, I quashed it.

'I'm starving,' Cal said. 'Got anything to eat?'

'No, sorry. I'll buy you some crisps on the way to the restaurant if you promise it won't spoil your appetite?'

He groaned. He didn't want to come, I knew that, but Alan had been away and this was a chance for the three of us to spend an evening together, special time. 'It's a quiet place. Cosy. I've booked a corner table,' I said, smiling and reaching for his wrist.

He pulled away. 'Bet you'd rather the window. Study the stares, second glances, people virtually tripping over as they turn back to gawp.' He pulled a face and the fist in my belly turned to acid.

'That's not fair,' I gasped.

'Isn't it?'

'I need the bathroom. Then we'll get going, otherwise we'll be late.' I wanted to be sick.

In the cubicle I dropped onto the toilet seat and removed a compact from the inner pocket of my jacket and reapplied my lipstick. I didn't need to but the waxy smell and pull on my dry lips was a strange comfort.

What the hell happened just now? You wanted Cal to be inspired, to be part of your work again. What have you been thinking?

I pushed myself up and returned to Cal.

He kicked the toe of his trainer against the floor, chin almost resting on his chest. Without lifting his head he mumbled, 'Sorry.'

I touched his shoulder and this time he didn't flinch. 'It's OK. Let's go eat.'

He tugged on the hood of his jacket and shrugged, pulling it over his forehead, obscuring his face, and strode towards the door, shoulders hunched.

Cal

Rain is thrashing against my window and it is so overcast my room is the colour of wet cement. I feel as if it could dry and harden around me and I will be stuck here for ever, encased in concrete dressings in a concrete room. There are days before the bandages are removed and I can see my face.

Eve bustles in. 'Beautiful day!' she jokes. But the brightness of her tone doesn't fool me. She is distressed. There's a puffiness about her eyes which suggests she's spent many hours crying. Her eyelids are shiny and swollen; there's a glimpse of vulnerability about her.

I humour her. 'Are you always so irritatingly cheerful, or is it a skill you develop when you're training?'

She laughs. 'I believe in making the best of things. No point moaning, each day comes only once, as my mother says.' She has my painkillers in a cup. Tablets now; I no longer have a drip.

'Is this a family trait then?'

Her eyes drop and she turns, quickly, to the jug of water on the side table, pouring a glass for me. She flinches at the sight of the CDs. I've said the wrong thing and I feel bad.

'Apart from my brother, yes. He can be a miserable

221

so-and-so, like someone else I know,' she says, turning back, smiling with her mouth, if not her eyes.

So that's why she's nice to me: I remind her of her brother. I wonder where he lives, if it is far away, if she misses him. Something in her voice tells me that she wishes she'd not told me this. She is worried about him; he is the source of her tears. I'd like to make her feel better but don't know how.

'My other name's Mr Happy.'

Jesus, that's so lame.

Left hand curled into a fist, the outstretched fingers of my right hand sitting in the grooves between my knuckles I lift my index finger, tapping out the rhythm of 'Smells Like Teen Spirit'. It's pathetic but tapping helps me think.

'What tune's that?' she says, pointing to my hands.

'Nirvana.'

She nods blankly. 'You play the drums.'

'How'd you know? Oh yeah. You know about me. You lied when you said you didn't.' I smile as I say it but she pulls a face and says sorry again.

'No worries. How much do you know then, Eve?'

She hands me the water and pills. I can take them myself now. Another improvement.

'Everything and nothing,' she says, surprised. Relieved to be thinking about something other than her brother I'm guessing. I've done well. 'I read everything I could when Mr McKenzie first told me that you were famous and everything.'

I huff at 'famous'.

'I hadn't heard about you, or Diana, or anything before. I'm not a complete philistine, but modern art's not my thing. I don't really understand it, if I'm honest.'

'Nor me.'

'You're not serious?'

'I am.'

'What are you into then?'

'Not all that much. Like Egon Schiele. Klimt.'

'All those gorgeous women!' She smiles.

'Thought you knew nothing about art?'

'They're really, really famous.'

'And I'm not!' I joke.

She laughs. I love to watch her laugh. Her laugh is gorgeous. She is gorgeous.

All the gorgeous women. Was that when everything began to disintegrate?

~

There is a poster of Beatrice Dalle on my bedroom wall, next to the old one of the FA and League Cup-winning Arsenal squad. Tony Adams and his team mates proud in their red shirts and too-short shorts. Dalle is washed in a beguiling midnight blue.

'Where'd you get the poster?' Stanley asks.

'Camden Town.'

'Cool.'

We're staring at the poster, imagining running our hands up her smooth pale arms, kissing her impossibly full mouth. I imagine running my tongue along her teeth, finding the wide gap between the front two, wrapping my tongue round hers. Dreaming. Of kissing. Not just Beatrice. Anyone.

'My brother's got a tape,' Stanley says, flicking through a copy of *Playboy*. The corners are curled and well-thumbed and not only because it's such an old copy.

223

Pamela Anderson's on the cover with tits like balloons and Dan Aykroyd with a head like a cone. Stanley tosses the magazine aside, 'Fucking freak.'

I look. 'Really?' I reply.

'Not like you. It's make up or something.' He punches my shoulder lightly.

'The video, dickhead. Did you get it?'

'Easy. He's got loads of porno.'

'*Betty Blue*'s not porn.'

Diana and Alan are out. They've gone to watch some arty-farty film in town. On the coffee table are a few cans of Vimto and some crisps. Stanley slips the video from his back pack. The cover's exactly like my poster. I take it from him and kneel to slide it into the player.

'It's in the right place, yeah?'

'Yeah. At the start. Start's the best bit.'

'You've seen it already?'

'Loads. Turn the light off.'

When it begins Stanley sits still and quiet next to me on the sofa. We lean forward, elbows on knees, as if to get a better look. The guy, I forget the actor's name, is talking in French, about Betty, and the screen is filled with the image of him doing it to Beatrice. The room on screen is dark and their bodies move like snakes over each other. Gleaming in the dulled light. He humps away at her then slips down between her legs, and she's moaning and writhing around. The subtitles obscure the view a little and Stanley leans further forward as if to peep behind the words. But it is the sound that I can't get over. The noises they make. She makes.

We replay the first few minutes over and over and over. In the end Stanley says we've got to move on, otherwise we'll wear the tape out. The film's OK, bit strange.

~

Alan's in my room asking what I fancy for supper. He points at the poster and sighs. 'Lovely, isn't she?' he says. I drop my head convinced he can see the lust in my eyes. That he knows.

Over supper he talks about the film they saw the other night. I've never heard of it.

'You might like it, Cal. Be good for your French. Bit like *Betty Blue*.' He winks.

'We could get *Betty Blue* out,' Diana says, brightly.

'It's an eighteen, isn't it?' I mumble.

'It's a beautiful love story. Bloody puritans. It's only sex. You're old enough.'

'I'm not quite fifteen.'

I look at the floor, dreading that she'll suggest that we all watch it together, but Alan nudges my arm and says, 'Leave the lad alone, he's probably seen it already.'

I hate that Diana is so liberal, that sex is so out there for her. I wish she was more like Stanley's mum who is much older. She never talks about it with Stanley, he says. She thinks his brother talks to him, and she is right, in a way, though Stanley has some weird ideas about sex. I wonder what his brother tells him.

I wake to a strange sound and in my half-conscious state I think there is a fight outside. Then I remember *Betty Blue*, and though I try to block it out, I see them, in my mind's eye; Diana splayed, naked, on their enormous bed, skin slippery and wet, her long, lean limbs writhing in ecstasy, Alan between her legs licking and sucking and caressing. I put my fingers in my ears.

225

If I block out the sound perhaps the pictures will go away. But it is hard. I do not have to imagine much; I have seen many images of Diana's body. Parts I wish I'd not seen. My body is taking over and I feel myself stiffen. I roll over, burying my face in my pillow, and rub until my hand aches.

In the morning I rip my sheets from the mattress and cram them into the machine before I leave for school.

There is a disco at school. It's the end of Year Ten and Stanley has a girlfriend, and I find myself hanging out with China more and more. She is still plump; she wears braces and her face is covered in spots. She tells me she has spots on her back and shoulders too, though I have to take her word for it as I've never seen her in anything other than a baggy sweatshirt, or jumper – even when it's boiling – and jeans that trail on the floor. When it rains a dark tidemark rises up her legs so that it looks as if her jeans are made from two different shades of denim.

We sit on the brown plastic chairs lining the edges of the drama studio and watch the dancers moving in the flashing lights. The DJ's playing 'Common People', but my favourite track's 'Pencil Skirt'. Jarvis Cocker's a dirty bastard. Stanley's wriggling around like a demented stick insect.

China leans across and shouts, 'Fancy a spliff?'

'OK.'

We slip out and sit up against the wall at the back of the sports hall, looking out over the tennis courts and athletics track. China pulls out a ready-rolled joint. I raise my eyebrows.

'Always prepared, me. I was a Girl Guide, would you believe it?'

I roll my eyes. 'No.' And it's true, I can't.

We finish the joint and we're stoned now. We sit

226

in silence for ages.

'Think I'll ever get a boyfriend, Cal?'

'Course.'

She is pretty underneath it all. Her spots will fade, the braces will come off and so will her puppy fat. I feel a childish urge to stomp my feet and scream. Rage bubbles at my core. I long to play my drums. I hear the bass beat of 'The Bends' thumping through the bricks. China pulls me to my feet and says, 'Let's dance,' and we pogo to Radiohead, flinging our frustration into the sweaty air.

Stanley has done it. On Monday morning, as we walk across the school from registration to our first lesson, I notice that he walks differently, proud, and I ask if he scored in the basketball match on Saturday. Stanley is very tall and he plays for a local team. The coach would like him to become a professional; he thinks Stanley has the potential, but Stanley wants to work with animals, endangered species abroad. The basketball is fun but not for life, he says.

'I scored, but not in the way you mean.' He laughs. He stops and looks at me, his eyes sparkling.

I want to ask him what it was like, but find that I cannot speak. He touches my shoulder and leans in. 'It's not all it's cracked up to be. But don't tell anyone I said that.'

I know he is only saying this, to make me feel better and I hate him for it.

I say, 'I don't need your fucking pity.' And I walk away and into the classroom without looking at him. It is French and the teacher is petite and pretty and always kind to me. When she smiles and says, 'Bonjour, Cal. Comment allez-vous?' I want to slap her. I am not a nice person, I'm really not.

Diana

The mirror wouldn't have looked out of place on the walls
of a Viennese palace. I found it in a run-down shop on Brick
Lane. Rays of light bounced off gemstones in the ornate
metal frame, cherubs trumpeted from the corners. It was
magical; if the mirror had spoken to me and granted me
three wishes I wouldn't have been surprised.

I pushed my nose up against the window for a closer
look, hands shielding my eyes. The glass was scratched
and peeling in several places, though this might well have
been part of the design – shabby chic was all the rage. My
reflection fractured, parts of my face and upper body
obscured by the brownish stains on the glass. For the first
time in my adult life, in the reflection of that glorious
mirror, I saw my future self, an old woman. It wasn't long
before my thirty-third birthday, and I was dreading it. I'd
sailed through my thirtieth, unlike friends and colleagues.
It might have been the responsibility of caring for Cal but
I'd felt like a 'proper' grown up for some years and even
looked forward to reaching an age when the number
matched how I felt inside.

But thirty-three was an ugly number, neither young

nor middle-aged. An in-between, unloved kind of number. I traced the faint lines across my forehead, examined the soft wrinkles fanning out from the corners of my eyes, a hint of tracks from nose to mouth. The imprint of the future was there, before me in the dusty summer light, and I saw my mother.

A bell tinkled as I pushed open the door. The shop smelt of garlic, jasmine and mothballs. A radio hummed in the background. I rubbed my fingers together to rib myself of the city grime I'd collected from the window.

'The mirror is for display only. It is not for sale, even to a beautiful lady,' the shopkeeper said firmly, nodding as he spoke, his forehead glistening with sweat in the heat.

'Everything's for sale,' I said, 'what's your price?'

'There is no price high enough, madam,' he replied.

'It's for my son's birthday,' I said, hoping to appeal to a love of family. I still stumbled over 'son', even after all these years. But I loved him as a son. I couldn't have loved him more and he was formally ours, mine and Alan's.

'Madam, there must be many things you could buy him. Walkman, trainers. All the young people love trainers, yes?'

I nodded. I'd already bought Cal a pair, just like the ones Damon Albarn wore, along with a jacket I'd found in Camden Lock. I'd bought too much, Alan said. I spoilt him, he said, and though I'd sworn to buy nothing else the mirror was tempting. I wanted it to be a special birthday, and this was a special mirror.

We haggled until, finally, I offered a price the shopkeeper couldn't refuse.

'Will you keep it here for a few weeks? I have nowhere to store it in my house.' I could have kept it at the studio but I was reluctant to pay for delivery twice. Alan would be cross enough as it was.

The shopkeeper smiled, head bobbing, as I handed over the cheque. 'No problem at all. When you want it you call. My son will deliver. You tell me where.'

Alan was in when I arrived home. Cal was in the bath.

'How was it?' he said, placing a coffee on the table in front of me. Fresh tiger lilies sat in a glass vase at its centre, the heavy scent both intoxicating and irritating in the sticky air.

'It's a great space. Good curator, knows what he's doing. Why the lilies?'

'Cal liked them. We went to Columbia Road market.'

'You don't have to get him everything he likes.'

'Steady. You're the one who spoils him.'

Contact sheets from Alan's recent trip to the Republic of the Congo sprawled across the table along with a viewing lens, the horror and brutality in the tiny images a sharp contrast to the beauty of the blooms. He looked tanned and healthy, though the haunted veil behind those blue eyes hadn't quite disappeared. Wires of grey shot through his hair and the extra weight he carried round his jowls and torso suited him. He exuded a gravitas and authority I'd never have thought possible when I first met him.

'We both spoil him,' I snapped, my good humour fading.

'You more than me.'

I shrugged, unable to retort. No way would I mention the mirror now.

'He was upset,' Alan said. 'Someone recognised him.' I flinched.

'Oh man, those bloody trendy shops. I should never have taken him in. It was my fault.'

I hated the way Alan said 'man' all the time. When we were younger it didn't matter so much; I barely noticed. But now? He was thirty-six. It was unbecoming. He sounded like an ageing hippy.

'They recognised him from the newspaper piece?' I said, annoyed with myself more than the editor. I shouldn't have agreed to an up-to-date portrait of Cal, shouldn't have agreed to the interview, period. The journalist had harped on and on about why a 'stunningly beautiful woman like Diana Brading insists on making ugly art.'

'Yes. The *Cal Patch* article.'

'Jesus.'

Cal Patch was inspired by those hideous soft toys manufactured and marketed in the eighties. In the main, it was an American phenomenon, but some had made it over here. They were limited edition dolls that were 'birthed' from cabbage patches and sold as individuals with names and shit like that to demented women who treated them like they were real babies. For the work I'd photographed a corner of a dilapidated, neglected garden and superimposed shots of Cal and myself as children, young adults and, in my case, as an adult onto the heads of the dying flowers and weeds. It wasn't one of my favourite pieces – it didn't say what I'd wanted it to –

231

and in certain moods I felt positively ashamed of it. I'd hoped it might lead to me being taken more seriously in the US, or at least give me much needed exposure. It did neither.

And Cal hated *Cal Patch*. He considered it 'beyond naff'.

'It's kinda old, anyway,' Cal had said when I mentioned the interview. 'Shouldn't you have talked about your more recent work?'

'Not exactly high art, is it?' I'd snapped. 'Commercial crap.'

'Popular with the buying public. Who cares what the critics think?' he'd said.

Me.

Alan continued telling me what had happened at the market. 'He dealt with it really well at the time. He answered her questions, polite, you know... But outside, oh man, he was upset. And then everyone was staring at him, or so he thought. And when I said it didn't bother him before – you know, trying to make things better – he said it always bothers him, always has done, and he wishes he was dead.'

I put my head in my hands and scratched at my scalp, pressing harder and harder till it hurt. 'I hate it when he says that. I thought we were getting there...'

'Lots of teenagers hate the way they look... I did.' He sighed, eyes watery.

'Me too.'

He was angry then. 'Oh, Diana. Don't go there,' he said, pointing at me. I held his gaze for seconds before looking away, ashamed. Damn him. How could it possibly be the same?

'Anyway he liked the lilies...' he said, tone conciliatory.

'I was never good enough,' I said. 'Not for Bunny.'

Again, he eyeballed me, mouth tight.

'But you're right. This isn't about me,' I added quickly.

I rested my arms on the table top. It was cool on my bare forearms. Alan took hold of my hands and rubbed his thumbs along my fingers. 'Don't use him in your work again. It doesn't help, turning him into a celebrity freak.'

'He's not a freak.'

'In the eyes of the world, he is. It's not right, but that's the way it is. And we need him to come to terms with his difference. Forcing him to celebrate it isn't helping. Something for the future. Maybe.'

He sounded sad, and serious, and maybe a little lost. Though my stomach knotted, I promised to find other ways for Cal to express himself, and for me to express myself. I thought of the mirror and it didn't seem like such a good idea after all. I squeezed Alan's hands and looked into his face. 'You're right,' I said.

'I know. I love you.'

'I love you too.'

'Then marry me.'

I sighed. 'We've been through this a thousand times. We're happy, let's not spoilt it.'

'We need to move on. We're stagnating. Let's have a baby.'

I let go of his hands, groaned. We'd talked about

233

this too, many times. There were so many reasons I didn't want a baby – I was terrified of the pain it could cause. Not the birth itself, but having another child might inflict terrible pain on Cal. Larkin had been one of Linda's favourite poets and though I'd forgotten most of what she read aloud to me during our Manchester days, the line about your parents fucking you up had stuck. Mine had, for sure. I was petrified I might love my own child more than I loved Cal, that I might love something perfect. I could not, and would not, risk hurting Cal. We had a son; we didn't need another to love.

'You guys having a baby?'

Cal slouched into the room, hands in jean pockets, shoulders hunched, head bowed.

'No, we are not,' I said, staring at Alan, before picking up the plastic bag from the sari shop and pulling out the fabric I'd bought at the same time as the mirror. 'You like this?'

'What's it for?'

'I don't know yet. Thought we might use it. Would you like to come to the studio after supper? Hang out?'

'I've got revision to do.' He shuffled towards the kitchen area. I heard the fridge door opening, the rustle of packaging, the gulping of milk straight from the carton.

'Use a glass!' I shouted across the large open plan space.

'Whatever.'

'Let him be,' said Alan.

But I couldn't. I could feel him slipping away,

pushing me away. There was a distance between us – had been for some time, and though I understood that this was an inevitable part of raising a child, letting go was proving difficult for me. Alan said I needed to trust that he would come back. He said all teenagers were distant and secretive, it's part of the process, but I didn't have that faith. Cal was almost an adult and he could walk away at any time. I couldn't bear the idea.

'A night off won't hurt. You're bright, you'll pass them all, no problem. They're not so important this year anyway,' I said, as I wandered over to the kitchen and hovered as Cal fixed himself a sandwich. I'd introduced him to the delights of peanut butter and jam sandwiches after a trip to the States. I went to hug him, but he flinched as my arm brushed his shoulder and I withdrew.

'Please come. I could use the company.'

He pulled a face. 'What about Al?'

'He's busy,' I said, asking Alan not to contradict me with my eyes. 'Don't make me beg. You owe me that much.'

He shrugged. 'OK.' He slid off back upstairs.

'You mustn't pressurise him like that. You'll drive him away,' Alan said.

'You're jealous,' I said.

'You're right, I am. I don't get to see him anywhere near enough.' Alan grabbed his coffee and followed Cal upstairs.

I sat alone downstairs, gazing at the artwork on the walls. It was mostly mine; Cal work. He surrounded me, as in an embrace. He was within me, everywhere. My spirits rose; we would have a lovely, special evening.

235

Cal

I gulp some water and throw the tablets to the back of my mouth. They are difficult to swallow, they stick in my throat and I have to take another gulp to push them down, choking afterwards, my throat scratched and throbbing. I lean back on my pillows. Physically I feel much better today, but I can't be bothered to get out of bed. As I crawl towards a new me, a new beginning, I'm weighed down by memories of the past. A beast with a heavy burden.

~

We are in the Hackney studio. Diana is preparing for an exhibition and a TV crew are following her journey. I do not choose to be here; I have to be. I am an important part of the film, as Diana's acknowledged muse. Diana is being interviewed. The presenter says it is unusual for an artist's muse to be male. Diana replies that artists – certainly successful ones – are still, sadly, usually male (she emphasises the sadly, looking direct to camera and smiling ironically) and so it would follow in most instances that the muse is a beautiful female.

'But you too are obsessed by beauty, like so many

236

artists, male and female, before you,' says the reporter.

'I am obsessed by notions of beauty, what we are told is beautiful or ugly, and challenging such assumptions,' Diana replies.

I switch off; I have heard this kind of crap before. Then I feel guilty so I perform really well for the director and everyone is really pleased with me.

There are advantages to my celebrity. People stare, but they don't call me freak out loud. I imagine that people stare at Kate Moss in the same way, because people think they know who she is, because they see her so often, and because she is so fascinating to look at.

A poster of Kate sits on my wall next to Beatrice and Yoda and the Gunners. Of course, more people stare at Kate than me. I am not a total idiot. Diana's world of art and artists is pretty small. They think they are the most important things in the universe, but they are misguided. The television programme will change all that, Diana says. She says that the programme will bring her work to a wider audience and this is a VERY GOOD THING. I will have to get used to more people recognising me.

Diana is inviting the director to supper. This geezer is divorced – aren't everyone's parents, China says – and he has a daughter. It is 'his' weekend, he says. Diana persuades him to bring her along and he agrees. Diana insists that Alan and I are present. She invites a single friend along too; I suspect that she is matchmaking.

Clothes are piled high on my bed. My hair isn't right and I'm pissed off. It's the one thing I can rely on to look OK, along with my hands. But who the hell looks at hands, at any rate? My hair is dark and glossy and hangs strong and straight to my shoulders. It falls in a centre parting quite naturally and I live with it like this because I can dip my head forward when I need to and my hair drapes over my face. Diana thinks I do it to stop unwelcome, hostile stares, and thinks I should make people confront difference, non-conformity, but I do it to protect others, not myself. I frighten small children and old ladies.

This evening I want to wear my hair in a side parting, swept across the worse side of my face, but my hair's not playing ball. I try tucking it behind my ear, but my ear sticks out too much and cannot hold the weight. I lean out of my bedroom window smoking a cigarette I stole from Diana's handbag. If she smells it, fuck it. What do I care? When I'm finished I flick the butt into the garden.

I look at my reflection in the mirror. I'm going for a Dead Kennedys look, punk/grunge scruffy, effortlessly cool, but instead I look lame, totally fucking naff.

I run my fingers through my hair again, scratch my scalp and peer into the glass. I hold my hands in front of my mouth and breathe. My breath smells of tobacco and mouthwash. I stick out my tongue; it's white and furry. My stomach rolls and rolls. I try to look at myself as someone else might. As a girl might. Fear hits my bowels like a punch. I dash to the bathroom.

As I'm coming downstairs I see Diana at the door, opening it wide and kissing the director on both cheeks. If I'd heard the bell I'd have stayed in my bed a bit longer. I freeze half way down.

Diana turns, her arm draped over the shoulder of a

girl, and looks up.

'Cal, this is Kathryn. Come down and say hello,' she says, like I'm six or something.

The director's daughter isn't drop dead gorgeous. Hardly surprising as he's no oil painting, as Alan would say, but I heard that her mother was a model. Diana says notions of beauty change. Maybe this is proof. The girl standing in the hall looks like a kid from an American TV show, and when she smiles she reveals a mouth full of metal.

I look for the shock, the flinch, the recoiling in her eyes, but it doesn't come. This girl's been well briefed. Maybe her dad showed her the rushes from the programme. Or she's an art fan. Ugh. I step down and offer my hand. She flashes another silver grin and takes my hand but rather than shaking it she leans in and kisses me gently on the cheek. A real kiss, light, but not an air one. Flesh on flesh.

Alan has prepared a spinach and ricotta pie with home-made filo pastry and I'm wondering if bits of spinach will get stuck in Kathryn's braces. She is very thin and doesn't eat much, so I'm thinking the braces will not turn green. I don't eat much either.

We are sitting opposite each other, Kathryn and me, and I discover that she doesn't much care for art. I like her for this. She's really into animation and hopes to become a film maker one day. She adores movies – especially Disney – and she's a fan of the Star Wars trilogy. She's a bit geeky about it but I let her talk because I'm not really listening fully. I'm watching her mouth. Her full lips changing shape as she forms the words. I can see her wet, crimson tongue and the downy hair on her top lip. I am wondering what it would be like to kiss those lips, to wrap my tongue round hers, swap bodily fluid. I catch a glimpse of a bra strap as she leans forward to pass the redcurrant sauce Alan has prepared for the dark chocolate tart. The strap is white and made of cotton, I think. It cannot be substantial because I can just about make out a small circular bulge through the silk of her blouse. I imagine that her nipples are small and perky, like Kate Moss's. I try to imagine what her tits would feel like; they look so very different from China's. Hers are big and soft like blancmange. I think Kathryn's will be firm, like not-quite-ripe peaches.

The tart is rich and it sticks to the roof of my mouth. I push it around with my tongue and hope that I haven't got smears of chocolate round my mouth. I pick up a serviette and dab at the corners. Like a right twat.

Afterwards, we stand, awkward, in our wide hall. Kathryn asks if I'm going to the preview in Soho in a few weeks' time, once post-production is done. I nod that I am, and then I think, 'Fuck it. What have I got to lose?' Full of reckless hope and bravado I say it, before I can change my mind and wimp out. 'Would you like to meet beforehand?'

She says, 'Yes.'

Yes! I can't believe it and I'm struck dumb with shock. I must look like such a prat. She'll change her mind in a minute.

'I know a place, round the corner. I can get us in. It's a private club ...' She pauses. We both know why private is good but neither of us can say it. 'I can get us in. Dad's a member. Then we can come on to the preview together.'

I know the club she mentions, Diana is a member too, but I do not say this. I cannot believe my luck. She would not do this just to be nice. She has done her duty; she has been polite and entertaining all evening. She must like me. As Kathryn walks down the path with her father I watch the movement of her buttocks and realise that I am in love with her. In love.

LOVE.

The world feels like another planet, where agony and ecstasy orbit like moons, pulling me back and forth like the tide.

Diana

Cal and I walked north through Hoxton towards the council estates and onto Hackney where I rented a studio. As was our habit we took the back streets to avoid the crowds spilling from the bars and cafes onto the pavements and into the stultifying air. London felt like a pressure cooker on a low heat, working its way to an explosion, a molecular change. A city bursting with energy; a city looking to the future.

Cal pulled the hood of his sweatshirt over his forehead, obscuring most of his face. He must have been hot, but I didn't say anything. I thought he had grown accustomed to people staring, believed that sometimes he even enjoyed it. But he had good days and bad days, and the incident in the market with Alan proved this one to be the latter.

When we stepped out together I often wondered what people thought of me. How they viewed me. As loving older sister? Devoted friend? Professional carer? Mother? After all, there were sixteen years between us. It wasn't inconceivable.

Unlike much of the city, the estates showed few

signs of economic buoyancy, and I felt vaguely depressed as we walked through them. It was as if nothing had changed in decades, though everything had. More often than not I avoided them altogether, but this was Cal's preferred route and I wondered if these estates reminded him of Manchester. He rarely spoke of Hulme, and neither Alan nor I raised it.

'Do you like living here, Cal?' I said.

'We don't live here,' he said, eyes fixed on the cracked, uneven paving slabs.

I laughed a high-pitched, nervous-sounding titter. 'I mean in London.'

'S'okay,' he replied.

'I mean, if you could live anywhere in the world, where would it be, and why?' I hoped I didn't sound desperate. 'Humour me.'

He hummed and ahhed, then said, 'America.'

'East coast or west?' I said, surprised. America was the most visual country in the world.

'New York.'

I was able to visualise myself living there one day. 'I love it. So diverse,' I replied.

'Full of fruits and weirdoes.' He turned to me and peeped from under his hood, a sly mischievous smile spread over his face. Tonight was going to be OK.

'What about Manchester? Ever think about going back?'

'Dunno. I hate Oasis.'

I laughed. 'Fair enough. It rains all the time too. We're nearly there.'

My studio was in a converted church. An artists' co-operative had found the place in the mid-eighties. Abandoned by all but the local pigeon population and falling apart from neglect and the damage inflicted by the birds, specifically their excrement, no one wanted anything to do with it. The artists acquired the lease for five years, renovated the place and worked out of it until church officials got wind of the profit to be made in renting spaces. When the five years was up the diocese refused to renew the lease. So much for Christian charity. They upped the rent and, only moderately successful, the co-operative artists could no longer afford the space they helped create. To rent the building was not prohibitively expensive and thanks to commercial success it had been my creative home for almost four years.

Only one stained glass window on the west face of the building remained. I was glad the first artists chose to keep it – there was enough light from elsewhere – and the vibrant blues, reds and yellows cheered me up. Rays of sunlight bisected the air as we padded across the stone slabs to the workstation positioned where the altar once stood. To the right was a huge cupboard where I kept my creative history. Everything from schoolbook squiggles to recent ideas scratched on pads, bits of wood, newspaper – anything I could lay my hands on. Cal wandered off to make something to drink as I rifled through the trays marked 'Ancient work – Diana'.

I'd not shown Cal any of my childish sketches, those drawings created in the make-up rooms and beauty parlours. They'd been my therapy, my salvation from boredom and creative starvation and they were intensely private. Bunny caught me once, at a fashion show, playing around with ideas on an A5 pad. I'd painted with nail lacquer from the selection lined up in front of the dressing room mirror and pieces of make-up scattered on the counter. She snatched the pad from my hands and flicked through the heavy sheets of paper with disdain. There were drawings in kohl pencil, skies painted with eye shadow and effects created with hair spray.

'No wonder we get through so many cosmetics. You'll pay for replacements out of your earnings,' Bunny said.

'I do anyway,' I replied. I had no idea where such insurrection came from. She went to slap me and stopped. Maybe she figured the mark might show. The show wasn't over; I had to take one more strut down the runway. Instead, she took my pad, tore out the sheets, set them alight, one by one, with her lighter, and threw them in the metal bin where tissues smeared with foundation and nail varnish remover sat. I watched the orange flames licking the air, crackling and spitting, the pain in my chest as intense as if my heart burned too.

'I never had the opportunities you have, you ungrateful little bitch,' she hissed, wiping her eyes. At the time I'd thought it was the smoke that made her eyes water, but later I realised it was her bitterness that had driven her to tears. She held onto my upper arm, her long fingernails clawing my flesh. The bruises took two weeks to disappear altogether. The bin was black with an oriental pattern in gold, and as the pages turned to ash the bin's inside turned from gold to black. In that moment my hatred for Bunny blazed white hot, like magnesium.

'Don't waste your time on that drawing rubbish again, baby,' she said as she closed the dressing room door behind her. I kept on drawing, but told no one, and showed no one, in case Bunny was right. In case it was worthless, better discarded or burnt.

From the 'Ancient work – Diana' tray I pulled out a piece I'd done at school for my O level Art. It had drawn praise from my teacher and fellow pupils but, looking at it now, I recognised it as terrible. I had no idea why my teacher, young, trendy Mr Bradshaw, encouraged me. He didn't fit in at the school, and maybe he recognised a fellow misfit. Without his faith I might have given up on the notion of a career in art altogether, instead gone into teaching or some other ghastly profession, only picking up a paintbrush again years later at a night class for the bored, elderly and underemployed, churning out insipid watercolours and paint-by-numbers landscapes or animals.

'Would you look at this?' I said, tossing it onto the floor at my feet. He squeezed two mugs of coffee onto the table, pushing aside jam jars, brushes, palettes; the effluent of a painter at work, left over from my last session, unusual in that I rarely painted. He crouched to look at the piece more closely.

I felt exposed. As if he'd see through the façade, that I'd got away with it so far, that he would see me for the chancer, the con artist, I was.

'Cool,' he said.

'You don't have to be polite. It's terrible,' I said.

'Well, the execution's not great, but the idea is awesome, it really is. That's your thing, concept—'

'A natural modern artist!' I laughed, embarrassed by his praise, unsure if it was genuine. 'Why the hell didn't you make real coffee? You know I hate instant.'

'I'll make some more. Sorry.'

'It's fine. Ignore me.'

'What else you got there?' he said, pushing himself to his feet.

'Let's take a look. I need inspiration for this show next year.' I pulled out the entire top drawer. Sketch pads, postcards, school project books, diaries, valentine cards and letters from Dad in Basildon Bond envelopes tumbled onto the floor.

Cal rummaged through the flotsam. He was excited. People always are when they get a glimpse into a private, hitherto secret world. I'd experienced it groping round in Bunny's underwear drawer one afternoon when she'd popped out shopping.

'This is way cool.' Cal held up a drawing. It was a self-portrait, done at school, which is why it had escaped destruction by Bunny. My irises weren't coloured blue, they were white and the whites of my eyes were painted blue. This mistake, I assumed it was a mistake, the date in the bottom right hand corner put me at eight and bit, gave the picture a power that it otherwise would not have had. It was perfectly ordinary and unimaginative, other than for those eyes. I looked like an alien.

'I wonder what that would look like in real life,' I said.

'Well weird. Got any biscuits?' Cal said, slurping on his coffee.

I shook my head. 'You've given me an idea.'

Cal turned back to rifling through the paper.

Is it possible to get white contact lenses or lenses to cover the entire eyes as opposed to the pupils only?

He'd sparked my imagination once again. The desire to recreate the image was overwhelming. To manipulate my own image, my body as canvas.

Cal played an acoustic guitar he'd left at the studio while I pottered. We talked trivia, and the silences were warm and comfortable. We drank more coffee and shared the only can of beer.

'I'll order pizza. We can slob out. I'll see if they'll drop a couple more cans over.'

He grinned.

'So long as it's weak,' I added.

We sat on the floor amongst the mess, ramming greasy slices into our faces. Afterwards, he picked up his guitar again. Certain he was utterly absorbed, I watched surreptitiously. Teenagers fascinated me, and not just Cal. In public places I'd find myself staring at groups of them, their outfits, make-up, haircuts. The way they held themselves, spoke with each other, the way they fluctuated between acting like a facsimile of adults and playing like children, free and unaware. Cal practised being a grown up too – awkward and clumsy on occasion, note-perfect on others. He wore his thick glossy hair long in the fringe, flopping over the left side of his face, covering most of his wide, flat forehead. The growths on his jaw and cheek were less alarming now that his chin was covered in downy hair, and the hump on his back was barely noticeable. The permanently

248

hunched slouch he affected, like all boys his age, disguised it.

In so many ways, Cal was like any other teenager and I congratulated myself and Alan for doing such a good job. Arguably, he was better adjusted and balanced than many, all things considered. Of course, I worried about all the usual things: sex, drugs. Especially drugs.

'Can I have another then?' he said, pointing at a can of lager.

I pulled a face, suddenly unsure.

'Not like it's crack or nothing.'

Cal knew how his mother had died; I had never kept this from him, though he showed little if any emotion whenever she was mentioned, which was rare. He barely remembered her, he said, and this made sense to me.

I shrugged a yes to his request and he ripped off the key and took a long gulp. I'd rather he drank with me, in a safe environment, than in a park with friends. 'Do you think addiction is passed on? You know, in the genes. Think I read somewhere that it might be,' he said, studying the can, turning it in his hands, before belching loudly.

'That's total and utter rubbish,' I replied, more sharply than I intended.

He stared at the teardrop-shaped hole in the tin. 'Do you think Michael will have kicked the habit by now?'

'Would you like to know?' I said, my throat dry. I opened the other beer.

'Dunno.'

'You're free to contact him. I'd never stand in your way.'

'What's the point? He could contact me. Not like I'd be difficult to find.'

'It wouldn't be easy for him to reach out,' I said. I didn't want Cal to think his father didn't care, though he probably didn't, assuming he still lived.

I had never spoken of Jim's revelation, not even to Alan. I paid Jim to stay away and I never, ever, wanted Cal to discover the truth about his parentage. His biological father's indifference would be so painful.

'Fathers can be crap, can't they?' he said.

I nodded. Most of the time my father pretended I didn't exist.

Dad and Louise had divorced in the early nineties. In the end it was Louise who decided to cut her losses and get out while she was still young and pretty enough to bag another fool. She took my half-brother Tom with her and though I got the odd letter from him – from his exclusive private school up north – we were worlds apart now.

'As well as mothers,' he added, crushing the can in his fist.

Bunny. I wonder how she is?

'You drank that fast. Too fast.'

I didn't want Cal and I to ever drift apart, to find that the gulf between us was too wide to bridge. I treasured evenings like this, when we hung out together as we did when he was younger, content to simply be with each other. I had to trust that he'd find his way back. He was almost seventeen, discovering who he was, what he wanted. I had to be patient, wait for him to return to me. It was hard; the impulse to wrap myself

250

about him was powerful, to say 'love me, love me,' over and over and over. To make him love me.

He picked up the guitar and began strumming.

I watched.

'What?' he said.

'Nothing. Carry on, don't mind me.'

He stopped playing, stood and wandered to the window.

'Come on. It's getting late; we need to get out of here. You've school in the morning.'

We closed up and faced the stifling night air, walking down the Murder Mile, keeping an eye out for a bus or a cab. Both were rare in this part of town at eleven fifteen. 'How do you feel when people stare?' he said. He didn't look at me.

'Depends. People can't help themselves, it's natural. But if they're gawping, or pulling a face, or just, you know, being totally insensitive jerks, then I get really, really pissed off. You know that,' I said, surprised that he'd opened up to me.

'Stare at you, not me,' he mumbled.

'People don't stare at me.'

'Liar. You know they do. Especially men.'

'Indifferent, mostly,' I said, finally, embarrassed that I was so transparent. Like most people, especially women, I was always aware when people looked, whether they were male or female.

'That must be nice,' he said. 'C'mon, you enjoy it.'

He was right. I did, in a way, and there was no point denying it or trying to gloss over it. He'd know. Cal was perceptive. Was he ashamed of me, embarrassed by me,

251

proud sometimes? I hoped so. I really, really did.

I stopped and touched his arm. He turned but his eyes remained downcast. 'I don't pretend to know how it must be for you, but I'd like to, I really would.'

He laughed, disbelief exuding from him like sweat. 'Oh, I bet you would. So long as you could go back. You'd probably use the experience as a piece of work.'

Hatred, rage, exploded like a bomb. I felt as if I'd been blown several feet backwards, hit by shrapnel. He marched off down the road, shoulders hunched, hands rammed in his pockets. I hurried after him, almost skidding on a puddle of pitta bread and finely chopped lettuce.

We jumped on a crowded bus, relieved that the crush rendered speech impossible. At home, he stomped straight upstairs, without so much as a 'goodnight' and my wounds continued to bleed, slowly, imperceptibly.

And, unseen, infection set in, turning good flesh bad.

I didn't give the mirror to Cal. After it was delivered to the studio, I tucked it away in the room where the choir boys used to change, where I dumped things I thought might, one day, be useful, and which, mostly, were never used. Every time I wandered into the room, I'd catch sight of myself in the tarnished glass and feel ever so slightly sick. In the end, I threw a dustsheet over it and when I moved out of the studio I left it there for the new occupier to deal with.

Cal

Pain has hijacked me today; it controls me. I'm wracked with it, and it's bad: a throbbing underneath the skin which I cannot ignore, cannot forget. It's given me a headache. My cheeks are tight and stretched, as if I'm in a wind tunnel, or jumping from a plane at altitude, the skin doing its best to free itself from muscle and bone and fly off into the glittering sky.

Eve warned me this would happen. She said recovery is a bit like climbing Everest: after the trial and dangers and hard work of reaching the summit, elation masks everything for a while, but then there's the descent, and that can be as difficult, if not more so, than the climb up.

'Do you need painkillers?' she asks.

'No thanks. I want to feel.'

'Are you sure?'

'You're talking to me like I'm a child.'

'Sorry.'

She's so lovely, inside and out. 'No, I'm sorry. Didn't mean to snap.'

'Pain makes everything hard.'

That smile again. It melts me. 'Physical pain's easy

253

compared to...,' I say as she's leaving the room.

'You're not wrong there,' she says, turning to face me as she grips the door handle and smiling with her mouth but not her eyes again. She turns to leave again, stops and leans on the half open door. 'And it can be useful – to channel emotional pain.' She pauses, as if she's wondering whether to say something more or not, then looks at the floor.

'I'm a good listener.' I want to help her, if I can. Ease her pain.

'My brother cuts himself.' She looks up, into my eyes. Her lashes are long and thick, like a doll's.

'I've never done that,' I say.

'I know; I've seen no scars.'

Her oblique reference to her intimate knowledge of my body, from the bed baths, causes me to wince. I can feel myself blushing, heat on my chest and neck, not my face which I cannot feel at all, masked as it is by this debilitating throbbing.

'He's in love but she doesn't want him. I needed to tell someone, that's all. Say it out loud, to make it smaller,' Eve continues.

'Has it?'

'I'm not sure.' And with that she leaves.

Pain courses through me, more powerful than before. I feel Eve's pain, her brother's. I remember the agony of first love. Or was it second?

~

Kathryn is wearing a gold satin skirt and a tight black T-shirt. The skirt is so short I will get a glimpse of her knickers when we climb the stairs. We meet at Tottenham

Court Road tube station. It is rush hour and there are bodies everywhere. People stare. Kathryn places her hands on my shoulders and kisses my cheek, before clutching my hand and leading me out onto the street. We walk up towards Oxford Circus before cutting through to Soho Square. I keep my eyes glued to the pavement and Kathryn tells me what's been going on for her over the past few weeks. She seems more assertive and sure of herself without adults around. I feel less so.

At the club she doesn't want to eat and neither do I. We sit in a dark corner of the bar and she orders orange juice. The barman says hello to me and I have to confess that Diana is a member and I have been here before. I apologise for not telling her and she laughs and tells me not to worry about it.

'Chill out,' she says.

I am so full of longing I can barely look at her face, let alone make interesting conversation. I have thought about her constantly since the dinner party. In my mind she gained the stature of some kind of goddess. I remember doing the Greeks at school. She doesn't remind me of one of the really, really beautiful ones, like Aphrodite, and anyway weren't the mortals usually more beautiful in the myths? She's more like Athena, or Hermes, with qualities that surpass mere physical loveliness. In the flesh Kathryn is more ordinary, more obtainable, but still I am dumbstruck. She is loveliness itself.

When the drinks arrive, in tall glasses with crushed ice and sprigs of mint and lime, Kathryn orders me to drink half a glass immediately and I do as I'm told. From a handbag she wears slung across her body, she pulls a half bottle of vodka and refills the glasses. I have never drunk a

255

spirit. Wine is served with meals at home and I am allowed a glass with supper.

We order more drinks – two tonic waters this time. I am feeling light-headed and reckless and my tongue is finally loosened. We talk and talk, and we laugh a lot. I touch her knee, briefly, as I deliver the punch line of a joke. Her bare skin is warm and sticky. I reckon she uses body lotion.

At the preview we are giggly, but controlled. In the darkness of the back row of the private cinema we sip from the vodka bottle. Afterwards I want to say goodbye alone. Kathryn agrees to meet outside on the street. I tell Diana where I will be. She will not let me travel home alone. Diana puts her arm round my shoulders, leans in and tells me to be careful. Like I'm some stupid kid or something. I shrug her off, feeling like a prick. I'd like to kiss Kathryn. I ache with desire.

Outside, when the cool air hits my face, I feel drunk and sick and wish that I'd eaten something. I lean against the wall and I cannot work out if the sickness is the vodka or anticipation mixed with hope. The desire actually hurts.

There is something different about Kathryn but I can't work out what. I need to get the words out before I lose my nerve.

'I had a great time tonight,' I say.

'Yeah, me too.' She is standing beside me, though she is not leaning against the wall as I am.

I push myself upright and turn so that I am facing her, though I do not look her in the eyes. I focus on her mouth instead. 'You like to hang out again sometime?'

'Sure.'

Her lips are full and sticky with gloss. I notice a tiny

mole just above her top lip. My mouth is so dry I wonder how I'll manage it. I'm drunk on the smell of her.

I lunge forward, clumsy, like a great stupid oaf, and push her back against the wall and press my mouth on hers. I cannot feel her lips. It isn't meant to be like this. I feel a shove to my chest and I'm staggering backwards, falling off the kerb and into the road. A cyclist serves to avoid me and shouts, 'Twat!'

'I'm sorry, I thought–'

She is crying and wiping her mouth, like she just ate something disgusting.

'I thought... I thought you liked me.'

Through her tears, tears of disgust I realise with horror, she shouts, 'I did. But not... not like that... I meant as a friend. How could you think...'

Did, not do. I do not hear anymore; I do not need to. How *could* I think that? Yeah, right.

The cab ride home is agonising. I try to pretend everything is fine, grunting when spoken to. Diana knows that it is not. At home I go straight to my room, but Diana knocks on my door after fifteen minutes. She has guessed what has happened; it's not rocket science after all. I am ugly. A freak. How could I ever think anyone would want me? I want to punch the wall. I want to play my drums but it's late and Diana will tell me to stop.

'Hey, Cal. It takes a while to find the right person.' She sits on my bed.

I grunt.

'Al was right in front of me for ages before I knew he was the one.'

I grunt again. I'm sitting on the stool, my kit in front of me, sticks in hand, waving them around, as if I'm playing, but I stop before the stick makes contact with the drum skin. I have to concentrate really, really hard to not make contact and create sound.

'You'll find someone special. You just might have to wait a while, that's all.'

I go to hit the cymbal.

'No one loves you like I do anyway.' She gets up and steps over the piles of clothes on the floor and stands next to me. I lower my sticks; I don't want to hit her accidentally and hurt her. She places her hand on the middle of my back, gentle, unsure – we do not have much physical contact these days – and I turn and bury my face on her shoulder, crying. I can smell her perfume mingling with the special smell that is all her own.

~

There's a different nurse. But it's not Eve's day off. I'm pissed off and uncomfortable. I'm used to Eve. It's irrational and childish but I long to shout: 'I want Eve. Only Eve.' I ask this new, strange nurse what's happened. Is Eve ill?

New nurse looks up from the chart over her tortoiseshell framed glasses and says, 'Her brother's not well. He tried to take his own life. He took some pills then changed his mind and telephoned Eve. More of a cry for help, really. She'll be back tomorrow.'

'And she all right with you telling me this? Kind of personal,' I say.

'"If Cal asks where I am, tell him. Everything." That's what she said.'

I'm flattered by this demonstration of trust and I'm concerned. Poor Eve. How awful. And for her brother too. To love and not be loved in return is the pits. But there are worse things, much worse.

I can relate to her brother. I understand what it's like to feel that life's not worth living. To stand at the edge and stare into the void.

The nothingness.

I wonder what he's got to be miserable about, Eve's brother, apart from the girlfriend thing. Lots of people talk about being depressed, but the term's used lightly these days. If you have a couple of crap weeks, you say, 'I'm so depressed.' You're not. Life is full of ups and downs, but without the downs how the fuck would you recognise the ups? Depression is sustained, relentless, and often chemical. A feeling of nothingness. Not crap.

~

I feel crap whenever I think about Kathryn. I feel like a total loser. I'm relieved that she doesn't go to the same school, know people I know. The humiliation would be gross, the pity even worse. How could I get it so wrong? How could I think that any normal girl would like me? I long for the days when my grasp on my difference was fragile. The days when I enjoyed the attention; from Diana, from school friends, adults, teachers. The fawning at exhibitions and the knowledge that people pay money to look at pictures of me.

With the passing days the pain subsides, but I am left feeling empty, and nothing Diana, or Alan, or China or Stanley can do makes me feel better. I cannot tell my friends why I'm so miserable. I am vile to them, and they tolerate it and this makes me even angrier. No way would they put up with such crap from anyone else; they'd tell them to fuck right off.

After school I come straight home and sit on the sofa in front of the telly, flicking through the channels so quickly the sounds and images merge together to form one mad, trippy mess. I can't even be bothered to play my drums. There's a magazine on the coffee table. I throw the remote down and pick the magazine up. It's one of those weekly, trashy ones you find in doctor's surgeries. It's full of celebrity gossip and other drivel. It is also full of freaks. Despite myself I'm drawn in.

There's an article about an American woman who is altering her appearance so that she looks like a pet dog that died some months ago. The surgeon says he sees her as a 'great challenge'. I laugh my face off and then it makes me crazy angry. I march upstairs to my room and start thrashing away on the drums. I'm working it so hard my shoulders begin to ache. I can't stop thinking about the article. Thump, crash, bang. I'm not even making music now, just noise. These people just don't get it. Diana is fascinated by people like this. I am raging.

How dare they alter perfectly normal, healthy bodies – have they no idea? Clearly fucking not. I hurl the drumsticks across the room and flop onto my bed.

I'm up again in an instant, the energy within me burning. I crash downstairs. In a cupboard in the living room is a box full of drawings of mine from when I was a kid. They're precious to Diana, she says. I remember I sat in front of a full-length mirror in my bedroom and drew – self-portraits – for hours and hours. Her idea, but I kind of got into it. Now I can barely look at myself when I comb my hair.

I pull the pictures out and study them. They're not lifelike. Not one bit. These images are of a child I don't recognise. A kid with a lop-sided smiling face and straight, thick hair and fingers like sausages. I pick up a drawing and tear it in two, then four, then eight, then sixteen. Pieces of paper, like confetti, scatter on the carpet. I grab another, and another, and soon it looks as if a weird snow has fallen. I gather the bits up in a carrier bag and take it to the garden. On the patio I strike a match and set the whole lot alight. Later I lie amongst the ashes of my artwork, and it feels good. So good.

~

My bandages come off in two days. I want to snap my fingers and propel myself into the future like magic. I want time to stand still. For the day to never come. I'm sitting in the hospital grounds watching clouds scud across a watery sky when I see Eve walking up the path to the main entrance. Her strides are long; she moves quickly, strength and purpose radiating from her like a Ready Brek glow. She's jabbering on her mobile and I wonder who she is talking to. The world is suddenly brighter. I notice the flowers, the green, green grass, freshly cut. I notice the smell – or imagine it – and the sound of birdsong.

I wave and Eve trots over.

'Back already? He all right then?'

'He'll be fine. Dad's with him.'

'What did you say to him?' I ask, 'To cheer him up?'

'I told him to get a grip. To carry on. For those that love him, if not himself. I told him there are so many people out there whose lives are so much harder than his, that he's lucky.'

'You told him about me.'

She lifts her shoulders, non-committal.

'Must be wicked to have you around. I bet he's glad you've gone back to work.'

That makes her smile. Then she becomes serious. 'He's bi-polar. Only the drugs can help him, and he forgets, or refuses, to take them. The highs are so good.'

'Perhaps he's comfortable with himself, being bi-polar and all. Maybe you need to accept him the way he is,' I say.

Where did that come from? Diana talks of acceptance, changing only what we can and what makes us happy. She's full of shit.

'Did Diana accept you the way you are? Do you?'

'She didn't want me to change. Not forever. Not for myself. '

~

The hospital is right in the centre of town and it doesn't really look like a hospital from the outside. Not to me. Does once we're in though. It smells of disinfectant. The tapping of clogs on shiny floors and the rattling of trolleys fills the cloying air. I want to be sick.

'Don't be frightened, Cal,' Diana says. 'We'll be out of here as soon as possible.'

'I'm not scared.'

'Of course you're not!' She laughs and I smile because she's right: I'm terrified. The headaches have been getting worse and worse.

Inside the consultation room a tall man with blue eyes and hair sprouting out of his nostrils talks to me like I'm an idiot.

'So, Cal. We're going to expand your skull again – give that big brain of yours room to grow. You'll get even better grades at school once I'm through with you.'

He's pointing at a screen with a diagram of a head on it, mine I think, showing me where they're going to cut open my head and insert another plate. He looks at Diana and smiles.

'There's the option to expand the forehead too. Given that we'll already have him on the operating table we could do some work here.' I hate it, the way people do that – talk like I'm not here. The image spins and he gestures at the flat profile. 'Give him a more rounded shape.' He wants to say 'normal', I feel it, but stops himself just in time. I want to be angry, but I'm intrigued by this idea. How normal could it make me?

'I don't want any unnecessary surgery. It'll be bad enough for him as it is. He's only twelve,' Diana says.

'I understand your concerns, Ms Brading, but we'll take very good care. Things have moved on so much since Cal last had any surgery, and when the time's right to do more, it will have progressed even further. Heart and lung transplants were inconceivable decades ago – imagine what could be achieved in the future.'

'He was a baby then. He doesn't even remember it. No, do what you have to do. Nothing more.'

I want to butt in, to say, 'Let's give it a go. I can't look any worse.' But I am frightened. Of the operation. Of the pain. In case I do look worse once they're done.

The doctor sighs and says, 'If you change your mind...'

'I won't,' Diana says.

Diana

'Aw thanks Alan, this is way, way cool.' Cal held out his right hand, admiring the ring on his middle finger.

It looked great. Cal's hands were still beautiful; his fingers were long and slim, the seashell pink nails flat and square, the skin smooth and unblemished. So different from my own, which on top of the usual signs of ageing showed evidence of an individual who worked with their hands.

'I'm really glad you like it, mate. It suits you. Happy birthday.'

'Yes, happy birthday, Cal. Eighteen! An adult now!' I reached over and hugged him, aware of his stiffening form. I brushed his cheek with the back of my hand but decided against kissing him.

'It's Russian, often called the bands of love. The three bands represent strength, spirit and love. I like to think it represents the three of us but maybe that's daft,' Alan said.

'It is daft, but I like it!' I said, with fake cheeriness.

I was annoyed with Alan. He'd bought the ring without my knowledge and presented it as an extra gift,

264

a surprise for Cal, and me. I did that sort of thing all the time, but this felt different. Like a betrayal, like he was nudging me out.

'Who's who?' Cal said.

'I have to be strength,' Alan said, puffing out his chest, 'and Diana love, so that leaves you as spirit, if you're happy with that?'

'Perhaps we could all be each one – kind of in rotation,' Cal said.

'You could have it engraved, with our initials on the bands,' I said.

'Good idea. Consider it done,' Alan said.

Alan crossed to kitchen, grabbed the cafetière, and mugs, and returned to the table, nudging the coffee between the torn wrapping paper, curling ribbon, scattered gifts and cards. Cal yawned and Alan poured. We'd had to shake Cal awake shortly after ten. Alan and I had been up for hours, excited.

I pushed the innocuous brown envelope across the table. 'For your coming of age. Something to help you on your way.'

'You've given me loads already.'

'It's never enough,' I said.

Cal opened the envelope and pulled out the cheque. I read the surprise in his face and waited for the usual 'it's too much,' mantra that he uttered each time Alan and I gave him money. He was determined to be independent, and it was a quality we admired, secretly believing we had imbued him with it.

But the mantra never came. Cal smiled and said, 'Thank you. This is amazing.'

'What you going to spend it on? Any ideas? A car, a holiday? You could save it for university,' Alan said.

'I don't know,' Cal replied, folding the cheque and placing it in the front pocket of his jeans. He took a gulp of coffee. 'This is good, thanks.'

I didn't believe him. Cal had the look of someone who knew exactly what they were going to do.

What is he concealing?

'Really?' I said, eyebrows raised, trying to keep it light.

'You shouldn't do that,' he said, pointing at my forehead. 'You'll end up with terrible wrinkles.' There was no humour in his tone, and I found myself touching the skin between my brows, rubbing the creases away.

Alan came to the rescue and lifted the atmosphere. 'Right then, what do you want for brekkers? I'll cook you anything you fancy, we've all your favourites. And Buck's Fizz!'

We ate a leisurely brunch and lazed about reading the papers. Cal had no plans for the day; a night out with China and Stanley and members of the band that evening to which we weren't invited. I'd suggested a surprise party but Alan had advised against and though I was disappointed, he was right. Cal wasn't one for crowds and although he still came to events with me when I pressurised him to do so, he was often surly and uncommunicative.

Alan had a meeting with his publisher that he'd been unable to postpone. A meeting to discuss his latest book – a project he'd been planning for years, photographing

266

the regenerated North, comparing it to his archive shots of the districts and people of Manchester, Leeds and Sheffield in the eighties. To document how the cities had fared in the intervening years, how they had changed and improved, from laid-to-waste industrial ugliness to service-industry, shopping mall centres of commerce and beauty, a pictorial history. Alan left shortly before two. I was feeling restless.

'Do you fancy a walk?' I said to Cal. 'We could visit the cemetery or pop into my studio? You've hardly been to my new one. We can take the back route; follow the old tube line from Finsbury Park. Spook each other out in the tunnel along the way!'

'I've not been there,' Cal replied.

'It's amazing. Deserted, derelict, wild. Irresistible.' I sounded over-keen but I didn't care.

'OK.'

In the end we didn't walk along the deserted railway line. We turned left out of the house and headed up the lane towards Highgate. Sunlight glittered through the gold-green leaves of the acacia trees, bounced off the silver-white of the birch trunks. The roses and hydrangea bushes splashed pinks and reds and white along the route. We had been in Hornsey under a year and I was still surprised at how much I enjoyed living in the leafy, affluent suburbs of North London.

The move from Hoxton had been Alan's idea. He was sick of all the grey buildings, how crowded and cramped it felt, and the unrelenting urban-ness. Even after gentrification it was pretty grim in places, and though I liked the merging of the ugly and the beautiful,

267

the grand and the prosaic, and would probably never have left were I on my own, I loved Alan and he was persuasive.

'Change is good,' Alan had said, and I hadn't been able to argue with that.

The lane wasn't all suburban gorgeousness. A couple of tower blocks stood tall and proud. Council-owned and rented to single people, they were originally built as a halfway house for ex-cons.

Along the lane there were pieces of litter here and there, empty beer cans rattling against the kerb, half full bottles sitting on garden walls, cigarette butts, and piles of dog shit crusted over in the heat. These imperfections comforted me but here, strolling with Cal, they reminded me of Hulme and Jim, and my stomach turned over with the cocktail of emotions such memories conjured. Years had passed since I'd seen Jim, though I felt his presence every time I read a bank statement.

'Will you miss it here?' I said, as we ambled along, the heat making a faster pace impossible.

'A bit. It's nice, pretty,' Cal said.

'Nice. I guess that sums it up.'

'Is it weird to be back?'

'How'd you mean?'

'You grew up close to here, you said.' Cal kicked a can up the road and we watched it bounce before it settled, still protesting, on the grid of a drain. I lit a cigarette and Cal tutted. He hated me smoking and I'd tried, and failed, to quit several times.

'I wasn't here long, and I was away at school a lot. What's weird is that I kind of like it, coming back. Hope you feel the same way after you've been gone a while,' I said.

'You might have moved on by then,' he said.

'Maybe,' I said. 'You'll visit wherever we are? Even if it's only to get your washing done or ask for cash.'

He half-smiled, knowing and thoughtful. 'Not as if you aren't making loads.'

I bristled. It was true; the money was flowing in, thanks to the commercial work. The work I wasn't interested in; the work I first developed to pay Jim his regular silencer; the work that had driven me further and further away from my true purpose – my passion. 'I'm going to concentrate on the less commercial stuff more and more now. This latest is only the beginning,' I said at last, waving a hand over my face.

'Got to get more ideas first,' he said, dismissive, almost aggressively, or perhaps that was me, imagining things. 'One's not enough.' The talk of money reminded me of the look that had washed over him when Alan and I asked how he planned to spend the money we'd given him.

'You've no idea what to do with your money?' I said.

'Sounds like you don't believe me,' said Cal.

'It's not that,' I lied, 'it's just there must be something you want. A new set of drums?'

'Money can't get me what I want.'

My head span. I thought of that old song, 'Can't Buy Me Love', and my heart ached for him. A girl, it must be a girl. Someone he likes, fancies, can't have.

'You'll find someone in the end. Someone who sees you for who you are.'

'Underneath all this?' He waved his lovely ringed fingers over his face.

'If you like.'

He laughed, mocking and hard sounding. 'That's not what I meant, actually.'

'Then what do you want? Maybe I can help.'

We were at the top of the lane, ready to cross the main road. The traffic rushed by, oblivious.

'You can't. It's not about money, though it'll help,' he said, stepping into the road, careless, thoughtless, like a child.

I grabbed his arm and pulled him back as a white van flew past. Clouds of dust billowed round us.

'Then what is it?' I shouted above the roar of the traffic.

'This.' He pointed at his face. 'I want to change all this.'

Finally, I understood. I gripped his wrist.

'Don't have surgery, Cal. It's not the way.'

He shook me off. 'What? You're gonna tell me that I'm beautiful as I am, that what counts is what's on the inside? You don't even believe that yourself!'

'It won't turn you into who you want to be,' I said. The technology wasn't advanced enough to help Cal. 'Or who you think you want to be.' I thought of the Californian celebrities, actresses, porn stars, pop stars. Many of them were as freaky as Cal; they weren't lovely, far from it. They suffered from a form of body dysmorphia. They needed a therapist, not a surgeon.

'You're such a hypocrite. Look at you, your mouth has only just gone back to normal,' he said, bending his fingers in the air, aping quotation marks, '"whatever that might be," as you're always reminding me.' We stood on the pavement, facing each other, screaming above the sound of the traffic.

What he said was true. Six months earlier I'd had two injections of collagen in my top and bottom lips as part of a body modification and cultural norms project. I filmed the procedure and took photographs of my swollen, distorted mouth and juxtaposed it with images of tribeswomen with plates in their bottom lips.

'You call it art. Others call it abuse, mutilation,' he continued. 'And you can go back to being lovely. You already are.'

'Please don't do this. Not now. Not yet. You're still growing. Notions of beauty alter. Four hundred years ago I wouldn't have been considered pretty. You only think of me as pretty because you're surrounded by images telling you I am.'

'I don't want pretty, I just want all right, not hideous, grotesque. You can't stop me.' He was defiant. He looked back to the road, turned his head left and right. A break in the traffic and over he went.

I scurried after him. 'You'll never find anyone who'll treat you,' I screamed.

'Don't bank on it.'

On the other side, he walked in the opposite direction to the studio. I raced to catch up.

'I'll stop the cheque.'

He came to a standstill.

'It's easy enough,' I yelled. I was angry, and worried, and I wanted Cal to stay as he was. Altering him would

271

be like painting over a Jackson Pollock. He was interesting and challenging and absolutely fantastic.

He looked at me with such hatred I began to cry. 'I don't mean that, I'd never do that, I don't know why I said it.' My voice was cracked, barely audible. 'I love you. As you are. Please don't do this.'

I reached for his hand and he let me take it. I pulled him towards me and we hugged there, on the pavement, with lorries speeding by so fast the ground shook.

'No one else does.'

'They do,' I said, 'they do.'

Cal

I'm standing in front of the bathroom mirror at home in Hornsey, tucking my hair behind my ears. I'm back from uni for the weekend. I stop. It's better flopping over my face anyway. But with my hair falling straight my ears poke out. Shiny and pink, the cartilage is accentuated against the dark brown. My hair sits on my shoulders and I love it. Hated it all short after the surgery on my head as a kid. Head's still a weird shape, despite the doctor's efforts, but my hair disguises this a bit.

Diana appears behind me. She's reaching towards the cabinet for something or other. I forgot to lock the door. That's what happens when you visit home after you've left.

'Who do I get my ears from?' I say.

'What?' She finds what she's after: a bottle of bright red nail varnish.

'My mother or my father. More likely my father, yeah?'

I swear I see her wince.

'Do you know, I can't remember. Your father, probably your father. Your mother was lovely. Why?'

273

'Just wondering.'

I'm having my ears pinned back at the Sussex next week, and it's no minor procedure, even if it is "cosmetic". The operation'll take three hours. Bandages will be wrapped round my head and under my chin and they'll stay like that for a whole week. Another three weeks before I can stop wearing the bandages at night. So that my ears stay flush against my head.

It's all pretty complex and although the doctor's advised me to, I'm not going to stay in overnight. No way. I'll order a cab to take me back to my halls of residence. Those rooms are so different to anywhere I've lived before. Stuck in the middle of nowhere, all green fields and singing birds, though Brighton's only a short bus ride away. The town is well known for being open and accepting, and it is quirky, full of fruitcakes and people from London who came here to lick their wounds and never made it back. It's full of therapists and new age practitioners. I thought about going to university up north – Leeds, Liverpool, Manchester – but I didn't get the grades. Too busy arsing around with music and doing Diana's shows.

She was pleased when I flunked out. She wanted me to study in London, live at home. No way. A teacher suggested Sussex and though I'd never considered it before, I said I'd do any course they had a space on and that was that.

'He's not a child. Let him find his own way, Diana, let go. You can't control him forever,' Alan had said.

Diana doesn't know that I'm getting my ears fixed and this gives me such a buzz. Pathetic really.

I twist my ring round and round. I'm excited at how I'm going to look with flat ears. It's the first step.

~

'That's a beautiful ring. Was it a gift from a girlfriend?' Eve says.

I laugh, more like a snort, and say, 'No. You can have it if you like. It's not precious.'

She touches the silver chain at her throat and shakes her head. 'I couldn't.'

'Sure you could.' It is difficult to pull the ring off, but I manage it. The skin which the ring covered is pink and puckered; it looks like pig flesh against the rest of my hand. The mole between my fingers looks paler too. I wonder if it will ever disappear. Probably not.

I offer Eve the ring on the palm of my hand. She picks it up and holds it to the light. She hands the ring back. 'It's lovely but you must keep it.'

I push it back onto my finger – it was a lie to say it wasn't precious. It is, and it isn't, and it *is* beautiful. I stretch out my arm and admire my hand.

'Your hand looks like yours again. It seemed strange without the ring. Incomplete somehow.'

'I'd have got used to it,' I say.

~

The pub is empty – unusual for Brighton – except for a skinny girl with purple hair wiping down the long, semi-circular bar. She looks bored and doesn't even look up when Si says, 'We're here to set up. We're the support.' She waves a filthy rag in the direction of the stage and carries on.

There's a PA here so it doesn't take too long to drag the gear from the van and set up. I'm sitting behind my kit in no time, feeling the space, looking out over the area where there'll be an audience in a couple of hours. I pick up one of my sticks and stroke it, running my fingers along the smooth wood.

I remember the first time I picked up drumsticks, the weight of them, the sound they made when I tapped, then bashed the drum in front of me that was held with a thick nylon strap tied round my neck. It was such a simple rhythm: ba-ba-ba. Ba-ba,ba. Bababa. Bababa. Ba-ba-ba. Love at first beat. The noise filled the room, enclosing me. The vibrations came from inside the very centre of me, radiating upwards and outwards, and it was all about the feel of it and the sound of it. Nothing else mattered. I forgot where I was, who I was. The rhythm took over and it was only when someone grabbed my arm and physically stopped me from beating on and on that I came to and stopped. Mrs Neilson was staring at me and when I lifted my eyes they met those of the entire class, who stared at me, open mouthed, like guppies.

'My, my. You have a talent, Cal Brading. I do believe we lost you to the rhythm for a moment,' Mrs Neilson said, and a few people sniggered, but I didn't give a shit. I was going to be a drummer in a band. I knew that at twelve years old, even though I learned to play the guitar as well because that was what Diana wanted.

The pub smells of stale ale and stale bodies and the walls are littered with band posters. Some of the corners are curled and torn. Most of them have white space at the bottom with the venue, date and time hand written in black marker pen. Just like ours. Diana always encouraged my musical ambitions, though she was surprised when I finally told her I didn't want to be a guitarist.

'You're so good. And you'd get all the attention as lead guitarist.'

But I like it here at the back, tucked out of the way. I don't want attention. I was trying to get away from attention then and I am now. At the back, I'm able to lose myself in the sound. I set the pace, keep the band on track. I am the gel and I like it this way.

The audience are mostly students as we expected and as we're on first no one's pissed enough, despite the cut-price beer, to heckle or throw stuff. This has happened a couple of times. Si went mental – lead singer for you – but I thought it was a like a rite of passage; having empty cans thrown at you is something every band should experience. Anyway, although the audience are pretty restrained they seem like they're enjoying us and no one's pointed at me or any of that crap.

We're thrashing out our third number when I see a couple of women walk into the bar. They stand out 'cos judging by their clothes they're richer than anyone else in the joint. I've no time to take a good look at them, because the number we're playing is hectic, really full-on, but as it comes to a close and the audience start clapping I realise that one of the women is Diana. She's changed her hair again – dyed it black and put in extensions – and there are loads of people staring at her. She's still gob-smackingly beautiful. I have no idea who her mate is. Never seen her before. The hair could be a wig.

I start to sweat even more. It's hot in here but I'm sweating because Diana has pitched up. She's done this before and it pissed me off then, but nowhere near as much as it's pissing me off now. I told her the first time that I'd invite her if I wanted her to come and hear me play, and I can't work out how the hell she found out. This is a good gig, for Brighton, but it's not what you'd call prestigious or nothing and it's not as if it'd be advertised in *NME*.

I hit the skins harder and harder. So much so that in a lull between songs bass player Spike asks me to cool it a bit.

We go down well, playing two encores, and though I want to enjoy this feeling I can't. It's irrational but I hate that Diana's here. I feel like I'm on show again. When we're done I rush off stage and out the back, lighting a fag before the fire doors have swung shut behind me. Inhaling deeply I try to understand what's going on with me. I should be pleased; she's come to support me.

Or has she?

She likes to parade her attachment to me. But why here? I'm being ridiculous. Just get out there and say hello, you stupid bastard.

I smoke my tab so low that I nearly burn my fingers. The nail on my index finger is stained brown and I make a note to myself to scrub it off. Stained fingers and nails are totally repulsive. I throw the butt on the floor and grind it into the pavement so hard it disintegrates, the tobacco spilling from its skin like a dropped kebab. I stuff my hands in my pockets and stumble back into the pub.

Diana and her friend are deep in conversation with a couple of dumb-looking girls. Diana grips a handheld camera, one of those small ones that dads usually carry on holiday, and she is pointing it at the girls. The other woman is making notes, a small pad clutched in her right hand. Both Diana and this woman look really, really intense. I edge towards them; I'm not sure if Diana realises I'm approaching, she has her back to me. I overhear her saying, 'So the band were great. Did anyone of them in particular stand out?'

I stop and turn my back. I don't want to be seen now.

278

One of the girls says, 'The lead singer, Si. He's totally gorgeous, like.' The other one titters. Nothing new here. Si gets all the girls.

'So it's not just about the music, the look of the band counts too,' Diana says.

'Well, yeah,' the girls say, like Diana's a cretin or something. I think about leaving her to it, and I cast my eyes around the bar when I catch her saying, 'And what about the drummer? What did you make of him?'

'He was really cool, awesome,' says one, and I glow with pride. 'He's so fast, like Dave Grohl or something.'

'Yes, he is,' Diana says, as if she knows who Dave Grohl is. 'So you found him attractive?'

'Attractive?'

'You were attracted to him? His talent?'

The girl hesitates, as if she's just cottoned on that she's being stitched up. 'I thought you were talking about the playing.'

Diana waits. Says nothing. The girl fills the gap. 'He's not really my type.'

'So you noticed how he looks?'

'Sure. Hard not to.'

'And did you find it interesting?'

'It' – I'm guessing by that she means me. I turn around. The girl says, 'I'm really here for the music...' and she starts to move away. She sees me and raises a hand as if to warn Diana. But Diana still has her back to me.

'Thank you so much.'

This is my band. My music. This is more me than anything. Inky black floods my vision, like I'm going blind. I feel invaded. The girls are moving forward, coming

279

towards me, closer and closer. As they pass, the one who spoke with Diana says, 'You were awesome. Totally awesome,' and her friend dips her head, as if she's not looking, but poking out from under her long fringe her eyes are fixed on my face.

Diana spins round, arms outstretched and yells, 'The star of the show. You were awesome!' She sounds phoney, and all wrong, like old people do when they try to sound street, and it feels like half the bar spin and stare at me. Diana's colleague is scribbling away and I want to knock the pencil right out of her bony claws.

'Cal, meet Lucinda, my new assistant.'

Lucinda waves, the pencil held between her fingers. 'Aren't you a bit old for all this?' I say.

They laugh nervously and Lucinda says, 'You're never too old for great music.'

'Or too ugly.'

Lucinda laughs again, though it's more like a shriek. I stare at Diana. 'Why are you here?'

'Because I'm interested.'

I raise my eyebrows. 'C'mon, I know you.'

'I'm doing a project about youth movements, the look, the music, etc. Good excuse to come and see you...'

The Lucinda woman is looking at the floor.

'I'd invite you if I wanted you here,' I say, and Diana looks crushed. Bad, guilty feelings rise up. I hate to hurt her, but I can't help myself. I turn and walk back to the front of the stage where the headliners are getting ready to begin. The last thing I hear is Diana asking Lucinda if she got all that.

280

Diana

Bunny sat at a table in the shade outside the restaurant. This struck me as odd because she'd always loved the sun. Perhaps recent publicity about melanoma had scared her, though it was more likely that her ageing skin was the more stark and powerful reminder of the ill effects of heavy duty sunbathing.

She looked cross. I was late. A constant churning in my lower abdomen had slowed me down and I longed to fold at the hips and knees into a crouched position, there on the pavement. We'd not seen each other in years – her move to California an irresistible excuse, which we both used shamelessly. After our last argument we'd made up quickly enough, though such repair was rather like putting a plaster over a hole in a dam.

It was clear Bunny hadn't seen me and I resisted the urge to run away. I couldn't visit the west coast and not see her.

I checked my watch. There were only a couple of hours before Alan would join us. I took a deep breath, stood and crossed over.

When, eventually, I'd told Bunny that Alan and I

were living together, I wasn't sure she even remembered him. I'd reminded her she'd been introduced in Manchester, and after an embarrassing pause – neither of us had mentioned that God-awful evening at the warehouse gallery since – she'd commented, 'Oh that funny-looking lad with the Marty Feldman eyes?' I'd retorted, somewhat defensively, that he'd grown into his looks and, actually, many people found him attractive. I'd wanted her to be pleased for me, to approve. After all, she'd gone on and on about me needing a man for years. Admittedly, that was because she thought it would divert me from 'all that stupid art stuff', but still.

As I approached the mid-point of the road a nervous Californian driver, no doubt unused to pedestrians, slammed on the brakes and a high pitched screech pierced the air. Bunny spotted me. She waved. I scurried over and we air-kissed.

'Well, hi there, sweetheart. Don't you look like a top model?'

'I'm thirty-seven.'

'You're right. Way too old now. Missed your chance.' She pursed her lips; fine lines fanned round her mouth. She laughed, flicking her head round the restaurant. 'And keep your voice down. I don't want people here knowing I have a girl that old!' she hissed.

'No one would believe you anyway. You look incredible.'

She covered one side of her face, palm out, and whispered, 'Face lift. A gift from Bobby.'

Bobby was husband number three – a moderately successful cosmetic surgeon she'd met at an international beauty convention some years back. I'd never met him.

'Great,' I said, looking for the scars round her ears. It was good work, though she remained every inch a woman in her mid-fifties.

We ordered chilled water and wine from a waiter with a deep, resonant voice. 'An actor?' I asked. Bunny was on first name terms with him.

'All the waiters here are in show business. He's going to be huge. I went to see him in a play downtown. Horrible flea-bitten place, but he was fantastic! And that's not the only thing he's great at.' She winked at me salaciously. From then on I couldn't look at him. I didn't want to think of them together. If they'd ever been together; it might well have been Bunny's overactive imagination. Her grip on the truth had always been loose.

I glanced around at my fellow diners. Everyone was tall and groomed and beautiful. In the young it might have been natural, in the old and older it definitely wasn't. I felt almost plain.

I've definitely come to the right place.

'So, sweetie. Why are you here?'

'A project.'

She arched her perfectly plucked eyebrows and sipped at her wine.

'I'm talking to surgeons.'

'Talk to Bobby.'

'No offence but I need the best.'

'None taken. I can see you do need the best.' She peered over the rim of her wine glass which was now welded to her face, eyes blazing. 'No offence.'

283

'None taken.' I snatched my water and drank like a camel that had been stuck in the desert for months.

This meeting is a mistake.

After another deep breath, I explained that I planned on having saline implanted in my forehead and in my cheeks.

'Now, the cheeks, I understand,' Bunny said. 'But the forehead? Why, for crying out loud? Botox can sort those wrinkles out.'

'It's for a project.'

From the expression in her eyes she'd have furrowed her brow were she able.

'The procedure will be filmed. It'll be shown in the gallery alongside images taken once the work is complete.'

'Sounds disgusting.' She shuddered theatrically.

The project was an extension of one I'd begun three years ago with collagen injections in my lips and I hoped it would attract enough attention to put me back on the map. Despite the commercial success of some work, I was yet to receive critical acclaim for my riskier projects and, more generally, what little interest there'd been in me was waning; there were too many bright new things on the scene. A few critics had been grudgingly admiring of later pieces but not completely won over. Nothing had matched the response to my early 'Cal' work. It irked.

We reverted to small talk and ordered lunch. I chose risotto and Bunny opted for a salad, commenting that she worked hard to keep her figure and she wasn't going to let my couldn't-give-a-damn British attitude tempt her. She took yet another gulp of wine. Evidently her health-consciousness had not extended to alcohol, quite unlike our neighbouring diners who drank an algae-like sludge. Pond water couldn't have been less appealing.

'The freak still at home?' she said, after an awkward silence.

'His name's Cal. And he's twenty-one, so no.' I chewed my lip. I was desperate for a cigarette and longed to be in London, where you could smoke outside without people treating you like a leper.

'Don't be so touchy.'

The wine was taking its toll; it was going to be a long lunch. I took a sip of my own wine and bit my lip again.

She carried on. 'It's what he is. No matter how much you dress it up as ART. He's still just a kid with a mashed-up face. Poor bastard. Though he looks a bit better now. He had work done?'

'He doesn't need your pity. And what makes you think that?' I said. She'd hit a nerve. I didn't know if Cal had been under the knife. He'd denied it when I'd asked him but he'd a distinct aura of perfidy. He'd not looked quite himself, but I'd rationalised it, persuading myself I wasn't so accustomed to his face now that I didn't see him every day. Alan denied knowledge of any surgery but I didn't entirely trust him either. 'And how come you know what he looks like?' I added.

'I've seen pictures. I check the World Wide Web. You got that yet?'

'Yes.' I grinned. 'So you do follow my progress. World Wide Web, indeed. Get you.'

How closely does she follow my career?

285

My forthcoming project was already attracting some attention in the press, mostly along the lines of why would a nice-looking girl like this go out of her way to make herself ugly, and was it art? Although I'd asked them not to, they'd dug up photos of Cal and run them alongside some of my early works. One hack even called him on his mobile phone and tried asking him a few questions. Cal phoned me immediately hollering and screaming, telling me to keep him out of my work.

Bunny smiled, revealing a set of teeth so perfect they could have been dentures, spoilt only by a sliver of lettuce trapped between an incisor and her gum.

'So what do you think?' I said, pointing to my teeth and rubbing a finger along them. She didn't take the cue.

'What of?'

'My work.'

'It's OK.' She paused, reconsidering her answer, then continued. 'Honestly?'

I nodded.

'It's a bit weird. Mostly. Prints are nice. And you've proved me wrong; you make a living and at least you can do this when you're old.' She patted my hand, her heavy rings rapping my knuckles.

'You're right, and it makes me happy.' The tight feeling in the pit of my stomach disappeared, the ache at the base of my skull faded, though that might have been the alcohol. To hear Bunny say something positive about my work was astonishing, and wonderful. After all these years I still sought her approval. I wanted to please her.

We talked on, warmer with each other than we'd been in some time. I asked if she'd heard any local gossip or feedback about the surgeons I was visiting. I was genuinely interested in her opinion and she liked to feel needed.

Time passed swiftly enough. I couldn't believe it when Alan breezed over, bashing his head on the umbrella over the table as he bent to offer Bunny his hand. Her face lit up. She grabbed his hand and pulled him close. 'Give Bunny a kiss now!' She was drunk.

He sat down and without preamble Bunny launched in. 'So what do you think about your girl messing with her face like this and making herself all ugly?'

I winced. This was a conversation I did not want to have. Not here, not now.

Alan didn't approve of the project, though he'd never said it outright.

'I love her whatever she looks like.'

Bunny raised her eyebrows sceptically.

'But I do worry that there'll be permanent damage. So much of what makes us who we are is in our faces. It's the first thing people see, it's what people remember, mostly.' I thought of Cal and my heart clenched.

Bunny touched Alan's hand and said, conspiratorially, 'But what I don't understand is what she gets from this. People pay good money to have work done, to make themselves look nice—'

'That's the whole point! That's the point I'm trying to make. What is beautiful? Can we truly reinvent ourselves? Cosmetic surgery gives us the ability to make ourselves look different, sure. But better? Who's to say?' I was shaking again, feeling queasy.

'It can be abused, for sure, but it can also be used for

good,' Alan said, looking at me.

'I don't follow,' Bunny said.

He took a swig of beer, direct from the bottle, and a number of people stared. He turned to Bunny, though his comments were for me. 'Why is it OK for some and not others? The origins of cosmetic surgery lie in plastic surgery, repairing soldiers blown to bits. Surgery can be a force for good.'

Bunny nodded, attempting sage-like and failing. She was flirting with him. 'I see. Diana here wants to make herself look all ugly, but she won't let the fr—, Cal, look normal.'

'Bang on.'

I was livid. 'I do not want to inflict months, if not years, of pain and discomfort on someone I love and care for with no guarantees that the eventual outcome will be what he desires. No amount of surgery could ever give Cal the result he desires.' I grabbed the wine bottle from the steel bucket and poured myself another generous glass. The waiter came over and Alan ordered another beer.

'But it could help him look more normal,' Alan hissed.

'Whatever that is.' The craving for nicotine was overwhelming. I forgot where I was and pulled a cigarette and lighter from my jacket pocket.

'I'm sorry, madam, but you can't light that here,' the waiter said, more aggressively than he needed to.

That did it. I exploded.

'Explain something to me,' I spat, crushing the cigarette in my palm, sprinkling tobacco strings onto the white table cloth. 'Why is it that you can inject chemical warfare or the cells of embryonic tissue into your face in this crazy town, but try and smoke one lousy cigarette and you risk the wrath of the health police?' I only realised how loudly I'd been shouting once I'd finished. The silence was like a noose, closing in on me, the eyes of dozens of customers cut into me like disembowelling knives. A public execution.

The waiter called his manager who asked us to leave. I rubbed the remains of the tobacco from my sticky palms onto the table as I stood. Bunny refused and remained seated.

Alan steered me into a cab, one hand pushing at the base of my spine, the other clutching my elbow. I shook free and flopped into the back seat, arms folded, like a petulant child. As the cab pulled away, I looked through the glass at Bunny. She waved limply, an inane smile on her face, like the queen mother.

Alan and I sat silent and fuming as the cab weaved through the highway traffic.

In the hotel room I descended on the mini-bar and poured a double vodka. Alan went to object, then stopped. I drained my glass.

'Why do you always side with Cal, huh?'

He turned his back on me and peeled off his shirt.

Enraged further, I hissed. 'You encourage him to change his face. He is fine as he is. Just fine.'

Still Alan said nothing.

'He needs to love and accept himself as he is.' I took another miniature from the bar.

'You might consider following your own advice,' Alan whispered.

'What did you say? What do you mean?' Fuelled by vodka and pain, I screamed like a banshee.

I said terrible things.

Alan sat on the bed, head slumped, chin resting on his chest, and stared at his lap. 'I want Cal to be content,' he whispered, 'and if you love Cal, if you really care for him, you will help him.' He pushed himself upright and loped to the bathroom.

I gulped the second drink and lay on the bed, staring at the ceiling, listening to the sound of water filling the kidney-shaped tub. Tears pricked. There was a time when the sight of such a bath would have had us both whooping with delight. It wasn't so very long ago that we lay in a hotel bath the size of a small swimming pool, surrounded by scented candles, sipping champagne. The occasion? Nothing special, a weekend away, just the two of us; Cal had stayed at China's. The sex was languorous and light-hearted; two people who loved each other, shared the same values, knew what worked for each other, who were considerate and respectful. Afterwards we lay nose to nose, laughing, planning the evening ahead.

A hairline crack zig-zagged the ceiling. I struggled to remember the last time Alan and I had laughed together, let alone made love. He never came near me. The running water stopped and I heard the sloop of him lowering himself into the bath. I imagined the bubbles caressing his skin and my body ached for his touch. I closed my eyes. Tears trickled from my eyes, wetting my temples and hair.

The room was empty when I awoke. Disorientated, eyes swollen and tender, I staggered to the bathroom. There was a note by the basin: 'Gone to get some air. Back later. Don't wait for me. Will order room service or eat out. Al. x'

The kiss was scribbled out of habit, of that I was certain. There was no apology – we'd said cruel things – and I knew that Alan was not going to relent. To accuse me of not loving Cal enough hurt and I loved Alan less for saying it. But I was remorseful, and the fear of losing Cal's love was stronger than the fear of his possible disappointment. He needed to discover for himself what surgery could and couldn't do. I had to allow him to change.

I wasn't lost to Cal. It was time to show him how much I loved him. What I could do for him. And perhaps Alan would forgive me too.

Once my surgeon and I had talked through the project, I showed him a picture of Cal and asked if he could help. Who was I to stand in Cal's way? He was growing up – he was an adult – he would do it anyway. I wanted what he wanted. And I'd had an idea. A brilliant idea. The thought of asking Cal to play his part turned my insides to jelly, let alone thinking about what Alan's reaction might be, but it was too good an idea to let it go, not to try.

If the project came off and worked as I dreamed it would, it would make my career. It would establish the reputation I deserved. It might even win awards.

I had to ask Cal.

I had to.

Cal

'**Tomorrow.** Would you like to see the pictures again? To give you an idea what to expect?' Eve says.

I shake my head. I've seen them already.

'How about a manicure?'

I nod and she turns and opens the drawer where the kit is and then fills the finger bowl with warm water from the basin.

'Are you interested to see how I look under all these?' I point at my bandaged face.

'No,' she says, smiling. 'I know who you are already.'

'Really? You're not even a tiny bit intrigued?' I say.

'Of course. But it doesn't matter. What will your face tell me that I don't already know? Nothing.'

'You talk like you've known me for ever. It's been months.'

Eve takes my hand and lowers it into the water. 'In a way, I feel like I have. Did I say you remind me of my brother?'

I nod and close my eyes. Brother. I enjoy the

293

manicures, I like how my hands will look afterwards but it's the intimacy I like best. Especially the massage at the beginning. I want this to never stop. The roof of my mouth tingles, my muscles relax, my head feels light, like candy floss.

I fade back in time again, memories playing like music, like a song that no one knows how to finish.

~

I stare at my ring, the bands of love, before closing my eyes. I can feel the bandages being unravelled. The hum of the camera is the only noise I hear. I've had the first operation; the first Diana has paid for; the first that hasn't been a medical necessity but a choice.

She filmed her own procedures (not for the squeamish) but she took photos of mine. Frame after frame after frame. She wants to put it together like those dirty moving images in Edwardian fairgrounds, hundreds of photographs flipping, like a deck of cards, moving so quickly they give the illusion of movement. She's filming the result though. Here we are.

A thought leeches across my mind: I am like Faustus; I sold my soul for a better life, a new face. Except I cannot enjoy my new face before the debt is called in. Even Faustus was given time. I should never have agreed to this; it's all so messed up. I should have waited, done it on my own terms.

Diana stops the camera and asks the nurse to stop removing the bandages. 'Turn it on again when I give you the sign,' she says to her cameraman.

Switching her attention to me, she says, 'Cal, I'm going to start filming. Be natural, but when I ask you a question I want you to look direct to camera before answering. Have you got that?'

I nod.

The camera rolls again and the bandages are unrolled some more. I tighten at my core, with excitement, with anticipation. I'm desperately trying to contain these feelings; I don't want them to sense how hopeful I am.

The bandages are off; I'm exposed. I feel different, free, the air on my skin, but I cannot judge the reaction of Diana and her small crew.

'Cal, how do you feel knowing that we can see your new face and you cannot?' Diana asks.

'I don't feel anything. I'm too busy trying to read your expressions.'

Nervous laughter bounces round the room, like a reverb.

'Would you like a mirror?'

'I'm not sure...'

'It'll take some getting used to.' Diana again.

'This is only the beginning,' I say.

I am handed a mirror. It rests on my lap, face down, for minutes, or is it seconds? It looks like an antique, this mirror, like something from a woman's dressing table, ornately moulded silver, cool handle. A looking glass. I clasp it and lift the glass to my face. I like the weight of it, the pull on my shoulder. I'm trembling, the mirror shakes, and I feel like an idiot.

Diana must be making some kind of point, for the face I see reflected in the glass is still me.

'First reactions?' Diana asks.

'Little difference. Same old ugly me. Uglier in a way.'

My face doesn't fit anymore, like when we patch holes in jeans, across the knees or arse, and they no longer hang right.

'I look all wrong, more wrong.' I sound detached, as if I'm talking about someone other than myself. I try not to look but find I am pulled back to the reflection. My forehead is smoother but livid red scars and stitches criss-cross above and around my eyes. I look like a patchwork quilt.

I'm waiting for Diana to say something, for her film, for her project, but she remains quiet. The room is bursting with controlled disappointment.

The moment of seeing is so intimate, so personal, and yet it will be devoured by a public hungry for spectacle, for so-called reality, for humiliation dressed up as art.

Desperation to conform, to fit in, to be something else, has allowed me to be moulded and shaped like clay. I am putty. And I am like this because I want to please her, to help her. She has helped me so much. She has never quite fulfilled her potential. She needs me, she says. And if I love her, I will help her, she says.

~

'There, what do you think?' Eve says.

I admire my nails. 'Champion, champion.'

'You sound like my granddad!' she laughs.

'I was thinking about Alan. It's something he used to say.'

'He's not dead. He probably still says it.'

Silence.

'You miss him?'

'Yeah, but he changed. He hadn't used that word in

296

years. Circles he mixes in. It reminds me of my childhood.'

'You could get in touch,' Eve says.

'He'd tell Diana. He loves her more than anything; he couldn't help himself.'

'That must be nice.'

'Yeah.' Changing the subject I say, 'How's your brother?'

'He's OK. Early days.' She brushes her hands down the skirt of her uniform, brisk, ready to leave.

And all I know is that she's lying, glossing over the truth. We all do it. Over matters big and small, especially the big. It's a cliché but the truth can be hard to face.

Diana

'I can't believe you're doing this! This is blackmail! Have you lost your mind?' Alan stood in the kitchen. He'd been preparing supper, chopping rosemary picked from the garden, ready to lace over lamb chops. He held the knife and for one laughable moment I imagined him coming at me with it.

'What's the big deal? Cal gets what he wants. A world-class doctor working on his face, making it better. Me paying.' I drew quotation marks in the air with my fingers when I said 'better'. 'It'd take him years to raise the cash for the range of procedures Mr Campbell says he can perform. This way he gets it done as soon as he likes. As soon as possible.'

'But at what price? You're using him again. You've conned yourself into believing it's a fair deal, but it's not. It really isn't. We can afford to help him. He doesn't need to strike a bargain. It's not what we agreed.' He pointed the knife at me, like a teacher with a ruler.

'I agreed to help Cal.'

'So in return he has to help you? The project doesn't need him.' He drew quotation marks in the air when he said 'help', mimicking me, mocking me.

'It raises the bar.'

'Linda'll never agree to it,' he said, 'she never liked the way you used Cal in your work. She thought it was wrong – she told me. And I defended you. I thought it was OK at first. That Cal enjoyed it—'

'He did—'

'But he doesn't now.'

I'd often suspected that Linda and Alan talked when we all lived together in Hulme but I was secure in the knowledge that she would not be able to turn him against me. Alan loved me too much then. Blinded, some would say. I wondered if she'd ever confided her suspicions about me and Jim, what passed between us, for I was sure she'd had them.

'She needs this exhibition to be a success as much as I do. There's already interest from the press.'

'No bloody wonder. They can smell a kill.'

'The concept is awesome. One metamorphosis from conventionally lovely to abnormal, the other in reverse. It's perfect and it asks searching questions about the nature of beauty and ways of seeing,' I said, writing the headlines in my imagination.

'For God's sake. Get a grip. This is madness and it could destroy Cal.' He threw the knife at the bread board. It bounced off the wood and sailed towards the floor narrowly missing his right foot.

'Jesus! You might have lost a toe,' I said.

'Shame I didn't, you could have filmed it, taken a photograph, made a sculpture. Another abnormality to add to your collection.' He stormed out of the kitchen,

299

brushing my shoulder as he went past.

I telephoned Linda.

'Hey, gorgeous, can't talk right now. Give us an hour or so and call me back.'

'Can I pop in? End of the day?'

'Course you can. See yas.'

Linda was the new curator at the gallery in Mayfair where the exhibition was to be held. She hadn't booked me, her predecessor had. But then the curator's mother died unexpectedly and she moved back to Norwich to care for her elderly father. Would I do the same for Bunny if her health failed? When I was informed that the incoming curator was an up and coming northerner called Linda Kelly, I thought I'd misheard. I made the gallery owner repeat the name.

'Good for Linda,' I'd muttered, while he continued to reassure me that all was well despite the sudden departure of a woman who felt passionately about my project. 'Ms Kelly has vision and passion and I'm sure you two will click.' Assuming it was *my* Linda Kelly.

Back at college Linda had expressed a desire to work in the art world – she'd studied Art History after all – but when I'd encouraged her she'd backed off, claiming that she didn't have the necessary contacts, the 'right' skin tone or accent. Privately, I'd thought she was using the race and class card as an excuse, so I'd been delighted to hear that she'd finally gone for it and was on her way to making it.

I'd called in at the gallery unannounced shortly after her start date. I heard the voice before I saw her face, and

300

though the accent was more refined, the pace slower, I recognised it immediately. The mass of curls was unmistakable too. She was sitting at a messy desk, her back to me. I stood in the doorway, unobserved. When I saw her skinny arm replacing the receiver I stepped forward and tapped her gently on the shoulder. She spun, scowling, before a wide smile cracked her face. She leapt up and threw her arms around me. The hug was strong and firm. Her fragile exterior was deceptive. This girl was a rock.

'Friggin' hell, I've been dying to see you as soon I saw what they had on. I had to get this job. I worked my arse off to get it! I've missed you, I really have. Lemme look at you.' The intervening years melted away.

'You could have called. I'm easy enough to find,' I said, not meaning to sound peevish. I'd never quite worked out why we drifted apart. Had she guessed about Jim? Was that what had broken the friendship?

'I thought about it, I really did. But it was never the right time, and then it was too late. How the frig would I explain?' she said. 'Christ! How long has it been? Twelve—'

'More.'

'You've not changed a bit!'

'Nor you.'

She was lying, as was I. The way people do when they've not seen each other for years. Why do we do that? Because it's kinder than saying, 'Jesus, you look like an old person!' or because we don't want to hear the truth about what's happened to our face and body. If we lie, they lie, and there's comfort in pretending that nothing's changed.

She was still stunning; her quirks accentuated with age. 'It's fantastic to see you, it really is,' I said.

She filled me in on what she'd been up to. She pretty much knew what I'd done and though it wasn't all accurate she had the gist. She wasn't surprised that Alan and I had ended up together. 'He fancied your keks off from the start. He adored you. And he was what you needed.'

'And what was that?'

'Unconditional love.'

I'd forgotten how insightful she was, how straight forward, no messing around. I trembled when she mentioned Alan, frightened I might burst into tears. I didn't want to tell her that it wasn't exactly Paradise Found between us right now.

She'd never married. Many lovers – no surprises there – but no one special enough. Or rich enough. She was still looking, still hopeful. She'd spent years in the Far East running bars and clubs, involving herself in the design of the interiors, 'Territory I know well!' she laughed, but couldn't make anything like the serious money she coveted. And then she met an artist who liked the way she'd organised the paintings in the bar. He needed a curator for a show and he paid handsomely. One job led to another.

Desperate to get out of the house and talk through my new idea with Linda, I left early and hung round till she closed the gallery. Only a handful of people came through the door while I was there. 'I hope we get a higher footfall for my exhibition,' I commented, only half joking. Alan was right, the press would get their knives out.

'You'll pull 'em in. No problem. Fancy a drink?'

'You bet.' I needed a drink, for courage.

We went to a local pub, ordinary for such a swanky part of town, and though it was freezing I asked if she fancied sitting outside. 'We can chain smoke, freezing our fannies off, like old times.'

'I've given up,' she said. 'I'm surprised you haven't.'

It sounded like a reprimand. Perhaps it was.

'Old habits are hard to kick.'

'Tell me about it!'

We drank cider as in our college days, though it was classier, and pricier, than the lighter fluid we used to slurp, and we laughed a lot. After a couple of pints I felt bold enough to ask if she didn't get in touch because of something I'd done. She pursed her lips and looked at the inky sky, faking thinking hard, avoiding answering.

I leapt in. 'Was it because of Jim?'

'Jim?' She seemed genuinely puzzled.

'Breaking up? You never said what happened, not really.'

'Didn't I?' She dropped her head and wiped some slopped cider off the table with her fingers. 'You really wanna know?' Perhaps the alcohol was making her bold too.

I nodded.

'Because of Cal.'

'Cal?' Now I was baffled, and perturbed. My insides churned.

'I never thought it was right, what you did. You have a good heart and your intentions were good, you thought you were doing the best thing for him, but...' Her voice trailed away.

'But what?'

'You swapped one prison for another.'

Heart beating against my chest I stared at my drink. Shit. She'd never agree to the new direction of the show — charting Cal's journey to normality. My mind spun.

Did it matter if Linda didn't agree? Her predecessor booked me. I was more powerful than she was. She couldn't refuse, could she? Success and the certain media coverage would reflect well on her. She was as ambitious as I was, and as desperate for the financial reward a leap up the career ladder would bring.

She coughed. 'There I've said it. It sounds horrible and judgemental, and I love you really. And I knew you loved Cal. And I was jealous. You were going places. Me, I had a good degree—'she continued.

'Fantastic degree! You got a First—'

'And nothing else.'

'You've done well. The gallery's good, got a reputation, this is a real break,' I said. She had visions of becoming a major player, dizzy ambitions: arts boards, national galleries.

'I want serious money, respect, admiration. I don't want to be living in a poxy one-bedroomed flat in Hammersmith all my life,' she said.

'You won't be. This is an important step,' I interrupted.

'I quite fancy a big house in leafy north London.' She

glanced at me out of the corner of her eye, mischievous, her reference to my Hornsey home not so subtle.

It was the doorway I needed. I launched into my idea, afraid if I delayed any longer I'd lose my nerve. I presented it as a way of cementing both our reputations. I truly believed that could be the case.

At first she was wary, though she disguised it well, but was soon persuaded of the sense of my proposition, tempted by the publicity and notoriety it would bring. I explained how much Cal had enjoyed being part of my work, and that this project had the added benefit of giving him what he craved.

'Adding this new dimension to the exhibition will lift it to another level,' I enthused. After all, I'd been using my body as canvas for some time, and others had followed. But this?

'This is totally new. Totally innovative.'

After a long pause, during which the cold air bit at my gloveless fingers, she said, 'And Cal is definitely comfortable with it?'

'He's fine. It's what he wants.'

'That's what I'm bothered about.'

'This will be my last ever request. He'll get the face he wants.'

Her mouth twitched; she smiled. She finished her second pint and, staggering to her feet, asked if I'd like another.

I didn't. I wanted to go home, warm up, and see Alan and Cal. But she had no one to go home to. 'Sit down. I'll get them in.'

She lifted her empty glass. I raised mine and clinked

it against hers. 'To our mutual success!'

'Success!' she chimed.

As I stood at the bar I thought about what she'd said. About trapping Cal, using him.

Had I done that? I'd cared for him, loved him, educated him. Where would he be without me? I'd made his life better, hadn't I? He'd enjoyed being involved in my work; he'd enjoyed the attention.

But Linda's words echoed in my brittle skull and like a pop song played over and over on the radio there was an annoying, nagging ring to it.

I had not hurt Cal. Bunny hurt me.

I felt sick contemplating the possibility that I had not treated him as well as I should have. That was not my intention. I loved Cal.

But I had not asked Cal if I could record his journey as part of the project. Not yet.

With trembling hands I dropped crisps onto the sopping table before placing the glasses down.

'Cheers,' Linda said, as she stuffed a handful of cheese and onion into her mouth. 'Speaking of Jim...'

I shook my head, struggling to keep up, the alcohol muddying my brain. What was she burbling about?

Brushing a stray crumb from the corner of her mouth, she recognised my confusion. 'You mentioned Jim a while back?'

My mouth dried. 'Did I?' I cursed my stupidity. Why on earth had I mentioned him? She would never have brought it up otherwise.

But as it turned out she would have. Because Jim had contacted her since I'd last spoken with her. He'd read about her appointment in the paper. He'd not long been back in the country; been working abroad for years, he said.

Linda snorted. 'He must scan the local papers, hardly what you'd call big news! Anyway, he's dying to see you again. And Cal.'

I pushed the crisps away – my hunger had vanished – and took a sip of cider. It tasted sour, like vinegar.

I'd hoped I was rid of him, rid of his shadow across my life.

Months ago I'd stopped the payments which bought his silence about Cal's parentage when I'd missed a payment after changing bank accounts and he never came after me. I reasoned that he must have felt I'd paid my dues. We'd had no contact. But it seemed he was coming for me after all and I hoped it was only money he was after.

'I think I'm going to throw up,' I said and ran to the bathroom with my hand over my mouth.

Jim could ruin everything.

Diana

I avoided asking Cal for his permission to take photos before, during and after his operations for as long as possible. Cal was home from university one weekend when he announced he'd spoken with Campbell and arranged a date for the first operation. I forced myself to confront the issue. Alan had remained dead set against the project so I'd have liked to speak with Cal alone, but despite some heavy duty hinting, Alan hovered like a hornet, pretending to be busy, sorting through magazines, one pile to keep, one to throw away.

I explained the concept behind the project to Cal and why his participation would be useful, and how much it would mean to me. It would be the very last time I asked, I promised.

'Like a gift from you to me. An early Christmas present if you like,' I said.

Cal sat on the sofa, flicking through the TV channels, going round and round and round, never settling on one, never prising his gaze from the screen.

'And if I refuse you this *gift*, you'll withdraw yours,' he said, without emotion.

'You're under no obligation. You can refuse, or change your mind at any time,' Alan said.

'I won't withdraw my gift,' I said. 'We'll pay for the operations whatever you decide.' Hot and strangled by my polo neck sweater I tugged at the neck and glared at Alan. 'The heating's too high, it's mild outside,' I said.

Cal switched off the television and placed the remote on the seat beside him. He turned his whole body towards me and stared into my eyes. I felt exposed and vulnerable, the seconds before he spoke passing like hours.

'We'll share our pain for the world to see,' he said.

And despite the heat of the radiators I shivered. 'There'll be joy too, Cal. Especially for you.'

'And if I refuse?'

'You will have as much done as you need.' I corrected myself, 'as much surgery as you want.'

'But you won't ever love me in quite the same way again,' he said.

'Diana loves you, no matter what,' Alan said. I was taken aback by this burst of loyalty.

'I do. I will. Promise,' I choked, emotion rising.

'You'll want to, but you won't be able to,' Cal said.

Cal agreed and yet I felt neither relief nor joy: no relief that I wouldn't have to explain to Linda, my agent and other staff, to back-track on my promise of an incredible project; no joy that I would have the project I planned, the project I dreamed of.

I felt only sadness and a hard, hollow fist in my stomach.

Cal stood and walked out of the living room.

'There's nothing on telly. I'm off out,' he said, slouching from the room.

The impulse to run after him, to say, 'Forget it. Who needs the lousy project anyway, all I need is you,' was almost overwhelming.

Almost.

~

Despite my physical discomfort, I was pleased with the images and with the film of the surgery itself. After much debate, I'd had a general anaesthetic so the running commentary came from Campbell and not me, which had been my original intention. This made it less interesting, but there was nothing I could do. Campbell wasn't a performer. I looked simian in many of the shots, with my high, protruding forehead and raised cheeks. In some shots I'd bared my teeth and when the lighting was right, creating flat grey shades, I looked especially otherworldly, alien and menacing.

The shots of Cal were great too. He had undergone his second round of treatment when I'd had the surgery to remove the saline. He wore huge bandages wrapped round his head, his eyes concealed behind mounds of heather-coloured bruising, but we could see that his forehead was smoother and smaller. He should have been delighted.

Instead he was more withdrawn than ever.

He'd moved back home while the operations took place. It made complete sense, though we were taken aback when he said he wouldn't return to university once he was healed. When I asked why, he said, 'No point. No jobs anyway.'

He no longer played his drums.

Throughout the winter, into the New Year, Cal remained compliant and passive.

Grey.

He did little except watch daytime television and spent hour upon hour in his bedroom. He didn't seem to care about anything other than the operations and how they would change his life. I tried to prepare him, to remind him not to set expectation too high. There was only so much a surgeon could do.

I expected his spirits to lift once treatment was over and he began to heal but if anything he seemed worse. I meant to talk with him on so many occasions, encourage him to visit our GP, see his friends, work on his music, but I was busy, and up and down physically and emotionally with my own procedures. I never found enough space to seek out the true cause of his unhappiness. Every time I asked how he was, he shut me down with alarming alacrity, slamming doors behind him, sleeping for hours on end.

I asked Campbell if the operations might have an adverse effect on Cal's general health, particularly his mental health. 'Probably not,' he said, dismissive.

'General anaesthetics can make some people a bit low but they soon snap out of it.' Campbell was old-fashioned, an army doctor before he set up his private practice, he was all boot-straps and stiff upper. And he was driven by commerce. He wasn't interested in saving lives, improving lives even. He wanted to mould and create his version of perfect people, people who paid handsomely for his services.

I was in a permanent state of nervous tension and exhaustion. Every time the phone rang I expected it to be Jim. I left the answer phone on at all times and screamed at Cal on the rare occasions he went to answer it. In the studio, I unplugged the landline and turned off my mobile. At the gallery, I was twitchy and irritable. I stopped arranging to meet Linda there in case Jim pitched up unannounced, choosing a near-by pub or café instead. I focused on the work, and the publicity, spending most of my time away from home. Alan didn't want me around anyway. He wore his disapproval like a heavy scent. When I came into a room he left, as if I were a cat and he was someone with an allergy. I trailed round him for a while, getting under his feet, but still he paid me no attention.

Cal and I withdrew into our shells.

I'd asked Linda not to give Jim my number, explaining that I was keen to see him, but that I needed all of the operations out of the way first, that as soon as I was back to normal and the exhibition was sorted I'd organise a proper get together. She could give me his number and I'd contact him.

Of course, I didn't.

Periodically, Linda said Jim hassled her, checking that I wasn't avoiding him. I laughed these conversations off, telling her to tell him not to be silly, though the clenched fist inside my stomach grew bigger and bigger, tighter and tighter. It was stupid to delay seeing him; I'd have to sooner or later. I was a coward.

And then, after months of preparation and waiting,

the exhibition opening loomed and I realised just how foolish I'd been, delaying our 'reunion'.

Jim had the potential to ruin months, years, of hard work. Cal seemed more vulnerable than ever. I couldn't protect him. He was ripe for the picking.

Diana

Daffodils peppered the garden with colour. Each day more and more bloomed, trumpeted a vibrant hello to the world, but despite the floral brigade's best efforts I remained miserable. My face was sore; red marks ran down the sides, along the hairline, like road markings on a map. Black stitches laddered my forehead. The keyhole marks on my cheek where Mr Campbell had sucked out the saline were raised and angry. I'd had the solution removed from my forehead and cheeks in one hit, against Campbell's advice, and I was paying the price. I felt lousy, but there was work to be done. The exhibition opened next month.

It was hard to believe that my face would repair itself in time. Campbell assured me it would, though I'd grown my hair to cover up the marks round my temples as a precaution. It was almost shoulder length, longer than I'd had it since art school and I liked it. It made me look younger and it was one of only a few things about me that Alan approved of. Linda joked that I should have asked for a face-lift while Campbell was stitching me back up.

'I'm going to age gracefully. Disgracefully, actually, but there's no way I'd have surgery,' I said, appalled.

'You're kidding me, right?' she said.

'No way. I do it for art and that's all. I make no judgement about others. That's up to them. Anyway, I'll have had my fill of hospitals and medics by then.'

'Maybe not. I reckon that by the time we're old ducks everyone'll be doing it. It'll be available on the NHS.'

'Linda, there won't be an NHS when we're crones if Blair has his way.'

'There'll always be healthcare of some sort.'

'Love your optimism. Cosmetic surgery has nothing to do with health,' I said. 'Clue's in the name.'

'Wrong,' she said, emphatic. 'Mental health. It has a huge impact on mental well-being.'

'Nutter,' I said, laughing and pulling a face. My smile soon faded.

~

Alan came into the bathroom as I lay soaking in a deep, frothy bath, the scent of lavender and geranium billowing in the moist air. I sank underneath the surface, relishing the tingle of pain as the hot water hit the tiny scars at my temples and on my cheeks; it felt like penance for something, some hidden, unspecified crime.

'All ready for your big night?' he said, as I emerged from the foam, sweeping water from my face, up and over my head. I scratched at my scalp, as if I were shampooing my hair. Anxiety rubbed at more than the fear of a negative reaction to the private view.

For almost a fortnight I'd been calling Jim, trying to

organise a meeting. But it was Jim's turn to avoid me. The gnawing fear that he would make himself known at the opening had grown steadily – it was Jim's style, ruining big nights. At least Cal wasn't going to be there.

It hadn't been part of the deal: Cal making an appearance.

His recent depression had deepened, he was even more withdrawn, and I worried about him in a way that I'd not done since Pru's death and the prospect of him being placed with a family who neither cared for nor understood him. Or, worse, ending up with Jim. I pledged to address it once the exhibition opened and I had more time. To find a therapist, a professional who could offer the help he needed.

Alan closed the lid of the toilet and sat down, fiddling with an elaborately spun silver ring he wore on his marriage finger. He'd bought it in a mining town in Mexico, on a working trip. He'd bought one for me too, joking that if I wouldn't marry him I could perhaps wear a ring so that only the most brazen lechers would come onto me when he wasn't around. I'd commented that wearing a ring attracted a different breed of man: those who liked a challenge.

Men like Jim.

I sat up in the bath, shy, my breasts floating on the water's surface, visible as the bubbles disappeared. It had been a long time since he'd seen me naked. I was about to comment to what did I owe the pleasure of his company but I didn't trust myself to control my voice so kept schtum. I ached for a big, generous hug. To be wrapped in those long, bony arms, to feel the flesh of his belly against mine. I looked at him, vulnerable, full of longing, then like a fly hitting glass I bounced away and folded my arms across my chest. The air felt cold against my wet skin. I could smell his aftershave and although it wasn't a favourite it was a comfort.

'Diana,' he sighed, 'can't you tell me what's wrong? Have we come to this... This silence?' His eyes were liquid. He sounded like a distant relative, formal, but concerned. Uncertain I would confide.

I felt my bottom lip tremble but I could not push the words out. Like fishhooks they pierced my throat and caught. He continued, 'I'm worried about Cal. I've tried to get him to see a doctor. You are too. Is that it? Or is there more?'

We dared to look at one another. Still I could not speak.

He went on, determined to elicit a response. 'He's clinically depressed. I am certain of it. He shows no emotion, about anything. Not even the surgery now. Yet his expectations remain unrealistically high. Campbell is filling his head with all kinds of baloney, encouraging him to undergo more work.' I wanted to laugh at the archaic 'baloney'. It was a word his father must have used.

Is he turning into his father?

He would never know. He was older now than his father had been when he died, was killed.

Does it matter that he never really knew his father?

A high-pitched cry split the air. Had it come from me? Alan looked at me with a crumpled brow, shook his head, and decided to ignore my bizarre outburst. He was

317

probably considering having me sectioned.

'We need help. We are not equipped to deal with this. When I suggested he lay off the surgery for a while, to give his bones a well-earned rest, he hit the roof. It showed some emotion, I suppose. But he was unhinged. I think he's unstable, I really do.'

Still I was unable to unlock my voice.

Alan stared at me, the floor. 'Man, I need to go and listen to some music,' he said, eventually. He stood, rubbed his palms over his face. 'He should go back to his music, to unlock his emotions, his loneliness, his despair. It works for me, always has done.'

'You were listening to *Your Love is King* when we first met. Do you remember?' The words were mine, but it was as if they came from elsewhere, from the end of a long tunnel. Tears welled in his bloodshot eyes, and I studied his face. I recalled his big, stupid, gormless face as it was almost twenty years ago when he opened the door of his scummy flat in Hulme, all frilly shirt, tatty trousers and outsized boots. Alan knew about loneliness and longing and getting through, becoming strong, learning to laugh through the pain.

He started to sing, badly. A soppy love song.

He was smiling, tears falling down his cheeks, voice quivering like an end-of-the-pier crooner.

I love you.

I'd always thought, like just about everyone I could think of, that ours was an unequal love. That he loved me more than I could ever love him. I was wrong, everyone was wrong. He loved me, I loved him and I needed him much, much more than he needed me.

The distance between us didn't seem so vast after all. It wasn't irreconcilable.

'What's happened to us, Al?' I began to cry.

He let me cry myself dry, and when I shivered, he helped me clamber out of the bath and wrapped me, like a child, in a towel. It was the one lying on the floor, the dirty one I'd kicked out of the way ready to put in the laundry bin. He was a slob, and I didn't care.

He steered me into the bedroom, sat me down on the edge of the bed. He peeled off his clothes before kneeling on the floor in front of me, resting his face in my lap, kissing my knees and thighs, the stubble on his cheeks and chin caressing me. I ran my fingers through his tousled hair, gripping it at the roots and lifted his head to kiss him.

He tasted salty and fresh and exciting. Our bodies pressed together, mine still damp and cool, his warm and inviting. Our fingers ran over each other, exploring, as if we had returned to a favourite room and were checking that much-loved furniture was still in place. Rivulets of water ran down my back. I ached for him to fill me with his energy and love. A great part of us had altered and yet so much was very much the same. Underneath the ageing skin was the man I'd fallen in love with. The man I still loved.

There was a comfort in the familiarity of his form. I remembered the first time we made love: it seemed so normal and right and good. It hadn't mattered that we were clumsy, out of step with each other, banging limbs and teeth with our inept fumblings. We'd laughed and we'd kept trying. That's what we'd forgotten to do: keep communicating, keep sharing, keep trusting, keep trying. I had known no other for almost fourteen years and wanted no other for the rest of my life.

Afterwards, we lay facing each other and I told him everything. What Jim had told me by the canal. The money I'd paid for his silence, all these years. How he'd been in touch with Linda, wanted to see Cal and me, that I had sex with him when he was seeing Linda, that I was frightened he intended to reveal everything, that he might even pitch up at the show.

I cared how Linda might take the news, the betrayal; I cared how Alan might take it. I was no longer his perfect, golden girl. But mostly I cared how the truth, if it came out, might affect Cal.

'You've not been my golden girl for a while. You're as imperfect as the rest of us, but I love you.' He held my head in his hands and kissed my forehead. 'But what were you thinking? His father. Keeping him away from blood. You have to tell him.'

'He's had a better life with us.'

'He might not see it that way.'

'Cal might not believe Jim.'

'We don't know that he'll tell him.'

'I've been stupid. Selfish. Greedy. Controlling. Ugly. Just like Bunny.'

Alan held my shoulders. 'You wanted to help, make things better for Cal. And you did, mostly. It's not too late.'

'I'm not so sure. And what about us? Where do we go from here?'

'We'll find a way,' he said.

'Let's hope we've not left it too late.'

'Don't be ridiculous. You're the light of my life. Now take a shower otherwise you'll be late for your own show.'

~

Dressed in a fifties frock complete with underskirt netting and kitten-heeled pumps, I stared at my reflection in the floor to ceiling mirror at the exhibition entrance. Across my mouth a gash of scarlet red, matching gloss on my fingernails. I was Marilyn crossed with one of the Italian sirens: Lollobrigida, Loren. If I was about to meet my nemesis at least I looked damn good. Alan stood by my side, his mobile in his palm.

As agreed, Cal wouldn't be joining us.

He'd disappeared as I was showering in the upstairs bathroom; Alan had been in the en-suite. As I'd towelled myself down I'd heard him on the landing, talking on the phone, then padding downstairs. I'd called out. 'You OK?'

'Yeah. I'm meeting China for a drink. Back later. Hope it goes well.'

He'd sounded happy, unnaturally so. I registered surprise that he was meeting China; he'd not seen her in months and I was about to ask how she was when I heard the front door slam. He'd gone.

Alan checked his watch. The gallery was rammed. Almost everyone who'd been invited had arrived. I was due to speak in thirty minutes. There were media people, arts administrators and policy makers, and a representative from probably the most influential privately owned gallery in New York. People milled, drinking, chatting, studying the work. There were appreciative nods and chin stroking, a few ughs (always a bonus) and one couple left almost immediately. A great sign.

My scalp was tight with tension.

Linda was nowhere to be seen and none of the staff had any knowledge of her whereabouts. I worried that she'd been hit by a car or something similarly melodramatic. Trying to memorise the speech I'd written only hours earlier, I kept one eye on the important people, remembering who to make a point of chatting with, and simultaneously kept a look out for Linda.

And Jim.

Jim might turn up.

Linda's assistant Felicity – a charming, empty-headed girl who looked fresh enough to have come straight out of secondary school, though in fact she'd recently left university – had spoken with Linda three hours ago and Linda had said that she'd be at the gallery for six.

Frantic, I scanned the space.

Alan squeezed my fingers reassuringly. He wandered off, to check the microphone – again – leaving me hovering at the door. I looked down at my shaking fingers and when I glanced up there was Linda, wild-eyed, her lips pale. Something was very, very wrong.

She grabbed my hand; she was ice cold and trembling. 'We need to talk. Now,' she said.

'Let me tell Alan.'

'Now.'

Terror robbed me of my voice. She was breathing heavily and the stench of tobacco hung around her. She pulled me through the crowd and upstairs, nodding and smiling efficiently and politely at the great and the good. I caught Alan's eye and gestured that we'd be back in two minutes. He gave me the thumbs up but his feigned cheerfulness wasn't convincing.

She knows. She knows.

In the office Linda opened her bag and pulled out a packet of cigarettes. I pointed lamely at the 'No Smoking' sign on the door. 'You've given up,' I said, voice cracking.

'Bollocks to that.' She handed the packet to me, lit up, inhaled deeply.

Perhaps she doesn't know.

She offered me a fag.

'I couldn't see who it was. The camera's busted.'

I shook my head. 'What?'

'I was getting ready when the door went. I'd never have let him in.' She took another deep draw on her cigarette.

'Jim?'

'Who else? He must have pressed all the flats' buzzers 'cos some pillock let him in. Next thing I know he's hammering on my flat door.'

Although surprised and a little suspicious – she'd not told him where she lived for one thing – she felt that she had to let him in. He marched through the living room and before she could object he lit a cigarette and sat at the table in the kitchen.

'"Thought you'd have somewhere bigger, posher like," he said, sneering at my kitchen. We made small

323

talk for a while, reminisced about Manchester, the usual crap. We'd been through it all before when we met for a drink,' Linda said.

I'd wondered why he didn't tell her then.

'He seemed to be making himself at home so I told him he needed to make himself scarce because I was off out. Polite, like.

"Going somewhere nice, are you?" he said, but he knew where I was going. With his free hand he pulled an invitation from his jacket pocket, turning it between the fingers of his skanky hands. I didn't even bother asking how he'd got hold of it. Once a thieving git, always a thieving git.'

She took greedy, shallow puffs on her shrinking cigarette.

My legs weakened and I sat on the chair facing the computer. 'So he'll turn up here.' My voice wobbled.

'But that's not the whole problem,' she said.

'Jim asked me for Cal's number. I lied and told him he didn't have a mobile, but he wasn't buying it. He sniggered and said that my loyalty to you – "the bitch" – was admirable, if misguided. I had no idea what he was talking about!'

'Linda, I'm sorry…'

'He recounted, in graphic, crude detail, what happened in the flat in William Kent, with you.'

I went to speak again, but Linda raised her hand. 'Like I give a shit. I knew he didn't love me. I wasn't even sure I liked him by that time. It was lust. I forgave you a long time ago. And right now there's no time to rake over old ground. It's history. It was such a cheap trick; I was so angry. I told him to go fuck himself.' For the first time since she'd begun the story her voice wavered. She paled and twisted a section of her gorgeous hair round and round her index finger.

'Linda?'

'He pulled a knife on me. A knife, Diana. He said he'd have his son's number whether I liked it or not. His son? I hadn't a clue what he was talking about and I was so scared I staggered backwards into the washing machine. He came right up to me – I can still feel the blade on my neck, the washing machine dials pressing against the back of my thighs, smell his rancid breath – and he laughed, saying that got me, didn't it? Little miss know-it-all.' She started to cry. I wanted to go over and comfort her, but my legs wouldn't move.

'I asked him, why now? Why not years ago? He snorted and said that he was busy trying to carve out a career for himself. I tell you what, Diana, I was shit scared but I still laughed at that, couldn't help myself. Career! He pushed the knife in a little – I can't believe it didn't cut me – and said it was all wrong, that you'd made a mint out of Cal while he didn't even have a bed every night. He was crazed. It's all been twisted and mangled in his warped brain. Never mind that he didn't give a toss about Cal, not unless you count throwing him a few sweets from time to time, that you've got talent, you've worked hard.'

Guilt seized me. I had made money out of Cal. Would I have got where I was without him? He was my muse, my inspiration.

'Not all my work involves Cal,' I said, gripping the

325

edge of the desk.

'I know that. He's crazy, deluded. And dangerous.'

Jim took Linda's phone, forced her to call Cal, to introduce him, before snatching the phone from her, and taking her keys from her handbag, trapping her in her own home by locking the mortis.

'I could hear him speaking to Cal. His voice fading as he went down the stairs. It took forever to get out. Banging on the flat door, hoping someone would hear. Lost my mind in the panic. Eventually, I came to my senses and called the freeholder on the landline. He took ages...'

I stopped listening. I wanted to be sick.

'He'll come here,' said Linda, 'Jim'll ruin everything we've worked for. Where's Cal?'

'He took a call while I was in the shower, said it was a friend...'

We looked at each other, both drawn, cheeks pinched. Her lips were dry, eyes black.

'Is it true that he's Cal's dad?'

A tear rolled down my cheek. 'I've no reason to believe he isn't.'

Composing herself she said, 'We have to get back downstairs. We've worked hard for this, that bastard's not going to ruin it. Cal might not even believe him. He's a lot of explaining to do. Father! Huh.'

I wiped away my tears, found my legs and we returned to our guests.

* * *

Downstairs the minutes creaked on. I delivered a shaky speech to a voracious audience and mingling in the crowd afterwards, I allowed myself to hope that perhaps Jim wouldn't come.

Engaged in conversation with a famously shy fellow artist I noticed two figures looming in the doorway. A murmur rippled across the room. Heads turned to look at the source of such excitement but I didn't need to look closer. I knew. I made my apologies and walked towards the open gallery door.

A crescent moon hung in the sky on its back, like a mean smile, mocking me. Jim draped an arm across Linda's stiff shoulders, and I wondered if he pressed a concealed knife against her ribcage with the other. Cal had already made his way across the floor to view the exhibits.

He had not seen any of them; he had shown no desire to, and I'd not encouraged him. He brushed people aside, ignoring the tutting. A sensation that was almost palpable spread amongst the audience, like an itch. People turned and stared, twitching – Cal, the real live work of art. There were many who had met him on a number of occasions, the first time as a boy, but their curiosity was as fierce as the next person's. People never tired of staring at difference, abnormality.

Even at a distance, I felt Cal's rage. I shrivelled, disintegrating with shame. For much of his life he'd tolerated such voyeurism, to please me. The audience parted as he swept by, as if his appearance might be contagious. He gave the images of me the most cursory of glances, ignored the film entirely, and paused in front

327

of the photographs of himself, before and after surgery. I approached Linda and Jim.

'Diana, nice to see you. You've done well for yourself. With Cal.' Jim whispered Cal's name. He held out a hand and I felt compelled to shake it, for appearances' sake. The same rough fingers, cheap rings. His nails were bitten. I wondered where and why he'd acquired the habit. The ends of his fingers were splayed and wide.

'Thank you. Linda said you traced us, wanted to drop by,' I said, mindful of flapping ears.

'It wasn't difficult.'

'I imagine it wasn't. What took you so long?' I waited for a reply but none came.

Instead Cal's voice cut across the room. 'Do you think I look better or worse than her?' He was pointing at an image of me and addressing a young, trendy couple whose expressions were a mixture of horror and deepest social agony. They looked like nice, gentle urbanites who would never be deliberately unkind to animals or children.

'Well?' Cal said. 'Uglier or prettier? It's a straightforward question.' He sounded as if he'd been drinking.

'Just different. Both unusual, interesting, challenging conventional norms of beauty,' said the woman, reciting the brochure blurb, a tight smile painted across her flawless, anodyne face.

'Not good enough. That's fudging it. Oi, you over there. Bloke in the bad tracksuit top. Yes, you in the green. What do you think? Or you? Or you? Or you?' Cal was spinning now, pointing at people and asking them to choose. All those who'd flocked round Cal to take a closer look, to introduce themselves, engage in conversation and have a good gawp, were regretting their nosiness. Those polite and afraid enough to keep their distance were smug.

'Cal, Cal. Neither is better or worse than the other, that's the whole point. You know that,' I said, taking him by the arm.

He shook me off and in a louder voice than ever said, 'I don't, Diana. I don't know anything anymore. Even when you're making yourself ugly, you're prettier than me. More NORMAL than me.' Everyone was staring at us. 'Wouldn't you agree?' He began pointing aggressively at people again.

'Beauty's in the eye of the beholder,' said Alan, who'd come to my rescue. A knight in shining Levi's.

'Is it fuck! You could chip away at me for a lifetime and no one would ever say I was pretty. C'mon, admit it, you bunch of fucking cowards. People like me make you feel better. Thank God it's not me, you think, AND you get to feel good about yourself when you're nice and kind and sympathetic to the freak. You're no better than those people who slinked down the side of the London Hospital, sneaking a peep at poor old John Merrick. Nice, polite, ever-so-grateful Mr Elephant Man. Wouldn't have had so much sympathy if he'd been a bit of a bastard though, would he? Or even if he was a nice guy but a bit of a bastard from time to time? Normal, you know. Like you smug-fucks.'

'That's enough, Cal. Let's get you home,' Alan had

hold of Cal's arm, but Cal resisted, the drink giving him a strength and flexibility that made him as slippery as an eel. Alan lost his grip. Cal moved towards Jim.

'And where exactly is that, Al? 'Cos this gent here,' he said, nodding towards Jim who stood unmoving on the side lines, 'says that I have family. Family that cares, that want me for who I am, not where I can get them, career wise.'

'Get him out of here,' I hollered, stepping forward with Alan. We held Cal's arms and manoeuvred him towards the door, pushing past journalists who scribbled in notebooks and babbled into dictaphones. Jim folded his arms across his chest and smiled. Journalists walked towards him.

The cold air seemed to stun Cal, like a slap across the face, and then he became loose and floppy, like a rag-doll. Alan flagged down a cab and we bundled him in.

'Can't take 'im if he's drunk, mate,' said the cabbie. ''E might be sick in me cab. Never get rid of the smell.'

'Triple your fare,' I said.

He shook his head.

'Quadruple it,' said Alan.

'Done, mate.'

And we were off.

At home we had to drag Cal in, locking the mortis behind us. He didn't want to stay; he banged his fists on the wooden door and I thought he might break it, such was the force. Worn out, finally he staggered into the living area where Alan and I waited like dead men walking, shuffling to and fro across the room, wringing our hands.

330

'Is it true? Is that man my dad?'

'Cal...'

'I remember him. He visited me, he was kind. He brought me food and videos, told me stories.'

'Cal...'

'So it is true. And you knew.'

I hung my head. There was nothing I could say.

'He said he wanted to take me, after my mum died. But you wouldn't let him. You wanted me for yourself, and for your art. To use me 'cos of the way I look. He's spent years looking for me—'

'It wasn't like that,' said Alan.

'And how the fuck would you know? You said my dad was in prison and he wanted you to take care of me, to give me a better life. I believed you. I was a child.' He was crying.

I remained silent. I could not, would not, tell him the truth: Jim hadn't wanted him, and he still didn't, not really. How could I tell Cal that his own father had abandoned him? Used him to blackmail me? To line his pockets?

I loved Cal the most; I'd proved it, hadn't I? I fought for him. The law agreed.

Jim could have come after Cal sooner. We would have been easy to trace. Jim didn't care. He didn't love Cal. I did.

I didn't point out the obvious flaws in Jim's story. Cal was intelligent, thoughtful. He'd sober up and work it out for himself.

And as we stood there in our comfortable, stylish front room on that April night with a mean moon

331

watching us through the French doors, I admitted I had done wrong by Cal.

He loved me unconditionally, as I had Bunny when I was a girl. But my love for Cal was conditional, and as children do, he sensed that my love came with terms, and he did all in his power to make me love him. He did my bidding, as I had for Bunny. For sure, I had a father, though he cared almost as little as my mother, or was unable to show it, and I had my looks. My good looks enabled me to feel the love and approval of people – strangers – albeit a superficial, fickle kind of love, and even though I abused that gift, making myself ugly, hoping that people would see beneath the surface to the real me, I had my beauty to fall back on and did so time after time.

I'd spent half a lifetime blaming the way I looked for my insecurities. Was I talented enough, good enough, clever enough?

But I was insecure because I wasn't loved enough as a child.

I had deceived us both. I would never be grotesque. I always chose to return to 'normality'. Cal had a chance at normality but I'd held him back by not allowing him to transform. I was as reliant on his looks as my own. I had given Cal the wrong kind of love.

I sat on the leather sofa and cried. For my lost childhood.

But most of all, for Cal.

Cal

Darkness shrouds the room in a misty grey. I have been lying awake for hours. Mr McKenzie is delighted with my progress and soon, within hours, I will see my new self.

My head is crowded with memories, especially those I have worked hard to forget. They burst in, uninvited, gatecrashers at a party. Some are visceral, like cobwebs catching in my hair and face as I push my way through the undergrowth, others sharp and brutal, brightly lit like a gallery or studio.

I hear Linda's voice, like an echo. 'There's someone who wants to talk with you.' She sounds odd – strangled.

'I'd love to see you,' a male voice says.

Love to see you. The expression amuses me momentarily because everyone loves looking at me, the freak, but no one loves me. My curiosity aroused, I agree to meet him, this man from my past. I long to escape from the house, from all the talk about the exhibition.

Diana is pleased with it. She is excited and nervous and frantic. She has forgotten about me and how I feel; it's all about her now. She is upstairs making herself beautiful. She will draw gasps of admiration from the men and envy from the women. I desire her and I hate her, and most of all I hate myself. For allowing this to happen. I did not have to agree.

I am a mess; an ugly bastard tied to the woman who created me, a modern-day Frankenstein, who doesn't know who he is and where he belongs. The procedures were a mistake, a waste of time and money. They didn't make me look like everyone else, and now even more people will be looking. I think about killing myself again. I could do it this time, I really could.

The man in front of me is tall, a bit overweight; there is a thickness around his middle that the loose shirt cannot disguise. I notice that he has a wattle, like a turkey's neck, and small creases at the sides of his head before his ears. He has no hair. I do not recognise him. Not one bit. After we talked on the phone, all I could conjure was an image of a thin man with yellow hair and flat vocal tones. He extends his hand and I notice the cheap rings before the bitten fingernails and know that it is him. The rings.

'I'm your father, Cal,' he says. He looks tense.

I'm silent. I can't look at him. Instead I look round the shitty café. The walls are covered in wood panelling, orange and shiny with too much varnish. Pictures hang on the panels: poorly executed countryside scenes, paint-by-numbers horses. It stinks of chip fat. Muzak buzzes at my ears. I hear the rattle and crash of the kitchen beneath his words. He is talking at me. I'm only half listening.

Stories of Manchester and midnight walks and regular visits.

I remember these things but it is Diana's voice I hear, not his. He talks of needing to work, to go away, not wanting to. The waitress hovering behind the counter looks tired. She holds a cloth and swipes at the counter with relentless monotony. I catch her eye and she turns to the clock hanging above her head. The day is over; she wants to go home.

'I've spent a long time looking for you,' he says.

This time I look at him. A child again, I remember the sweets he brings and the shape of him in my blackened room. The feel of his leg against my chest is powerful.

Standing up to leave, I take his hand, this man who claims to be my father, and pull him towards me in an embrace, excusing his stiffness as a sign of a man who rarely hugs other men. I don't understand why I do this. He pats my back and eases me away, saying, 'What 'ave they done to you, Cal?'

Shaking, I tell him I have to go. I hurt all over. He tilts his head and smiles. Says he'll come too.

Dawn is breaking. I climb out of bed and open the blinds. The sky is like cherry blossom; it's going to be a beautiful day.

Lying back down I close my eyes and wonder if my lack of sleep will show in my new skin.

The clock on the side table reads five forty-five. Soon the night shift will be over. I hear the click of the handle, the door opening and sit up. It is Eve, with dark circles round her eyes. She's been up all night with her brother. He's gone off on one again, I bet. I'm surprised she's here.

335

'Big day,' she says, holding onto the handle, leaning forward. She does not enter. 'Buzz if you want anything.'

'Cheers.'

She probably can't wait to have a butcher's at my new face, despite what she said about not caring, about knowing who I was inside. Just like everyone else, she can't resist the opportunity to take a good look at the freak. Why I am so horrible? Eve is lovely; I like her; I trust her. I am as ugly beneath the skin as above.

~

When I am certain Alan and Diana are asleep, I step out into the sharp night air and head for Linda's flat. He called me from Linda's phone earlier. She will know where he is. It is late and the tube has stopped and I don't know the night bus routes so I walk. My hangover kicks in. It is dawn before I am pressing the bell by the wide door with coloured glass in the panels. A voice crackles through the intercom, it buzzes and I am in.

Linda offers me a coffee. I refuse. She looks terrible. It must be one hell of a hangover she's got. She warns against searching for him, says I shouldn't expect too much. He's had a hard life; he is a hard man. I persist. I say it is my right, which it is, but it's not like I've shown any interest in looking up my father, any father, till now. Till Jim showed up. He's not the man I've always been told is my father. Diana lied to me. Why? To use me, to keep me as her living, breathing work of art? They all lied to me: Diana and Alan and Linda.

In the end Linda gives me a hotel card with a room number scratched on it in untidy writing and says this is where he is staying, she thinks. He dropped the card when he came to see her.

I ask her why. Why didn't he come for me earlier, if he loves me so much, like he said? Why did he let Diana take me? Why was Diana the one who was there for me, who fed me and cared for me, who taught me about reading and writing and music, who showed me another life? Linda cannot answer. She says Diana did what she thought best.

Best for her, or me, I wonder?

I punch the wall, over and over, and Linda doesn't tell me to stop. He may or may not be my father; I don't give a fuck. He doesn't care. He doesn't now and he didn't then. But I go anyway.

The hotel is in a dodgy part of Pimlico. It's falling to bits and seedy and it won't matter that I'm scruffy as hell. On the reception counter is what looks like a doorbell. It is white and rectangular, though it doesn't appear to be wired up. I press it and wait.

An old man in trousers and a vest – no shirt – materialises from a side door. He does not flinch at my appearance. What sights he must have seen. He does not speak and a tip of the chin suggests he expects me to talk first.

'I've come to see a guest, Mr Jim...' I realise I do not know the man who says he is my father's name. 'The guest in,' I check the card squashed in my hand, 'room thirty-four.'

'Gone,' the old man says. 'Didn't pay the bill. You come to settle up?'

'I don't have any cash.' This is a lie but I don't have

Diana

I woke late to a glorious morning. The golden haze of
the sunlit bedroom felt like an insult to the gloominess of
my mood, as memories of the previous evening surfaced.
The house felt unnaturally still. Alan snored lightly
beside me and I slipped out of bed, careful not to wake
him.

In the kitchen I made coffee and toast, placed it on a
tray and made my way to Cal's room. It was a pathetic
attempt at an apology but I had to start somewhere.
Dispensing with knocking – it had never woken him and
was unlikely to start now – I eased open his door and
stepped in.

His bed hadn't been slept in. I opened the wardrobe
– there was no evidence he'd packed a bag. Shirts swung
gently on plastic hangers; the fug of old trainers stole
into my nostrils. In his bathroom the toothbrush rested
in the glass beaker on the windowsill. I raced downstairs,
desperate to convince myself that he'd only popped out,
for more milk, for a walk, to see friends? As was his
habit, Alan had emptied his pockets before we retired to
bed, dumping loose change and a couple of fivers on the

coffee table. It had gone. The French doors were ajar. Cal had gone. I was certain.

Back in Cal's room, I searched for a note, a clue, something to hint at where he might have headed. There was nothing. I shook Alan from his slumber.

'He's not left his ring?' he said, as we stood in Cal's room, looking for I know not what.

The tightness in my chest and throat loosened and I began to shake, to cry.

'It's a good sign. He's wearing the bands of love,' Alan said as he pulled me into an embrace. 'It means something. He'll come back. Those three rings, that one ring, is us.'

I didn't have that faith, but I said nothing.

He probably forgot to take it off, that's all.

We raced around North London in the car, looking for a short, hunched guy in a black hoodie and jeans. There were thousands of them. Back home we called China and Stanley, former band members, his old university, his university digs. The manager of the packing company where Cal worked part-time before he couldn't be bothered to turn in, depression holding him hostage to inertia.

No one had heard from him in months.

The day went from bad to worse. Once we'd exhausted the obvious options, Alan made a cup of tea and sat down in the living room with the newspapers which had been collected from the mat and thrown onto coffee table before we'd dashed out. He opened one of the broadsheets and studied the front page. I paced about, unable to focus on anything.

'Sit down,' Alan said, lowering the paper.

'I can't.'

'You must. I need you to see something.'

I sat next to him. He opened the paper and pointed at an article in the bottom left-hand corner. 'Ruckus at Gallery.' It was a short piece, mostly factual, with a reference to another artist whose son had published a memoir of his childhood in which he chronicled his feelings of vulnerability and abuse at being studied and drawn by his father.

'They must have been short on news,' I said, though my fingers quaked.

The following morning, there was still no word from Cal. Sick with sleep deprivation, guilt, and the knowledge of what Jim was capable of, I walked into our local newsagents and bought the leading tabloids.

As I feared, Jim had talked to the press, driven by his greed and his desire for revenge; greed was possibly the greater motivation. I wasn't a household name – not then – but I was well-known enough for the story to appear on page five. Days later I occupied a double-page spread. Our story was perfect tabloid fodder and how they loved it.

A proper freak show.

I was portrayed as a fruitcake and an exhibitionist tart – the irony of them sneering at the explicit shots of me only pages after an image of a half-naked girl passing the editor by. Phoney, bonkers artist propped up with public – taxpayers' – money. Criminal, said one. Jim profiled as a hard-done-by, caring father, who'd made a few mistakes in life ('Who hasn't?' they said) but had come good in the end. Salt of the earth bloke hoodwinked by a manipulative female and denied his parental rights.

'What a load of utter bollocks,' Alan raged.

'They didn't even mention where the exhibition's on. Might have driven some people through the doors at least.'

Alan stared at me. 'You're not serious?'

I harrumphed. 'No. But notoriety isn't all bad. There are collectors who like that, the kudos. No such thing as bad publicity.'

'Do you not see how this will affect Cal? He's less likely than ever to come back.'

'Of course I do. I don't actually mean it.' I burst into tears.

My comment about publicity proved to be prophetic. The crowds poured into the exhibition and work sold to private collectors for eye-watering sums. After years, I'd finally achieved my ambition: I was a fully-fledged famous artist.

Days drifted into weeks and still we heard nothing from Cal. We called the police to report a missing person. The duty sergeant was sympathetic and took details but we came unstuck when it became apparent that Cal was an adult – I'd talked as if he were a child.

'There's very little we can do I'm afraid, Mrs Brading.'

'Ms Brading.'

343

'I'm sure he'll come back when he's ready. You could put up a few posters, that might help,' he said, tired, bored, keen to get off the phone and get on with real police business.

Linda and I met only once after the exhibition closed, at the pub round the corner from the gallery and I drank too much, too quickly. Some habits never change. She was angry. With time to reflect she blamed me for the assault at her flat: if I'd met with Jim earlier, if I'd brought Cal to him, as promised, Jim would never have come chasing after her. She had no idea what she was getting herself into, she said.

'I should never have got involved with him. I can only say sorry. Sorry, sorry.'

'Don't go on about the affair,' she said. 'It's not about that.'

I wouldn't have called what Jim and I had an affair but I let it go.

'Deep down, from the start, I knew I was second choice. He fancied you more, but I was pushier,' she said. Threatened by my beauty, and perceived class, she'd gone all out to get him, and she was surprised that I gave in so easily.

'I'd never let a bloke come between a friendship. You're beautiful and you're not pushy,' I said. I didn't tell her what Jim had said: that she was more straightforward. Less fucked-up – my words, not his.

'Look, I'm angry with myself as much as you. I feel ashamed because I made excuses. I allowed myself to believe it was OK. But in here,' she tapped her chest, 'I knew it wasn't what Cal would have wanted. Not really. Just like the old days. I've been complicit. I used Cal too.'

'You didn't.' I reached for her hand but she pulled away.

She laughed, rueful, and slugged her drink. 'You're not the only one to benefit from this show, the publicity. It's not done me any harm either, has it?' she said.

'I'm going to donate the money to charity. I've found one that helps kids in the developing world with hare-lips and other facial deformities,' I said.

She turned and stared at me. 'It's not about the money.'

'Of course not.'

She polished off her drink, picked up her expensive handbag and stood. 'Artists have a history of fucking up their muses.'

'Or marrying them,' I said, a final attempt to lighten the atmosphere.

'Take responsibility. Admit it.'

'I do. I have.'

'Good.' She bent and air-kissed one cheek, both of us stiff, then set off down the street. Wondering if I'd ever see her again, I remained seated until she disappeared round the corner.

We emailed, always planning to meet, but never making a firm arrangement. 'Getting together' was always in some distant, indistinct future. After numerous mails, we admitted that each reminded the other of events and decisions that were still raw, painful. I sought atonement and wouldn't get it from Linda. Perhaps she just wanted

345

to forget. After all, her part was such a small one. Finally, we agreed that we needed to give one another space and would make contact when it felt right.

Time rolled on and no time was ever the right time. And judging by her silence, so it was for her too.

Cal

Mr McKenzie is late. What's keeping him? I can't bear being alone; too much time to think. I cannot imagine what it would have been like here without Eve.

Eve.

She has made everything bearable. No, so much more than that.

I want it over with – I want the bandages off now. For much of my life I've been good at being alone. I've had to be. There was a time when I wanted to be with people all the time, surrounded non-stop, by Diana, Alan, Linda. There's only one person I'd like to be with now.

Diana isn't a monster. In my mind, I built her as one, but she's not. My shrink has helped me see this. Diana's misguided, self-serving, as damaged as me. But she loved me, loves me, in her own way. She doesn't know how to love me right. Does she have regrets? I bet she does.

After I walked away from my old life, I read about Diana's childhood. She never spoke of it and when I did ask she was vague. Maybe it was meeting Jim that made me want to dip into the past, I don't know. There were hours and hours to kill as an all-night security guard, sitting in front of all those screens, watching all those empty grey images captured by the cameras placed strategically around the factory and offices. In over four years I never once saw anyone. The occasional rat, the factory cats prowling. But no burglars, no arsonists. I read novels at first, devouring them. But I grew tired of fiction, became hungry for facts.

I read an interview with her mother in a magazine. One of those horrible, voyeuristic ones. It'd been left on the desk by the guy who covered the day shift. Never got to know him properly. Kept myself to myself. It's no wonder that Diana's messed up, her mother's bat-shit crazy. I remember the first time I met Bunny. Though she greeted me with a smile and offered me sweets her warmth was forced – and so was mine. She was one of the few people I didn't trust back then. Nowadays I don't trust easily; I trust no one.

Almost no one. There's one I do.

Fear washes through me, charging through my veins. I'm glad Mr McKenzie is late. I never want him to arrive.

The door clicks. I jump.

Eve.

'All right? He won't be long now!' She's smiling. I can hear her excitement.

'I'm not sure I want the bandages off.' The words spill out. 'That sounds pathetic... I've got used to them. No one knows what's under here, and I like that. I could stay like this.'

'It's what's under the skin that matters. You can't

run away forever,' she says, bending to collect the uneaten breakfast: the soggy cornflakes and rubbery egg. She holds the tray in front of her and looks into my eyes.

She is beautiful.

'Have you never wanted to reinvent yourself? To begin again?'

She shrugs. 'I dyed my hair once.'

'Why?'

'I overheard a boy saying, "Brunettes are mysterious and exotic." I was fourteen. He didn't know I was in love with him. So I bought a home kit from Boots. After it was done my hair was so black it was almost blue.'

'Did it work? Were you alluring? Did he fall in love with you?' I say, trying to imagine Eve all sultry with dark hair. I can't.

'No! I still giggled at his jokes, smiled too much, blushed too much.'

'Did you ever tell him how you felt?'

'No. He went off with a blonde from the year above. They left school at sixteen and married a couple of years later when she fell pregnant.'

'They still together?'

'Yes. What we think we want and what we really want aren't always the same thing.'

I nod, and she checks her watch. 'I've got to go, but I'll be back.' She reaches over and squeezes my hand. Her skin feels very soft and I don't want her to take it away. I want to hold onto her.

When she has gone I get up and walk to the mirror by the basin. I look ridiculous, like a mummy in a cheap made-for-TV film. More people would stare if I went out like this than before. Before all the surgery, and after it, before the attack. I cannot stay like this though part of me wants to.

I touch the dressing covering my cheek. Whose face was this? I didn't even realise people could donate their faces till recently. How did he die? Have other bits of him been distributed all over the place?

He might have been ugly.

I am grateful to my donor, this man whose identity I will never know. This generous, big-hearted man who chose to give another – me – a second chance. Hope. Part of you will always be with me and I will always be thankful. I owe you that.

I turn my head, study my profile. A strong nose, I think. I like that.

Is my need as great as the man who gets his heart, with a wife and two small children who depend on him? The woman who receives his kidneys? Who's to say? Perhaps the normality of this new face will only serve to highlight the bad bits about me. It's only a partial transplant after all. Doc says it'll be years before fulls are possible. Perhaps it doesn't matter.

This is a lie. It matters enormously. I want to be rid of the Cal that adorns gallery walls, who enjoyed the attention, then hated it, and Diana.

How did I get here? In this hospital awaiting a new face?

How I sank.

~

The smell of fried food and sick lingers long after the clubbers have staggered home. Pulling my sleeping bag over my head, I wish that I didn't exist. Why did I come back here, to London? I could have found another job, far, far away from Diana and my past. I'm a sucker for punishment.

Dawn is breaking, throwing a shadowy light onto the pavement. I need to find somewhere to hide before the shoppers arrive. I surface from my sleeping bag like a snail emerging from its shell, taking care to look around. I roll up the bag and tie it to my rucksack, which I sling over my shoulder and drag my blistered feet down the street. My little dog Peg, another stray, at my side.

At a corner a gang of youths appears from an alleyway. From their attitude I know they are drunk and cruising for trouble. A memory from my childhood flashes. Dé jà vu. But this time, I am alone. Unprotected.

Dropping my head I stare at my hands, pondering whether or not to clench them. I notice how dirty and cracked my fingers are. My once beautiful hands with their slender fingers and flat pink nails.

The gang moves closer. I am rooted to the spot. They holler, foul-mouthed. I keep my head low and shuffle forward. To turn and run would incite them. Peg whines at my heels. She feels the threat.

Chin pushed into my neck, hood up, I force one foot in front of another. They are close, so close.

They are behind us.

We have escaped.

Then, a tug at my back. Peg yelps, flies in front of me. She has been kicked. Animals, I try to scream. Too late.

A kick to the back of the knee, another tug at my rucksack and I am falling onto the ground. I am an upturned insect, the soft, vulnerable part of me exposed. I am flaying about, kicking the air. I cover my face with my arms and the punches and kicks rain down. On my head, my back, my legs, my arms, my face. I hear the jeers. Peg's barks grow louder and louder, more and more desperate. Blackness closes in; I can defend myself no longer. I no longer care. This is it. I am gone.

I wake beside a sea of blood. Peg's muzzle pushing against my face. My blood.

    And then, the screams. They are not mine.

    'You got a mobile?'

    'Call an ambulance. An ambulance.'

    'Poor little dog.'

    'Help the beast.'

At the hospital I hear the whispers, 'He's lucky he didn't lose his sight, just millimetres from his eyes.'

    Lucky bastard, I think, before losing consciousness once more.

Diana

The summer wilted to an end. It had been hot, almost as hot as a childhood summer when standpipes held streets to ransom and the days went on forever.

The cemetery was my favourite place for walking and thinking. Dad had been a Friend of Highgate for years, though he no longer lived on the doorstep. The old boy who looked after the place, like a park keeper or caretaker, remembered me from the days when, as a lonely teenager visiting for the occasional weekend, I'd wander round the stones doodling, while Dad weeded or tended to the neglected graves, preferring the company of the dead to his daughter's. The park keeper wasn't the sort of man who'd read the arts pages of the broadsheets, or watch the South Bank Show, let alone visit a gallery. He knew me only as Mr Brading's daughter, and he would allow me into the West Cemetery whenever he could.

'Evening,' he said, from behind the gates. 'Come for a stroll?'

'Hi, Bill. How's you?'

'Fine, fine.' He opened the side door and I went in.

353

There was comfort in the quiet and cool of the land of dead. I headed for the Circle of Lebanon, past ostentatious mausoleums, weeping angels and statues of urns and lions. The beloved. It was a place of beauty and not forgetting. I thought of Cal, where he might be, if he was happy, if he was still alive.

Often I wondered if Jim looked for Cal too. If he had decided to try and become a real father to him, and occasionally I'd search for Jim as well as Cal, trying to find out what he was up to.

Mostly I hit dead ends until, one day, when I was recovering from a bad dose of 'flu and good for nothing apart from sitting in front of the TV or computer, the search threw up an article in the *Manchester Evening News*. Jim had been involved in a shooting in Moss Side and, along with five others, was facing a murder charge. Portrayed as a habitual criminal with a history of petty crime ranging from house robberies to drug dealing to his final, fatal foray in the seedy world of Yardies and gun crime, he'd served time in jail in Spain and the UK already.

The article had given me an idea. Perhaps Cal had returned to Manchester after all? Initially we'd dismissed this as extremely unlikely – too many difficult memories.

So Alan and I went back, for a weekend break we said, but we both knew why we were there. Great swathes of the city centre were unrecognisable. Piccadilly Gardens, the shopping arcade, the Northern Quarter, the gloomy streets of abandoned warehouses backed by the canals had all been transformed. We walked from our hotel in the fashionable gay village, close to the building we'd hijacked for a gallery, down the Oxford Road past the School of Art and into Hulme, unsure what we were looking for. If anything.

Hulme no longer existed. Not as we remembered it. No crescents, no burnt-out cars, no walkways. Bar a few tower blocks, the entire estate had been demolished in the early nineties. It was too ugly, too troubled, with too much history. The council had redeveloped the area but it wasn't what you'd call genteel. And, to my eyes and Alan's, it had lost its energy. The sun was shining; the sky was a crisp blue; we saw the new, improved Hulme in the best light possible and we agreed we preferred it the way it had been: ugly, vivid, vigorous.

There was no sign of Cal.

A cemetery tour marched past me, visitors with cameras, clutching leaflets, heading towards the terrace and the catacombs, the guide speaking of plans the Victorians made for their deaths, the money they spent, the care and attention lavished on their legacy. I checked my watch; it was time I returned to my studio. My legacy. I was preparing for another exhibition, though art mattered less to me now.

After an extended sabbatical I'd returned to my studio, to begin a new journey of artistic discovery, without the young man I called my muse. At first, I couldn't bear to be inside, holed up in my studio on Jackson's Lane. I'd wanted, needed, had to be out there.

Just in case I found him.

So I'd walked and walked and walked, always

355

searching, and along the way I collected lost things and abandoned items – taking inspiration from another hero of mine, Robert Rauschenberg – and this led me into my new project.

Obsessed with beauty, and finding it in unusual places, I'd also been listening to a lot of popular music. Cal had left his CDs, along with everything else. I wanted art to be as accessible, ephemeral and everyday as music. And music brought me closer to Cal, reminded me of him. I tore beautiful images from glossy magazines in ragged shapes and stuck them onto dog-shit smeared pavements with fag ends wedged in the cracks between the slabs. In rubbish dumps, I clambered over the discarded remains of modern life and placed a single white rose in a crushed cola can. I took photographs and uploaded them onto my ever-changing website.

Gathering my own camera, I looked again at the cemetery tourists, scouring the faces of the young men, searching.

Because wherever I was, wherever I went, I kept one eye open for Cal.

Cal

Mr McKenzie and some members of his team march into the room. You wouldn't believe how many surgeons were involved in my procedure. Dozens. They are followed by a small battalion of acolytes. He told me he would do this: bring people in to marvel at his handiwork, show me off to journalists when he is sure the procedure has been a success, my only caveat that I am not named in any publication. Not the name I've been using for five years, not my real name. It is part of the deal we have struck. Ours is a mutually beneficial relationship – not the first I've had, of course. I didn't like him, the first time we met. I was totally off surgeons, fed up of their empty promises.

~

He stands before me, as I lie on the trolley, inspecting me like I'm a piece of steak he's about to carve and devour, lifting the make-shift A&E dressings with little concern for the pain this causes me.

'You did well to bring him to my attention. Well done.' He talks to the nurse like she's a child. I'm expecting him to offer her a sticker. He can't even be bothered to read her badge, find out her name. He has not asked me mine. 'I'd say he's quite au fait with surgery, judging by the scar tissue here. Just the sort I'm looking for.'

If I had the energy, if I wasn't floored by loss of blood, agony, fear, I'd punch him. All I can muster is a snarled, 'He is present, you rude bastard, and he's got a name, knob-end.'

'Point taken. Delighted to make your acquaintance, knob-end.' He studies the chart. 'I'm Mr McKenzie.'

Despite myself I laugh, and it hurts like hell, and although he's not won me over, he's on his way. He tells me he is a reconstructive surgeon; he has a private practice and he is the best in the field, with an excellent team around him.

'Modest too,' I say.

'Merely honest,' he says, 'and don't you want the best?'

'I've no cash.'

'There's no need. You can pay another way.'

~

'Good morning, Cal. All set?'

'As I'll ever be.' I look at the people before me. I cannot see their faces; they all wear masks – to protect me, my new skin, from infection. My palms are sweating. Mr McKenzie approaches the side of the bed, leans in and begins to peel away the mask, talking as he does so. His audience nod and make notes.

The bandages are off; I can feel the air on my skin, I think, it's all so weird. Mr McKenzie puts his gloved hand under my chin and turns me from side to side. There are approving nods and sounds, but I catch the expression of an audience member and it is one of thinly veiled disgust. An expression I know well. My heart thuds. I look at Eve, to see if I can read her expression.

I can't.

'You may take a look now,' Mr McKenzie says. He asks Eve to pass him a mirror.

'With everyone here?' I stammer, my new lips still tight, the words almost choking me. The excitement, the anticipation, the dread is great. This wasn't part of the deal; I'm not sure I want a room full of witnesses; I'm not sure I can cope.

'Don't you want to see?' he says, turning and chuckling with his disciples at the petulant child. He can still be a dick.

I nod, and Eve takes the mirror. She looks at me and asks if I'm ready. Unable to form words, anxious my voice will reveal my fear, I nod again and she lifts the glass in front of me.

I raise my hands to touch the cheeks of the person before me. Eve shakes her head. I cannot touch yet, I'd forgotten. I turn my head from side to side. It is the only way I can be sure the man I see is me.

Who is this? Where have I gone?

The eyes. The eyes are mine. And the forehead. But I am wearing a mask once more. I am different but the same. It is the weirdest thing ever.

Alone again in my room I gaze out of the window. The green of the distant trees is dazzling against the blue of the sky. Even the plastic bins in the back courtyard look shiny and bright. Mr McKenzie warned me that my new skin will be extremely sensitive to UVA rays, that I must wear sunblock, take painkillers. I would like to feel the sun on my skin. I touch my cheek; it is soft and smooth. My fingers wander to the grooves and crevices of the scars across my non-existent eyebrows; they are tender and I withdraw, frightened I might do some damage. To my surprise I find I want to look again, to check if it really is as it seemed, to check that I've not morphed back into a beast. I turn to walk over to the basin mirror. The door clicks open; it is Eve.

'I'll go if you like?' she says.

'Stay. I was about to have another look.'

'Take your time.'

She appears beside me in the reflection; we are a similar height. I try to smile with my new face; it looks more like a grimace, but only because it is so forced, so false. She takes hold of my shoulders and says, 'So what do you think?' I shrug, like a teenager, not a grown man.

She tracks a scar with a finger without making contact with my skin. I want to feel her skin on mine. 'These will fade and your eyebrows will grow back. Your hair will grow long again and the marks at the side of your face will barely be noticeable. As for the old scars on your forehead – get a fringe. It'll suit you,' she says.

I do not respond.

'Your eyes are as lovely as they ever were, and we can see them more clearly now, and your mouth...' She frames my lips with her hands, as Diana and Alan used to do before taking a photo, 'is beautiful.'

'Huh.'

All I can think of are the words she has uttered:

lovely, beautiful. These words have never belonged to me.

She thinks I am disappointed and I fear she is losing patience. Is she disappointed? Did she expect me to look totally normal?

'What did you expect? You had virtually no face left, and from what you told me you hated the old one anyway.'

'I wanted to look normal. Like everyone else.'

'You will.'

'I can see that from a distance I'll look like everyone else, but not close up I won't. I longed for the impossible.'

'Maybe.'

I grasp the edge of the basin; it is cool and hard. 'I am tired of being defined by the way I look. I want an identity outside of my appearance. Outside of being Diana Brading's muse, outside of being Mr Stuart McKenzie's latest project, success story, and so on and so forth,' I say. I turn my back on the mirror and face Eve.

'Then get on with it. It's up to you.' She is sharp. Her impatience is a knife wound.

'Easy for you to say. Eve with the pretty face, good job, nice family. Doing a worthwhile job, helping those less fortunate than herself. Are you nice to me because you're paid to be?' I sound bitter and cruel, but I cannot stop.

'I'd slap your face if it wasn't so new.' She spits the words out. 'You're the one obsessing about your looks. No one else. You can't go on forever changing your appearance. It's not the answer. You've a good mind and,' she waves her arm in front of my face, 'there's a nice guy in here. Get out there.' She points to the window. 'Make something of yourself, people will forget the way you look, accept it. As you should.' She storms out of the room and I turn and stare at my reflection once more.

With each passing day, I grow more and more accustomed to my face. The reporters have arrived today. As promised I pose with Mr McKenzie and I say all the right things. That my new face is sweet, that without the doc my life wouldn't be worth living. And so on and so forth. We agree that I will never disclose my identity, and before they arrive I slip my ring, the bands of love, into the drawer of my bedside table. I do not put it back on.

Cal

Autumn is my favourite season. As a boy of eleven, maybe twelve, I loved walking through Victoria Park kicking the leaves piled in bundles under the trees, spreading them out to be blown by the wind. Freeing them.

In autumn everyone hibernates, withdrawing into homes and dens. Birds migrate. In autumn hats and scarves come out and collars are lifted and faces are buried into chests cloaked in thick coats. The trees are gold and red and I should be happy that this is so, but I'm not. For the first time I mourn the loss of the lightness of summer, the heady tang of honeysuckle, the long days and small nights. I'll cheer when spring returns, like all normal creatures.

Brockwell Park is quiet. The only people I see are mothers with pre-school children and a couple of drunks who hang around the café come rain or shine. The October sun is low in the sky, hazy and drab. I walk past the drained paddling pool and long for days when I can sit on the parched grass and watch the children play, and with my eyes caress the golden limbs of the girls and women who splash in the water beside them.

I think about summer and the lido on the other side of the park, of bodies slipping in and out of turquoise water. Next summer I will swim there, underwater, watch all the bodies sliding by, like beautiful eels. In goggles and hat and sunblock I will pass for ordinary.

Loneliness is a killer. I do not find it easy to make friends, and few approach me. I miss Diana and Alan, and China and Stanley, but this is my life. I make the decisions, make the choices. Right or wrong. I am in charge of my destiny. I've joined another band. Just for fun.

The door to the walled garden is closed and I panic. Perhaps it is locked. Perhaps essential works are being carried out on the ponds and benches and flower beds and walls that enclose this little Eden buried in the heart of Brixton. If it is closed, where should I wait? Will she find me? Perhaps she has already gone, or perhaps she changed her mind and never came at all?

Eve.

Eventually I plucked up courage and I called the hospital, asked to speak with her. Her shift was over and she had gone home. The receptionist told me to call back in the morning.

'Will she definitely be here?' I said.

'She will.'

At first she didn't sound like herself; she was formal and reserved. I asked if it was OK to talk, and before she finished answering I said that I was sorry. That I am a self-obsessed, miserable bastard who doesn't deserve her friendship and I totally understood if she wanted to hang up and never hear from me again.

She laughed and said it was OK. She was pleased to hear from me.

'I'm learning to be content,' I said. 'But I could do with a friend.'

'You'll have to pay me,' she said, 'I don't come cheap.'

'I've got a job.'

'Good.'

I twist the metal handle and the door to the garden opens. It reminds me of a church door. The garden is quiet and I marvel how the sounds of the city disappear here. Brown leaves float on the ponds, the trees are bare. In a gazebo covered in evergreens in the far corner sits a lone figure. It could be Eve, but I'm not sure.

When she stands I know it is her and as I enter the thicket I realise I do not know how to greet her, outside of the hospital, outside of a patient/nurse relationship. I offer my hand, which she takes. Her handshake is firmer than mine. We sit on the bench in the semi-dark.

'What's the job?' Eve says, as if there hasn't been a gap of four days since our telephone conversation.

'It's only a filler, to get some cash,' I say.

'What is it?'

'An orderly. In a hospital.'

She laughs. 'Haven't you had enough of hospitals? You can't stay away can you?'

'I like the nurses.' I am taking a risk.

365

'Oh, I bet you do, Cal Brading, or whatever you call yourself these days.'

I don't call myself a freak, I want to say, but instead I shrug and ask how life is treating her. She talks about work and the decorating she's doing in her flat. I tell her about my job, my plans to go back to university once I've saved a little money, the room I rent in a knackered house on Josephine Avenue. The odd collection of fellow tenants, their stories and problems. The band.

'What are you going to study then?' she asks.

'Psychology or psychotherapy. I'd like to work as a therapist one day. Unless I become a rock star.' We both laugh.

'Help others?'

'My therapist is amazing. And I reckon I've got something to give.'

'I reckon so too.'

'How's your brother?'

I almost wish I'd never asked, the atmosphere changes so sharply.

'He attempted suicide again. At the end of the summer. Took some pills, but he bottled out in the end.' She laughs ruefully at her own pun.

'I'm sorry.'

'I wish there was something I could do, but there isn't. Nothing anyone can do. It has to come from him, from within,' she says, rubbing her hands together. It is cold and we have been sitting here for ages, though it feels like seconds.

What she says is true. I know that now. Finally I am free of myself, of my appearance. I accept that I will never be 'normal', but I can live a normal and happy life. This is down to me and me alone. I cannot and will not rely on others.

'Give him this. I've been trying to get rid of it for months. But I couldn't give it away to anyone. I have to know where it's gone. Crazy, huh?' I pull the bands of love from where it's been for months, in the inside front pocket of my jacket. I intended always to give it to Eve, I tried once, but it was never meant for her, but for her brother.

'Tell him what it means. Strength, love, spirit. Tell him that it's OK to be different, but not to let that difference destroy you, take over, if that makes sense.'

'Sort of,' she says, uncertain, but taking the ring nevertheless.

'Do you think it'll fit him?' I say.

'You're a very similar size. In fact, you remind me of him. Did I tell you that?'

'Once. Shall we go for a coffee? You look freezing.'

We stamp our feet, mine are almost numb, and we wander out of the garden.

It's gloomy inside the café, and despite our stinging toes we sit outside. There's pigeon waste all over the seats and we hover by a table hugging our polystyrene cups, sipping the sludgy liquid even though it burns our lips and tongue.

'Let's walk,' I say, 'it'll keep us warm and if we go to the top of that hill there's a great view of the city.'

'That's not a hill, it's a gentle incline,' says Eve, pointing dismissively at the bump in the landscape.

'Trust me, the view's awesome.'

Even though it's not as clear as I'd like she's impressed. The skyline is bathed in a fuzzy light and we take it in turns to point out the landmarks: Battersea Power Station, St Paul's. We are looking north.

'Is that Ally Pally?' Eve says.

Alexandra Palace is close to where Diana lives. Or lived. Eve knows this.

'I don't hate Diana,' I say, 'in many ways I still love her. I think of her often enough. But we're better off without each other.'

'I'm glad. Hatred is destructive and pointless and ugly. Like despair.' I know she is thinking of her brother. 'And the world is so beautiful.'

She is right, it is.

I slip my hand round hers and we stand there, admiring the view.

Diana

Winter 2007

I am wandering through the cemetery when my phone rattles. Alan is abroad on an assignment. The mobile is on silent, so there is no trilling, only a reverberating. I do not recognise the number but I hit answer, my heart pounding. Sales people love me because I always pick up.

It isn't Cal. It never is.

It's a police officer. I do not hear his name. They have a suicide, clinging on to life. He doesn't have long. They're struggling to identify the body; he has nothing on him and dental records take time. But this detective likes art; he's a fan, he says. Bit of a connoisseur. There's a ring on the victim's finger. He recognises it. He saw it on a photograph of a boy, a deformed boy, by the artist Diana Brading, and this ring, on the suicide, is engraved; the bands are marked with an A, a D and a C. Could I come to the hospital? I need to be quick.

From my contacts I pull up Linda's number and hope that it's not changed.

Linda and I embrace again. I slip Cal's ring onto my thumb; it's too big. I will wear it on a chain around my

369

neck. We walk towards the detective who is waiting for me outside the hospital relatives' room.

Before we reach him I am overcome with a desire to say goodbye. The need is pressing, urgent.

'I want to see Cal,' I say.

'No, Diana. He's not there,' Linda says.

'I have to see him.'

Linda takes my hand and tells me, as gently as she can, there is nothing left of Cal. That it could destroy me to see him.

'Remember him as he was. It's a terrible image to carry,' she says.

I am undeterred.

The ring is clenched in my right fist which I press against my chest. I push open the door. I ask the nurse to leave, to let me do this alone. She says she will be right outside the door.

I see the feet, poking out from beneath the sheet. This is strange because Cal was short and the sheet should be long enough. I move towards the head. As I reach across to pull back the cover an arm swings from beneath the cotton. I jump, horrified at first.

I take hold of the arm; there is still warmth and I am surprised. I expected it to be cold. It could be Cal's arm.

I move the ring from my fist and into the front pocket of my jeans. I will never give it away. I take hold of Cal's hand with both of mine. He has such beautiful fingers. There are no broken bones as far as I can tell. I lift it up and kiss it.

But something is wrong, something about this

370

hand is unfamiliar. I look at the nails. Cal's half-moons were white-white, perfect semi-circles. These are not. Can nails change like this? I move to the other side of the bed and slip my hand underneath the sheet. I pull out the other arm and look for the tiny, raised mole on the web-like flesh between his ring and middle finger. It is not there.

This is not Cal.

I weep.

My studio is bathed in a soft light. It's dusk and I'm surrounded by half a lifetime's work. The room is full of distorted images: transformations of Cal, of me, of the world we inhabited. I run my fingers across photographs and drawings and ceramics and models, searching for a pulse. But I cannot find him here, in these works of art, these beautiful things. They conceal and disguise him.

But as I look and look, images escape from the cracks between the artworks, fluttering into life: a young and dishevelled Alan with heavy heart and kind eyes; Linda with saucer-sized earrings and short, short skirts; Jim, golden and hard; Pru and Michael and technicolour filthy Hulme; Manchester, wet and red and funky. And there, parading through them all is Cal. Smiling his crooked grin, brown eyes glimmering. A hobgoblin boy with beautiful hands and the power to enchant.

And this vision is no longer painful because I know he's out there, alive. I hope that he's really living, embracing it all, going for what he wants, what makes him, and others, feel good.

Most of all, I hope he knows that he is loved, that he is a beautiful creature, inside and out.

Author's Note

The Hulme portrayed in the first part of the novel no longer exists. The estate was a 70s social housing disaster. Within a decade of completion the glorious 'streets in the sky' were a breeding ground for vermin, crime and anti-social behaviour; the families it had been built for had been moved out. The four crescents and the 'safer' rows were flattened in the early 90s to make way for more appropriate housing. I studied for my degree in Manchester and lived in a Hulme flat in a similar time-frame to Diana. I did not live in the notorious crescents but on Harvington Walk and I was fortunate in that I was never mugged or burgled.

If the description above makes it sound like a nightmarish place to live, nothing could be further from the truth. In my experience. Yes, crime was rife, the cockroaches and damp were a pain, but Hulme was a vital, creative (and cheap) environment in which to live. Artists thrived there and it was, without a doubt, the most extraordinary place I've ever lived. Ever since, I wanted to write about Hulme and Manchester but it was decades before I found my story.

I can't draw or paint for toffee but I am a fan of art, particularly modern art. Whilst copywriting for a charity which helps children damaged by congenital deformity, I became aware of the work of French performance artist ORLAN and American shape-shifting photographer Cindy Sherman. Both women use themselves as canvas and both are, to my eyes, beautiful. The germ of the story which grew into Skin Deep was seeded. It's perhaps worth noting that Cal's disfigurement is fictional and deliberately non-specific. I took inspiration from a number of conditions, all of which are extremely rare.

If you're interested in Hulme — as it was — and the work of the artists from which I drew inspiration you might like to check out my Skin Deep Pinterest board or take a look at some of the links detailed below. I cannot include everything I happened upon during my research but I hope this gives you a taste.

https://www.timeout.com/manchester/art/23-fascinating-photos-of-old-hulme-from-al-baker

http://www.mancky.co.uk/?p=1978

http://www.albakerphotography.com/

https://www.flickr.com/photos/mmuvisualresources/sets/72157625038079675/

https://www.youtube.com/watch?v=S1qpf9hogI0

https://www.moma.org/interactives/exhibitions/2012/cindysherman/#/11/

http://www.orlan.eu/exhibitions/

About Laura

Laura Wilkinson lives in Brighton with her musician/carpenter husband, ginger sons and a cat called Sheila. She is the author of four novels: *The Family Line*, *Public Battles Private Wars*, *Redemption Song* and *Skin Deep*.

For more information visit:

www.laura-wilkinson.co.uk

@ScorpioScribble

/LauraWilkinsonAuthor

/Laura1765

/Laura_WilkinsonWriter

Secrets in a family are like moths in cashmere;

They **dig** themselves in and **eat** their way out …

If knew your dreams were trying to tell

you something, would you listen?

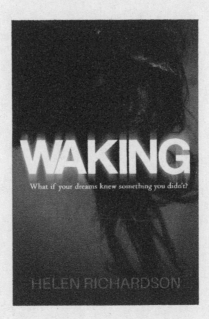

Anna Caldwell is terrified going to sleep.

She knows her nightmare will be there waiting

for her ...

Perfect for fans of Lisa Jewell.

Can you really trust her?

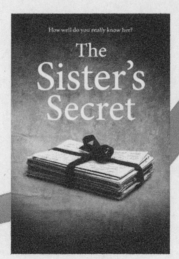

A psychological thriller that tests
the power of trust and the very
people you hold close.

For more information about **Laura Wilkinson**
and other **Accent Press** titles
please visit

www.accentpress.co.uk

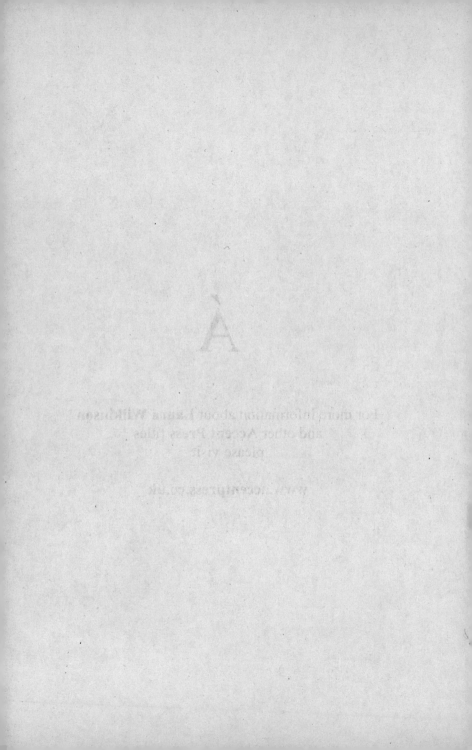

For more information about Laura Wilkinson
and other Accent Press titles
please visit:

WWW.ACCENTPRESS.CO.UK